Alexandria

Lindsey Davis began writing about the Romans with *The Course of Honour*, which tells the real-life love story of the Emperor Vespasian and Antonia Caenis. Her best-selling mystery series features laid-back First Century Roman detective Marcus Didius Falco and his partner Helena Justina, plus friends, relations, pets and bitter enemy the Chief Spy. She has also written *Rebels and Traitors*, a serious novel on an epic scale, set in the English Civil War and Commonwealth. Her books are translated into many languages, recorded for audio serialisation on BBC Radio 4. She has won the CWA Historical Dagger, the Dagger in the Library, and a Sherlock for Falco as Best Detective. She has been Honorary President of the Classical Association and is a past Chair of the Crimewriters' Association. In 2009 she was awarded the Premio de Honor de Novela Historica by the Spanish City of Zaragoza, for her career as a historical novelist.

ALEXANDRIA

Lindsey Davis

arrow books

Published in the United Kingdom by Arrow Books in 2010

1 3 5 7 9 10 8 6 4 2

First published in the United Kingdom in 2009 by Century

Arrow Books
The Random House Group Limited
20 Vauxhall Bridge Road, London, SW1V 2SA

Addresses for companies within The Random House Group Limited can be found at:
www.randomhouse.co.uk/offices.htm

The Random House Group Limited Reg. No. 954009

www.rbooks.co.uk

A CIP catalogue record for this book
is available from the British Library

ISBN 9780099515623

The Random House Group Limited supports The Forest Stewardship Council (FSC), the leading international forest certification organisation. All our titles that are printed on Greenpeace approved FSC certified paper carry the FSC logo. Our paper procurement policy can be found at www.rbooks.co.uk/environment

Typeset in Ehrhardt MT by Palimpsest Book Production Limited,
Grangemouth, Stirlingshire
Printed and bound in Great Britain by CPI Bookmarque Ltd, Croydon, CR0 4TD

To Michelle
With thanks for being an intrepid travel companion and guide
and apologies for the culture shock,
the sandstorm,
the closed museum
and *that* airport

PRINCIPAL CHARACTERS

Marcus Didius Falco	fixer, traveller and playwright
Helena Justina	his well-read wife and tour-planner
Julia Junilla, Sosia Favonia, Flavia Albia	their well-behaved poppets
Aulus Camillus Aelianus	Helena's brother, a diligent student
Fulvius	Falco's enigmatic uncle, a negotiator
Cassius	his life partner, a wonderful host
M. D. Favonius, aka Geminus	Falco's father, who was ordered not to come
Thalia	who will regret bringing him, an artiste
Jason	her python, a real curiosity

At the Royal Palace

The Prefect of Alexandria and Egypt	highly renowned (name not recorded)
A bunch of dim rich boys	his admin staff, typical high-fliers

Legionaries

Gaius Numerius Tenax	a centurion who gets the awkward jobs
Mammius and Cotius	his back-up, hungry for glory
Tiberius and Titus	on duty at the Lighthouse, bored (not for long)

At the Alexandria Museion

Philetus	the Museion Director, uplifted on merit?
Theon	Librarian of the Great Library, downcast
Timosthenes	of the Serapeion Library, hungry for promotion
Philadelphion	the Zoo Keeper, a ladies' man

Apollophanes	virtuous Head of Philosophy, a toady
Zenon	Chief Astronomer and not accountable
Nicanor	Head of Legal Studies, honest (honestly!)
Aeacidas	a self-assured tragedian, as good as anyone
Pastous	a library assistant, closely taking stock
Chaereas and Chaeteas	zoo and autopsy assistants, good family folk
Sobek	a Nile crocodile, hungry for action
Nibytas	an obsessive old reader and book-lover
Heras, son of Hermias	a Sophist scholar, none too wise
Students	as you would expect
Aedemon	an empirical physician (purges and laxatives)
Heron	a *deus ex machina*, earthly god of machines

Colourful Alexandrian characters

Roxana	an admired young woman, with poor sight
Psaesis	a litter-bearer (deserves a raise)
Katutis	in the gutter, gazing at the stars
Petosiris	an undertaker (knows where the bodies are)
Itchy and Snuffly	his helpers (stitching people up)
Diogenes	an ambitious man of commerce
A box-maker	his sidekick

<u>Also</u>

The legendary catoblepas	not appearing, but deserves a mention
The gnu	pure nostalgia

There were various ancient lists of the Seven Wonders of
the World, some counting the Walls and Gardens of
Babylon as two but omitting the Pharos. We use the more
conventional list of:

* The Great Pyramid at Giza
* The Hanging Gardens of Babylon
* The Statue of Zeus at Olympia
* The Temple of Artemis at Ephesus
* The Mausoleum at Halicarnassus
* The Colossus of Rhodes
* The Pharos at Alexandria

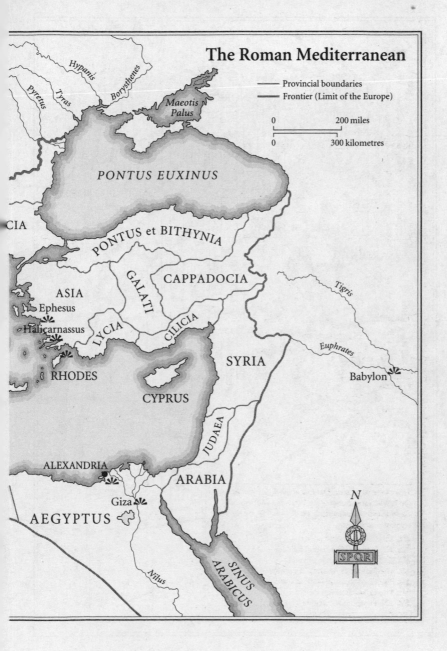

The Roman Mediterranean

Provincial boundaries
Frontier (Limit of the Europe)

0 — 200 miles
0 — 300 kilometres

Hypanis
Pyretus
Tyras
Borysthenes
Maeotis Palus

PONTUS EUXINUS

CIA

PONTUS et BITHYNIA

GALATI
CAPPADOCIA

ASIA
Ephesus
Halicarnassus
LYCIA
CILICIA
Tigris

SYRIA
Euphrates

RHODES
CYPRUS
Babylon

JUDAEA

ALEXANDRIA
ARABIA

Giza
AEGYPTUS
Nilus

SINUS ARABICUS

N

SPQR

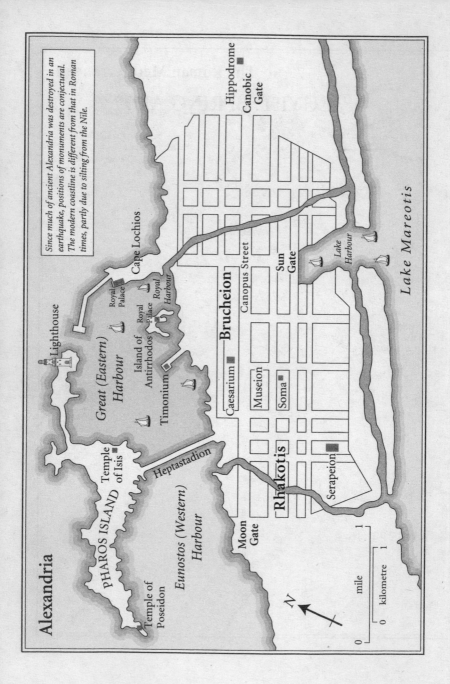

Alexandria

Since much of ancient Alexandria was destroyed in an earthquake, positions of monuments are conjectural. The modern coastline is different from that in Roman times, partly due to silting from the Nile.

Lighthouse

PHAROS ISLAND

Temple of Isis

Temple of Poseidon

Eunostos (Western) Harbour

Heptastadion

Great (Eastern) Harbour

Island of Antirrhodos

Timonium

Cape Lochios

Royal Palace

Royal Palace

Royal Harbour

Moon Gate

Rhakotis

Serapeion

Caesarium

Museion

Soma

Brucheion

Canopus Street

Sun Gate

Hippodrome

Canobic Gate

Lake Harbour

Lake Mareotis

N

0   1   mile

0   1   kilometre

EGYPT: SPRING AD77

I

They say you can see the Lighthouse from thirty miles away. Not in the day, you can't. Still, it kept the youngsters quiet, precariously balancing on the ship's rail while they looked for it. When travelling with children, always keep a little game in hand for those last troublesome moments at the end of a long journey.

We adults stood close by, wrapped up in cloaks against the breeze and ready to dive in if little Julia and Favonia accidentally plunged overboard. To add to our anxiety, we could see all the crew making urgent attempts to work out where we were as we approached the long, low, famously featureless coastline of Egypt, with its numerous shoals, currents, rocky outcrops, suddenly shifting winds and difficult lack of landmarks. We were passengers on a large cargo boat that was making its first lumbering trip south this season; indications were that over the winter everyone had forgotten how to do this journey. The dour captain was frantically taking soundings and looking for silt in seawater samples to tell him he was near the Nile. Since the Nile delta was absolutely enormous, I hoped he was not such a poor navigator he had missed it. Our sailing from Rhodes had not filled me with faith. I thought I could hear that salty old sea god Poseidon laughing.

Some Greek geographer's turgid memoirs had supplied oodles of misinformation to Helena Justina. My sceptical wife and tour-planner reckoned that even from this far out you could not only see the Lighthouse, shining like a big confusing star, but also smell the city wafting across the

1

water. She swore she could. True or not, we two roman-
tics convinced ourselves that exotic scents of lotus oil, rose
petals, nard, Arabian balsam, bdellium and frankincense
were greeting us over the warm ocean – along with the
other memorable odours of Alexandria, sweaty robes and
overflowing sewage. Not to mention the occasional dead
cow floating down the Nile.

As a Roman, my handsome nose detected this perfume's
darkest under-notes. I knew my heritage. I came fully
equipped with the old prejudice that anything to do with
Egypt involved corruption and deceit.

I was right too.

At last we sailed safely through the treacherous shoals
to what could only be the legendary city of Alexandria.
The captain seemed relieved to have found it – and
perhaps surprised at his skilful steering. We pootled in
under the enormous Lighthouse then he tried to find
one empty space to moor amongst the thousands of
vessels that lined the embankments of the Eastern
Harbour. We had a pilot, but pointing out a spare stretch
of quay was beneath him. He put himself off into a
bumboat and left us to it. For a couple of hours our ship
manoeuvred slowly up and down. At last we squeezed
in, shaving the paint on two other vessels with the joggle-
mooring method.

Helena and I like to think we are good travellers, but we
are human. We were tired and tense. It had taken six days
from Athens, via Rhodes, and an interminable time out
from Rome before that. We had lodgings; we were to stay
with my Uncle Fulvius and his live-in boyfriend – but we
did not know them well and were anxious about how we
would find their house. In addition, Helena and I were
well-read. We knew our history. So, as we faced up to disem-
barkation, I could not help joking about Pompey the Great:
how he was collected from his trireme to go ashore to meet
the King of Egypt – and how he was stabbed in the back

by a Roman soldier he knew, butchered with his wife and children watching, then beheaded.

My job involves weighing up risks, then taking them anyway. Despite Pompey, I was all set to lead the way bravely down the gangplank when Helena shoved me out of her way.

'Oh don't be ridiculous, Falco. Nobody here wants your head – yet. I'll go first!' she said.

II

Foreign cities always sound so loud. Rome may be as bad, but it is home and we never notice the racket.

Groaning on a strange bed as I flexed beneath unusual coverlets made from no fleece I recognised, I awoke from dreams where my body seemed to be still rocking on the ship that brought us, to find unsettling light and noise. At my movement, an extremely unusual insect flew away from just beside my left ear. Agitated voices rose from streets outside, through those wobbly shutters with latches that I could not close last night upon our arrival, too exhausted to solve the incomprehensible riddles of strangers' door- and window-furniture. I had made some joke about us being set a life-or-death test by a winged Greek Sphinx, and my clever partner had pointed out we were now in the territory of the lion-bodied Egyptian Sphinx instead. It had not struck me there was any difference.

Thundering Jupiter. The inhabitants of this new place conversed at the tops of their voices, as they held harsh, pointlessly long arguments – though when I looked out hoping to see a knife fight, they were all just shrugging casually and strolling off with loaves under their elbows. The level of street sound seemed absurd. Unnecessary bells clanged to no purpose. Even the donkeys were noisier than at home.

I fell back into bed. Uncle Fulvius had said we could sleep in as long as we liked. Well, that got the maids clattering up and down the stone stairs. One even burst in on us to see if we were up yet. Instead of vanishing discreetly, she just stood there in her shapeless shift and sloppy sandals, grinning.

'Don't say anything!' Helena muttered against my shoulder, though I thought her teeth were gritted.

When the servant or slave left, I raved for a while about how many loathsome indignities are imposed upon blameless travellers via that filthy phrase, *remember, darling, we are guests!*

Never be a guest. Hospitality may be the noblest social tradition of Greece and Rome, possibly of Egypt too, but stick it straight back in the sweaty armpit of whatever helpful relative wants to bore you to death with his army stories, or the very old friend of your father who hopes to interest you in his new invention – whichever menace has invited you to share his inconvenient foreign house. Pay your way in an honest *mansio*. Preserve your integrity. Keep the right to shout *get lost*!

'We are in the East,' Helena soothed me. 'They say the pace of life is different.'

'Always a good excuse for foreigners' ghastly incompetence.'

'Don't be bitter.' Helena rolled into my arms and snuggled, becoming once more comfortable and comatose.

I had a better idea than sleeping. 'We are in the East,' I murmured. 'The beds are soft, the climate balmy; the women are sinuous, the men obsessed with lust –'

'And don't tell me, Marcus Didius – you want to put a new entry on your list of "cities where I have made love"?'

'Lady, you always read my mind.'

'Easy enough,' suggested Helena cruelly. 'It never changes.'

This was the life. We were in the East. We had no pressing business and breakfast would go on being served all morning.

*   *   *

5

I knew the arrangements for breakfast because Fulvius had told me. As a man with a past he never talked about, who was engaged in trades he kept mysterious, my maternal uncle tended to be terse (unlike the rest of our family), so he imparted vital information with unsparing clarity. His house rules were few and civilised: 'Do what you like but don't attract attention from the military. Turn up for dinner on time. No dogs on the reading couches. Children under seven to be in bed before dinner starts. All fornication to be conducted in silence.' Well, that was a challenge. Helena and I were enthusiastic lovers; I was eager to see if it was feasible.

We had left my dog in Rome but had two children under seven – Julia, approaching five, and Favonia, two. I had promised they would be exemplary house guests and since they were fast asleep when we arrived, nobody yet knew otherwise. With us too was Albia my foster-daughter, who was probably about seventeen, so sometimes she attended formal meals like a very shy grown-up or sometimes she stormed off to her room with a murderous scowl, taking all the sweetmeats in the house. We had found her in Britain. She would be a poppet one day. So we told ourselves.

Albia was a fixture, on her second major trip with us. Helena's brother Aulus was an unexpected addition to my party. He could be a trial when he wanted to be; since he was an abrasive character, that was frequent. Aulus Camillus Aelianus, the elder of Helena's two brothers, had worked as my assistant in Rome before he took himself off to learn law at Athens, after (for the fourth or fifth time, to my knowledge) he was blindingly struck by his 'real' vocation. Like all students, immediately his family thought he was finally settling down in a prestigious, extremely expensive university, he heard through some grapevine that there was better teaching at another one. Or better parties and the chance of a better love life, anyway. When we dropped in to visit him last month, he hitched a free ride on our ship, saying he passionately wanted to study at the Alexandria Museion. I said nothing. His father would pay for it. The senator, a diligent, tolerant man, would just be thankful that Aulus had not – so far – expressed a wish to be a gladiator, a master forger or a writer of ten-scroll epic poetry.

Fulvius could not have known I would bring my wastrel brother-in-law, but he expected the rest. My mother's brother, the most complicated of a crazy trio, years ago Uncle Fulvius ran away from home to join the cult of Cybele in Asia Minor. After that, he was not seen for a good two decades, during which he was known as 'the one we never talk about' – though of course he always came under avid discussion at family parties, once enough wine had been drunk and people got on to insulting absent members. I grew up with many a dainty auntie chewing on bread rolls toothlessly while speculating whether Fulvius had actually castrated himself with a flint, as devotees supposedly did.

I had encountered him a year back, in Ostia. I had been fully accompanied on that mission, so he knew I came with a tribe. His reappearance in Italy was a shock at the time. He now engaged in suspicious-sounding overseas activities, which presumably continued in some form now that he lived in Egypt. Being Fulvius, he had not bothered to explain why he moved here. At Ostia he and his crony Cassius took to Helena; at least, it had been to her that the couple addressed an invitation to stay in their Alexandrian house. They knew she wanted to see the Pyramids and the Pharos. Like me, Helena Justina had mental lists; a methodical tourist, she aimed to one day see all the Seven Wonders of the World. She liked numbered aims and ambitions; for a senator's daughter, those ambitions were extravagantly cultural, which – she joked – was why she married me. We had done Olympia and Athens on a trip to Greece last year. *En route* to Egypt we had added Rhodes.

'And how was the dear Colossus?' Fulvius asked, when we joined him on the flat roof of his house. There the promised breakfast was indeed still being served, and judging by the crumbs on the tablecloth it had been going on for at least the past three hours.

'Tumbled down in an earthquake, but the broken pieces are phenomenal.'

'He's a cutie – don't you adore a man with thirty-foot thighs?'

'Oh Marcus is muscular enough for me . . . Fulvius, thank you so much for inviting us – this is heavenly!' Helena knew how to biff aside rude talk.

Fulvius allowed himself to be diverted. A paunchy figure in pristine Roman dress – ankle-length full whites – he was the kind of tetchy expatriate who did not believe in trying to fit in. Abroad, he wore a toga even on occasions when he would never have dreamed of bothering in Rome. Only his enormous cameo ring hinted at his exotic side.

Looking north across the ocean, Helena gazed out at the panorama of gorgeous sea views that simmered beneath a hot blue sky. My astute uncle had somehow acquired a house in the Brucheion region, once the royal quarter and still the most magnificent and sought-after place to live. Now that the incestuous royal Ptolemies had been kicked into oblivion by us Romans – deftly cleansing the world of rivals – the district was even more desirable to those with taste. We had glimpsed its atmospheric assets on arriving last night, for Alexandria was home to an enormous lamp-manufacturing industry; the streets here were gloriously lit at night, unlike every other city Helena and I had lived in – Corduba, Londinium, Palmyra, even our own dear Rome, where if lamps were hung up the burglars immediately doused them.

Our ship had berthed very close to my uncle's house. This good luck was unlikely to last. After more than ten years as an investigating informer, I expected Fortune to allot me kicks, not caresses. But we had even managed to find a trustworthy guide, which suggested the citizens of

Alexandria were strangely friendly to foreigners; I doubted it. I was born and bred in a city, the best in the world, and I knew all cities shared the same attitude: the only thing to admire about foreigners is the innocent way they part from their travel money. Still, with the guide's help, we had found the house so fast, all we saw was that Alexandria was expensive, expansive and extremely Greek in style.

Helena always devised lecture notes. So I knew Alexander the Great had come here towards the end of his conquering adventures, found a clutch of fishermen's huts decaying beside a deep freshwater lake, and spotted the potential. He was going to build a mighty port to dominate the eastern end of the Mediterranean, where safe harbours were few and far between. You don't spend years beating up the world's famous cities without acquiring a sense of what will impress visitors – and what will last. Alexander had incentives. If you are founding a new place and putting your own nametag on it, you get it right.

'He laid out everything himself.'

'Well you don't become the greatest general in history unless you know to *never* trust subordinates!'

'Apparently,' Helena informed me, 'he had brought no chalk – or, since his satchel was full of maps of Mesopotamia, there was not room for enough. So some ingratiating courtier told him to use bean flour instead, to mark out the street plan. He went to endless trouble over the alignments – he wanted the cooling, health-giving winds from the sea to waft in for the inhabitants – they are called Etesian winds, by the way –'

'Thank you, dearest.'

'Then when Alexander had finished, a huge dark cloud of birds rose up off Lake Mareotis and devoured all the flour. The books say –' she was frowning – 'Alexander was persuaded by soothsayers that this was a good omen.'

'You disagree?' I myself was busy devouring – the array

of bread, dates, olives and sheep's cheese that Uncle Fulvius had provided.

'Well, obviously, Marcus. If the birds ate the markings, how did Alexander's nice Greek grid of streets ever get built?'

'No allowance for myth and magic, Helena?' asked my uncle.

'I cannot believe Alexander the Great let himself be bamboozled by a bunch of soothsayers.'

'You chose an extremely pedantic wife,' commented Fulvius.

'She chose me. Once she made her views known, her noble father handed her over *very* quickly. This should perhaps have worried me. Still, her attention to detail comes in handy when we work.' I enjoyed alluding to our work. It kept Uncle Fulvius on the alert. The old fraud liked to imply *he* was involved in undercover dealings for the government. I myself had taken on tasks as an imperial agent but I had never found anyone official who knew about this uncle of mine. 'Informing needs scepticism as well as good boots and a high expenses budget, don't you find, Uncle Fulvius?'

He jumped up. 'Marcus, my boy, can't sit around chatting! Cassius will look after you. He's around somewhere; he likes to flap and he loves being domestic! We have a grand treat laid on this evening – I do hope you will like it. Dinner is in your honour – and I've invited the Librarian.'

III

Once Fulvius had bustled out of earshot, Helena and I both groaned. Still drained by travel, we had been hoping for an early night. The last thing we wanted was to be paraded as Roman trophies in front of some uninterested provincial dignitary.

Don't get me wrong. I love the provinces. They supply us with luxury commodities, slaves, spices, silks, curious ideas and people to despise. Egypt ships at least a third of Rome's annual corn supply, plus doctors, marble, papyrus, exotic animals to kill in the arena, fabulous imports from remote parts of Africa, Arabia and India. It also provides a tourist destination that – even allowing for Greece – must be unparalleled. No Roman lives until he has scratched his name indelibly on a timeless Pharaonic column, visited a Canopus brothel and caught one of the hideous diseases that have led Alexandria to produce its world-famous medical practitioners. Some visitors pay up for the extra thrill of camel-riding. We could miss that. We had been to Syria and Libya. We already knew that to stand near a spitting camel is a loathsome experience, and one of the ways all those doctors keep in business.

'Fulvius is only excited that we are here.' Helena was the decent, kindly one in our partnership.

I stuck to vitriol. 'No; he's a social-climbing snob. He'll have some reason to ingratiate himself with this big scroll-beetle; he's using us as an excuse.'

'Maybe Fulvius and the Librarian are best friends who play board games every Friday, Marcus.'

'Where does that put Cassius?'

*   *   *

We soon found out where Cassius was: in a hot kitchen in the basement; in the middle of organising menus; and in a tizz. He had a cohort of puzzled staff working for him, or in some cases against him. Cassius had clear ideas how to run a party, and his system was not Egyptian. Since I believed Fulvius might have first met him cavorting with the worshippers of Cybele on the wilder shores of Asia Minor, his businesslike approach to a lie-down banquet surprised me.

'We ought to be nine couches, to be formal, but I'm settling for seven. Fulvius and I don't believe in touting invitations around the baths, just to make up numbers. You attract fat bores with no morals, who will be sick in your peristyle. It goes without saying, they never ask you back . . . I thought your father would be here with you, Falco?'

'Did he write and tell you that? No chance, Cassius! He did suggest imposing himself – I forbade the devious old bastard to come.'

Cassius laughed, the way people do when they cannot believe you are serious. I glared. My father and I had spent half of my life estranged, and that was the half I liked. He worked in the antiques trade, in that specialism where 'antique' means 'put together yesterday by a man with a squint in Bruttium'. My smooth-tongued father could make 'doubtful provenance' sound like a virtue. Buy from him and you would get a fake, but so flagrantly overpriced you could never admit to yourself that he diddled you. Ten to one a handle would fall off while you lugged the object home.

'He is not coming. I am serious!' I declared. Helena snorted. Cassius laughed again.

Despite greying hair, Cassius was sturdily built; he went weightlifting twice a week. If ever Fulvius got into bother, Cassius was supposed to fight their way out of it, though I had seen this bodyguard in action and had no faith in him. A handsome chunk, he was about fifteen years younger than my uncle, who must be ten years older than my parents; that put Fulvius well into his seventies, Cassius late fifties. They claimed they had been together for a quarter of a century. My mother, who always knew everyone's private business, swore her brother was a loner who had never set up house. That just showed how elusive Fulvius could be. For once Ma was wrong. Fulvius and Cassius had anecdotes that went back decades, involving several provinces. Certainly Cassius was getting flushed over his canapé recipes like a man who had spent years having mental breakdowns over parties he had hosted. His act was polished and he was heartily enjoying it.

Helena offered to help, but Cassius sent us out sightseeing.

As soon as we stepped outside, the customary local who knew strangers had arrived jumped up from the gutter where he was patiently waiting. We knew better than to hire a guide for the sights. We elbowed him aside and headed away briskly. He was so surprised, it took him some moments to gather himself together to curse us, which he did with sinister muttering in a strange language.

He would be there every day. I knew the rules. Eventually I would weaken and allow him to take us somewhere. He would get us lost; I would lose my temper; the unpleasantness would convince him that foreigners were loudmouthed, insensitive braggarts. In a couple of centuries the accumulated loathing from such incidents would lead to a vicious revolt. I would be part of the cause, just because I had wanted an aimless hour or two, walking hand in hand in a new city with my wife.

Today at least we escaped by ourselves. Aulus must have been up with the light and had hoofed to the Museion to try to convince the academic authorities he was a worthy scholar. If students had to have rich fathers, he would barely qualify. If brains were required, he was on even stickier ground. Albia was sulking because Aulus went out without her. Our two little daughters also rebuffed us; they had discovered where the servants hung out waiting for cute little girls in matching tunics to happen along looking for raisin cakes.

For Aulus to play the intellectual was fine with me. He wanted the kudos of saying he had studied at Alexandria, whilst I could use an agent in the Library. If he failed to worm his way in by himself, I would have to fix it with the Prefect, but our cover would look better if Aulus got his feet under the reading-tables independently. Besides, I hate prefects. Begging for official favours never works for me.

Egypt has been kept as a personal jewel case for the emperors, ever since Octavian – subsequently renamed Augustus – sank Antony's ambitions at the Battle of Actium. Since then, emperors have clung on to this glittering province. Others are governed by ex-consuls, but not Egypt. Every emperor sends trusted men of his own to run the place – equestrians, often ex-palace slaves – whose task is to siphon its rich resources straight into the imperial purse. Senators are officially forbidden to set foot in Nile mud, lest they get ideas and start plotting. Meanwhile, Prefect of Egypt has become a sought-after job for middle-rank officials, second only to heading the Praetorian Guard. These men can be political heavyweights. Eight years ago it was a Prefect of Egypt, Julius Alexander, who first acclaimed Vespasian as Emperor and then, while Vespasian manoeuvred to clinch his accession, provided his power base in Alexandria.

I disapproved of emperors, whoever they were, but I had to earn a living. I was a private informer, yet from time to time I carried out imperial missions, especially where they helped fund foreign travel. I had come here on a 'family visit' but it did contain a chance to do work for the old man. Helena knew that, naturally, and so did Aulus, who would help me with it. What I was not sure about, was whether Vespasian had bothered to inform the current Prefect I had been informally commissioned.

Let's say meeting the Librarian this evening was a little too soon for me. I like to get the measure of an investigation by myself, before I tangle with the principals.

But tourism came first: Alexandria was a beautiful city. Neatly laid out, it made Rome look as if it had been founded by shepherds – as indeed was true. The Sacred Way, meandering into the Forum Romanorum with grass between its haphazard stone slabs, was like a sheep track compared to glamorous Canopus Street. The rest was no better. Rome has never been given a formal street grid and that's not just because the Seven Hills get in the way. In domestic situations, Romans do not take orders. I doubt if even Alexander of Macedon could instruct an Esquiline copper-beater how to orientate his workshop; it would be inviting a sharp blow with a hammer to the heroic Macedonian skull.

Helena and I wandered through as much of this noble city as we could manage, given that I became grumpy as an admiring visitor and she was four or five months pregnant – another reason we had rushed to accept my uncle's invitation. We came as early in the year as we could sail. Soon Helena would cease to be mobile, our mothers would insist she stayed at home, and if we waited until the birth was over there would be – we hoped – an extra infant to drag around with us. Two was quite enough, and having a relative's house here to dump them in was a boon. This might be the last time sightseeing was feasible for the next ten or twenty years. We threw ourselves into it.

Alexandria had two main streets, each two hundred feet wide. Yes, you read it correctly: wide enough for a great conqueror to march all his army past before the crowds got sunburned or for him to drive along several chariots abreast, chatting with his famous generals as they occupied their own quadrigae. Clad with marble colonnades for its entire length, Canopus Street was the longest, with the Gate of the Moon at its western end and the Canobic Gate in the east. We hit it around the middle, from where the gates would be just distant dots if we could see past the milling crowds. Running through the royal quarter, Canopus Street intersected with the Street of the Soma, named for the tomb to which Alexander the Great's embalmed body had been brought after he died of wounds, weariness and drink. His heirs struggled to possess his remains; the first of the Ptolemies snatched the corpse and brought it to lend renown to Alexandria.

If the tomb of Alexander seemed rather familiar to us, that was because Augustus copied it for his own Mausoleum, complete with plantings of cypress trees on its circular terraces. Alexander's was substantially larger, one of the tallest buildings at the city centre.

Naturally we went in and inspected the famous body, covered with gold and lying in a translucent coffin. Nowadays the coffin lid was sealed, though the guardians must have given access to Augustus after the Battle of Actium, because when that reprobate pretended to pay his respects, he broke off part of Alexander's nose. All we could make out was the hero's blurred outline. The coffin seemed more like sheets of that stuff called talc than moulded panes of glass. Either way, it needed a sponge down. Generations of gawpers had left smeary fingerprints while sand dust had blown in everywhere. Given that the illustrious corpse was now almost four hundred years old, we did not complain about lack of closer contact.

Helena and I had a witty discussion about why Octavian, Julius Caesar's great-nephew, had taken it upon himself to destroy Alexander's best feature – that nose so gloriously embodied in elegant statues by his tame sculptor Lysippus. Octavian/Augustus was obnoxious and self-satisfied, but plenty of Roman patricians have those faults without attacking corpses. 'Horseplay,' explained Helena. 'All generals together. One of the lads. "You may be Great – but I can tweak your nose!" – Oh dear, look; it's come off in Octavian Caesar's hand . . . Quick, quick; stick it back and hope no one notices.' Undeterred by convention, my darling leaned down as close as she could get to the opaque dome and tried to see whether custodians had glued the nose back on.

We were asked to move along.

The Soma was just one feature of the grandiose Museion complex. A Temple to the Muses sat in a huge area of formal gardens, within which stood phenomenal buildings dedicated to the pursuit of science and the arts. It had a zoo, which we left for another day when we could bring the children. It was also home to the legendary Library and other handsome accommodation where scholars lived and ate.

'Tax-free,' said Helena. 'Always an incentive to intellectuals.'

I was not yet ready to explore the seat of learning. We refreshed ourselves strolling among the shady terraces and water features, admiring the stork-like ibises who dipped their curved beaks in the elegant canals, where lotuses were in flower in brilliant blue. I plucked an opening bud to present to Helena; its scent was exquisite.

Later we strolled towards the sea. We came out at the end of the narrow causeway that linked the mainland to Pharos Island. This causeway was called the heptastadion because it was seven Greek stades long – about four thousand feet, I reckoned by eye – more than we wanted to tackle that day. From the docks on the Great or Eastern Harbour, we had a good view of the Lighthouse. When we sailed in yesterday, we had been too close to look up and see it properly. Now we could appreciate that it stood on a spur of the island, set within a decorative enclosure. Overall, it rose to about five hundred feet. The tallest man-made structure in the world, it had three storeys – an enormous square foundation, which supported an elegant octagon, which in turn held up a round lantern tower, topped off with a great statue of Poseidon. Back in Italy, the lighthouse at Ostia was built to the same pattern, but I had to concede it was no more than a feeble imitation.

Part of Pharos Island, together with the heptastadion, formed one enormous arm around the Great Harbour. On the shore side, where we were, lay various wharfs; some encircled sheltered docking areas. Then away to our right, near where we were staying with Fulvius, another promontory called Lochias completed the circle. On this famous peninsula, we knew, many of the old royal palaces stood, the haunt of Ptolemies and Cleopatras long ago. They had had a private harbour and a private island they called Antirrhodus because its gorgeous monuments rivalled Rhodes.

The main part of Pharos Island turned in the opposite direction to form the sheltering mole around the Western Harbour. This was even bigger than the Great Harbour, and was known as the port of Eunostos, with its inner basin Kibotos, supposedly all man-made. Way out of view behind us, on the other side of the city, was Lake Mareotis, a huge inland stretch of water where yet more wharves and moorings served the export of papyrus and other commodities that were produced around the lake.

For Romans all this was a shock.

'We are so used to thinking that Rome is the centre of the trading world!' Helena marvelled.

'Easy to see why Alexandria was able to pose such a threat. Just suppose Cleopatra and Antony had *won* the Battle of Actium. We could be living in a province of the Egyptian Empire, with Rome just some unimportant backwater where uncultured natives in crude tribal garments

18

insist on speaking Latin instead of Hellenic Greek.' I shuddered. 'Tourists would rush straight through our town, intent on studying the curious civilisation of the ancient Etruscans instead. All they would have to say for Rome is that the peasants are rude, the food is disgusting and the sanitation stinks.'

Helena giggled. 'Mothers would warn impressionable daughters that Italian men might look handsome, but would get them pregnant then refuse to leave their Campagna market gardens.'

'Not even if the girl's uncle offered the fellow a good job in a papyrus factory!'

As we turned back for home, we walked by an absolutely enormous Emporium that made the central warehouse in Rome look like a collection of cabbage stalls. Also beside the waterfront we found Cleopatra's Caesarium. This monument to Julius Caesar, at the time still unfinished, had become the place of refuge where the Queen hauled up the wounded Mark Antony to die in her arms after he tried to kill himself in his own refuge, another impressive monument by the harbour which was called the Timonium. Then the Caesarium was the scene of her own suicide as Cleopatra pipped the gloating Octavian's hopes of flaunting her in his ceremonial Triumph. For that alone I liked the girl. Unfortunately Octavian turned the Caesarium into a shrine to his own dreadful family, which spoiled it. It was guarded by enormous old red granite obelisks, which we were told he had brought from elsewhere in Egypt. That was one advantage of this province. Exotic outdoor ornaments littered the place. Had these obelisks not been such dead weights, Augustus would undoubtedly have shipped them off to Rome. They were begging to be used in trendy landscape gardening.

We gazed at the Caesarium, and felt the pang of standing next to history. (Trust me; it is extremely similar to the pang of badly wanting a sit-down and a drink of cold water.) We found a giant sphinx against whose lion paw we could lean weakly until guards chased us off. Helena was at pains to assure me that Cleopatra's mystique had derived not from beauty but from wit, vivacity and vast intellectual knowledge.

'Don't disappoint me. We men imagine she bounced about on scented satin pillows, wildly uninhibited.'

'Oh Roman generals like to think they have seduced a clever woman. Then they can fool themselves they have done it for her own good,' Helena mocked.

'Anything less frigid than the average general's wife would have seemed hot stuff to Caesar and Antony. An hour of Cleo throwing her sceptre at the ceiling and doing erotic back-somersaults would pass pretty pleasantly.'

'And the Queen of the Nile could tickle their fancies while simultaneously showing off how she had read natural philosophy and was fluent in foreign languages.'

'Linguistic ability was not the kind of kinky taste I meant, Helena.'

'What – not even to shriek, *"More! More, Caesar!"* in seven languages?'

We went home for a rest. We would need energy that evening. We had to endure a formal dinner with a dignitary. That was nothing. Before it began, according to my uncle's house rules, we had to persuade Julia and Favonia to go to bed much earlier than they wanted to – and stay there.

IV

Cassius had thrown himself into the evening. Most of it worked. The decorations and some of the dishes were superb.

He served grilled fish in Sauce Alexandrian. Although Cassius saw it as a compliment to Egypt, I reckoned any local guest was bound to feel this recipe fell short of his mother's cherished version. Cassius was asking to be informed that stoned damsons were now a cliché and everyone who was anyone used raisins in their sauces . . . On the other hand, Cassius whispered that he could never have trained the cooks in time to do fine Roman cuisine. He was afraid that the pastry chef would knife him, if asked to try. Worse, he suspected that the chef had sensed the possibility of being asked to change his repertoire, and might already have poisoned the fried honey cakes. I suggested Cassius should eat one to check.

The Librarian did come, though he was late. We had to endure an hour of Fulvius getting agitated as he thought he had been snubbed. Then, while the man shed his shoes and was made comfortable, Fulvius pretended to us that arriving late was a custom here, a compliment that implied a guest was so relaxed he felt time was of no consequence . . . or some such waffle. I could see Albia staring, wide-eyed; she had already been startled by my uncle's outfit, which was a loose dining-robe of the type called a synthesis, in vivid saffron gauze. At least the Librarian had brought Fulvius a gift of potted figs, which would solve the dessert problem if Cassius keeled over after my pastry test.

His name was Theon. He looked acceptable on the surface but his clothes were a fortnight overdue at the laundry. They had never been stylish. His workaday tunic hung on a thin frame as if he never ate properly and his beard was sparse and straggly. Either he was too poorly paid to live up to his honourable position, or he was a natural slob. As a natural cynic, I presumed the latter.

At dinner, Cassius hung us all with special garlands then positioned us carefully. It was intended we should have three formal courses, though service was curious and distinctions became blurred. Still, we ploughed diligently through the correct rota of conversation. The appetisers were given over to my party's voyage. Helena, acting as our spokesperson, gave a humorous oration on the weather, the mercenary ship's captain and our stop-off in Rhodes – with its highlight of looking into the gigantic pieces of the fallen Colossus and seeing the stone and metal framework that would have held it upright, but for the earthquake.

'Do you suffer many earthquakes here?' Albia asked Uncle Fulvius in extremely careful Greek. She was learning the language and had been instructed to practise. Nobody would think that this grave and neat young girl had once roamed the streets of Londinium, an urchin who could spit 'Get lost, you pervert!' in more languages than Cleopatra elegantly spoke. As adoptive parents we viewed her proudly.

Helena had created a Greek phrasebook for our foster-daughter, including the question on which Albia had sweetly ventured as an ice-breaker. I regaled the company with further examples. 'The next continues the volcanic theme: *Please excuse my husband farting at the dinner table; he has a dispensation from the Emperor Claudius.* A footnote reminds us this is true; all Roman men enjoy that privilege, courtesy of our frequently maligned ex-Emperor. There was a good reason why Claudius was deified.'

Albia dragged back decorum into the conversation: 'My

favourite phrase is *Please help; my slave has expired from sunstroke in the basilica.*'

Helena smiled. 'Well, I was particularly proud of: *Can you direct me to an apothecary who sells inexpensive corn-plasters?* which then has a follow-up: *If I need anything of a more delicate nature, can I trust him to be discreet?*'

Uncle Fulvius displayed unexpected good nature, informing Albia in slow phrases, 'Yes, there are earthquakes in this country, although fortunately most are mild.'

'Do they cause much damage, pray?'

'It is always a possibility. However, this city has existed safely for four hundred years . . .' Albia was having trouble with Greek numbers; she started panicking. The Librarian had listened inscrutably.

When the main dishes came, of course we switched topics. I applied myself politely to local questions. Hardly had I broached how hot was the weather likely to be during our stay, when Aulus interrupted, launching into how he had fared that morning at the Museion. Aulus could be crass. Now the Librarian would assume he had been invited tonight so we could beg a place for Aulus.

Theon glared at the would-be scholar. What he saw would not impress: a truculent twenty-eight-year-old, overdue for a haircut, with so few social graces anyone could see why he had not followed his father into the Senate. No one would guess Aulus had nonetheless done a routine stint as an army tribune and even spent a year in the governor's office in Baetican Spain. In Athens he had grown a beard like Greek philosophers. Helena was terrified their mother would hear about it. No honest Roman wears a beard. Access to good razors is what singles us out from the barbarians.

'Decisions about admissions are taken by the Museion – it is out of my hands,' warned Theon.

'Not to bother. I used my charm.' Aulus smiled triumphantly. 'I was accepted straight away.'

'Olympus!' I let slip. 'That's a surprise!'

23

Theon appeared to think the same. 'And what do you do, Falco? Here for education or commerce?'

'Just a trip to visit family and put in some gentle sight-seeing.'

'My nephew and his wife are intrepid travellers,' beamed Uncle Fulvius. He was no slouch himself at touring, though he kept to the Mediterranean whereas I had been to more remote areas: Britain, Spain, Germany, Gaul . . . My uncle would shudder at those grim provinces, with their heavy legionary presence and absence of Greek influence. 'Your activities are not unconnected with imperial business, eh, Marcus? And I heard you were involved with the Census not so long ago? Falco is *very* highly regarded, Theon. So tell us, nephew, who is due for a penetrating audit here?'

Had Cassius not placed himself between us on the dining couches I could have kicked Fulvius. Trust relatives to open their mouths. Up until that point, the Librarian had viewed us as the usual ill-read foreigners wanting to look at pyramids. Now, of course, his gaze sharpened.

Helena helped him to pork-stuffed-two-ways and dealt with it briskly. 'My husband is an informer, Theon. He did carry out a special investigation into Census avoidance two years ago, but his work in Rome is mainly background checks on people's intended marriage partners. The public have the wrong perception of what Falco does, though in fact it is commercial and routine.'

'Informers are never popular,' Theon commented, not quite sneering.

I wiped sticky fingers on my napkin. 'Mud sticks. You will have heard about the crooked ones among my colleagues in the past, who pointed out rich men to Nero; he had them hauled into court on trumped-up charges so he could plunder their assets – with the informers taking a cut, of course. Vespasian put an end to that scam – not that I ever dabbled. Nowadays it's all small beans. Disputing wills for hopeful widows or chasing after runaway partners from debt-ridden small businesses. I help members of the public avoid pain, yet for the world at large my work still has the fragrance of a blocked drain.'

'So what *do* you do for the Emperor?' The Librarian would not let it go.

'The public is correct. I poke a long stick into noxious blockages.'

'That takes skill?'

'Just a strong shoulder and knowing when to hold your nose.'

'Marcus is being modest.' Helena was my best supporter. I winked at her wickedly, implying that if we had been couched alongside, I would have given her a squeeze. Against convention – but convention never bothers me. She was wearing dark red, a colour that gave her a luscious glow, with a gold necklace I had bought for her after a particularly profitable mission. 'He is a first-class investigator with exceptional skills. He works quickly, discreetly and with unfailing humanity.' *And he's all hands*, said her dark eyes back to me across the half-circle of couches.

I sent over more private eye-messages to Helena. Theon had spotted something going on, but had not worked out that it was lechery. 'The noble Helena Justina is not just my wife, but my accountant, business manager and publicist. If Helena decides you need an enquiry agent – good references and cheap rates – then she will prise a commission out of you, Theon!'

Helena then shot us all a beaming smile. 'Oh not this month, darling! We are in Egypt on holiday!'

'All-seeing Argos never sleeps!' Now it was Aulus pompously giving the game away. I was surrounded by idiots. No one had any discretion; well, except Cassius, who was so worn out by his exertions all day he had nodded off with his chin on his forearm. Protruding from a wide-sleeved robe of some African design, the forearm was extremely hairy.

25

'Classical allusion? Oh really!' Helena rapped her brother playfully with the end of a shellfish spoon. 'Marcus promised he would be all mine. He has come away to spend time with me and the little ones.'

I tucked into my foodbowl, looking like an innocent domestic treasure.

Helena then swerved neatly and started polite smalltalk about the Great Library. Theon ignored Helena. He favoured me with a professional grumble: 'You might think the Library is the most important institution here, Falco, but for administrative purposes, it counts less than the observatory, the medical laboratory – or even the zoo! I ought to be fêted but am harassed at every turn, while others take precedence. The Director of the Museion is by tradition a priest, not a scholar. Yet he includes in his title, "Head of the United Libraries of Alexandria", whereas I – in charge of the most renowned collection of knowledge in the world – am merely its curator and secondary to him. And why should the Pharos be so famous – a mere bonfire at the top of a tower – when the Library is the true beacon, a beacon of civilisation?'

'Indeed,' Helena humoured him, ignoring in her turn his exclusion of women. 'The Great Library, *Megale Bibliotheca*, should be one of the Wonders of the World. I have read that Ptolemy Soter, who first set out to found a centre of universal scholarship here, decided to collect not only Hellenic literature, but "all the books of the peoples of the world". He spared neither expense nor effort –' Theon was clearly unimpressed by her research. Women were not permitted to study in his Library and I reckoned he rarely mingled with them. I doubted if he was married. Helena's attempts at flattery met only a downcast expression of bad temper and bad grace. The man was hard going. Probably desperate, she jangled an armful of bangles and asked the obvious question: 'So how many scrolls do you have?'

The Librarian must have bitten on a peppercorn. He went white and choked. Fulvius had to pat him on the back. The disturbance woke Cassius from his nap, so he too was treated to Theon's look of reproach and thought the food was being blamed. Catching up with the conversation as if he had never been asleep, Cassius muttered under his breath, 'From what we hear of the famous Library, the freeloading scholars have a stinking lack of morality and all the staff are so disheartened they have almost given up!' It was the first time I saw my uncle's partner show his dyspeptic side. That's dinner parties for you.

Then, just as Aulus was forcing a beaker of water down the Librarian – with a grip that showed our boy really had been in the army – two pathetic little barefoot figures appeared in the doorway: Julia and Favonia were bawling their eyes out, having woken in a strange house all alone.

Uncle Fulvius growled. Helena and Albia jumped up and rushed from the room, carrying the children back to bed. Albia must have stayed with them. By the time Helena returned to the dining room, the third course had been brought and the slaves had withdrawn. We men had redoubled the pace of our wine intake and were talking about horse-racing.

V

Horseflesh, surprisingly, was the Librarian's best topic. Aulus and I could hold our own, while Fulvius and Cassius spoke of legendary contests run by noble beasts in international hippodromes, using colourful and sometimes off-colour anecdotes.

Helena commandeered the wine flagon, to forget us being sports bores. Roman men magnanimously take their women to dinner parties, but that doesn't mean we bother talking to them. But Helena would not tolerate staying in the women's quarters like a good Greek wife, letting her man go out to be entertained by a professional party girl. She had had a husband once, before me, who tried to go solo: she served him with a divorce notice.

We were a team: she refrained from nagging me, and when the party broke up, I made sure I found her buried among a pile of cushions and hauled her to bed. I can undress a woman who says she is too sleepy. Anyone can see where sleeve-buttons are. Helena was sober enough to flop around in the right directions. She just liked the attention; it was good fun for me too.

I spread her red dress neatly on a chest, placing earrings and so forth upon it. I threw my tunic on a stool. I crawled into bed beside Helena, thinking how good it would be to have a lie-in next day, before another of my uncle's leisurely all-morning breakfasts on his gently sunlit roof terrace. Afterwards, perhaps, now that I had met him, I might go and annoy Theon by poking around his Library and asking him to show me how the catalogue system worked . . .

No luck. First, our daughters found out where our room was. Still feeling neglected, they made sure we knew it. We were woken by two hard artillery rocks plummeting at our prone bodies then squirming between us. Somehow we had produced children with iron heads and fast-kicking powerful rabbits' feet.

'Why do you not have a nursemaid to look after them?' Uncle Fulvius had asked, in genuine bafflement. I had explained that the last slave I bought for that purpose found Julia and Favonia such hard work she announced she would be our cook instead. It added to his incomprehension. Fulvius should have known all about family chaos; he grew up on the same crazy farm as my mother. His brain seemed to have blanked out the misery. Perhaps mine would one day.

The next horror was a disturbed breakfast.

Barely had we slumped under the pergola, than we heard footsteps thumping loudly up the stairs. I could tell they meant trouble. Fulvius also seemed to recognise military boots. Given that his house rules were firm about not attracting this kind of attention, it was remarkable how fast he reacted. He struggled to get up, intending to take the newcomers downstairs somewhere private, but after his night of revelry was just too sluggish. Three men stomped out on to the terrace.

'Ooh – soldiers!' Helena murmured. 'What have you been up to, Fulvius?'

As far as I remembered from desultory checks before we left Rome, there were two legions in Egypt, though supposedly they exercised control with a light hand. Having the Prefect in Alexandria meant troops had to be permanently stationed here to show he meant business. Currently, those who were not up-country occupied a double fort at Nicopolis, the new Roman suburb on the eastern side that Augustus had built. Geographically, this fort was in the wrong place – right in the north of a long, narrow province while the brigands were a long way south, preying on the Red Sea ports, and any over-border incursions from Ethiopia and Nubia were even further away. Worse, during the Nile floods, Nicopolis was inaccessible except by punt. Still, the Alexandrian mob had a rowdy reputation. It was useful to have troops close by to cover that, and the Prefect could feel big, going around with armed escorts.

Apparently the militia also carried out certain law enforcement duties that in Rome would fall to the vigiles. So instead of the equivalent of my friend Petronius Longus, we had a visitation from a centurion and two sidekicks. Before they even said what they wanted, my uncle assumed the look of a naughty stable-boy. He rushed to lead away the centurion to his study – though the soldiers pretended they thought it was more discreet for them to stay behind on the roof terrace to supervise the rest of us. They had spotted the food, of course.

Good ploy, noble squaddies! I immediately questioned them on what had brought them to annoy my uncle.

They were commendably demure – for all of five minutes. Helena Justina soon softened them up. She filled fresh bread rolls with sliced sausage for them, while Albia passed around olive bowls. No soldier has been born who can resist a very polite seventeen-year-old girl with clean hair and dainty bead necklaces; she must have reminded them of their little sisters back at home.

'So what's the big mystery?' I asked them, grinning.

Their names were Mammius and Cotius, a long streak of wind with a broken belt-buckle and a short pot of pig's fat with his neck-scarf missing. They wriggled with embarrassment, but through mouthfuls of breakfast they inevitably told me.

Theon, the Librarian, had been found in his office that morning. A garland of roses, myrtle and green leaves, the garland with which Cassius had bedecked all of us last night at dinner, was lying on his work-table. This garland was a special order, about which Cassius had been meticulous, personally selecting the choice of leaves and style. It had led their centurion to the flower-seller who made it – and she fingered Cassius from the address where she delivered the foliage. Egypt was a bureaucratic province so the house was on some register as rented by Uncle Fulvius.

'What was up with Theon?'

'Dead.'

'Dead! But he never ate any of the pastry chef's poisoned cakes!' Helena laughed to Albia. The soldiers became nervous and pretended they had not heard her.

'Foul play?' I asked, making it casual.

'No comment,' announced Mammius with great formality.

'Does that mean you were not told, or you never saw the body?'

'Never saw it,' swore Cotius self-righteously.

'Well, nice lads don't want to go looking at corpses. It might make you queasy . . . So why was the army called in? Is that usual?'

Because, the lads informed us (lowering their voices), Theon's office was locked. People had had to break the door down. There was no key, not in his door, on his person, or anywhere inside the room. The Great Library was stuffed with mathematicians and other scholars, who were drawn to the commotion nosily; these great minds deduced that someone else had locked Theon in. In the traditions of the academic world, they loudly announced their discovery. A rumour flew around that the circumstances were suspicious.

The mathematicians had wanted to solve the puzzle of this locked room themselves, but a jealous philosophy student who believed in civic order, reported it to the Prefect's office.

'The snitching beggar must have scampered there on

31

very fast little legs!' As soldiers, my informants were fascinated to think anyone would ever involve the authorities voluntarily.

'Perhaps the student wants to work in administration when he gets a real job. He thinks this will enhance his profile,' Helena sniggered.

'Or perhaps he is just a nasty sneak.'

'Oh that would not debar him from government administration!' I could see Mammius and Cotius thought Helena an extremely exciting woman. Sharp lads.

Anyway, the sneak had landed us in it. At this moment, the centurion was instructing Fulvius to produce yesterday evening's menu and confirm whether any of us had suffered ill effects. My uncle would be quizzed on whether Cassius or he had had any grudge against Theon.

'Of course,' the soldiers admitted to us frankly, 'as visitors to the city, you people are bound to be the first suspects. When any crime happens, it helps public confidence if we can say that we have arrested a suspicious bunch of foreigners.'

VI

I left Helena and Albia to keep the soldiers occupied and hoofed downstairs. I found Fulvius and Cassius calm. Cassius looked slightly red in the face, but only because his qualities as a host were in question. Fulvius was as smooth as pounded garlic paste. Interesting: had these old boys had to answer to officialdom before? They operated in tandem and had a fund of tricks. They knew to sit wide apart, so the centurion could only look at them one at a time. They commiserated and pretended they were eager to assist. They had ordered up some very sticky currant pastries, which he was finding hard to eat while he tried to concentrate.

They waved me away, as if there was no problem. I stayed.

'I am Didius Falco. I may have a professional interest.'

'Oh yes,' said the centurion heavily. 'Your uncle has been explaining who you are.'

'Oh well done, Uncle Fulvius!' I wondered just how he had described me – probably as the Emperor's fixer, hinting it should give Cassius and him immunity. The centurion seemed unimpressed, but he let me nose in. He was about forty, battle-hardened and well up to this. He had forgotten to put on his greaves when he was called out in a hurry, but otherwise he was smart, clean-shaven, neat – and he looked observant. Now he had three Romans pretending they were influential citizens and trying to baffle him, but he kept his cool.

'So what do we call you, centurion?'

'Gaius Numerius Tenax.'

'Which is your unit, Tenax?'

'Third Cyrenaïca.' Raised in North Africa, the next patch along from here. It was customary not to station troops in their home province, just in case they were too loyal to their cousins and neighbours. So the other legion at Nicopolis was the Twenty-Second Deiotariana: Galatians, named for a king who had been a Roman ally. They must spend a lot of their time spelling it for strangers. The Cyrenians probably watched and jeered.

I made my pitch to win his friendship: 'My brother was in the Fifteenth Apollinaris – he was based here briefly, before Titus collected them for the Judaean effort. Festus died at Bethel. I heard the Fifteenth were brought back afterwards, but temporarily.'

'Surplus to requirements,' Tenax confirmed. He stayed polite but the old-comrade routine had not fooled him. 'Packed off to Cappadocia, I believe.'

I grinned. 'My brother would think himself well out of that!'

'Wouldn't we all? We must have a drink,' Tenax offered, making the effort though probably not meaning it. Fortunately he did not ask where I myself had served, or in what legion; if I had mentioned the disgraced Second Augusta and ghastly Britain, he would have frozen up. I did not push him now, but I intended to take him up on the friendly offer.

I subsided and let Tenax run the show. He seemed competent. I myself would have begun by finding out how Fulvius came to know Theon, but either they had covered that already or Tenax assumed that any foreigner of my uncle's standing automatically moved in those circles. This begged the question: what standing? Just who did the centurion think my wily uncle and his muscular partner were? They probably said 'merchants'. I knew they engaged in procuring fancy art for connoisseurs; back in Italy my father had his sticky fingers in it. But Fulvius was also an official negotiator for corn and other commodities, supplying the

Ravenna fleet. Everybody knows that corn factors double up as government spies.

Tenax chose to start by asking what time Theon left us last night. After a few arguments, we worked out when it was; not late. 'My young guests were still tired after travelling,' scoffed Fulvius. 'We broke up at a reasonable hour. Theon would have had time to return to the Library. He was a terrible work-slave.'

'The responsibility of his position preyed on him,' added Cassius. We all exchanged pitying glances.

Tenax wanted to know what had been served at dinner. Cassius told him and swore that we had all tried all the dishes and drinks. The rest of us were alive. Tenax listened and took minimal notes. 'Was the Librarian drunk?'

'No, no.' Cassius was reassuring. 'He won't have died of overindulgence. Not from last night.'

'Any signs of violence?' I put in.

Tenax shut off. 'We are looking into that, sir.' I could not complain about his avoidance tactics. I never gave out unnecessary details to witnesses.

'So what's all this about a locked room?'

Tenax scowled, irritated that his men had talked. 'I am sure it will turn out to be immaterial.'

I smiled. 'Probably the key bounced out while they were battering down the door. It will have slithered under the floorboards –'

'Ah, if only the Library was not such a handsome building, with great slabs of marble everywhere!' Tenax muttered, with only the slightest hint of sarcasm.

'No gaps?'

'No bloody gaps that I could see, Falco.' He sounded glum.

'So apart from the locked door – which may of course have an innocent explanation – does this death look unnatural in any other way?'

'No. The man could have had a stroke or heart attack.'

'But now the scholars have raised the issue, you will have

35

to come up with explanations? Or would the authorities like it discreetly hushed up?'

'I shall carry out a thorough investigation,' replied Tenax coldly.

'Nobody is suggesting a cover-up!' oozed Fulvius. He then made it plain that unless there was a good reason for further questions, he was terminating the interview. 'You can rule us out. The man was alive when he left our house. Whatever happened to Theon must have happened at the Library, and if you couldn't find answers when you looked at the scene, it may be that there are none.'

The centurion sat staring at his note-tablet for a few moments, chewing his stylus. I felt sorry for him. I knew the scenario. Tenax had nothing to go on, no leads. The Prefect would never directly order him to drop the investigation, yet if he did drop it and there was an outcry, then he would get the blame, whilst if he carried on, he could not win either; his superiors would suggest he was time-wasting, over-pernickety and straining the budget. Still, some niggle kept him worrying at it.

He did eventually leave, and he took his soldiers, but there was unhappiness in the way he loped off. 'It would not surprise me if he leaves a watch on our house,' I said.

'No need!' Fulvius exclaimed. 'This is a city of suspicions – we already have official eyes on us.'

'That fellow who sits on the kerb outside, waiting to harass people?'

'Katutis? Oh no, he's harmless.'

'What is he? A poor peasant who scrapes a living with offers of guiding visitors?'

'I think he comes from a temple,' said Fulvius offhand-edly.

Well, now I knew I was in Egypt. You had not lived in this province until you were haunted by a sinister, muttering priest.

*   *   *

Another curse landed on me that afternoon. Fulvius must have given me a seriously ornate curriculum, which Tenax reported back to base. I was summoned to the Prefect's office. There, I was greeted as some kind of high-ranking imperial emissary; I was inspected by a senior flunkey, given hearty best wishes from the Prefect (though he did not emerge to impart these effusions himself) and asked to take over the investigation into Theon's death. It was put to me that if they brought in an imperial specialist, this would calm potential agitation among the Museion élite lest they imagine the matter was not being taken seriously.

I understood. My presence was handy. By making these arrangements, the Prefect and Roman authorities would look suitably concerned. The academics would be flattered by my presumed importance to Vespasian. If Vespasian heard I had been given the job, *he* would be flattered that his agent was so well thought of (the authorities were wrong about his views on me, but I did not enlighten them). Best of all, for them, this had the makings of a tricky case. If I bungled it, an outsider would be carrying the blame. They would look as if they had tried their best. I would be the incompetent.

On my return to the house Helena heard what had happened and smiled with huge, loving eyes. 'So, this is well up to your usual work, my darling?' She knew how to deflate my self-satisfaction with a hint of doubt. She sipped mint tea a little too thoughtfully. A silver bangle flashed on her arm; her eyes were just as bright. 'A ridiculous puzzle, with no obvious way to clear it up, and everybody else just standing by to watch you make a mess of it? Dare I ask what they are paying you?'

'The usual government rates – which means, I am just expected to be honoured that they place so much faith in me.'

She sighed. 'No fee?'

I sighed too. 'No fee. The Prefect assumes I am on a

retainer already for whatever Vespasian sent me out here to do. His official did not ask what that was, incidentally.'

Helena put down her tea bowl. 'So you said you were insulted by their offer?'

'No. I said I assumed they would pay my expenses, for which I claimed a large advance immediately.'

'How large?'

'Large enough to fund our private trip to the Pyramids, once I've sorted out this case.'

'Which you are confident you can?' asked Helena with her usual gentle courtesy.

I kissed her, with my normal air of bluff.

VII

Aulus came in from the Museion, not long afterwards, eager to recite the strange fate of our dinner guest. He was annoyed that we already knew. He calmed down when I told him not to unbuckle his boots; he could come back out with me to inspect the crime scene. If it was a crime.

As a courtesy, Cassius had sent Theon home last night in the litter he and Fulvius used for getting about. Cassius now called up the bearers and we ordered them to take us to the Library, or as near as they could go, by exactly the same route. Retracing Theon's steps brought us no clues, but we convinced ourselves it was expert sleuthing. Well, it kept us out of the sun.

The head bearer, Psaesis, had a name that sounded like a spit but he was fairly pleasant for a man who was stuck with transporting rich foreigners to earn his bread and garlic. He spoke enough Greek to get by, so before we set out we asked him if the Librarian had seemed himself last night. Psaesis said Theon struck him as a little moody; in a world of his own, maybe. Aulus reckoned that sounded normal for a librarian.

My uncle's conveyance was a florid double palanquin with purple silk cushions and a heavily fringed canopy. It would have made passengers feel like pampered potentates, had the bearers not been different heights so as they got up speed the unstable equipage rocked around wildly. Cornering was treacherous. We lost three cushions overboard as we clung on. This must be routine, because the bearers stopped to retrieve them almost before we shouted. When they dropped us off, they grinned triumphantly as if they thought filling us with terror was the point.

Aulus led the way. A thickset figure, he marched off boldly across the Museion grounds. He wore a white tunic, a stylish belt and expensive boots, all with the grace of a young man who believed himself a born leader – thereby persuading everyone else to treat him as if he was. I always marvelled how he did it. He had no sense of direction, yet he was the only man I knew who could lure road-sweepers into telling him the way without mischievously sending him straight to the local midden. As my assistant in Rome, he had been slapdash, ignorant, lazy and too well spoken, but when a case interested him, I had found he bucked up and became reliable.

Approaching thirty, Aulus had behind him all the necessary moments of hard drinking, unsuitable friends, loose women, flirtations with religion and dubious political offers; he must be ready to settle down into the same kind of pleasant life on the fringes of high society that his easygoing father led. Once he tired of study, Rome would welcome him back. He would have a few good friends and no other close associates. Presumably a well-behaved wife would be found for him, some girl with a half-decent pedigree and an only slightly scathing attitude to Aulus. She would run up bigger dress bills than the Camillus estates could cover, though Aulus was so inventive he would somehow cope.

I had no idea what kind of intellectual he was. Still, he had chosen to study, so he may have applied himself better than young men who are forcibly sent to Athens just to get them out of trouble in Rome. In Greece I had met his tutor, who seemed to think well of him, though Minas was worldly – a heavy drinker. He might say anything to keep his fees. How had Aulus become accredited to the Museion? Perhaps through sheer bluff.

'This centre,' said Aulus, disparaging the Egyptian jewel like a true Roman, 'was founded by the Ptolemies to enhance their dynasty. It is a huge learning complex that forms part of the royal district of Brucheion.' I had seen yesterday that the Palace and Museion complexes took up almost a third of the city – and it was a large city. Aulus continued briskly: 'Ptolemy Soter started it about three hundred and fifty years ago. A career soldier, Alexander's general – fancied himself as a historian. Hence his big ambition: not just to create a Temple of the Muses to glorify his culture and civilisation, but to have in it a Library which contained all the books in the known world. He wanted to be tops. He set out deliberately to rival Athens. Even the catalogue is a thing of wonder.'

Aulus had walked me through some of the gardens where Helena and I sauntered yesterday. He did not stop to smell the flowers. He was athletic and moved fast. His guided tour was succinct: 'See the pleasant outside areas: cool pools, topiary, colonnades. Inside: marbled lecture halls with speakers' podia, rows of seats, elegant couches. Excellent acoustics for music and reading recitals. A communal refectory for the scholars –'

'Tried the food?'

'Lunch. Edible.'

'Scholars don't come to pamper themselves, lad.'

'We have to feed our busy brains, though.'

'Hah! So what else have you found?'

'Theatre. Dissecting rooms. Observatory on the roof. The biggest zoo in the world.' This zoo made its presence felt. Any walk among the shady porticoes was orchestrated by disconcerting animal roars, squawks and bellows. They sounded quite close by.

'Why in Hades do scholars need a zoo?'

Camillus Aelianus gave me a sad look. Clearly I was a barbarian. 'The Museion facilitates enquiry into how the world works. These beasts are not some rich man's trophies.

41

They are gathered here deliberately for scientific study. The whole place, Falco, is intended to attract the best minds to Alexandria – while the Library –' we had reached that edifice – 'is designed to lure them most of all.'

It was arranged around three sides of yet another garden. At the centre of the lush green planting lay a long straight-sided rectangular pool. The limpid water drew the eye towards a grandiose main entrance. Two side wings rose up double height, with an even more stupendous main building that towered directly in front of us.

'So in there,' I mused, 'is all the knowledge in the world?'

'You bet, Falco.'

'The greatest scholars alive today gather to read there?'

'Best minds in the world.'

'Plus a dead man.'

'At least one,' answered Aulus, with a grin. 'Half the readers look embalmed. There could be other stiffs that nobody has noticed yet.'

'Ours had eaten an excellent meal in friendly company, with decent talk and enough good wine, yet he still wanted to bury himself in his workroom late that night, surrounded by the inert presence of hundreds of thousands of scrolls . . . Poor home life?'

'He was a librarian, Falco. No home life at all, most probably.'

We walked up to the imposing marble-clad entrance. Inevitably it was flanked by stupendous pillars. Both the Greeks and the Egyptians are superb at monumental pillars. Put them together and the Library had a heart-stopping, heavyweight porch and peristyle. Huge statues of Ptolemy Soter, the 'Saviour', flanked the entrance. Coins showed him as curly-haired and mature, thicker-set than Alexander – though he lived much longer; Ptolemy died at eighty-four whereas Alexander only made thirty-three. Polished in granite, Ptolemy was smooth and serene in the style of the Pharaohs, smiling, with the flaps of a traditional head-dress behind his long ears and the merest hint of eye makeup. Alexander's closest general, he was a Macedonian, a fellow-student of Aristotle, but in the big share-out after Alexander died he grabbed Egypt, which he ruled with respect for its ancient culture. Perhaps it was because Ptolemy was a Macedonian that he made it his mission to establish Alexandria as a rival to Athens, to spite the Greeks who viewed Macedonians as crude northern upstarts. So Ptolemy not only built a library to outdo those in Athens, but he stole the Athenians' books to put in it – 'borrowing' them to copy, then keeping the originals even though he had to forfeit his surety of fifteen gold talents. This tended to prove what the Athenians thought: a Macedonian was a man who did not care if he lost his deposit.

Demetrius Phalereus had built for Ptolemy one of the cultured world's great statement buildings. Oddly, its core material was brick. 'Cheapskates?'

'Helps air circulation. Protects the books.' Where did Aulus find that out? This was like him; whenever I condemned him as lackadaisical, he came out with some gem. The main library faced east; that, too, was better for the books, he said.

We craned up at enormous polished granite columns, topped by exquisitely carved capitals, florid in the Corinthian manner but earlier and with distinct Egyptian overtones. Around their mighty bases, clusters of off-duty readers littered the well-planned architecture in untidy groups – younger members of the academic world, all looking as if they were debating philosophical theories, but in fact discussing who had what to drink last night, and in what horrendous quantities.

Passing through the shadow of the intimidating porch, we entered the grand hall. Our feet slowed reverently; the floor, made from enormous sheets of marble, was so highly polished it showed our blurred images. A pervert could look up your tunic; a narcissist could look up his own. I slowed down cautiously. The interior space was enormous, sufficient to impart hush through size alone. Beautiful marble veneers cooled the air and calmed the spirits. A colossal statue of Athene as goddess of wisdom dominated the far wall, between two of the magnificent pillars that decorated the lofty lower area and supported the upper gallery. Behind this colonnade, which was repeated above with lighter pillars, were tall niches, each covered by panelled double doors. These housed some of the books. Occasional open doors showed wide shelves of scrolls. The cupboards were set above a triple plinth; its steps ensured that anyone approaching the scrolls would be fully visible. Library staff could discreetly monitor who was consulting what valuable works.

The upper gallery was protected by elegant latticed banisters with gilded bosses. The lower floor had half-columns at intervals, bearing bearded busts of famous authors and intellectuals. Discreet plaques told us who they were. Many would have worked here in their day.

I laid a hand on Aulus' arm and we stood for a moment watching. This alone should have drawn attention to us, though no one seemed to notice. The scholars ignored activity around them. They worked at two rows of handsome tables running down each side of the great hall. Most were lost in concentration. Only a few talked; it caused a *frisson* of irritation among the others. Some had mounds of scrolls on their tables, which gave the impression they were deeply involved in lengthy research – and also stopped anybody else trying to use the same table.

Men came in and looked around for empty seats or for staff to fetch scrolls from store, but rarely did anybody gaze directly at other people. Without doubt, some of these blinkered types avoided being sociable; they crept around unobtrusively and were nervous if anybody spoke to them. Some, I thought, must be well-known, but I reckoned others liked anonymity. In most public buildings, everyone has a common interest: they work as a team on whatever the building exists for. Libraries are different. In libraries, each scholar toils privately on his thesis. Nobody else need ever find out who a man is, or what his work entails.

I had used libraries. People condemn informers as low blockheads but I not only read for pleasure, I regularly consulted the records in Rome for my work. My main haunt was the Library of Asinius Pollio, Rome's oldest, where citizens' details are held – birth, marriage, citizenship status, death certificates and opened wills – but I had other favourites, such as the Library on the Porticus of Octavia, for general research or consulting maps. In just a few moments' stillness, I began to recognise familiar types. There was the man who talked long and loud, oblivious to the bad feeling he caused; the one who came and sat right next to someone else, even when there were plenty of free seats; the fidgety one who seemed to have no idea how much he rustled and clattered his stuff; the one making furious long-hand notes with an extremely scratchy stylus; the one who breathed maddeningly. Moving around quietly with requested scrolls were staff members doing a thankless task.

We had already encountered the students hanging around outside, those who never did any work but just came to meet their friends. Inside were the weirder scholars who *only* came to work and consequently had no friends. Outside were the flighty souls who sat around discussing Greek adventure novels, dreaming that they could one day be authors of popular fiction, earning a fortune from a rich patron. Inside, I spotted the teachers who wished they could give it up just to be scholars. As a market gardener's grandson, I admit I hoped that somewhere lurked a brave soul who dared wonder if he would be happier and more useful if he went back to run his father's farm . . . Probably not. Why would anyone give up the fabled 'freedom from want and freedom from taxes' that scholars had enjoyed at Alexandria since the Ptolemies?

Theon had told us that although he worked in such a glorious place he was 'harassed at every turn'. I wondered if he was being chased by some number-crunching administrator who was trying to cut back funds. He had muttered against the Museion Director for undermining his kudos. From what I knew of public administration, he was also likely to have had an underling who saw it as his mission to disrupt. Institutions always possess administrative creeps. Should there be any suggestion of foul play in the Librarian's death, I would be looking for whatever up-and-coming greaser had jealous eyes on Theon's job.

I sighed. If we had shouted 'Fire!' many of these beings would have looked up vaguely, then gone back to their reading.

I did not relish making enquiries here for witnesses.

Aulus was more impatient than me. He had collared a library assistant.

'I am Camillus Aelianus, just admitted to the Museion. This is Didius Falco, who has been asked by the Prefect to examine the death of your director, Theon.'

I noted that the assistant was unfazed. He was not disrespectful, but nor was he awed. He listened like an equal. He was about thirty, dark like a Syrian rather than an African, square face, curly hair cut short, wide eyes. He wore a plain, clean tunic and had mastered walking silently in his loose sandals.

Whatever we said here would be overheard by many, even though the readers were all keeping their heads down, apparently. I asked, 'If we are not interrupting, could you show us Theon's room?'

Unusually for public servants, library assistants believe they exist to help people find things. This one put down an armful of scrolls and led us off immediately. Once away from the audience, I got talking to him. His name was

Pastous. He was one of the *hyperetae*, the staff who were responsible for registering and classifying the books.

'How do you classify?' I asked, quietly making conversation as we crossed the mighty hall.

'By source, author and editor. Then each scroll is labelled to say it is mixed or unmixed – whether it contains several works or only one long one. Each is then listed in the Pinakes, which were begun by Callimachos.' He looked at me, uncertain how educated I might be. 'A great poet, who was once head of the Library.'

'Pinakes? This is your famous catalogue?'

'Yes, the tables,' said Pastous.

'Defined by what criteria?'

'Rhetoric, law, epic, tragedy, comedy, lyric poetry, history, medicine, mathematics, natural science and miscellanea. Authors are arranged under each topic, each with a brief biography and critical account of his work. The scrolls are stored alphabetically too, according to one or two initial letters.'

'Do you specialise in a particular section?'

'Lyric poetry.'

'I won't hold that against you! So the Library has holdings of books – and books about the books?'

'One day,' Pastous agreed, showing a sense of humour, 'there will be books about the books that are about the books. An opening for a young scholar?' he suggested to Aulus.

My brother-in-law scowled. 'Too futuristic for me! I don't see myself as original. I am reading law.'

Pastous saw that Aulus' surly manner hid some wryness. 'Precedents! You could write a commentary on the commentaries on precedents.'

I broke in. 'He is earning no fees currently. Would there be money in it?'

'People write for *money*?' Pastous smiled lightly, as if I had put forward a strange concept. 'I was taught that only the rich can be authors.'

'And the rich do not need the work . . .' Then I asked the question Helena had asked Theon yesterday: 'So how many scrolls are there?'

Pastous reacted calmly: 'Between four hundred and seven hundred thousand. Call it half a million. However, some say considerably less.'

'For a place that is so heavily catalogued,' I sniffed, 'I find your answer oddly vague.'

Pastous bristled. 'The catalogue lists every book in the world. All of them have been here. They are not necessarily here now. For one thing –' He was not above a gentle jibe – 'Julius Caesar, your great Roman general, burned a great number on the quayside, I believe.'

He was hinting that Romans were uncivilised. I glanced at Aulus and we let it pass.

We had reached an area behind the reading hall. Dim corridors with lower ceiling heights ran here like rabbit burrows. Pastous had brought us past one or two large, narrow rooms where scrolls were stored. Against the long walls, some were in big open pigeonholes, others contained in closed boxes. Smaller rooms had clerks working and craftsmen, all slaves I guessed, engaged on maintenance: mending torn sheets, adding scroll rods, colouring edges, applying identification tags. From time to time we were assailed by scents of cedarwood and other preservatives, though the main aura was timeless and dusty. Some of the workers were the same.

'People stay here for decades?'

'The life claims them, Falco.'

'Was Theon enraptured by this life?'

'Only he could have said,' returned Pastous gravely.

Then he came to a stop and made an elegant arm gesture. He had indicated a pair of tall wooden doors that had recently suffered damage. One now stood half open. He did not have to tell us: we had reached the dead Librarian's room.

VIII

A small black slave had been left to guard the room. Nobody had explained to him what that entailed. He let us go in with no attempt to check credentials. So comforting.

The corridor was otherwise deserted. All the milling sightseers described by the centurion Tenax must have gone away, bored. Aulus coughed nervously; he asked Pastous if the Librarian's body was still here. The assistant looked shocked and assured us it had been taken for burial.

'Who gave the order?' For once a vague expression came upon Pastous. I asked if he knew where the remains had gone.

'I can find out for you.'

'Thanks.'

I pushed at the double doors. The one that moved was solid and heavy, none too level on its great hinges; the other was stuck fast. This was a grandiose entrance. One man's arms would not be long enough to place the doors in the full open position simultaneously; they were designed to be ceremonially moved by a matched pair of flunkeys.

Someone had gone at them like a developer's wrecker on double time for fast demolition. 'They made a good job of it!'

'I heard a natural science student was fetched.' Pastous had a pleasing dryness. 'They tend to be large healthy young men.'

'The outdoor life?'

'Few lectures, so most spend their spare time out at the

49

Gymnasium. On field trips, they build up their legs running away from rhinoceroses.'

Aulus and I sidled through the half-open door and entered the room. Pastous remained on the threshold behind us, watching with a curiosity that managed to be polite yet sceptical.

We inspected the doors. On the outside of the room they had a formidable lock of great antiquity, a wooden beam that was held shut by pin tumblers; with much squinting I made out there were three of those. Whenever the doors were closed and the beam put in place, gravity would make the tumblers fall and act as a lock. Inserting the correct key would lift them out of the way, then the beam could be withdrawn using the key. I had seen other locks where the operator removed the beam by hand, but Pastous said this was the traditional Egyptian kind, as used on most ancient temples.

There was one disadvantage: the wooden key must be about a foot long. Aulus and I knew that Theon had not been carrying anything like that when he came to dinner with Uncle Fulvius.

I reckoned no one used the old wooden beam lock now. Perhaps because of the inconvenience, someone had much more recently installed a Roman lock. It was metal, beautifully ornate with a lion's head, and fixed on the inside of one of the doors. Its beam shot into a post that had been specially fixed to the other door to receive it. This lock would have a slotted turning key. Operated through the door, from outside in the corridor, the key would turn, moving pins inside the lock. However, a ward plate also inside the lock ensured the slots on the key had to line up; only the correct key was able to turn through this plate – and it had to be inserted right on line. I had seen keys that were made with hollow stems, so they were pushed in over a guide to keep them straight.

If Theon had been carrying *this* key last night, he could

have hidden it about his person, on a string around his neck maybe, and we would not have seen it. It must be bigger than a ring-key, but still manageable. 'And this key has disappeared?'

'Yes, Falco.'

The lock was damaged; this was probably done when people broke in to find the body. Double doors are vulnerable to pushing in. Pulling them open from the inside if you had been locked in would be more difficult. But there was no sign of that.

'Too much to hope that the key just fell somewhere!' Aulus hated puzzles. As Tenax had told us, there was nowhere for a key to have fallen. We looked up and down the corridor, just in case it had been kicked across the floor, but no.

I had no patience with mystery features myself, so I turned back into the room and looked around. It had been purpose-built for a notable incumbent. Half as high again as the corridor outside, it had a coffered ceiling and ornate classical covings. The walls were inset with yet more book cupboards, in expensive wood but plain; all the spaces in between were richly painted and gilded in colourful Egyptian style. A dramatic desk was supported on two elegant carved leopards. Behind it was a seat more like a throne than a clerk's writing station, ornamented with enamel and ivory. My father would have made an offer to auction it on sight.

Pastous watched me considering the grandeur of the furniture. 'The Librarian was called "Director of the King's Library" or "Keeper of the Archives".' He paused. 'Traditionally.' He meant, before the Romans came and finished the line of the Kings. I looked back over my shoulder at him, wondering if that rankled. It seemed impolite to ask.

'So how well did you know Theon?'

'He was my superior. We spoke often.'

'He thought well of you?'

'I believe so.'

'Are you prepared to tell me what you thought of him?'

Pastous ignored my invitation to be indiscreet. He replied formally, 'He was a great scholar, as all Librarians have been.'

'What was his discipline?' enquired Aulus.

I knew. 'Historian.' I turned to Pastous. 'Theon had dinner with us at my uncle's house last night and I asked him. To be honest, we found him hard going, socially.'

'Well, you said he was a historian!' chortled Aulus, half under his breath.

'He was a shy man by nature,' Pastous exonerated his leader.

I defined him differently. I had thought Theon unfriendly, even arrogant. 'Not good for someone in his elevated position.'

'Theon would mingle with important people and overseas visitors when it was required,' Pastous defended him. 'He carried out his formal duties well.'

'He warmed up when the talk got on to the hippodrome! He seemed quite a racegoer.'

The assistant made no comment. I gathered he knew nothing of Theon's private interests. Equality within the Library went no further than the reading room. Outside, there was a social gap between officials and their staff which I imagined the gruff Theon had been happy to sustain.

'Where was the body found?'

'In his seat at his desk.'

Aulus took up a position there, facing the door, some ten feet away from it. He would see anyone who came in as soon as they opened the door. I looked around. The room had no other exits. It was lit by clerestory windows, high in one of the walls. Though they were unglazed, they had metal grilles, with very small spaces. Aulus then played dead, arms flung across the desk, head down on the wood.

Pastous, still in the doorway, looked nervous as the lordly young man occupied the chair. Ever an impatient type, Aulus soon moved, although not before he had sniffed the desk like an uncontrolled bloodhound. He left it and paced to the book cupboards, which he opened and closed one after another; their keys were in the locks, though whether they were locked or unlocked seemed random. Perhaps it was thought safe enough for the Librarian to lock his room when he went out. Apparently aimless, Aulus lifted out one or two scrolls, then put them back askew, while gazing into the shelf spaces, inspecting their corners and staring up at their tops.

I stood beside the portentous desk. It held a small selection of writing styluses and pens on a tray, an inkwell, a stylus knife, a sand sifter. To my surprise, nothing bore the written word. Apart from the implements, which were shoved to one far corner, the surface was completely clear. 'Has anything been removed from this room today?'

Pastous shrugged; he clearly wondered why I asked.

'No handy suicide note?' chaffed Aulus. 'No hastily scrawled declaration of *"Chi did it!"* Written in blood, perhaps?'

'Chi?' I scoffed.

'Chi the unknown quantity. Chi marks the spot.'

'Ignore my assistant, Pastous. He is a wild man, reading law.'

'Ignore my brother-in-law,' Aulus retaliated. 'He is an informer. They are uncultured and prejudiced – and boast about it. It is reasonable, Falco, to hope at least for a reminder saying *"meet Nemo after dark"*.'

'Save us the Homeric references, Aulus. Theon's rather cosy office hardly equates to a Cyclops' cave with Odysseus calling himself "Nobody" and thinking it extremely clever. If Theon met with foul play, it was executed by *Some*body.'

'Have any sheep been seen walking out of the Library with seagoing adventurers clinging to their wool?' Aulus merrily asked Pastous.

The library assistant winced as if he thought us a couple of clowns. I suspected he was more astute than he let on. He watched us closely enough to see that while we were fooling, both of us absorbed information from our surroundings. He was interested in our procedures. That curiosity was probably harmless, just natural to a man who worked with information. Still, you never know.

We asked him to find out where the corpse had been taken, thanked him again for his help and assured him we could be left to carry on by ourselves.

Once we were alone, we sobered up. I took a turn in Theon's chair. Aulus continued his search of the book cupboards. Nothing on the shelves caught his attention. He turned back to me.

'Something is missing, Aulus.'

He quirked up an eyebrow. We were quiet now. Thoughtful, businesslike, and serious. We assessed the room professionally, considering possibilities. 'Documents, for one thing. If Theon really came to work, where is the papyrus?'

Aulus breathed in slowly. 'Someone cleaned up. There is nothing significant in the scroll cupboards; not now.'

'What scrolls does he have?'

'Just a catalogue.'

'So, if yesterday's work involved documents, they have been snaffled. If it's relevant to how he died, we have to find them.'

'Perhaps there was no work.' Aulus had an imagination and was applying it for once. 'Maybe he was depressed, Marcus. Sat for a long time with an empty table in front of him, thinking about his sorrows – whatever they were. Stared into space until he could bear none of it any longer – and then committed suicide.' We both imagined that silently. Reliving the last moments of a suicide is always unsettling. Aulus shivered. 'Perhaps he died naturally . . . Alternatives?'

I let a ghost of a smile hover. 'I won't tell Cassius, but his Sauce Alexandrian last night was heavy enough to give gripping indigestion. Maybe Theon sat here, unable to get his guts comfortable, until nature carried him off.'

Aulus shook his head. 'As sauces go it had, for my taste, too much pepper. A piquant little condiment. But hardly lethal, Marcus. Any other possibility?'

'One.'

'What?'

'Theon may not have come here for deskwork. Maybe he planned to meet someone. Your Nemo may have existed, Aulus. If so, we have the usual question: did anybody else see Theon's visitor?'

Aulus nodded. He was glum. Neither of us relished such an enquiry, given that hundreds of people worked here. If any of the staff or scholars was observant enough to notice who went to the Librarian's office (not a hope I relied upon), finding the witness among the rest would be difficult. Even if we succeeded, they might not be willing to tell us anything. We could waste a lot of time, yet never get anywhere. Besides, at night, with everywhere quiet and the back rooms deserted, any mysterious associate who knew how to tiptoe could have reached the Librarian without being noticed at all.

'Something else is missing,' I remarked.

Aulus gazed around the room and failed to work it out. I waved an arm. 'Look again, my boy.' Still no good. He was a senator's son and took too much for granted. His brown eyes were as wide set and good looking as Helena's, but he lacked his sister's rapid intelligence. He was merely bright. She was a genius. Helena would herself have spotted the omission, or when I asked the question she would have followed my train of thought doggedly until she worked it out.

I gave up and told him. 'No lamps, Aulus!'

IX

Following my lead, Aulus saw that indeed there were no oil lamps, no sconces, no freestanding candelabra. If this room really was just as it had been found, then Theon sat here at his desk, and died, in pitch darkness. More likely we were right earlier: someone had cleaned up.

We went out to the corridor to ask the little slave. He had scarpered.

Three-quarters of a day had already passed since the Librarian was discovered. We needed to act fast. I hailed a craftsman in a scroll-worker's apron and asked who Theon's deputy was. He did not have one. On his death, the running of the Library was taken over by the Director of the Museion. He was accommodated near to the Temple of the Muses. We went to see him.

His name was Philetus. A room was not enough for him; he occupied his own building. Statues of his most eminent predecessors were lined up in front of it, headed by Demetrius Phalereus, the founder and builder, a follower of Aristotle who had suggested to Ptolemy Soter the idea of a great institution for research.

Uninvited visits were discouraged. But as the secretaries began their tired rebuffing routine, the Director popped out of his sanctum, almost as if he had been listening with an ear pressed to the door. Aulus shot me a glance. Staff wittered that we had come about Theon; although the Director stressed what a busy man he was, he conceded he would find time for us.

I mentioned the statues. 'You'll be next!'

Philetus simpered 'Oh, do you think so?' with so much false modesty I saw at once why Theon had disliked him. This was the second most important man in Alexandria; after the Prefect, he was a living god. He had no need to push himself. But pushing himself was what Philetus did. He probably believed he pushed with elegance and restraint – but in truth he was mediocre and bumptious, a little man in a big man's job.

He made us wait while he bustled out and did something more important than talking to us. He was a priest; he was bound to be manipulating something. I wondered what he was fixing. Lunch, maybe. He took long enough.

Some holders of great public office are modest about it. Surprised to be chosen, they carry out their duties as effectively as the wise folk who chose them anticipated. Some are arrogant. Even those can sometimes do the job, or their cowed staff do it for them. The worst – and I had seen enough to recognise one – spend their time in deep suspicion that everybody else is plotting against them: their staff, their superiors, the public, the men who sell them their street foods, maybe their own grandmothers. These are the power-crazed bastards who have been appointed far beyond their competence. They are generally a compromise candidate of some kind, occasionally some rich patron's favourite, but more often shoved into this post in order to extract them from somewhere else. Before their time is up they can ruin the office they hold, plus the lives of all with whom they come in contact. They stick in their place using loyal toadies and threats. Good men wilt during their demoralising tenure. Fake reputations glue them dangerously to their thrones of office where they are suffered to continue by government inertia. To his credit, Vespasian did not appoint such men – but sometimes he was stuck with those his predecessors had wished on him. Like all rulers, sometimes he saw it as too much effort to ditch the duds. All men die eventually. Unfortunately, dreary failures live long lives.

'Settle down, Falco!'

'Aulus?'

'One of your rants.'

'I never spoke.'

'Your face looks as if you just ate a chicken liver that a bile duct broke over.'

'Bile duct?' The Director of the Museion came bustling back in. Overhearing us, he looked perturbed.

I gave him my happiest *Good evening, sir; I am your chef for the evening!* grin. We had waited so long, it seemed appropriate to greet him again. 'Philetus – what an honour this is for us.' That was enough. I switched off the simpering. He had smooth features of an anonymous kind. Trouble had not marked him. His skin looked very clean. That didn't mean he lived morally, only that he spent hours at the baths. 'The name's Falco. Marcus Didius Falco; I represent the Emperor.'

'I heard you were coming.'

'Oh?'

'The Prefect confided that the Emperor was sending out a man.' The Prefect overstepped the mark, then.

I played it straight. 'Good of him to clear my path . . . This is my assistant, Camillus Aelianus.'

'Have I heard that name?' Philetus was sharp. Nobody made it to Director of the Museion without at least some mental ability. We must not underestimate his self-preservation skills.

Aulus explained. 'I have just been admitted as a legal scholar, sir.' We all liked that 'sir', for different reasons. Aulus enjoyed shameless bluffing, I looked good for my respectful staff, and Philetus took it as his due, even from a high-class Roman.

'So . . . you two work together?' The Director's eyes glittered with wary fascination. As I had suspected, he had a stultifying fear of conspiracy. 'And what exactly do you do, Falco?'

'I conduct routine enquiries.'

'Into what?' snapped the Director.

'Into anything,' I breezed cheerily.

'So what did you come to Egypt for? It cannot have been Theon! Why has your assistant enrolled at my Museion?'

'I am here on private business for Vespasian.' Since Egypt was the Emperors' personal territory, that could mean business on the imperial estates far outside Alexandria. 'Aelianus is on a sabbatical, taking a private course of legal study. When the Prefect invited me to oversee this business of Theon's death, I called him in. I prefer an assistant who is used to working with me.'

'Is there a *legal* problem?' Philetus would be a nightmare to work with. He picked up on any irrelevance and needed soothing every five minutes. I had been in the army; how I knew this type!

'I hope,' I said gently, 'I shall find there is *no* problem . . . Would you like to tell me what happened at the Library?'

'Who else have you asked?' A paranoid's answer.

'Naturally I came to you first.' That flattered him – yet left him on his own with finding a story. To save time, I helped him start: 'Can you create a general picture for me – Was Theon well liked at the Library?'

'Oh everyone loved him!'

'You too?'

'I had great admiration for the man and his scholarship.' That rang false. If Theon had loathed Philetus, as he implied to us last night at dinner, almost certainly Philetus had loathed him back. Loyalty to his deceased underling was one thing; trying to blow smoke in my eyes served nobody.

'So he had a good academic reputation and was popular socially?' I asked drily.

'Indeed.'

'Normally, do Librarians retire, or go on until they die in post?'

'It is a lifetime position. Occasionally we might have to suggest a very elderly man has become too frail to continue.'

'Lost his marbles?' Aulus piped up cheekily.

'Theon was not too old.' I waved him down. 'By any standards he died prematurely.'

'Terrible shock!' fluttered Philetus.

I stretched in the wicker chair his staff had provided. As I did so, I fetched out a note-block from a satchel, opening it upon my knee though maintaining a relaxed attitude. 'Explain to me this business of finding him in the locked room, will you? What had made people go looking for him?'

'Theon failed to appear at an early morning meeting of my Board. No explanation. Quite unlike him.'

'What was the meeting? Special agenda?'

'Absolutely routine!' Philetus sounded too firm.

'Subjects that related to the Library?'

'Nothing like that . . .' He stopped meeting my eye. Was he lying? 'When he failed to arrive, I sent someone to remind him. When there was no answer –' He looked down at his knees demurely. He clearly ate well; under a long tunic, with expensive widths of braid on the hems, the knees he was surveying bulged chubbily. 'One of the scholars climbed up a ladder outside and looked in. He saw Theon sprawled across his table. Some people broke the doors down, I believe.'

I smiled, still treating him with friendliness. 'I am impressed that Alexandrian scientific enquiry extends to climbing ladders!'

'Oh we do much more than that!' rasped Philetus, misjudging my tone. Aulus and I nodded politely. Aulus, who had a vested interest in the Museion's good reputation for study, made himself look particularly obsequious. Sometimes I wondered why he did not rush home and apply for election to the Senate straight away.

At this point, Philetus suddenly decided to take charge. 'Now listen, Falco – far too much is being made of this missing key nonsense. There is bound to be a rational explanation. Theon happened to die, before his time maybe, but we must bury him decently, while those whose duty it is must appoint a successor.'

I foresaw problems there. I guessed Philetus was jittery about making decisions; he would put it off until the last minute, endlessly consulting other people until he was so flummoxed with contrary advice he jumped on the least good solution.

'Indeed.' He thought I was beaten. I had hardly started. 'The Emperor will let you take the lead producing a short-list for the Librarian's post. The Prefect will be grateful to receive it as soon as possible.'

Philetus was visibly put out. He had not expected, and clearly did not want, official involvement. 'Oh! Will you have a hand in this, Falco?'

'It would not be usual. Since I am here,' I murmured, 'the Prefect may appoint me as a consultant.' There was not a chance in Hades that the Prefect would allow me near this decision – but I had fooled Philetus. He had thought he controlled the Librarian's post. Perhaps he did. Unless he tried to appoint a three-legged nanny-goat from the low end of town, most prefects would be happy to sit back and allow whatever the Director wanted. Now he believed I had muscled in on him; he never suspected I had no power to do so.

'I shall have to consult the Academic Board, Falco.'

'Fine. Tell me when and where.'

'Oh! We never normally allow strangers to hear confidential discussions.'

'I very much want to meet your Board.' Normally I flee from committees but I wanted to meet this group, because if anything odd had happened to Theon they must be the men who stood to gain from it professionally. 'Is it daily?

Shall I attend tomorrow morning? You mentioned they meet early – I can manage that.'

Panic showed on Philetus' face.

Looking casual, I kept pressing: 'Now, were you responsible for Theon's body being removed from his office? Can you tell me which funeral director has the corpse?'

This caused more anxiety. 'You surely do not wish to view it?'

'We may just look in on the undertaker,' Aulus weighed in with a mollifying tone. 'Didius Falco always likes to mention names in his report. It gives a good impression if Vespasian believes we carried out a full personal check.'

Aulus managed to imply we probably would not really go there. He played the dozy and unreliable student so successfully that before the Director knew it, he squeaked out the information for us.

As we were leaving, I turned back unexpectedly – that old tired trick, but it has been known to work. 'Just one last point, Philetus – routine question: can you tell me where you were and what you were doing yesterday evening?'

He was furious. But he was able to say he had been at a long poetry recital. Since it was apparently hosted by the Roman Prefect, I could check. And much as I would have liked to make the Director my chief suspect, if the Prefect – or more likely some minion on his staff – confirmed this, I would have to believe the story.

X

The Director had named a local undertaker. His embalming salon was close to the Museion. One of the secretaries took us, leading us outside the complex, through early afternoon streets full of Alexandrian flatbed carts, each with its mound of green fodder for the horse or donkey. The beasts all had nosebags. The drivers all looked half asleep, until they spotted us to stare at.

There was fine dust everywhere. We walked through a small market, teeming with pigeons, rabbits, ducks, geese, chickens and bantams; all were for eating and were either caged or kept on pallets with their feet tied together. Behind the market, which remained highly audible, lay the dim premises we sought. Curious locals watched us going in, just as they would back home on the Aventine.

The head of the outfit was called Petosiris.

'I am Falco.'

'Are you Greek?'

'No fear!'

'Jewish? Syrian? Libyan? Nabataean? Cilician? –'

'Roman,' I confessed, and watched the undertaker lose interest.

He catered for all tastes, except Jewish. The Jews had their own quarter, alphabetically called Delta, near the Gate of the Sun and the Eastern Harbour. They conducted their own rituals, which Petosiris assumed were unpleasantly exotic, compared with good Nilotic tradition. Likewise, he spoke disparagingly of Christians, whose dead were kept for three days in the deceased's house while their own

friends and family washed and clothed them for burial –
all deeply unhygienic – before mysterious ceremonies were
performed by a priest amidst sinister lights and chanting.
Christian priests were viewed askance in Alexandria, since
a certain Mark the Evangelist had denounced Egyptian
gods fifteen years ago; he was set upon by the mob and
dragged by horses through the streets until he needed a
grave himself. Petosiris saw this as a fine moment in history.
He had not asked if we were Christians, but we thought it
advisable to indicate a firm negative.

Otherwise Petosiris was extremely versatile. He could do
you a nine-day mourning and cremation Roman-style with
a full feast at your family tomb. He could fix up a respectful
two-day Greek viewing, ashes in a traditional urn and
enough ritual to ensure your soul would not hover between
this world and the next as a disrespected ghost. Or he would
bandage you up as a mummy. If you opted for mummification, once your brain had been hauled out through your
nose with a long hook and your body organs were drying
out in natron in a decorative set of soapstone jars, he could
hire an artist from the south to paint your face extremely
realistically and put it on a wooden plaque over your bandaging to identify you inside your coffin. Needless to say,
for all of these systems there were numerous kinds of
sarcophagus to choose from, and an even greater variety of
memorial steles and statues, most of them horrendously
expensive.

'Will Theon's family foot the bill?'

'He was a public official.'

'The state will bury him?'

'Of course. He was the Librarian!'

'Excellent,' said Aulus. 'So let's have a look at him, may
we?'

I thought there was a pause. However, Petosiris soon led
us to a body, which he displayed quietly enough. Assistants
stopped their ministrations and stood back for us.

Aulus walked up to the top of the bier, cocking his head slightly as he considered the dead man's facial features. I stayed halfway down. Aulus stuck his thumbs in his belt. I kept my arms folded. We were thoughtful, but I concede that the way we posed may have looked unduly critical. Petosiris did not know we had met Theon when he was alive.

Before us lay a body, naked, with its head shaven. The nose was hooked, the cheeks rotund, the chin treble. A linen cloth had been placed across its middle for reasons of ritual or modesty. Beneath it, the belly rose abundantly, even with the man lying on his back. His fleshy arms lay at his side, his legs were short and sturdy.

People change in appearance when they die. But not that much.

Aulus turned and looked at me, puzzled. I signalled agreement. We nodded our heads as we counted to three, then we leapt into action. Aulus shoved Petosiris up against a wall, crushing his windpipe with one forearm. I indicated that the assistants should not intervene. 'My young friend who is attacking your leader has a kind nature. If I did it, I'd rip that lying bastard's head off.'

I grinned at the frightened embalmers, making it bloodthirsty.

Aulus then put his mouth right up to Petosiris' left ear, and yelled: 'Don't mess with us! We asked to see Theon – not some poor three-days-dead cucumber-seller from Rhakotis!' The undertaker squawked. Aulus lowered his voice, which only stepped up the terror: 'Falco and I met the Librarian. The man is an aesthete – he's all skin and bone. Whoever it is you're washing with Nile water for his trip to eternity in the beautiful fields of reeds, we know *this is not Theon*!'

XI

For a moment it went wrong.

There were two mortuary assistants; Aulus subsequently named them Itchy and Snuffly – a dark, pudding-faced, slow-moving dreamer and an even darker, thin-featured, jumpy fellow. While Petosiris stood trapped, once they got over their surprise they reacted. Itchy stopped scratching and squealed with hysteria. It was annoying but harmless. Snuffly was the trier. He leapt on me, knocked me over and sat astride my chest. A gleeful leer said he was going to demonstrate how they removed dead men's brains with their nose-hook.

While he waved this extractor, he foolishly left my arms free. I parried the hook as it threatened my nostrils, then punched him in the throat. These fellows were used to passive customers. He was taken aback. I bucked violently, forced him aside, struggled upright and when he refused to surrender, I hit him harder. Snuffly went out like a pinched wick. I laid him on the bier beside the body of the man Aulus had called a cucumber-seller, leaving him to recover in his own time.

Itchy was wondering feebly whether he too should be an action man. I pointed to him, pointed to his unconscious colleague and shook my head slowly. This proved to be international sign language.

Wincing, I examined the nose-hook.

'Nasty!' remarked Aulus to me. 'How much not to tell my sister you were nearly mummified?'

We both then tackled Petosiris. It was short; we were

irritated and brutal. After pretending he had no idea he had shown us the wrong corpse, he admitted that Theon's body was expected here later, but had yet to be brought to him.

'Why did you need to lie about it?'

'I don't know, sir.'

'Somebody told you to?'

'I can't say, sir.'

I asked where Theon really was. As far as Petosiris knew, still at the Museion.

'Why would that be?'

Petosiris reluctantly admitted why, and then we understood the reason people had wanted him to try to bamboozle us: 'They are conducting a "See for yourself".'

Aulus scoffed. 'An autopsy? I don't think so, man!' He became the self-righteous legal scholar: 'Under Roman Law, the medical dissection of human remains is illegal.'

'Well, this is Egypt!' countered Petosiris proudly.

XII

We found our own way back to the Museion, then set about trying to discover where this outlawed procedure was happening. Naturally there were no advertisements scrawled up on walls. At first all the halls seemed to be hosting ill-attended lectures and anaemic lyre recitals. Aulus spotted a young man who had befriended him in the refectory. 'This is Heras, son of Hermias, who is studying under a Sophist – Heras, have you heard anything about a dissection today?'

'On my way there!' A typical student, he was dawdling; he had no idea of time. As we tagged along, willing Heras to hurry, I learned that Sophistry was a branch of declamatory rhetoric that had been practised for four hundred years; the Alexandrian version was famed for its florid style. Heras looked like a pleasant Egyptian from a wealthy family, well-dressed, with gentle features; I could not see him being florid. Aulus was studying judicial rhetoric of a more subdued variety with Minas of Karystos, though from what I had seen in Athens it mainly involved partying. Having brought money from his father to Aulus in Athens, I was aware that the Senator hoped I would help restrict his son's expenditure. (How? Blameless example, tiresome speeches – or just thumping him?) I didn't ask Heras if Alexandrian Sophistry involved the good life. No one should give students bad ideas.

We found the place. They were not selling tickets to the public. We had to bluff our way past a couple of bored doorkeepers. Security was not their strong point, so luckily they were a pushover.

Just in time, we three sidled into the back of a demonstration theatre. It was old, purpose-built, with a smell of apothecary's apron. A gentle half-moon of seats looked down on a work-table, behind which stood a handsome man in his late forties, flanked by two assistants. It was obvious that a human body lay on the table, so far fully covered by a white cloth. A small plinth nearby probably held medical instruments, though they too were covered over. The room was packed with an eager audience, many with note-tablets at the ready; most were young students, though I noticed a proportion of older men, probably tutors. It was already warm here, and buzzing.

'The Head of Medicine?' I whispered.

'No, that post is vacant. Philadelphion – the Zoo Keeper.' Aulus and I both registered surprise. 'He does regular dissecting,' explained Heras. 'Though of course, normally animals . . . Are you intending to stop this?' he asked, clearly aware of the legal position.

'Not diplomatic.' Besides, I too wanted answers.

Philadelphion made a small gesture to indicate he would begin. Instant hush fell. I would have liked to move closer, but every seat was filled.

'Thank you for coming.' Modesty made a pleasant change. 'Before I start, a few words about the special situation today, which has drawn such a large crowd of you. For those who may be new to this, I shall first review the history of dissection in Alexandria. Then I shall explain why this body, which you all know is that of Theon, the Keeper of the Great Library, seems to require an examination. Finally I shall perform the necropsy, assisted by Chaereas and Chaeteas, my young colleagues from the royal zoo, who have worked with me here before.'

I liked his style. There was nothing florid here. He just had the knack of straightforward exposition, backed by a will to educate. Members of the audience were furiously scribbling down all he said. If what he intended to do was illegal, Philadelphion was making no attempt to do it furtively.

'When the Museion in Alexandria was first established, its far-sighted founders gave unprecedented freedom to scholars – a freedom that we still enjoy in many disciplines. Eminent men came here to use unrivalled facilities. They included two great medical scientists: Heraphilus and Erasistratus. Heraphilus of Chalcedon made profound discoveries in human anatomy, concerning the eye, liver, brain, genital organs, vascular and nervous systems. He taught us to appreciate the pulse of life which you will feel if you lay fingers across the wrist of whoever is sitting next to you. Heraphilus used direct investigation techniques – that is, dissection: dissection of human corpses.' There was a murmur among the audience, as if the pulses they had tested now raced faster. 'He was permitted to do that. His motive was benign. As a result of his greater understanding of the human body from examining the dead, he developed a regimen of diet and exercise to maintain or restore human health in the living.'

Philadelphion paused, to allow note-takers to catch up. While he spoke, his assistants stood completely still. Either he had rehearsed this, or they were already familiar with his approach. He spoke extempore. He was calm, audible and utterly compelling.

'Erasistratus of Ceos also believed in research. He carried further the work of Heraphilus, who had learned that the arteries carry blood, not air as had been wrongly thought previously. Erasistratus identified that the heart works like a pump, which contains valves; he believed the brain to be the seat of our intelligence and he identified its different parts; he disproved the false idea that digestion involves some kind of "cooking" procedure in the stomach, while showing that food is propelled through the intestines by smooth muscle contractions. In his investigations of the brain, Erasistratus demonstrated that damage to certain parts would have a direct consequence on movement. For that, you will realise, it was necessary to experiment on live brains, both human and animal. His human subjects were criminals who were taken from the city's jails.'

Again a pause for catching up – and for the reaction to subside. Aulus and his friend sat frozen in their seats. They saw themselves as tough young men. They went to the gym; they were up for an argument. Aulus had been an army tribune – though on peacetime duties. Still, as the bodily descriptions became more vivid, they grew more subdued. Everyone in the room was now envisaging old Erasistratus sawing open the head of some live convict and, while his victim screamed and squirmed, calmly observing what happened.

Undeterred by his audience's cringes, Philadelphion continued: 'Aristotle – the teacher of Alexander the Great, of Ptolemy Soter and of Demetrius Phalereus, the founder of the Museion – had taught that the body was a shell, housing the soul, or psyche. That did not excuse vivisection. But many of us believe that when the soul departs, the body loses all we regard as human life. That makes dissection after death legitimate, where there are reasons. I myself prefer not to countenance vivisection – experiments on the living, whether human or animal. Since that brief period when Heraphilus and Erasistratus flourished, all such experiments are seen as regrettable, or outright repulsive, by right-thinking people. Distaste for any kind of necropsy also rules. Cutting up our fellow-humans, we feel, lacks respect for them and may dehumanise ourselves. It is, therefore, a long time indeed since anyone conducted a "See for yourself" on a human corpse at the Museion.'

One or two people cleared their throats nervously. Philadelphion smiled. 'If anyone feels he would rather *not* see for himself, leaving the room will be no disgrace.'

Nobody left. Some people may have wanted to.

'So why is this case exceptional?' asked Philadelphion. 'We all knew Theon. He belonged to our community; we owe him special regard. He was physically fit, a lively debater, good for more years in his post. Perhaps of late he had seemed preoccupied. That could have had many causes, including illness, either known or unrecognised. But his complexion was good, his manner still zestful. I was startled to hear he had died, and I suspect so were many of you. Witnesses noted odd features when he was found. We can either bury him and think no more about it – or we can do him the service of trying to discover what happened to him. It is my decision to undertake a necropsy.' The two assistants stepped forward quietly. 'We shall proceed,' Philadelphion instructed, 'always with respect and with gravity. Our actions will be conducted in a spirit of scientific curiosity as we enjoy the intellectual prospect of discovering answers.'

One of the assistants gently removed the cloth that had covered Theon's body.

First, Philadelphion did nothing.

'The first procedure is close visual examination.'

Aulus turned to me and we nodded: this was the genuine body of Theon. He was naked – no modesty cloths here. Even from several rows back, his thin frame was instantly recognisable and so were his features and beard shadow. Unlike the undertaker's false corpse, he still had his hair, thin, dark and lank. After their master's inspection of the front, Chaereas and Chaeteas stepped forward and rolled the body for inspection of the back, then laid it down face-up again. The top of the head and the soles of the feet were scrutinised. An eyelid was pulled up. The mouth was opened and peered into for some time. Philadelphion used a spatula to hold down the tongue and look closer.

'There are no wounds,' he eventually pronounced. 'I can see no bruises.'

'Any asp bites?' Aulus called out from our back row. He had a clear senatorial accent with a pristine Latin diction;

his Greek had never been as fluent as his brother's or his sister's but he knew how to make himself heard well enough to start a riot. In the silence that fell you could have heard an asp slither. Every head in the room turned towards us. Everyone now knew there were two Romans in the room, just as insensitive as the cultured Egyptians and Greeks had always thought us. Aulus himself winced. 'Because of the locked room, I just thought snakes ought to be considered,' he mumbled, apologetically.

Philadelphion fixed the source of the crass interruption and replied with some coldness of tone that there were no snake, insect, dog or human bites. He continued methodically: 'This is the body of a fifty-eight-year-old man, somewhat underweight and with poor muscle tone, but unmarked by anything that would explain sudden death.' He touched the corpse. 'Temperature and coloration imply that death occurred within the past twelve hours. We know, in fact, that Theon was alive until late last night. So! There are no answers yet. It will be necessary to dissect the corpse, if light is to be shed on what killed our esteemed colleague.'

At the words 'esteemed colleague' an elderly man on the front row snorted loudly. A large, jerky figure with unkempt hair, he lolled over two seats, arms and legs flung wide. His manner was proud; he took no notes; even from the set of his head we could tell he was watching as if he expected no good to come out of this.

'Who is that?' I asked Heras.

'Aeacidas the Tragedian.'

Easy to get his measure. A long-time academic who did not expect to have to introduce himself and whose snide attitude had been apparent from the start. It was no surprise when he demanded, 'Do you have a reasonable expectation that opening the body will solve any mystery?'

'I have *some* expectation.' Philadelphion spoke firmly. He was courteous but not prepared to be bullied. 'I have hope.'

The tragedy expert did subside, which may have been

unusual for him. It was clear he thought zoology a lesser discipline than literature; scientific experiments were just a low sport. But standing up to loudmouths often quells them, so Philadelphion still dominated the scene.

The second assistant had lifted away the cloth covering the instruments. Sharp knives, saws, probes and scalpels glinted; the last time I saw an array like it, an over-eager surgeon in an army hospital was threatening to amputate my leg. These were laid out amongst a pile of hemispherical bowls. Bronze buckets were also visible beside the plinth. Both assistants had quietly assumed aprons, though Philadelphion worked in his tunic, which was short-sleeved and unbleached.

He was handed a scalpel and, almost before the audience was ready, made a Y-shaped incision, cutting from both shoulders to the centre chest then straight down to the groin. He worked without drama. Anyone who expected flamboyance, and I fancied that included Aeacidas, would have been disappointed. I wondered how many times Philadelphion had done this before. In view of the questionable legality of these proceedings, I did not intend to ask. However, it was clear his two assistants were confident about their duties. He never needed to prompt them. Those zoo keepers knew just what to do.

The skin, then a layer of yellowish fat, was peeled back on both sides. Philadelphion explained that there would be little blood, because the flow ceases upon death. The incision must have pressed right down to the bone. Now, his assistants held back the flesh, one each side, while Philadelphion severed the ribs from the breastbone by sawing through the connecting cartilage. We could hear the saw. At this point there were gasps. Aulus was leaning forward with his hand pressed to his mouth, possibly to stifle cries of amazement; well, that was what he claimed afterwards. I did wonder if those discard-buckets were provided in case spectators threw up. Someone nearer the front did suddenly keel over in a faint; he was spotted by Chaeteas and unhurriedly laid out in an aisle to recover. When he came round, he stumbled from the theatre.

Squeamish or not, the rest of us were gripped. We watched Philadelphion carefully remove and inspect the heart and lungs, then other solid organs – the kidneys, liver, spleen and smaller items. He named each dispassionately as he handled it. Particular attention seemed to be paid to the stomach and the reams of intestine. Their contents were investigated, with predictable results. A couple more members of the audience remembered prior appointments and fled.

It was all dignified, all methodical. Anyone with a modicum of religious attendance had seen similar proce-dures with animals, though often conducted out of the direct line of vision of all except the gods. (When acting as a priest, you try to hide your mistakes.) The dissector here was completely open but he had the same manner – that formal reverence of an officiating priest as he inspects the innards of a sacrifice, looking for omens. His calm assis-tants pattered around as attentively as altar boys.

It was not gentle. Though not butchery, it was a muscular activity. Even to de-bone a chicken needs exertion. No one who had been a soldier would be surprised at the physical strength needed to open flesh and dismantle a human skeleton. Philadelphion had to hack and rip. Young men who had spent their lives poring over scrolls were visibly shocked.

They were more disturbed when we reached the part where the skull was sawn open and the brain removed.

Philadelphion completed the procedure fully without making pronouncements. He worked steadily. Once he had finished, he asked Chaereas and Chaeteas to replace the organs in the body and reassemble it for sewing up. While they did that, we all shifted in our seats, stretched our limbs and tried to recover our composure. Philadelphion washed his hands and forearms thoroughly then dried them on a small towel, as if politely preparing to eat dinner. Afterwards, he sat by himself, making notes.

This did not take long. His assistants removed the bowls and instruments, and pushed the table with the body to an exit door; I thought I glimpsed Petosiris the undertaker, with his mismatched assistants, Itchy and Snuffly, waiting outside to receive the cadaver. Chaereas and Chaeteas closed the door and took up positions there for the announcement of discoveries, still moving unobtrusively and as if they were minor guardian deities.

Philadelphion stood for his oration. He held his notes, though he only rarely referred to them. His manner remained calm and confident.

'I shall give you my conclusions now. You are welcome to ask questions.'

Aeacidas, the big dissenter fidgeted abruptly. He was beside another, quieter man, also older than the students. 'Apollophanes,' whispered our young friend Heras, himself a much healthier colour now. 'The Head of Philosophy.' Aeacidas did not in fact interrupt; even his bumptiousness seemed to have been deflated by the clinical choreography.

'Much of what I found was normal for a man of Theon's age,' pronounced Philadelphion. 'The rib cartilage, for example, is beginning to coalesce into bone, which we know happens as the years pass. But there was no sign of disease in the organs, nor any significant encroachments of age. The heart and lungs clearly failed, but it is not possible to determine whether that was a specific cause of death or part of the process. I found nothing worthy of comment in the brain.'

There was laughter at that – not from Aeacidas, in fact, but from Apollophanes. His laugh was gentle, almost sympathetic. The Head of Philosophy enjoyed a joke, it seemed, but was not strident.

Philadelphion himself smiled. He had not intended to be witty, but accepted that his straight remark could be taken two ways. 'The areas I consider significant are concentrated in the digestive system. The liver, for instance, is larger and heavier than it should be, and when I sliced it through, the internal structure suggested that Theon had been drinking hard recently. This could be an indication of anxiety. As his colleague, who knew him professionally and socially, I would not have described him as a devotee of Bacchus.'

'More fool him!' commented Aeacidas. Philadelphion ignored it.

'The condition of the liver was not enough to cause death. In fact, my observations failed to find any explanation for what we would consider a "natural" demise. We have, therefore, to determine an unnatural reason. No violence had occurred. So did he, in common parlance, eat or drink something that disagreed with him? It is known that Theon went out to dinner last evening. Those of you on the front rows are particularly aware that I found evidence of a large, rich and varied meal having been eaten; the food was consumed over a period of time, some hours before the Librarian died.'

'How can you say the time?' demanded one of the note-taking students.

'I could tell from the food's state of digestion and position in the organs. If everyone else is prepared to take my word for it, I can talk you through it later, young man; come and see me privately –' Most of us were quite prepared to skip the details. 'I shall be weary this evening; I suggest tomorrow morning at the zoo.'

'How much can you ascertain about the meal?' one of the other young men asked. Philadelphion looked uneasy and shrugged.

Aulus stood up. 'There is no need to speculate. Details of the meal are known, sir.' He gave a full breakdown of the menu, adding, 'It has been established that all dishes were eaten by more than one person, with no other diner suffering any ill-effects. Two of us, indeed, have a strong enough stomach today to watch your necropsy.'

'And much wine was drunk?' the second student asked him.

Grinning, Aulus scratched his ear. 'We drank the quantities you would expect at a meal of that kind, given that there were visitors from overseas and an important invited guest. I would say Theon kept up well, though he did not outpace the rest of us.'

'As far as you remember?' quipped Philadelphion. Clearly he too had a sense of humour. Aulus acknowledged the comment with another relaxed grin, and sat down again. 'Since he was the honoured guest, we presume Theon would have been served as much as he wanted. A witness says his behaviour seemed unexceptional. So if he regularly *over*-drank,' Philadelphion suggested, 'this was done in private. Secret drinking, particularly when it has not been the drinker's prior custom, is to be regarded as significant. I referred earlier to Theon seeming preoccupied, and this would reinforce my remark that he may have been experiencing mental anguish of some kind. Why am I concentrating on this supposition? Because in his stomach and oesophagus were intriguing remains – something he had eaten or drunk later than his dinner. I have saved samples, which I shall be discussing with our botanist colleagues. It is plant material, apparently leaves, and perhaps seeds. I am qualified to comment on the circumstances, inasmuch as we at the zoo examine animals – our own or those that are brought to us – animals that die when they have eaten poisoned feed. I recognise similarities.'

This caused a stir. Someone asked quickly, 'When you began the necropsy, were you anticipating poison?'

'It was always a possibility. Those of you who are alert will have noticed the body was unclothed. Normally in such a case, examining the clothes worn at the time of death would be part of the initial procedure. On this occasion Chaereas and Chaeteas had removed the tunic for aesthetic reasons; there was vomit present. I examined it prior to the necropsy.'

'Did you find more plant material?'

'Yes. Given that Theon had eaten well already, if he was poisoned I doubt he had unwisely picked and chewed some foliage he passed by, daydreaming. So, if he ingested this plant material while he sat at his table, and if he did so voluntarily, then we must decide he was so troubled in his mind, he committed suicide. Otherwise —' For the only time that afternoon Philadelphion paused dramatically. 'Otherwise someone else gave him the poison. If they knew what they were giving him — and why do it unless they knew? — then for reasons we cannot immediately say, our Librarian was murdered.'

XIII

The reaction lasted some minutes. During the uproar, as men turned to each other and exchanged ideas excitedly, I slipped from my seat and walked down to the central area.

'Philadelphion, greetings and congratulations on your work today. My name is Didius Falco —'

'The Emperor's man!'

I raised an eyebrow. He must have seen there was a stranger in the audience – nothing wrong with his vision; those large, good-looking eyes could do both close focus and distance – but this was inside knowledge. 'You heard I was coming?'

Silver-haired and svelte, the handsome lecturer smiled. 'This is Alexandria.'

The noise was dying down. Questions were now being put to Philadelphion, including 'Why would Theon have been locked in?'

Philadelphion raised his hands for hush. 'Answering this is not in my remit. But here is the Prefect's special investigator – Falco, do you mind? – who may be able to explain more.'

I noticed he did not identify me as coming from Rome, Vespasian's agent. Nice courtesy.

Philadelphion withdrew to a seat, leaving me unexpectedly with the floor.

'My name is Didius Falco. As Philadelphion said, I have been asked to run the enquiry into Theon's death. You have all been sitting here a good while, and what we have seen was harrowing, so I won't prolong the agony. But I am glad to introduce myself. While we are all together here, may I ask that if any of you know anything useful about what happened, please see me privately as soon as possible.'

There was some shuffling, as people who had never helped a law and order investigation before looked nervous. I dealt with some low levels of society where everyone knew all too well how it worked. I had to remind myself there were polite circles where the witnesses would feel uncertain what was expected of them.

'One of you just asked: why would Theon have been locked in? His room, which I have seen, can only be locked from outside. So if he committed suicide, that locked door is odd. If he was murdered, it makes sense; it would ensure he could not seek help before any poison took effect. Philadelphion, did your examination give any clues to the length of time between ingestion and death?'

He did not trouble to rise but answered, 'No; it depends what the poison was. I hope to find out more tomorrow. Plant poisons can take from minutes to several hours, or sometimes days.'

'Long-acting ones are less attractive both to murderers and suicides,' I commented.

'Is there not another possibility?' asked a bright-looking youth at the side of the room. 'That the leaves and seeds could have been eaten by Theon in the hope they would be an antidote to some other poison?'

Philadelphion turned in his seat. 'That, too, will depend upon identification – assuming it is possible.'

The lad was in his stride. 'Theon might not even have swallowed any poison, merely feared he had. The antidote leaves might then themselves have caused more reaction than he wanted –' This young man had a vigorous imagination, the type that likes things really complicated.

'I shall bear those factors in mind,' replied Philadelphion patiently.

We were starting to go around in circles. I intervened. 'Now listen – it's late, we are all exhausted. I am satisfied that Philadelphion's excellent examination has isolated a substance that could well have killed Theon. Without proper identification, further speculation this evening is pointless. Know when to let things take their time,' I warned, taking the role of a hoary professional. 'Let me say this. Even if Theon killed himself, somebody else locked the door on him. I want to know who, and why. I need any information you can give me. Who saw it happen? Who saw anybody going to see Theon? It has been suggested he was anxious recently. Who knows why? Who talked to him and heard him let slip some worry about his health, his work, his private life? And, if there was foul play here, who was his enemy? Who was jealous? Who wanted his research, his written treatise, his unique collection of black–figure vases, the mistress he kept secretly or the mistress he stole from somebody else and flaunted openly? . . .' Philadelphion gave me a bright look, as if he was shocked by the suggestion. Aeacidas and Apollophanes were half laughing; Theon was definitely not a ladies' man. 'Who wanted his job?' I asked in a neutral tone. Now *that* could be more than one person present.

Nobody volunteered answers. That would come later, if I was fortunate. I knew they would hotly debate the questions. I knew people might start sneaking up to me from tomorrow – possibly even tonight. Some would want to help, some would want attention, some would undoubtedly be keen to dish dirt on their esteemed academic colleagues.

Philadelphion and I made it clear the meeting was to break up. I invited him home with me to dinner; he said he had a prior engagement in a private house. It must have been with established friends because *he* invited *me* to go along with him. By then I needed to go home to reassure Helena. Aulus and I took his young friend Heras with us.

When we left the Museion building, we had lost all sense of time and space. The necropsy had been so intense we felt we had been in another world.

Out of doors, the sky still retained some light, but darkness was steadily falling. It increased our feeling that we had been rapt for much longer than a few hours. We were drained. We were hungry. We were overwhelmed.

The audience dispersed quickly. Many of the others were hurrying off to the refectory. Some were in small groups, though a surprising number went alone. Scholars seemed to huddle into themselves more than people in most large groups.

Aulus, Heras and I walked back from the great Museion complex, through the well-lit streets of Brucheion to my uncle's house. We made our way together in silence, with a great deal to remember and to think about.

Alexandria was alive and vibrant at night, though to me did not seem threatening. Businesses were still open. Families were in their shops or strolling through their neighbourhoods. This was the largest port in the world, so sailors and traders were inevitably roistering, but they were close to the wharves and the Emporium, not so much in the broad avenues. There, daily life continued long after dusk as half a million people, of many nationalities, hailed one another, ate street food, chattered and dreamed, worked and gambled, picked pockets, exchanged goods, held assignations, complained about Roman taxes, insulted other sects, insulted their in-laws, cheated and fornicated. As the restive wind came off the sea, it brought the tug of the Mediterranean. We passed a temple and heard the shiver of a sistrum. Soldiers marched by us, with the familiar legionary tramp. We were in Egypt, yet only on the northern edge of it. We caught glimpses of its strangeness, yet were half in the world we thought we knew.

The necropsy had affected me. I was glad to step into the blaze of my uncle's house, to be met by the howls of my children, who had had a fractious day. Then I was enfolded in Helena Justina's warm embrace. She leaned back, quizzing me silently. She would be eager for news of today, and in the hearing, she would soften its inhumanities with her gentle sanity.

XIV

Fulvius and Cassius were out pursuing some business interest, so our meal that night was a family occasion. That suited me.

We dined on the roof, but the servants had made a cosy area under awnings. We three men slumped weakly at first on baggy cushions and the rich but worn coverlets that adorned the ancient couches. To me, Fulvius and Cassius had a rich but worn look too. I wondered whether the furnishings came with the house or were theirs. Julia and Favonia were at the meal, but after a hard day of squabbling, the tear-stained twosome soon fell asleep. Albia sat by Aulus, punching him awake when he forgot to be sociable. I ate and drank slowly, thinking.

Helena patted the couch beside her. 'Come and talk to me, Heras!'

The friendly young man took up the offer at once. He had excellent manners, was probably the product of a good mother, and looked flattered by the attention. He cannot have known that the nice Roman lady, at sight so safely married and pregnant, was a dangerous witch. Helena would pick his brains as adroitly as she had already picked the flesh from shellfish and the seeds from pomegranates. 'Tell me about yourself,' she smiled.

Heras was all obedience. So Helena discovered he came from Naukratis, an old Greek city; his father was rich, and anxious for his boy to make his way successfully. Heras had been sent on his own to Alexandria, to find a study course. The results had caused discomfort in his relations with his father. 'So does your father disapprove of your tutor or your subject?'

'Pretty much both, madam.'

Heras explained that Sophistry was required study for anyone who hoped to be a leader of society here. Learning to be a persuasive public speaker was a vital skill; it would fit him for the highest levels – to be a senator, magistrate, diplomat, public benefactor. Unfortunately, Sophist teachers had become far too aware of their value to the wealthy – who were by definition their best source of students. Sophists charged high fees. Very high, in most cases, since to demand less than a rival might imply mediocrity. 'Their teaching is supposed to encourage virtue, a selfless ideal; so some people take the view that to charge fees at all is wrong. My father can pay –' All adolescents think that. I glanced at my little daughters, wondering how soon these sleeping cupids would be expecting a bottomless purse from me. Not long. Julia could already price a toy. 'But Father is shocked how much my tutor wants.'

'Socrates always spoke in public, for all comers.' Helena surprised Heras with her knowledge and her easy confidence in sharing it. I knew how widely she read. Senators' daughters are not normally educated to the standard of senators' sons, even where the daughters are brighter. But when Helena was growing up, with two younger brothers, there were schoolmasters in the house, not to mention a private library. She had grabbed every opportunity. Nor was she discouraged. Her parents both took the view that she would be responsible for the upbringing of future senators. Their only misjudgement was that Helena chose me instead of a stuffed patrician. Our children would be middle-rank. I had no objection to her teaching them anything valuable, but if the baby she was expecting was a boy, and if he survived birth and childhood, I would not send him overseas to pick up bad habits and serious diseases in a foreign university. Born plebeian, I wanted returns on my cash. I had earned the money myself. I was capable of wasting it myself too.

'So tell me about your studies, Heras.' Helena was talking to the student and simultaneously watching me. I hid a smile. I liked my women versatile. I liked this one much more than others I had known.

'We learn the rules of rhetoric, good style, voice training, and correct stance. Part of the regimen is declaiming model speeches in the classroom. My father says these involve false, sterile subjects, divorced from life – he sees it as no more than oral trickery. We also observe our master giving public orations, through which he wins the admiration of the city – and my father is just as suspicious of that. He argues that teachers now cultivate the art of virtuoso rhetoric for incorrect reasons. Their lifestyle offends against the good qualities they are supposed to be teaching: they make orations to gain reputations; they want reputation only in order to earn more money.'

I leaned on my elbow. 'To say knowledge cannot be bought and sold like corn or fish sounds virtuous. But philosophers have to put clothes on their backs and food in their bellies.'

'Not in Alexandria,' Helena reminded me. 'The Museion promises them "freedom from want and taxes". Even in Rome, our Emperor, Vespasian, has sought to encourage education by granting immunity from municipal obligations to grammarians and rhetoricians. And he provides schoolteachers' salaries.'

Heras laughed shyly. 'This is the same emperor who, at the beginning of his office, exiled all philosophers from Rome?'

'All except the esteemed Musonius Rufus,' agreed Helena.

'What was special about him?'

'My father knows him slightly, so I can answer that – he is a Stoic, who argues that the pursuit of virtue is a philoso-

87

pher's aim. Nero sent him into exile – which is always a sign of quality. When Vespasian's armies were advancing on Rome at the end of the civil war, Musonius Rufus pleaded with the soldiers to exercise peaceful behaviour. What I particularly like about him is that he says men and women possess exactly the same capacity for understanding virtue, therefore women should be taught philosophy equally with men.'

Both Aulus and Heras guffawed at that. I could not see it going down well with the academic establishment in Alexandria. Come to that, few Roman women would take up the idea, especially if it required the pursuit of virtue. That does not mean I disapproved of the equal-education principle. I was prepared to sneer at bad philosophers of either sex.

'We regard Vespasian as stingy,' Heras confided. Uncle Fulvius kept a good cellar. Heras had drunk wine with us, perhaps more than he was used to and certainly more than made him wise. 'We call him the Salt-fish-seller. Because,' he thought it necessary to add, 'when he was here, it is said he did that.'

'Better not insult the Emperor too loudly,' Aulus warned him quietly. 'You never know who may be listening. Do not forget: Marcus Didius works for the man.'

'You are in his power?' Heras asked me. I chewed a date thoughtfully.

'Who knows?' shrugged Aulus. 'Perhaps Marcus Didius also seeks reputation in order to earn money – or perhaps he has enough character to remain his own man.'

Old and wise, I remained silent. Sometimes I had no idea myself how much I had capitulated and sold my soul to keep my family, or how much I simply played along and guarded my integrity.

Helena's eyes were on me again, shadowed in the lamplight. Full of thoughts, full of private assessment; if I was lucky, still full of love.

*　　*　　*

I rolled, grasped wine and water flagons one in each hand, and refilled beakers. Helena declined; I kept Albia's share minimal; I gave Aulus and Heras more water with it than they probably wanted. Then I took up the talk myself.

'So tell me, lads –' I included Aulus, so it looked less like a grilling of Heras. 'What do you know about the running of the Library?'

Heras had round eyes. 'You think there is a scandal there?'

'Whoa! It was a neutral question.'

'Neutral?' Heras considered the concept. He was as wary as if I had just landed a deep sea monster, never seen before.

'This is empirical research,' I explained gently. 'I seek evidence then draw conclusions from it. In this system, you are not given a set answer to which you must frame oratorical delivery. The objective is discovery, without preconditions or prejudice. A simple *How? What? Where?* and *Who?* All to be answered before you can even start on *Why?*'

The lad still seemed worried. I was perturbed myself, by his narrow attitude. Far too many people shared it: the false belief that you could only ask questions when you knew the answers. I talked him through it gently: 'I use libraries in my work in Rome. We have grand ones – Asinius Pollio's public collection, the Library of Augustus up on the Palatine – and Vespasian is building a new overspill Forum in his own name, which is to have a Temple of Peace, alongside a matched pair of Greek and Latin libraries.' There seemed no harm in mentioning that. It was not a secret. Vespasian's programme of Roman beautification was to be world famous. 'Now here I am in Alexandria. Alexandria and Pergamum have the best libraries in the known world – but, let's admit this: who in Hades knows where Pergamum is? So for a man who is curious about all things, naturally in Alexandria I want to know about the Great Library.'

'This is independent of the suggestion that its Keeper was murdered? Even though you investigate such things?'

'I cannot know whether the Library is relevant until I first find out what is normal there.'

'So what are you asking me?' Heras quavered weakly.

'What have you noticed? How well does it all work?'

Heras looked shy and hung his head. No doubt he usually bluffed when he was quizzed by his tutor or his anxious father, but to me that night he told the sorry truth: 'I am afraid I am rather lax. I do not go to the Library as often as I ought to, Falco.'

Well, he was a student. Helena sent me a look that said I should have known.

XV

Next morning, waking early was hard. But I had to beard the Head of the Museion and his colleagues at their morning meeting. It would be vital. I thought they were bound to discuss Theon's death.

Besides, when I take against someone, I continue the pressure. I found Philetus, the Director, as savoury as steaming stable manure. I intended to fork him over until he squeaked.

Aulus was still snoring. So were most other people in the house.

Helena came with me. She was meeting Albia later to show the children the zoo, but as a thoughtful mother she would reconnoitre first.

'Excellent woman. If Alcmene had been as careful, the infant Hercules would not have had that tricky moment jumping out of his cradle to strangle two snakes . . . I can offer you another kind of zoo,' I said. 'There will be unbelievable wild beasts – it's a human menagerie.'

'The academics? They won't let me in, Marcus.'

'Stick with me, fruit.' I took a linen napkin, made a sling, said I would claim I had damaged my hand and my wife was the only person I would trust to take notes faithfully or to keep it confidential afterwards. 'Walk behind me. Sit very still. Don't speak at any time.'

'I am not a Greek woman, Falco.'

'Don't I know it! You are a handful, my darling, but the woolly intellectuals need not be told. If you can bear to keep your mouth shut, they may never realise.' The chances were slim. She would burst out with indignation the first time they waffled unworldly twaddle. I beamed at her as if full of confidence. Helena knew herself; she looked wry.

'They still won't let me in.'

They would. Philetus had not arrived yet. This was a typical large organisation. The others were keen to do anything to get up their Director's nose.

There was a good reason Philetus had not arrived. He was keeping aloof from unpleasantness: unpleasantness that he had caused. He had reported Philadelphion to the Prefect. Tenax and his sidekicks had come to arrest the Zoo Keeper for conducting an illegal human dissection. We found them on the steps of the Director's building. The culprit was with them, standing with his handsome head thrown back, daring them to march him off.

I greeted the centurion easily. 'Gaius Numerius Tenax! And Mammius and Cotius, your excellent operatives. *Smart turnout, boys!*' They had burnished their breastplates for this formal occasion. I do like to see trouble taken. The centurion had his greaves on this morning and gripped his swagger-stick as if he was afraid some naughty monkey might jump down from a gutter and snatch it from him. The monkeys were the ones wearing the Greek beards here, I was beginning to think. 'Are we filling cells on this beautiful morning?'

'There has been a complaint,' complained Tenax. For once the complaint was not about me. (That could yet change.) Tenax spoke to me in an undertone, sharing his disgust with a fellow-Roman. 'The prick in charge could have had a quiet word with me about it, but he just had to go straight to the Old Man, didn't he?'

'He's a priest. No idea of form. Well, if you arrest the zoologist, Tenax, you must arrest me too. I was there when he sawed up Theon's corpse.'

Tenax was fascinated. 'So what did you think, Falco?'

'I thought it was justified. It produced results – the

Librarian had taken poison. We wouldn't have known without unravelling his guts. I reckon you can assure the Old Man this necropsy was a one-off; view it as intended to be helpful. Also, go against it, and there may be bad feeling at the Museion, due to Theon's popularity –'

'What popularity?'

Helena giggled. 'His colleagues will praise him like mad, hoping the same is done for them one day.' Tenax took it well. He liked Helena.

'Besides,' I warned darkly, 'this could escalate.'

'What?' Tenax still stood at Philadelphion's shoulder, as if arresting him.

'You know the Alexandria mob – taking a man into custody could blow up into a public order issue in five minutes.'

'So what can I do, Falco?'

'Go back and tell the Old Man you came down and assessed the situation. It's your belief you should just caution the perpetrator, explain to him that such experiments are alien to the Roman tradition, get him to promise to be a good citizen – and effect a strategic withdrawal.'

Strategic withdrawal was not supposed to be the Roman army way, but Tenax saw Egypt as a soft posting, where the army kept out of trouble. 'Can I say you concurred?'

'Say whatever you like,' I allowed graciously. 'He will not re-offend.'

Tenax looked at Philadelphion. 'Got that, sir? Caution, tradition, promise – and don't do it again. Please don't, or the Prefect will mince my nuts for offal gravy!'

Philadelphion nodded. He showed no reaction to the lewd remark, perhaps because he and his little dissecting knife were no strangers to testicles, of all types. The soldiers marched off smartly. We went indoors.

Philetus bumbled up soon afterwards. He looked astonished to see Philadelphion still at large. Of course he could say nothing, without admitting it was he who had grassed.

He found something else to be indignant about: 'Do I spy a *woman*?'

'She's with me. Director, meet my wife. As a senator's daughter, Helena Justina represents the glorious best of Roman womanhood. She has the rectitude and acumen of a Vestal Virgin. She is a confidante of Vespasian and holds the long-term admiration of Titus Caesar.' Vespasian might be called a salt-fish salesman here, but his son and heir, Titus, was a golden boy in Alexandria. Good-looking young generals, hot from triumphs in the East, reminded them of their founder. Implying that Helena was the hero's moll could only gild her prestige. I waved my sling. 'She has *my* admiration and will take my notes.'

Furious, Helena was about to speak, but our unborn baby gave a fearsome lurch. I knew it from her expression so put an arm around her kindly. (It had to be a boy; he was on my side.)

'Bear up, dear girl . . . Do not fret, Philetus. She will be invisible and silent.' She would slam me with plenty of vocals once we were home, but Helena took the hint temporarily.

Philetus enthroned himself like a particularly uninspiring magistrate. The others slunk into a circle of armchairs that were like the marble seats assigned to senators in amphitheatres. I managed to get one for Helena. A folding stool was fetched for me. Needless to say, it had unequal legs and kept trying to refold itself. As an informer I was used to this trick. It was better than being made to stay standing like a slave.

'Didius Falco will observe proceedings.' Philetus pecked at the announcement spitefully. Any good nature he had ever possessed had wizened like a diseased plant. 'We must keep the Emperor's man happy!'

While I was busy stabilising my stool, Helena Justina took notes. I still have her documents, headed by who was present. Nobody had introduced us – manners were not on the curriculum at this institution – but she concocted her own cast list:

Philetus: Director of the Museion
Philadelphion: Zoo Keeper
Zenon: Astronomer
Apollophanes: Head of Philosophy
Nicanor: Law
Timosthenes: Curator of Serapeion Library

Normally there would have been two more: the Head of the Great Library and the Head of Medicine. Theon was detained at the undertaker's. Heras had said the medical post lay vacant for some reason. Helena scribbled queries as to why literature and mathematics were unrepresented; subsequently she arrowed all branches of literature, along with history and rhetoric, to the Head of Philosophy while the Astronomer had a remit for mathematics; I saw her scowl. For a start, she loathed the demotion of literature.

One thing struck me immediately. None of the names were Roman, or even Egyptian. They were all Greek.

As the morning wound on, Helena added opinions and pen-portraits. An 'L' meant Helena considered that man a candidate for the job at the Great Library. Those were the ones I watched most carefully. I had every faith in Helena's judgement on them. If Theon had been murdered, the shortlist would be my suspects.

Philetus: MDF's bugbear. And mine! Priest and poltroon.
Philadelphion: cheekboned charmer; ladies' man? No, just thinks he is. L
Zenon: Never speaks. Dumb or deep?
Apollophanes: Lofty. Director's toady. ?L
Nicanor: Pompous. Thinks himself a cert for L – no chance.
Timosthenes: Too reasonable to survive here. Should be L

The agenda for the most part followed the pattern it must have had most days, which at least allowed those who hated meetings to nod:

Director's report: potential VIP visits
Faculty matters
Budget
Acquisitions: Librarians' reports (deferred from yesterday)
Discipline: Nibytas (deferred)
Progress on new Head of Medicine
New item: appointment of Chief Librarian
AOB: drama performance

It was typical of the Director's unfitness for office that he thought it more important to panic about the possible appearance in two months' time of a deputation of town councillors, on a spree from some Greek island, than to tackle Theon's demise yesterday. His only expressed interest in that incident was wittering about a replacement. The Library could have been full of bloodthirsty assassins and all Philetus wanted to do was put the next victim in a position to be attacked. He was a psychopath's dream. I did consider the possibility he might himself be a psychopath. (Was he uninterested in Theon's fate because he already knew what had happened?) Philetus certainly failed to understand or relate to other people. But I decided he lacked precision, compressed energy and the cold desire to kill.

Faculty matters were as boring as you think and went on twice as long as you imagine is possible. The Museion had no set teaching programme, which at least saved us endless wrangling between hidebound devotees of an Old Syllabus and thrusting exponents of some New; nor did they nitpick about removing the works of one old minor philosopher nobody had ever heard of in favour of another nonentity whose name would make the scholars groan. Philadelphion indulged in a ramble about how they ought to try to deter scholars' parents from approaching them full of unwise hopes. 'Better if they just send gifts!' commented Nicanor, the lawyer, cynically. The Director bemoaned the low standard of students' handwriting; he beefed that too many were so wealthy they were submitting theses that had been copied out for them by scribes – which increasingly meant that the scribes had really done the work. Philetus cared less that the students were cheating than that the scribes – mere slaves – were being permitted to acquire knowledge. Apollophanes boasted snidely that *his* scholars could not cheat because they had to declaim philosophy in front of him. 'If what they have to say is interesting enough to keep you awake!' scoffed Nicanor, implying with legal subtlety that it was not just the *students* in the philosophy faculty who were tedious.

Timosthenes wanted to talk about hosting public lectures, but they all pooh-poohed that.

The budget was dispatched briskly. The astronomer, Zenon, with his watching brief over mathematics, presented the accounts to the meeting, without any explanations. He just handed them round, then gathered them straight back in. Nobody else understood the figures. I tried to snaffle a set, but Zenon whipped all the copies away fast. I wondered if there was a reason. Helena wrote *Money???* on her notes. After a moment she drew a circle around it for added emphasis.

Acquisitions had to be deferred because Theon was dead. However, Timosthenes reported on book matters at the Serapeion, which we deduced was an overspill library; it sounded well run. He offered to cover Theon's responsibilities at the Great Library on an *ad hoc* basis, but Philetus was too suspicious to let him. It was clear from Timosthenes' understated way of speaking, and his grasp of his own report, that he would have been a good stand-in. Philetus therefore feared him as a threat to his own position; nor would he appoint anybody else. He preferred to leave everything in limbo. Apollophanes made some flattering comment that it was 'wise not to over-react, wise not to be precipitous' (these carefully balanced lumps of sycophancy helped Helena and me to identify Apollophanes as the Director's toady). Everyone else at the meeting slumped despondently. It looked habitual.

They skipped discipline, so we never found out who Nibytas was or what he had done. Well, not that day.

There was absolutely no need to have the Head of Medicine appointment on the agenda every day, other than to allow Philetus to fidget pointlessly over a matter that had already been resolved. Philadelphion stifled a yawn and Timosthenes let himself close his eyes briefly in despair. A candidate had been chosen and appointed. He was on his way by sea. I asked where he was coming from: Rome. That seemed a radical move, until I heard he had trained in Alexandria: Aedemon, who worked for the well-to-do in Rome. Amazingly, Helena and I knew him, though we kept quiet. Association with us could damn the man before he stepped ashore.

When they reached the appointment of a new Librarian, everyone sat up. Waste of effort: Philetus only mumbled half-hearted regret over Theon. He made much of his own important role in composing a new shortlist for the post. He had no timescale. He had no finesse either. He enjoyed himself by saying, 'Some of you will be considered!' with a mischievous twinkle that made me feel ill. 'Others may be surprised to find themselves omitted.' He managed to suggest that those who slighted him need entertain no hopes.

Philetus sent out a clear invitation to engage in gruesome flattery and to give him expensive dinners. It stank. Still, Helena reminded me that in most of public life, in Rome too, that is how things work.

The discussion of the Librarian's post took less time than an endless wrangle under Any Other Business about some students wanting to produce a version of Aristophanes' play *Lysistrata*. The Board's objections were not to its saucy language or its dangerous theme of ending war, nor even to its portrayal of women organising themselves and debating their own role in society. There was serious doubt about the wisdom of allowing the actors, all male, to dress in women's clothes. No one mentioned that the play turned on withholding sex as a way for the female characters to influence their husbands. I overcame some of my boredom by looking around the board and wondering which of them even knew what sex was.

I might also have wondered whether any of these cultured beings was familiar with the play. But implying they might discuss a text they had not even read would of course be sacrilege.

The meeting broke up. It achieved nothing tangible. I had the impression that this daily torture never did.

Philetus sailed off to his room to be served mint tea. Apollophanes found an excuse to beg fawningly for a few words with his master. I was disappointed with this philosopher, who had seemed reasonable yesterday at the necropsy. That's how it goes. Decent men demean themselves in the hunt for career advancement. Apollophanes must have known that Philetus had an inferior mind and reprehensible ethics. Yet he sucked up to the man openly, in the desperate hope of the Librarian's job.

All of the attendees seemed demoralised. Some looked shifty too. For a great and historic institution to be so badly run and so low in spirits was doleful.

There was only one way for Helena and me to recover. We went to the zoo.

XVI

By arrangement we met Albia, who was being towed through the gardens by Julia and Favonia.

'Aulus has gone to play as a student.'

'Good for him!' enthused his sister, heaving Favonia on to one hip in the hope that close proximity would help with controlling her.

'He's a tough boy,' I reassured Albia. I put Julia into a sophisticated wrestling hold. She made a good effort at the extrication move, but as she was still not quite five, I managed to win by sheer strength. 'Aulus won't let a little spot of education ruin him.'

Helena flapped at me with her free wrist, bangles jingling. 'He's ferreting around on your behalf, I take it?'

'Under cover with the scroll beetles. We can't all take our ease, staring at elephants.'

The zoo did have elephants, a couple of them cute babies. There were aviaries and insect houses. They had Barbary lions, leopards, a hippopotamus, antelopes, giraffes, chimpanzees – 'He's got a *horrible* bottom!' – and, most marvellous of all, an absolutely enormous, highly pampered crocodile. Albia was honestly entranced by everything. My infants pretended to be offhand throughout, though the marked improvement in their behaviour as they stared at the animals told its own story. Julia's favourite was the smallest baby elephant, who tossed grass with a bad aim and trumpeted. Favonia lost her heart to the crocodile. 'I hope it doesn't indicate her future choice in men,' murmured Helena. 'He must be thirty feet long! Favonia, if he munched you, it would just be like eating a sweetie for him.'

We were still stuck looking down into the crocodile pit, unable to tear our lovelorn Favonia away, when the Zoo Keeper came by. 'His name is Sobek,' he told my daughter gravely. 'A god's name.'

'Will he eat me?' Favonia demanded, then shouted the answer to her own question, 'No!'

Setting down the child, Helena murmured, 'Only two, and already distrusting everything her mother tells her!'

Philadelphion went into an educational lecture. 'We try to make him eat only fish and meat. People bring him cake, but that is bad for him. He is fifty years old and we want him to live healthily to a hundred.'

Noting his patience, Helena asked, 'Do you have a family?'

'Back home in my village. Two sons.' So he had a Greek name, but was not Greek. Had he changed it for professional reasons? Uncle Fulvius had told me that the different nationalities lived peaceably together, most of the time, but at the Museion it was clear which culture ruled.

'Your wife looks after them?' It sounded like chit-chat, but Helena was probing. Philadelphion duly nodded.

Favonia and Julia both tried to climb the fence on the edge of the crocodile's deep pit while we urgently instructed them to get down. 'Will Sobek escape?' squealed Julia. She must have noticed that inside the fence the zoo staff had a long access ramp to the deep pit, protected by metal gates

'No, no,' Philadelphion assured us. As my two excitable girlies bounced about on the fence, he helped me lift them down. 'There are two gates between Sobek and the outside. Only I and members of my staff have keys.'

Helena told him how we had once met a traveller who told us about the crocodile at Heliopolis, a tame beast in a temple, which was covered with jewels and regularly fed sweetmeats by pilgrims until he had become so fat he could hardly waddle.

'Also called Sobek,' Philadelphion replied. 'But we keep ours in more natural conditions for the purposes of science.' He wooed the girls' attention with facts about how fast the gigantic crocodile could run, what good mothers the females were, how rapidly the babies grew once they broke out of their eggs and how Sobek knew his wild companions lived on the shores of Lake Mareotis. 'He yearns for them. Crocodiles are sociable. They live and hunt together in large groups. They will co-operate to herd fishes against the shore so they can catch them –'

'Will he run back to the lake if anybody lets him out?'

'No one will be so silly as to let him out,' Helena told Julia.

In his pit, Sobek lay down on his belly with his powerful legs crouching, as he basked with his snout up at right angles against a wall. His body was in shades of grey, his underbelly yellower; his great powerful tail had darker bands around it. All were covered with scaly hide, patterned in rectangles, with crenulations running along his spine and tail. He looked as if he knew what we were thinking.

Philadelphion took us into his office, where they had babies, a couple of months old, which had been snatched as eggs while their scaly mother left their nest to cool off. The children were thrilled by the little squeaking monsters. The smiling staff, Chaereas and Chaeteas from the necropsy yesterday, supervised very closely. 'Even this young they could bite you badly. Their jaws are tremendously powerful,' warned Philadelphion. Julia snatched her arm, with its colourful bead bracelets, back close to her body; Favonia waved a hand at the little snappers, daring them to grab her. 'Yet crocodiles have weak jaw muscles in some ways. They cannot chew; only rip off pieces of meat then swallow lumps whole. A man can sit astride even a large one like Sobek, and hold his mouth closed from behind. But a Nile crocodile is extremely strong; he would writhe and twist his body, rolling over and over again, to throw the man off or drag him under water and drown him.'

'Then would he eat the man?'

'He might try to, Julia.'

Two little human jaws dropped, showing a variety of white baby teeth.

Philadelphion suggested that Chaereas and Chaeteas who were, as he drily remarked, good with young animals, should look after the girls so he and I could talk. Whether he intended to include Helena was uncertain, though not to her. She came to play with the boys.

Albia stayed behind to practise her Greek on the staff. She probably thought they were gentle, helpful, harmless fellows. Unlike me, she had not seen Chaereas and Chaeteas hauling on the dead Librarian's dead flesh to expose his ribcage yesterday.

Mint tea was served. I jumped straight in and asked Philadelphion if he had had any success with identifying the leaves Theon ate.

'I consulted a botanist, Falco. His tentative identification is oleander.'

'Poisonous?'

'Very.'

Helena Justina sat up. 'Marcus, the garlands!' She explained to Philadelphion: 'Our host, Cassius, had special garlands made for the dinner party; they had oleander wound in them.' She must have noticed the varieties; I can't say I did at the time.

Philadelphion raised his eyebrows in an elegant gesture. 'My colleague told me it would certainly be possible to murder someone with this plant, though you would somehow have to persuade them to ingest it. He thought the taste would be very bitter.'

'Try it?'

'Not brave enough! Taken in sufficient quantities – not unmanageable amounts – it acts within an hour. It works well. I am told it is a favourite choice of suicides.'

'Was Theon's dinner garland found with his body?' I asked.

Philadelphion shook his head. 'Perhaps – but not sent to the necropsy.'

'Someone cleaned up Theon's room and may have thrown it out. Know anything about that?' Again he signalled a negative.

I could see one flaw. Neither Theon, if he felt despairing, nor a potential murderer could have known in advance what foliage would be in our garlands. Cassius had made his selection only the afternoon before the dinner. 'Would Theon know anything about plants? Would he recognise these leaves or be aware of their toxicity?'

'He could have looked them up,' Helena pointed out. 'After all, Marcus, the man did work in the world's most comprehensive library!'

'We have botany and herbal sections,' confirmed the Zoo Keeper, favouring my wife with one of his very handsome smiles. Unlike Theon, I decided, he *was* a ladies' man. Leaving the wife back home in the village must have advantages.

I stretched my legs and asked about that morning's meeting. 'You are not the only expert with surgical implements, Philadelphion! Your colleagues had the knives out a few times at the academic board.'

'They were on good form,' he agreed, settling down as if he enjoyed gossip. 'Philetus has a good grasp of essentials – essential being defined by him as that which enhances his own grandeur. Apollophanes devotedly seconds whatever Philetus thinks, regardless of how low it makes *him* look. Nicanor, the Head of Legal Studies, hates their ineptitude, but is always too wily to say so. Our astronomer has his head in the stars in more ways than one. *I* try to maintain balance, but it is a lost cause.'

In view of how scathing he had just been, that last comment should have been ironical. Philadelphion failed to see his own bias, and was not one for self-mockery.

'What was Theon's usual role?'

'He argued with Philetus, particularly recently.'

'Why?'

Philadelphion shrugged, though gave the impression he could have made a good guess. 'Theon started to seize upon pretty well every subject that came up, as if he wanted to disagree with Philetus on principle. I would imagine he had told Philetus what his grievance was. But unlike most of us, who tend to seek support in numbers at the board, he would approach Philetus privately.'

Helena said, 'He spoke to us of his regret that the Director was viewed as his superior even though he, Theon, held such a famous post.'

'Call it more than regret!' Now Philadelphion was more frank. 'We are all senior men and loathe bending the knee to Philetus, but for the Librarian it is bitterly galling. A previous Director of the Museion – Balbillus, who was in post about ten years ago – took it upon himself to have his title expanded to include oversight of the united Alexandrian libraries.'

'He sounds Roman?' I suggested, narrowly.

'An imperial freedman. Times have changed since the Ptolemies,' Philadelphion acknowledged. 'Once, the post of Librarian was a royal appointment, and not just that – the Librarian would be the royal tutor. So originally the Librarian had prestige and independence; he was called "The President of the King's Library". Through schooling his royal charges, he could become a person of great political influence, too – effectively chief minister.'

I could see why the Roman Prefecture would want to change that. 'Knowing how things had worked in the past, Theon felt he had been deprived of status.'

'Exactly, Falco. He suspected he was not taken seriously

enough, either by his colleagues here – chiefly by Philetus – or even by your Roman authorities. Forgive me; I cannot put that more delicately.'

It was my turn to shrug. 'As far as Rome goes, Theon did himself down. The Great Library of Alexandria carries enormous prestige in Rome. Its Librarian is automatically held in reverence – which I can assure you the Prefect of Egypt upholds.'

The Zoo Keeper appeared not to believe me. 'Well, his reduced position was a long-standing grievance. It wore him down. And I believe there was administrative friction too.'

Since he had nothing to add, we moved on. 'I gained a good impression of Timosthenes at the meeting – he is in charge of the Serapeion, isn't he?' Helena asked. I won't say she thought I was flagging, but she lifted her stole over her shoulder and smoothed down her shimmering summer skirts like a girl who has decided it is her turn.

'Up on the hill, over towards the lake. It is a complex devoted to Serapis, our local "synthetic" deity.'

'Synthetic? Someone deliberately *invented* a god?' Privately, I thought it must have made a change from counting the legs on millipedes and producing geometry theorems. 'Tell us!' Helena prompted, apparently as full of glee as our girls had been at the crocodile pit.

I doubted he approved of formal female education, but Philadelphion liked lecturing women. Folding her hands in her lap, Helena tipped her head on one side so a gold ear-ring tinkled faintly against her perfumed neck as she encouraged him shamelessly. 'Noble lady, this was a deliberate attempt by the Ptolemy kings to conjoin the ancient Egyptian religion with their own Greek gods.'

'Far-sighted!' Helena's clear smile included me. She knew I was exuding bile.

Philadelphion apparently missed the moment between

us. 'They took the Apis bull from Memphis, who represents Osiris after death, and created a composition with various Hellenistic deities: a supreme god of majesty and the sun – Zeus and Helios. Fertility – Dionysos. The Underworld and afterlife – Hades. And healing – Asklepios. There is a sanctuary, with a superb temple – and also what we call the Daughter Library. Timosthenes can tell you the exact arrangements, but it takes scrolls for which there is no room at the Great Library; duplicates, I imagine. The rules are different. The Great Library is only open to accredited scholars, but the Serapeion can be used by members of the public.'

'I imagine some scholars look down on public access,' I suggested. 'Timosthenes' ideas for open lectures were quickly shouted down at the board meeting.' Philadelphion produced one of his airy shrugs. I did not have him down as a snob and I thought he was just avoiding controversy.

Time was pressing. Helena gave me one of those meaningful looks that husbands are taught by their wives to act upon. We could not abandon our two infants for much longer; it was unfair both on Albia and the zoo staff. But Philadelphion was in a good mood to talk. As the race for Theon's post hotted up, such a moment might not happen again, so I slipped in a last question: 'Tell me who is in the running for this shortlist for the librarianship. I presume you yourself must be a favourite?'

'Only if I can keep myself from wringing the Director's neck,' Philadelphion admitted, his tone still pleasant. 'Apollophanes thinks *he* will walk away with the prize, but he has no seniority and his work lacks prestige. Aeacidas – whom you may have noticed yesterday, Falco – is pushing to be considered, on the grounds that literature is the most relevant subject.'

'He is not a member of the Academic Board, though?'

'No, Philetus has a low opinion of literature. When the rest of us want to be mischievous we point out to the

Director that Calliope, the Muse of epic poetry, was by tradition the senior Muse . . . Nicanor could get it. He's pushy enough – and rich enough. He can afford to smooth his own path.'

'Is his wealth the proceeds of his legal profession, or a private income?' Helena enquired.

'He says he earned it. He likes to make out he is sublime, in court or on the teaching rostrum.'

'How about Zenon?' I asked.

'We haven't had an astronomer in charge since Eratosthenes, as far as I recall. He believed the earth was round and calculated its diameter.'

'You have had some great minds here!'

'Euclid, Archimedes, Callimachos . . . None of them would have counted for much with Philetus!'

'And what about Timosthenes, my wife's favourite? Will he stand a chance?'

'None! Why is he her favourite?' Philadelphion was probably thinking that Timosthenes was nowhere near as handsome as him.

'I like a man who is intelligent, organised and speaks well,' Helena answered for herself. From loyalty or absent-mindedness, at that moment she took my hand.

Her attitude may have been too much for the Zoo Keeper. He acquiesced when I said we should recapture our children. I thanked him for his time. He nodded, like a man who thinks he has had a lucky escape from something he had expected to hurt a lot more.

I had not quite got his measure. Either this fellow was unusually open by nature, and keen to assist the authorities, or we had just witnessed a clever bout of wordplay.

Helena and I agreed one thing had come out clearly: Philadelphion believed the Librarian post should be his, on merit. Would he have had enough ambition to kill Theon to make the post available? We doubted it. In any case, he seemed to expect the appointment would go elsewhere, either through his colleagues' manoeuvring or the Director's favouritism. Besides, he seemed too liberal to commit murder. But that could just be the impression the wily Zoo Keeper intended us to have.

XVII

I had a late lunch with my family, outside the Museion complex, then they went off back home. Lunch had been happy, but noisy with so much excited chatter about the exotic animals.

Even Albia wanted to show off: 'There has been a public zoo in Alexandria for thousands of years. It was first founded by a ruler called Queen Hatshepsut –'

'Chaeteas and Chaereas been giving you history lectures? I hope that was all they taught you!'

'They seemed very nice boys from the country,' sniffed Albia. 'Good family people – not gigolos, Marcus Didius. Don't be silly.'

I was a true Roman father, manically suspicious. Soon I was hunched over my flatbread and chickpea dip, full of paternal gloom.

'You are a *good* father,' Helena reassured me in an undertone. 'You simply have too much imagination.' That could be because I had once been a flirtatious and predatory bachelor.

Outside the Museion complex stood rows of enterprising pedlars who sold wooden and ivory models of animals, especially snakes and monkeys, which sharp-eyed children could plead with their parents to buy. Fortunately Julia, who already knew the going rate for articulated bone dolls at home, thought these were too expensive. Favonia went along with Julia. On toy-purchase, they co-operated like crocodiles herding shoals of fish.

*　　*　　*

I returned by myself to the Library. After the hubbub of my family, the internal hush seemed magical. I entered the great hall, alone this time, so I was able to enjoy its stunning architecture at leisure. Rome's marble was predominantly white – crystalline Carrara or creamy Travertine – but in Egypt they had more black and red, so to me the effect was darker, richer and more sophisticated than I was used to. It produced a sombre, reverential atmosphere – though the readers seemed unawed by it.

Once again I had the impression that each man here moved in his private space, engaged in his unique studies. For some, this great place must provide a home, a retreat, even a reason for existence they might otherwise not have. It could be lonely. Its subdued sounds and respectful mood could seep into the soul. But the isolation was dangerous. It could, I had no doubt, drive a vulnerable personality quite mad.

If that happened, would anybody else ever notice?

In search of general information, I strolled back outside and fell in with one of the groups of young scholars who clustered in the porch. When they heard I was investigating Theon's death they were fascinated.

'Will you tell me about the routines here?'

'Is that so you can spot inconsistencies in witness statements, Falco?'

'Hey, don't rush me!' Like Heras last night, these lively sparks were snatching at answers far too soon. 'What inconsistencies do you know about?'

Now they failed me: they were young; they had not paid enough attention to know.

However, they gladly filled in details of how the Library was supposed to operate. I learned that official opening hours were from the first to the sixth hour, which was the same as at Athens. This covered about half the day, on the Roman time system where day and night are each always divided into twelve hours, which vary in length depending on the season. A good citizen will rise before dawn to catch the light; even an effete poet will be spruced up and parading in the Forum by the third or fourth hour. In the evening men bathe at the eight or ninth hour and dine after that. Brothels are forbidden to open before the ninth hour. Manual workers down tools at the sixth or seventh hour. So scholars can be stuck at their work for a similar period to stokers or pavement-layers. 'Also ending up with stiff backs, cramp in the calves and serious headaches!' giggled the students.

I grinned back. 'So *you* think it healthier to work reduced hours?' At the sixth hour, in Alexandria during most of the year, it would still be light. No wonder they had to organise music and poetry recitals, and rude plays by Aristophanes. 'Listen. When the Library is closed to readers, are the doors locked?' They thought so, but I would have to ask the staff. None of these youthful characters trying out their first beards had ever stayed late enough to find out.

They were bright, excitable, open-minded – and willing to test theories. They decided to come along tonight and see whether the place was locked or not.

'Well, promise not to go tiptoeing through the great hall in the dark. Somebody may have committed murder in this building, and if so, he is still at large.' They were thrilled by my statement. 'I suspect it will be locked. The Librarian would be able to come and go with keys, so too perhaps some senior academics or select members of the staff, but not all and sundry.'

'So who do you think did it, Falco?'

'Too early to say.'

They quietened, nudged one another surreptitiously, then one bold – or cheeky – soul piped up, 'We were talking among ourselves, Falco, and we think it was *you*!'

'Oh thanks! Why would I top him?'

'Aren't you the Emperor's hit-man?'

I snorted. 'I think he sees me more as his boot-boy.'

'Everyone knows Vespasian sent you to Egypt for a reason. You cannot have come to Alexandria to *investigate* Theon's death, because you must have set out from Rome several weeks ago . . .' Under my hard stare my informant had lost his nerve.

'You've studied logic, I see! Yes, I work for Vespasian, but I came here for something quite innocent.'

'Something to do with the Library?' the scholars demanded.

'My wife wants to see the Pyramids. My uncle lives here. That's all. So I am fascinated that you knew I was coming.'

The students had no idea how the word had spread, but everyone at the Museion had heard about me. I supposed that the Prefect's office leaked like the proverbial sieve.

This could be either vindictiveness or simple jealousy. The Prefect, and/or his administrative staff may have felt they were perfectly equipped themselves to answer any questions from Vespasian without him needing to commission me. They may even have imagined my story about the Pyramids was a cover; perhaps I had a secret brief to check how the Prefect and/or his staff were running Egypt . . .

Dear gods. This is how bureaucracy causes needless muddle and anxiety. The result was worse than a nuisance: putting out false stories locally could get agents into trouble. Sometimes the kind of trouble where a poor mutt doing his duty landed up losing his life in a back alley. So you have to take it seriously. You never think, *'Oh I am the Emperor's agent, so important the Prefect will look after me!'* All prefects loathe agents on special missions. 'Looking after' can take two forms, one of them filthily unpleasant. And of all the Roman provinces, Egypt probably had the worst reputation for treachery.

While I was musing, the scholars leaned against column bases quietly. These young men showed respect for thought.

It was unsettling – quite different from my normal work

at home. If I was trying to identify which of three grasping nephews stabbed some loose-tongued tycoon who had foolishly admitted he had written a new will in favour of his mistress, I had no time to think; the nephews would scarper in all directions if I paused, and if I appeared vague, even the indignant mistress would start screeching at me to hurry with her legacy. Tracking stolen art was worse; to play 'find the lady' with chipped statues at some dodgy auction in a portico required keen eyes and close attention. Stop to let the mind wander, and not only would the goods be whipped away on a handcart down the Via Longa, but I could have my purse lifted by a thieving ex-slave from Bruttium, together with the belt it was hanging on.

I pulled myself back to the present. 'Sorry, lads. Off in a world of my own . . . Alexandrian luxury is getting to me – all this freedom for daydreaming! Tell me about the library scrolls, will you?'

'Is that relevant to Theon's death?'

'Maybe. Besides, I am interested. Anybody know how many scrolls are in the Great Library?'

'Seven hundred thousand!' they all chorused immediately. I was impressed. 'Standard lecture they give all new readers, Falco.'

'It's very precise.' I grinned. 'Where is the spirit of mischief? Don't renegade staff ever put about conflicting versions?'

Now the scholars looked intrigued. 'Well . . . Alternatively there are *four* hundred thousand – possibly.'

One pedantic soul who collected boring facts to give himself more character then informed me gravely, 'It all depends whether you believe the rumour about when Julius Caesar set fire to the docks, in his attempt to destroy the Egyptian fleet. He had sided with the beautiful Cleopatra against her brother and by burning his opponents' ships as they were at anchor, Caesar gained control of the harbour and communication with his own forces at sea. It is said that the fire swept away buildings on the docks, so quantities of grain and books were lost. Some people believe this was most or all of the Library itself, although others say it was only a selection of scrolls that were in store ready for export – maybe just forty thousand.'

'Export?' I queried. 'So what was that? – Caesar grabbing loot – or are scrolls from the Library regularly sold off? Duplicates? Unwanted volumes? Authors whose writing the Librarian personally hates?'

My informants looked uncertain. Eventually one took up the main story again: 'When Mark Antony became Cleopatra's lover, it is said *he* gave her two hundred thousand books – some say from the Library at Pergamum – as a gift to replace her lost scrolls. Afterwards, perhaps, Cleopatra's library of scrolls was taken to Rome by the victorious Octavian – or not.'

I made a bemused gesture. '*Some say* and *perhaps* . . . So what do you think? After all, you do have an operational library now.'

'Of course.'

'I can see why the Librarian seemed a trifle put out when the conversation flagged awkwardly and my wife asked for figures.'

'It would reflect on him badly if he was unable to say what his stocks were.'

'Is it possible,' I suggested, 'that at various times, when threatened, wily librarians misled conquerors about whether they had taken possession of all the scrolls?'

'Everything is possible,' agreed the young philosophers.

'Could there be so many scrolls, nobody can ever count them?'

'That too, Falco.'

I grinned. 'Certainly no one man can *read* them all!'

My young friends found that idea quite horrible. Their aim was to read as few scrolls as possible, purely to tickle up their debating style with learned quotations and obscure

references. Just enough to obtain flash jobs in civic administration, so their fathers would increase their allowances
and find them rich wives.

I said I had better not keep them from that laudable aim
any longer. 'I just remembered I forgot to ask the Zoo
Keeper where he was the night Theon died.'

'Oh,' the students told me helpfully, 'he's bound to say
he was with Roxana.'

'Mistress?' They nodded. 'So how can you be so sure
that he had an assignation that night?'

'Maybe not. But isn't "with my mistress" what all guilty
parties tell you, when they are fixing up an alibi?'

'True – though colluding with the mistress requires them
to admit to a racy way of life. Philadelphion may need to
be circumspect; he has a family somewhere.' I saw the young
men were envious – though not of the family. They wanted
to hook fabulous mistresses. 'So what is Roxana like? Bit
of an exotic specimen?'

They came alive, making voluptuous gestures to indicate her curvaciousness and seething with lust. I had no
need to go back to Philadelphion. Whether or not he had
something to hide, he would make Roxana swear he was
with her all night and any court would believe him.

When he had finished the necropsy, he had told me he
was going to dine somewhere. I gained the impression at
the time that, wherever it was, Philadelphion was well in.
After cutting up dead flesh, he must have welcomed the
warm delights of living.

I wondered at which hour of the day a citizen of
Alexandria could decently visit his mistress.

I asked one last question. Remembering the item on the
Academic Board's agenda on discipline (which they had
deferred very eagerly), I asked: 'Do any of you fellows know
somebody called Nibytas?'

They looked at one another in a way I found puzzling,

but said nothing. I made my gaze sterner. At last, one replied shiftily, 'He is a very old scholar, who always works in the Library.'

'Know anything more about him?'

'No; he never speaks to anyone.'

'No use to me then!' I exclaimed.

XVIII

The young man took me indoors and pointed out where Nibytas generally sat – a lone table at the very end of the great hall. I would not have found it unaided; the table had been pushed right into a dark corner and set at an angle as if creating a barrier to others.

The old man was absent from his place. Well, even the studious have to eat and pee. A mass of scrolls littered the table. I walked up to have a look. Many of the scrolls had torn strips of papyrus stuck in them as markers, while some were lying half unrolled. They looked as if they had been left like that for months. Unruly piles of private note-tablets were jumbled in among the library scrolls. The reading position reeked of intense, long-winded study that had been going on for years. You could tell at a glance the man who sat here was obsessive and at least a little crazy.

Before I could investigate his weird scribbles, I spotted the tragedy professor, Aeacidas. I wanted to interview all the likely candidates for Theon's job, and do it as quickly as possible. He had seen me; afraid he would decamp, I walked over and asked for a few words.

Aeacidas was big, lolloping, bushy-eyebrowed, with the longest beard I had seen in Alexandria. His tunic was clean, but had worn nap and was two sizes too big. He refused to leave his work station. That didn't mean he would not speak to me: he just stayed where he was, no matter how much annoyance his booming baritone caused to others nearby.

I said I had heard he was on the Director's shortlist. 'I

118

should damn well hope so!' roared Aeacidas unashamedly.

I tried to murmur discreetly. 'You may be the only outsider, the only one not from the Academic Board.'

I was favoured with an explosion of disgust. Aeacidas claimed that if Philetus was given his head, the Museion would be run by archaic representatives of the original arts assigned to the Muses. In case I was the ignoramus he took me for, he listed them, both good and bad: 'Tragedy, comedy, lyric poetry, erotic poetry, religious hymns – *religious hymns!* – epic, history, astronomy and – the gods help us – song and bloody dance.'

I thanked him for this courtesy. 'Not much room at the moment for literature.'

'Damn right!'

'Or the sciences?'

'Stuff bloody science!' All charm.

'If you wanted to get added to the Board to speak for your discipline, how are people elected? Dead men's shoes?'

Aeacidas made a restless movement. 'Not necessarily. The Board steers Museion policy. Philetus can co-opt anyone he thinks has a contribution to make. Of course he doesn't. The ridiculous little man just can't see how much help he needs.'

'Drowning in his own incompetence?'

The big, angry tragedy teacher stopped and gave me a hard look. He seemed surprised that anyone could come in as a stranger and immediately grasp the institution's problems. 'You've met the bastard, then!'

'Not my type.' Aeacidas was not interested enough in other people to care what I thought. He only wanted to stress that in *his* judgement the Director lacked skills. That was old news. I cut him off. 'So, wasn't the death of Theon fortunate for you? Without it, you wouldn't stand much chance of wriggling in among Philetus' tight little clique. By putting yourself forward for librarianship, you may join the Board as of right.'

Aeacidas immediately caught my drift. 'I would not have wished Theon dead.' Well, tragedy was his medium. I guessed he understood motive; no doubt fate, sin and retribution too.

I wondered how good he was at spotting the essential human flaw that tragic heroes are supposed to have. 'What's your assessment of Theon?'

'Well-intentioned and doing a decent job according to his abilities.' Always, this man managed to suggest the rest of the world failed to meet his own grand standards. Under his rule, everything would be different – assuming he ever won the post. If sympathetic man-management was a requirement, he stood no chance.

I asked where he was when Theon died. Aeacidas was astounded, even when I said I was asking everyone. I had to point out that failing to answer would look suspicious. So he grudgingly admitted he was reading in his room; nobody could verify his whereabouts.

'What were you reading?'

'Well . . . Homer's *Odyssey*.' The tragedian admitted this lapse of good taste as if I had caught him out with a racy adventure yarn. Forget that; the *Odyssey* is one. Say, caught with a pornographic myth, involving animals – sold under the counter in a plain wrapper by a seedy scroll shop that pretends to be offering literary odes. 'Sorry to disappoint you, Falco – that's all I can do to clear myself!'

I assured him only villains took elaborate precautions to establish their movements; to have no alibi could indicate innocence. 'Note my gentle inflection on *could*. I adore the subjunctive mood. Of course in my trade the *possible* does not necessarily embrace the *feasible* or *believable*.' Helena would tell me to shut up and stop being clever now; her rule was you have to know somebody extremely well before you engage in wordplay. To her, word games were a kind of flirting.

Aeacidas gave me a filthy look. He thought sophisticated

verb deployment should be barred to the lower classes – and informing for the Emperor was definitely menial. I sneered like a thug who didn't mind getting his hands dirty – preferably by wringing suspects' necks – then I asked where he thought I might find Apollophanes so I could try out my grammar on him.

The philosopher, the Director's sneak, was reading, on a stone bench in an arcade. He told me it was forbidden to remove scrolls from the complex, but the walks, arcades and gardens that linked the Museion's elegant buildings were all within bounds; they had always been intended as outdoor reading rooms for the Great Library. Works had to be returned to staff at the end of opening hours.

'And scholars can be trusted to hand them in?'

'It's not inconvenient. The staff will keep scrolls until the next day, if you still require them.' Apollophanes had a weak, slightly hoarse voice. At the Academic Board he had had to wait for a pause to open up and then jump in, in order to be heard.

'I bet quite a few go missing!' He looked nervous. 'Steady! I'm not accusing you of book-stealing.' He was so jumpy he was quivering.

Perhaps Apollophanes had a good brain, but he hid it well. Away from the Director's protection, he looked hunched and so unassuming I could not imagine him writing a treatise or teaching pupils effectively. He was like those idiots with absolutely no *bonhomie* who insist on running a bar.

I asked the usual questions: did he see himself as a short-list candidate and where was he two evenings ago? He fluttered that oh, he was hardly worthy of high office – but if considered good enough, of course he would take the job . . . and he had been at the refectory, then talking to a group of his pupils. He gave me names, apprehensively. 'Does this mean you will question them about whether I have told the truth, Falco?'

'What is truth?' I demanded airily. I like to annoy experts by wading into their disciplines. 'Routine procedure. Think nothing of it.'

'They will believe I am in some sort of trouble!'

'Apollophanes, I am sure your pupils all know you as a man of impeccable ethics. How could you lecture on virtue, without knowing right from wrong?'

'They are paying me to explain the difference!' he quipped, still flustered but yet taking heart as he sank back into his discipline's traditional jokes.

'I have been talking to some of the young scholars. I liked their style. As one would expect at such a renowned centre of learning, they seemed exceptionally bright.'

'What have they been saying?' Apollophanes anxiously pleaded, trying to gauge what I had found out. Anything I said would go straight back to his master. He was a good toady. Philetus must find him invaluable.

'Nothing your Director needs to worry about!' I assured him with a fake smile as I took my leave.

I could not find the lawyer. I asked a couple of people, suggesting that Nicanor might be in court. Both times this notion was greeted with bursts of hearty laughter.

Zenon the astronomer was easier. By now dusk was falling, so he was on the roof.

XIX

The purpose-built observatory was at the top of a very long flight of winding stone steps. Zenon was fussily adjusting a long, low seat which must be what he used when he gazed at the heavens. Like most practitioners who use equipment, astronomers have to be practical. I suspected he himself designed the star-watching lounger. He may have constructed it too.

After a swift glance at me, he lay down holding a notebook, tipped his head back and looked skywards like an augur out bird-spotting.

I tried being topical: '"*Give me a place to stand and I will move the world!*"' Zenon received my quotation with a thin, tired smile. 'Sorry. Archimedes is probably too earthbound for you . . . I'm Falco. I'm not a complete idiot. At least I didn't ask what your star sign is.' He still gave me the silent stare. Men of few words are the bane of my job. 'So! What is your stance, Zenon? Do you believe the sun orbits the earth or vice versa?'

'I am a heliocentrist.'

A sun man. He was also balding early, his gingery curls now providing a ragged halo around the top of an oval head. Above the obligatory beard, the skin on his cheeks was stretched and freckled. Light eyes surveyed me unhelpfully. At the Board meeting, he had been so quiet that compared with the others he had appeared to lack confidence. It was misleading.

'Your arm seems to have mended rather quickly, Falco.' I had ditched the napkin sling as soon as Helena and I left that morning's meeting.

'An observant witness. You are the first to notice!'

On his own ground, or his own roof, he had the autocratic attitude so many academics adopted. Most were unconvincing. I wouldn't ask a professor the time; not even this man who probably fine-tuned the Museion's sundial groma and knew what hour it was more exactly than anyone else in Alexandria. Zenon certainly did not view time as an element to be wasted: 'You are going to ask me where I was when Theon died.'

'That's the game.'

'I was here, Falco.'

'Anyone confirm it?'

'My students.' Briskly, he gave me names. I wrote them down, checking in my notes that they were different names from those Apollophanes provided. Without prompting, Zenon then told me, 'I may have been the last person to see Theon alive.' He jumped up and steered me to the edge of the roof. There was a low balustrade, but not what I call a safety barrier. It was a long way down. We looked over at the rectangular pool and the gardens that lay adjacent to the main entrance of the Great Library. 'I tend to be here until late. I heard footsteps. I looked and saw the Librarian arrive.'

'Hmm. I don't suppose you could make out whether he was chewing leaves? Or holding a bunch of foliage?'

Zenon's derision was tangible. 'No – but he had a dinner garland looped over his left arm.'

Word had got out that the garland was critical. 'It seems to be lost . . . Still, that's the kind of clue I like – what a geometrist would call a fixed point. All I need are a couple of others and I can start formulating theorems. Did you see anyone else, Zenon? Anybody following him?'

'No. My work is looking up, not down.'

'Yet you were curious about the footsteps?'

'We have intruders at the Library sometimes. One does one's duty.'

'What kind of intruders?'

'Who knows, Falco? The complex is full of high-spirited young men, for one thing. Many have rich parents who supply too much spending money. They may be here to study ethics, but some fail to embrace the ideas. They have no conscience and no sense of responsibility. When they get hold of wine flagons, the Library is a lodestone. They climb in and lie on the reading tables as if they were symposium couches, holding stupid mock debates. Then for a "lark" these boys break into the carefully catalogued *armaria* and jumble all the scrolls.'

'Regular occurrence?'

'It happens. Full moon,' said the astronomer mischievously, 'is always a bad time for delinquency.'

'My friends in the vigiles tell me so. According to them, they don't just experience more members of the public going crazy with axes, but increased dog bites, bee stings and absconding from their own units. This could be a ground-breaking topic for research – "Social consequences of Lunar Variation: Observed Effects on Volatility of the Alexandrian Mob and Behaviour of Museion Layabouts . . ." Was there a full moon two nights ago?'

'No.' Helpful!

Zenon now changed his suggestion; he was playing with me – or so he thought. 'We Alexandrians blame the fifty-day wind, the Khamseen, which comes out of the desert full of red dust, drying all in its path.'

'Are we in the fifty days?'

'Yes. March to May is the season.'

'Was Theon affected by red dust?'

'People hate this wind. It can be fatal. Small creatures, sickly infants, and – who knows? – depressed librarians.'

'So he was depressed, you'd say?' I moved away from the edge of the roof. 'How did you regard Theon?'

'A respected colleague.'

'Wonderful. What kind of indemnity must I offer to obtain your real opinion?'

'Why should you think I am lying?'

'Too bland. Too quick to answer. Too similar to the nonsense all your esteemed colleagues have fobbed me off with. Were I a philosopher, I would be Aristotelian.'

'In what way?'

'A sceptic.'

'Nothing wrong with that,' replied Zenon. Night had drawn in. There had been one small oil lamp burning up here where he wrote his notes; now he pinched the wick. It prevented my note-taking, and it stopped me seeing his face. 'Questioning – especially to reassess received wisdom – is the foundation of good modern science.'

'So I'll ask you again: what did you think of Theon?'

My eyes adjusted. Zenon had the quicksilver intelligence of a drover selling rustled mutton, just far enough outside the Forum Boarium to avoid notice from the legitimate traders. Any minute now he would halve his price for a quick sale. 'Theon did a respectable job. He worked hard. He had the right intentions.'

'And?'

Zenon paused. 'And he was a disappointed man.'

I scoffed quietly. 'That seems common around here! What caused Theon's disappointment?'

'Administering the Library was too great a struggle – not that he lacked the energy or talent. He faced too many setbacks.'

'Such as?'

'Not my field of expertise.' That was a cop-out. I asked if the setbacks might be caused by colleagues, specifically the Director, but Zenon went celestial on me: he refused to dish the dirt.

I tried another tack. 'Were you friends with Theon? If you saw him eating a meal in the refectory, for instance, would you take your bowl alongside?'

'I would sit with him. And he with me.'

'Did he ever talk about his private life?'

'No.'

'Did he talk about being depressed?'

'Never.'

'Were you after his job? Are you up for consideration now he's dead?' Perhaps the wrong wind blew in from the desert just then. As I probed his own ambition, the astronomer took umbrage suddenly and flared up: 'You have made enough insinuations. If I had been Theon's enemy, you would now find out, Falco! I would hurl you off the roof!'

I was glad I had stepped back from the edge. 'How painfully normal to find suspects offering threats!'

That got to him. Maybe too much starshine had invaded his brain. At any rate, Zenon snapped. It was quite unexpected in an academic. In a trice the man was on me. He leapt behind my back, locked his arms around my chest and marched me back to the head of the steps.

He would have made a good bouncer in a rowdy tavern where the stevedores are massive, over by the quays where the grain ships were loaded. If he tipped me downstairs it would be a long, hard fall. Probably a cracked skull and a premature entry ticket to Hades.

I co-operated just long enough. I was fit. I had recently spent the long days on shipboard catching up on exercise. Recovering myself, I dropped forward abruptly, pulled him off his feet, bucked him right over my head and dumped him on the ground. I made sure I did not pitch him down the staircase.

Zenon got up, winded, yet barely embarrassed. I watched him brush down his tunic, one-handed. I think he hurt the other wrist when he landed. He was hiding the pain from me.

I wondered if I had made an enemy. Probably. Since there was no point holding back, I snapped, 'I want to see those budget figures you whipped away in the meeting this morning.'

'Not a chance,' replied Zenon, as mildly as if he was refusing a tray of pastries from a street-seller he saw regularly.

'The Emperor runs this Museion now. I can get a warrant from the Prefect.'

'I await your subpoena,' the astronomer retorted, still calm. He went back to his observation chair. I stood at the top of the stairs for a moment, then I left him.

Those figures must be worth scrutiny. There was no chance I would ever see what was suspicious. Zenon was too relaxed about it. I guessed he had had that accounting document fixed up and fiddled to look clean, straight after he noticed my interest at the Academic Board meeting.

XX

I was ready for a rest.

Help appeared to be at hand. When I left the Museion complex, I saw Uncle Fulvius' palanquin waiting to collect me. Aulus was standing beside it. 'Olympus, I'm whacked. Transport is welcome!' I said. Then distrust cut in. 'Nothing wrong, I hope? What's up?'

Aulus chuckled as he tucked me into the curtained conveyance. 'Oh, you'll find out!' He was staying behind. He had palled up with a group who were going to see Aristophanes' *Lysistrata*.

'It's all about sex!' I said, as if warning a prude.

I did not tell him it was about men being *refused* sex by stroppy wives. A twenty-eight-year-old unmarried man was too young to find out that could happen. Well, he wasn't going to hear it from me.

Aulus deserved a hiding. When he came across the bearers, they must have told him why Helena had sent the litter to speed me back home. Aulus, that jester, could have warned me.

The bearers deposited me at my uncle's house, though they made no attempt to move off again. I assumed Fulvius and Cassius needed the palanquin for another evening out with business cronies. All I wanted was a quiet night, with a good dinner and a peaceful woman to hear the story of my day and tell me what a clever boy I was.

The house was one of a group, arranged on a series of levels. There was no central atrium in any of them; all the

129

buildings in the complex opened on to an enclosed courtyard that was shared communally. We came in through an
outer gate with a porter then the bearers dropped me in
the yard outside my uncle's personal doorway. For private
outdoor space everyone used their flat roofs. Indoors, all
the internal rooms opened off the stairs, as if whenever
they ran out of space they just built upwards. I went up
the doglegs slowly, aware from a hum of activity that
everyone was gathered near the top. As I reached it, the
salon door opened and young Albia slipped out. She must
have been on the alert for me. She was about to speak,
perhaps to give me a chance to flee . . . Too late, the door
whipped fully open. My children burst out: Julia was playing
at crocodiles, with her arms stretched out ahead of her like
snapping jaws. She was grappling Favonia, who was acting
as some animal that roared and head-butted doors open.

'Come here nicely and give your father a kiss –'

Neither stopped. Julia twisted madly as she tried to
subdue her sister, while Favonia sturdily kept on roaring.

I had been spotted from within. Ahead lay a warm glow
of lamps, a blur of conversation. I heard a familiar voice,
loudly deriding my commission on the Theon death:
'Murdered in a locked room? You mean Marcus has
convinced himself someone got a trained serpent to slide
in and stab the man, using an ivory-handled dagger with
a strange scarab on its hilt?'

Helena spoke calmly: 'No, he was poisoned.'

'Oh, I get it! A trained ape crawled down a rope from
the ceiling, bringing a curiously carved alabaster beaker of
contaminated borage tea!'

I exploded. Albia winced and held her head in her hands.
I strode in. It was him all right. That voice and attitude
could not be disguised: wide-bodied, grey-haired and well
into a winecup but still capable of obnoxiousness, without
the grace of slurring. He was tanked up and tearing into
it – but he did stop when he saw me.

'Uncle Fulvius has a new house guest, Marcus!' Helena cried brightly. 'Just arrived tonight.'

'When are you leaving?' I snarled at him.

'Hades!' Albia, at my heels, hated trouble.

'Don't be like that, my boy,' he whined. Marcus Didius Favonius, also known as Geminus: my father. The curse of the Aventine, the dread of the Saepta Julia, the plague of the antique auction porticoes. The man who abandoned my mother and all his offspring, then tried to snare us back to him two decades later, after we had learned to forget he existed. The same father I had strictly forbidden from coming to Alexandria while I was here.

And there was more.

We were going to a party. It was diplomatic, at the Prefect's residence, the kind no one can escape. Fulvius had accepted for me, so failure to show would be remarked upon. We were all going. Helena, Albia and me, Uncle Fulvius and Cassius – plus Pa. There was no chance that bastard would plead weariness after long travel, not when there was free food, drink, company and entertainment on offer, in a place where he could show off noisily, try to sell the wrong people dubious art, be indiscreet, upset the top man and amaze the staff – and above all, cause me irreparable embarrassment.

XXI

Tiberius Julius Alexander, the previous Prefect of Egypt, helped the Flavians acquire the Empire nearly ten years ago. He then made sure Vespasian rewarded him with a really worthwhile sinecure back in Rome. Helena thought he led the Praetorian Guard, though it cannot have been for long, because Titus Caesar took that over. Still, it was good going for a man who was not just Jewish by birth but Alexandrian. Provincials usually struggle more.

Prefect of Egypt was not part of the senatorial lottery for governorship of provinces, but in Vespasian's personal gift. Private ownership of Egypt was a serious perk for an emperor. The intelligent ones took great care in appointing their Prefect, whose main job was to ensure that the corn flowed, to feed the people of Rome in their Emperor's name. Another vital task was gathering in tax money and the gemstones from the remote southern mines; then again, the Emperor would be loved at home because of his stupendous spending power. Vespasian's huge building programme in Rome, for example – most famous for its amphitheatre, though it also included a library – was financed partly from his Egyptian funds.

The current Prefect was a typical Vespasian man – lean, competent, a measured judge and very hard worker. I had heard no rumours of him being anything but ethical. His ancestors were new enough men for him to suit Vespasian's family, the equally new Flavians. He had a good past curriculum; a wife who was never named in scandal; health; courtesy; a brain. He went by three names, none of which

I bothered to learn. His full title was Prefect of Alexandria and Egypt, which stressed that the city was mysteriously separate from the rest, sitting like a bunion on the north coast. You don't find a governor of 'Londinium and Britannia' – and if you did, a man of this intense superiority would still think the posting a cruel punishment. But the Egyptian job made him purr.

When we arrived at his bash, the Prefect headed a formal receiving-line, where he greeted Fulvius and Cassius like wholesome commercial visitors and seemed strangely taken with Pa. My father knew how to ingratiate himself. Helena and I were received with practised indifference. His Excellency must have been briefed by his bright-eyed boy assistants, but he could not remember who I was, what I had been sent to do for the Emperor (if anything), what his centurion had got me to take on at the Library instead, who my noble wife's noble father was and whether it mattered a green bean – nor indeed whether he had already been introduced to us last week. However, after thirty years of such bluffing, his act was oiled. He shook our hands with his limp, cold fingers and said how nice it was to see us here and do please go on in and enjoy the evening.

I was determined not to enjoy it, but we went on in.

The surroundings made up for everything. This was one of the Ptolemies' palaces – of which they had a glorious clutch, all opulent and intended to intimidate. Halls and doorways were graced with huge pairings of pink granite statues of gods and pharaohs, the best of them forty feet tall. Anywhere that could be approached by a wide flight of steps was. Marble pools of awe-striking dimensions reflected the soft glimmer of hundreds of oil lamps. Whole palm trees served as house plants. There had been Roman legionaries on guard outside, but in these halls where Cleopatra once walked, we were attended by discreet flunkeys in Egyptian kilts, characteristic head-dresses and glinting gold pectoral adornments on their oiled bare chests.

Everything was done to the highest diplomatic standards. The usual enormous trays of peculiarly concocted morsels. Civic canapés: a cuisine unknown anywhere outside the lukewarm ambience of large-scale catering. Wine that was all too familiar: from some unhappy Italian hillside which even though it was in our fine home country failed to get enough sun. This mediocre vintage had been carefully transported here – our dross, imported to this city whose own superb Mareotic wine was deemed fit to grace the gilt tables of the very rich in Rome. Always insult the people you are ruling. Never take advantage of their wonderful local produce, lest it seem you are rotting with unpatriotic enjoyment of your overseas tour.

Fulvius and Cassius soon went off to canoodle with businessmen. Traders always know how to angle for invitations. There were plenty here. We shed Pa – or rather, he shed us. It might be his first night, but he already had someone to see. My father possessed the knack, which my late brother Festus also mastered, of making himself seem an *habitué* of any place he found himself. In part, Pa was sufficiently insensitive never to worry about whether he was welcome; the rest was winning over startled locals with sheer weight of personality. Strangers took to him eagerly. Only his close relatives shrank away. Fulvius was one exception. The first time I ever saw them together I knew that Fulvius and Pa met on equal, equally shady terms.

I managed to identify the Prefect's admin staff. Most were clustered around Albia. They probably all kept mistresses locally, but a polite girl from home with flowers in her hair was a treat. She was telling them about the zoo. None had been there; they just assumed they would get around to it later. Who goes out to work in a foreign province and ever sees the sights? Each of the plump women for whom they bought flowers and fancy necklaces was after sex with some clean, virile youth, exciting because he was

134

foreign and because he would be off home by the time they were bored with him. Going out to the zoo when they could be eating pastries in their apartment love-nests and complaining about the weather was beneath such cultured Alexandrians.

As for these young men on the brink of their public careers, they were at least more impressed by an imperial agent than their master had been. One even winked, as if my presence in Alexandria was some insider secret. 'Only a fact-finding mission,' I bluffed – and even that was pushing it.

'Are you making progress? Can we smooth your path? Remember, we are here to help.' The old lies were flowing. Every time a new boy came out on detachment, the well-thumbed bureaucrats' lexicon must be passed on, along with the inkwells and the petty cash for bribes.

'I am bogged down working on your suspicious death.'

'Oh *you* landed that!' Gaily he pretended not to know.

'I landed that.' I was grim. 'Actually you could speed my task; something would help me incredibly –' I saw Helena flash approval of my diplomatic phrasing, though she looked suspicious. 'I need to see the financial budget of the Museion, please.' I nearly choked on 'please'. Helena smiled wickedly.

The golden bureaucrat pursed his lips. I knew what was coming. It was too difficult. To know where to lay hands on a document was far beyond the vague, floppy-haired senatorial brats who came out to the provinces. For them, this was a twelve-month posting that would clinch their next move up the ladder. The one I was talking to only wanted to survive it without getting Nile mud on his white tunic. He was here for a year of sun, wine, women and collecting exotic stories, then he would go home to the next elections, taking the lifetime patronage of the particular Prefect he had served and sure of a bench in the Curia. Daddy would have a rich bride waiting; Mummy would have ensured the selected heiress was, or could pass herself of as, a virgin. The new wife would face a marriage, whether short or long, full of dreary stories about Sonny's triumphal experiences in Egypt, where according to him he ran the place single-handed, fighting off local ineptitude and graft, plus the obstructions of all his Roman colleagues. Probably with Barbary lion hunts and a narrow escape from a rhinoceros thrown in.

Think again, highborn aide-de-camp. Who really ran Egypt for Rome were the centurions. Men like Tenax. Men who acquired geographical knowledge, legal and administrative skills, then used them. They would resolve disputes and root out corruption in the thirty or so old Ptolemaic local districts, the *nomes*, where appointed locals supervised local government and taxation but Rome was in overall charge. No twenty-four-year-old son of a senator could safely be let loose on embezzled land, sheep-stealing, house burglary or threats against a tax collector (especially if the taxman's ass was stolen or he himself had gone missing). How could this thumb-sucking juvenile decide whether to believe the word of the witness with the scar on his thigh who smelt of sweat and garlic or the word of the man with one leg and a scar on his cheek who smelt of sweat and horses – both speaking only Egyptian, looking shifty and signing their names with just a mark?

'I'll check, Falco. That request might be a smidgeon tricky.'

See what I mean? Useless.

I gave the sign that he need not bother. Quickly, he sidled out of reach.

Somewhere must be a tribune, who was nominally in charge of finance. Better still, I knew from experience, in a small accounts office off a poorly decorated corridor, plying his abacus furiously, would lurk an imperial freedman who could find me what I needed.

*   *   *

136

'You're tired.' Helena had read my expression. Before we came, I had been allowed to go out to the baths, which enlivened me, but the effect was temporary. On the way here I had given her the gist of my afternoon's investigations so she knew my head was whirling with facts to digest – not to mention our joint experiences at the Board meeting and the zoo. Plucking a triangular cheese tart from a passing tray, she fed it to me. Tiny shreds of onion invaded the gaps in my teeth. That would give me something to play with if I was bored. 'Come along; I've found out where the entertainment room is. You can loll on cushions like Mark Antony and doze off while someone plays a lyre at us.'

Helena jerked her head; Albia shed her covey of admirers and scampered after us. I was sure I heard my foster-daughter mutter, 'Prunes!'

'You are talking about the cream of Roman diplomacy, Albia,' I said.

'Not all young men are idiots,' Helena soothed her.

'No; I remain an optimist.' Helena had taught Albia the knack of sounding strait-laced while being satirical. 'Thanks to you, I am travelling large distances and seeing very many foreign lands. I am sure one day I shall meet the only fellow in the world who has a drip of intelligence. I learned today,' breezed Albia, grazing a salver of almond fancies as we passed, 'the earth is a sphere. I only hope the one man with a brain has not fallen off the other side while I am looking.'

'You made her like this,' I grumbled at Helena.

'No, the men she knows did that.'

'Your views are just as scathing.'

'Perhaps – but I believe my role as a mother is to instil fair-mindedness and hope. Anyway –' Helena's fine dark eyes gleamed with reflections from the many lights on a mighty candelabrum – 'I know men can be good, bright and honest. I know you, dearest.'

You could rely on a Ptolemaic palace to have long, wide, apparently deserted corridors, with handsome statues on enormous plinths and with shiny floors up which you could chase women, sliding along and larking about with squeals of glee.

'There is probably a wily eunuch spying on us!' Helena whispered, pulling up.

'A priestly conspirator, who will send us to a lingering death to satisfy his raven-headed god's demands!' Albia must have been reading the same myths. She was enjoying herself this evening and darted around us like a scatter-brained butterfly. More attendants appeared, so we all slowed to walk more sedately; I placed Helena's right hand formally upon my own as if we were a pair of bandaged corpses going to the Egyptian underworld.

'Nuts, Albia. Your conspirator is going to be that man who lurks outside Uncle Fulvius' house, forever trying to guide us to the Pyramids.'

The women collapsed, giggling, until Albia became serious. 'He followed you and Helena Justina when you went out to the Museion this morning,' she told me, a little anxiously. I had taught her that my work could involve danger, and she must report anything suspicious.

'Uncle Fulvius calls him Katutis.' I never saw him tailing us. We must have lost him along the route. I gave both my girls a reassuring squeeze.

We let ourselves be steered by the hired-in party managers, who shooed us into the great hall where music, dancing and acrobatics were to take place for our entertainment. Half-naked Nubians waving ostrich feather fans confirmed the clichéd taste of the current Prefect. Fortunately there was more wine; by now I was ready to drink anything that came along in a goblet.

A large group of Alexandrian glass exporters had arrived ahead of us and ensconced themselves in the best seats. They were perfectly friendly, however, and happy to move up for a pregnant woman and an excitable young girl; even I got a look-in, because they thought I was Helena and

Albia's escort-slave. They were talking in their own language but we exchanged greetings in Greek, then nods and smiles, and passed each other titbit bowls from time to time. Less approachable were a pair of well-dressed women, in attire so expensive they had to keep rearranging skirts and bangles in case anyone had missed their price-tags. They continued gossiping together the whole time and never spoke to anyone else. It could be that one was the wife of the Prefect, or they were just from that tiny top layer of society in Alexandria who were settled Romans. They could not be senatorial, but they were solidly wealthy and incurably snobbish. Apart from commercial visitors, everyone else here was from the next layer down, either Greek or Jewish – people with enough money and status to become Roman citizens (they had to call themselves Alexandrians). Needless to say, I saw none of the native Egyptians who toiled at useful trades and were stuck fast at the bottom of the social pile.

The two women eyed up Helena Justina coolly. They were absolutely blatant, taking in each detail of her silk gown with its deep embroidered hem, the way she draped her lustrous stole, her gold filigree necklace with pendant oriental pearls, the gold net with which she attempted to control her fine, flyaway dark hair. She let them stare, murmuring under her breath, 'Right clothes, right jewels – I am doing well – but no; a desperate error! See their fascination dwindling now . . . Marcus Didius, this is just no good. Your generosity must become much more elastic – I must travel with a hairdresser.'

'You look adorable.'

'No, love – I am damned. *Wrong hair!*'

Albia joined in, exclaiming that nobody in polite Alexandrian society would now invite them to a poetry soirée or a mint tea morning. We were shamed; we must go home immediately . . . It suited me. Sadly, she was only winding the joke further. Besides, the music was starting. Until we were saved by an interval, we were unable to leave.

More people arrived to swell the audience. Among them were Fulvius and Cassius, who waved to us across the room grandly. They must have made friends with a flunkey, because extra-plump cushions in expensive-looking fabrics were obsequiously laid for them to recline upon, while a small wooden table with satyr's legs was positioned before them. Upon this, drinks in elegant cups and saucers of nuts appeared, placed with graceful gestures. My uncle and his partner picked at the saucers politely. They looked as if they enjoyed this kind of attention all the time. Every few moments the saucers were removed and replaced with full ones. Once Cassius smilingly refused the replenishment and signalled for the little dish to be brought across to my party. We were given more wine, and it seemed better quality. Everyone else leered jealously at this special treatment.

The music was bearable. Jugglers juggled with not too many foul-ups. The room grew warm. My eyes were heavy. Albia wriggled. Even Helena had the set expression of intense interest that meant she was growing restless.

One of the glass exporters leaned across and imparted eagerly, *'Special dancing!'* Bright-eyed, he nodded at the curtained arch through which the various acts were being released to amuse us. Could it be that even at this farther-most point of the Mediterranean, we would find the ubiquitous Spanish girls? Would the sophisticated Alexandrians like their back-breaking romps with tambourines, even though they had the option of scintillating Syrian flute-players, who could whiffle and undulate at the same time?

My father shouldered his way through the main doorway, looked around as if he owned the place, then joined Fulvius. Clued in to our presence he gestured towards the arch and jerked a thumb at his tunic proudly, as if whatever was about to follow was his responsibility.

'Are we going to like this?' enquired Helena apprehensively. 'Does Geminus dabble in entertainment, Marcus?'

'Seems so. Is it an advert for his business?' I could picture my father putting on a show that had touts handing the audience flyers for statues that idiots could add to their art galleries. 'Can he be selling cut-price *moving* statues?' I groaned. We were in the city where automata had been invented. 'The combination of Pa and the dread words "special dancing" suggests we should start gathering ourselves for a discreet departure . . .'

No such luck.

The audience livened up, full of expectation. Possibly prompted, the Prefect chose that moment to drop in. He and his private entourage now blocked the exit; there they smiled and waited for what was clearly to be the high spot of this otherwise rather staid reception. I hoped whoever made the booking had thought it wise to ask to see a demonstration. If they had, they must have been stuck without a cancellation clause in the contract. Knowing Pa, though, there was not even a written contract. Just some blithe words on his side and a vague understanding of the kind that with my father could so easily go wrong . . .

Exotic instruments stepped up their fevered beat. Tambourines of a sturdily non-Spanish kind. Desert drums. The hissing rattle of sistrums. Soft-booted tumblers leapt unexpectedly into the room, leading other performers in odd shapes and sizes. Insofar as they were wearing costumes, these were brightly hued and spangled. Spangles inevitably fell off. Anyone who knew how to wear a feather in their hair was doing so with panache, even if the routine involved somersaulting in a large circle all around the room. There were child dancers. There was a small troupe of monkeys, some of whom sat in miniature chariots pulled by well-trained performing dogs. The standard was high and, to me, somehow reminiscent of other occasions. Only one of the chariots had its little wheels stick and only one dog ran after a treat someone threw to distract them.

His monkey got him back in line. We were still cheering

that when the main spectacle started. A cod Roman general in painted Medusa armour, rather dark-skinned, strutted across the performance area. His scarlet tunic was rucked up, by a rather large backside. He struck a pose, efficiently covering up his arse with a luxuriant circular cloak. Next, a man-mountain with a whole amphora of oil splurged on his bulging muscles broke through the curtain. Intimidated, we cheered. Over his shoulder he carried a vast rolled carpet. The carpet looked bedraggled, as if it belonged to a travelling theatre group at the end of a long season touring very hot countries. Fringe hung off one end raggedly. In fairness, it was rolled inside out, as a carpet must be when it is meant to be unrolled as a moment of drama.

The hulk circled the room, giving us a good look at his superb physique and his heavy burden. He ended before the general, and hailed him as Caesar. Caesar responded with a haughty gesture. The giant dumped the carpet on the floor, then sprang back; he made a conjuring gesture. Of course we knew what was happening. We had all heard the story of the very young Cleopatra having herself delivered so provocatively to the susceptible old Roman general.

Well, we knew more or less. The cod Caesar pointed with his swagger-stick. In response, the carpet was unrolled by the big man, a yard at a time, to jerking drumrolls that were timed to derisive kicks of his enormous foot. Almost at the end, the audience gasped. Something appeared within the roll – and not what most people expected.

A large snake poked its head out, reared up suddenly and eyed us with a nasty expression. It had madder eyes than most and it definitely enjoyed scaring us.

It was not an asp. It had the distinctive diamond markings of a python.

Albia jumped back against me and I put an arm around her. Helena's expression became quizzical; she was almost laughing.

The giant bearer flung the rest of the carpet open. A figure unravelled slowly, with balletic grace. Once revealed as a spectacular piece of womanhood, she burst into life.

Up leapt this Amazon of stupendous presence, wearing more eye paint than the best-equipped pharaoh. She boasted faux-gilt sandals and a red and blue Cleopatra necklace that could be real enamel. It adorned a bosom on which weary kings might rest their head in gratitude. Snake-headed bracelets were tight around better biceps than those of the monster who had carried her in the carpet. There was an explosion of draped white costume, very short and so transparent my eyes watered.

'Aaah! What is she doing?'

'She will dance with the snake, Albia.' Helena murmured faintly. 'All the men will think it very rude, while the women just hope they are not asked to volunteer to go and touch her snake. He is called Jason, by the way. Her name is Thalia.'

'You *know* them?'

To prove it, the snake-dancer recognised us. She favoured Helena with a huge, lascivious wink. This was not bad, given that when she did it, our friend Thalia was lying on her back with her legs around her neck, while the snake – who was, in my opinion, not entirely to be trusted – coiled himself three times around the tender parts of her person and stared up her loincloth. Assuming she was wearing one.

I never gamble, since it is of course illegal for a good Roman – but if I had, then from what I knew of Thalia's racing form, I would have placed a large bet that underwear was absent.

XXII

Due to the late hour, much remained unsaid. After the performance ended, to wild applause, we signed to Thalia that we had to take young Albia home. Thalia waved gaily, mouthing back that she and I would talk soon – a mixed thrill, given my unease at the possibility that this wild woman had shared a ship to Egypt with my father. I could see that they knew each other; the timing of their arrivals might not be coincidence.

Nothing daunted Thalia. She turned up at our house for breakfast, her daywear only slightly less amazing and her manner only marginally less loud. Thank the gods she did not bring the snake.

'He is tired. But he would love to see you, Falco. You must drop by – we have our tents by the Museion. Thalia was one of the Muses,' she said educationally to Albia. I filled in for her that Thalia was an extremely successful businesswoman, who traded in animals, snakes and stage people.

'Isn't that dangerous?' wondered Albia, owl-eyed.

'Well, the people can bite.'

'I am surprised they dare.'

'Only when invited to, Falco!'

'Not in front of the children, please . . . Thalia was the Muse of Comedy and rustic poetry,' I spelled out. 'The "blooming" one! How appropriate. Thalia, blossom, I can't believe they let you pitch a circus tent in the Museion complex. The Director's a pontificating bastard; he'll go nuts.'

Thalia let out a feral laugh. 'So you know Philetus!' She did not elucidate. 'So – Flavia Albia, was it? – how do you come to be with these dear old friends of mine, my poppet?' Albia was not yet aware she was being eyed up skilfully as a potential acrobat, actress or musician.

'Compared with your exotic charms,' I told Thalia, 'for Albia merely to have been orphaned as a baby during the Boudiccan Rebellion in Britain – as we think she was – seems a tame start. Don't get ideas. Even in those hot-headed moments when she hates us for not understanding her, my foster-daughter is never going to run away to the circus. Albia has already had enough adventure. She wants to learn secretarial Greek and book-keeping.'

'I could use a bent accountant,' Thalia joked back. She must be doing well. 'You'd have to be versatile and tickle up the python when he's bored.'

Albia looked interested but I cut in firmly. 'Is Jason still a handful?'

'Worse than a man, Falco. Talking of being a menace, your father is a right case.'

I breathed carefully. 'So how did you hook up with Pa?'

Thalia grinned – a wide, rascally grin that she shared with Helena. 'He heard I was coming out here and fixed a berth on my ship. Of course, your name swung it.'

'I suppose he paid no fare? Well, you'll know next time.'

'Oh Geminus is all right . . .'

Had I not been sure that Thalia had a full-time old flame called Davos, I might have worried. Pa had a past. Even the bits I knew about were lurid. He had always been up for barmaids, but now Flora, his girlfriend of thirty years was dead, he seemed to think he had extra freedom. Yes, my mother was alive. No, they had never divorced. Since she and Pa had not spoken or been in one room together since I was about seven, she did not inhibit him. In fact Ma reckoned she had not counted for much when they lived together either. According to Pa, that was vindictive and unjust. So probably true, then.

'How is the trusty Davos?' I asked. He was a traditional actor-manager, with some talent. I had found him congenial.

Thalia shrugged. 'Touring tragedy in Tarentum. I opted out. I like that play with the bloody axe murders, but you can have too much gloom thrown at you by a chorus of black-robed women. Besides, there are never good parts for my animals.'

'I thought Davos was a good thing.'

'Love of my life,' Thalia assured me. 'I can't get enough of his thundering virility or the way he picks his teeth. I've known him for years, which is cosy and familiar . . . But good things are best kept in a fancy box for festivals. You don't want them to go stale, do you?'

'What brings you to Alexandria?' Helena then asked Thalia, smiling.

'The future lies in lions. That monstrous new amphitheatre creeping up in Rome. It's almost up to roof level and they are planning a grand opening.'

'Plenty of wild beast importers will make fortunes,' I said, picking up her lion reference. It was a trade I had investigated once. I was working on the Census at the time, so I knew all about the fabulous sums involved. 'But I never saw you as selling meat for slaughter, Thalia.'

'A girl has to earn a living. It's a damn good living or I would opt out. I don't really agree with going to all the trouble of capturing and keeping complicated wild animals if you just want them to die. It's hard enough to keep them alive in captivity in any case. But I'm no sentimentalist. The money's too good to ignore.'

'So now you're in Egypt, are you travelling south where the beasts live?' Helena asked.

'Not me. I like the easy life. Why struggle, when there are men daft enough to hunt them for you? I have special contacts, some of them at the zoo.'

I wondered if 'special contacts' were as exotic as 'special dancing'.

'Not Philadelphion?' queried Helena.

'Him? He's a dry stick.' From what I knew of Thalia that meant the handsome Zoo Keeper had rejected her advances. 'No; mostly I come to see Chaereas and Chaeteas. When the dealers are bringing them specimens, they organise extras for me.'

Did Thalia's specimens appear in the Museion ledgers? 'I'm looking for fiddles at the Museion.' I decided Thalia and I were good enough friends to be frank. 'I won't land you in it, you know that – but who pays for these extras, if I may ask?'

'*I* pay – the going rate!' snapped Thalia. 'And it's damned expensive. The lads just put dealers in contact. And if the dealers come up with some beast I'm not familiar with, Chaereas and Chaeteas advise me how to handle it. There's no fiddle, Falco.'

'Sorry; I'm just working on a problem. You know me. A case makes me suspicious of everybody.'

Helena waded in. 'You can help Marcus, Thalia. What do you know about finances at the Museion? Do they have any money troubles?'

Mollified immediately, Thalia sniffed. She had saved Helena's life once after a scorpion bite, so they shared a special fondness. 'The zoo always seems flush. They don't get privileges, mind you – it may have been different in the pharaohs' day, when everything belonged to the man on the throne, but now the man on the throne is a tight-arsed tax collector's son back in Rome. When they buy a new animal, *they* have to pay the going rate! They moan – but they still get whatever they need.'

I grinned. 'The same going rate as you pay?'

'No fear. *I* have to beat the dealers down, so I can afford to pay Chaereas and Chaeteas for their kind assistance.'

'So would you say –' Helena posed the critical question – 'the way the zoo is run is straight?'

'Ooh, I should think so, darling! After all, this is the one city in the world that's stuffed with geometrists who know how to draw a straight line . . . Mind you,' said Thalia darkly, 'if a group of us went out for a fish supper, I wouldn't trust a geometrist to work out the bill.'

At this point Uncle Fulvius appeared with Cassius and Pa. Pa had introduced the others to Thalia last night. She was just the kind of colourful element that Fulvius and Cassius liked. Pa took all the credit for bringing her into their orbit; Helena and I, who had known her for years, were sidelined.

In this gathering of entrepreneurs, I felt an outsider. I picked up my notebooks and after arranging to meet Helena later for a visit to the Serapeion, I went out.

At the Museion I tidied up unfinished business.

I was still looking for Nicanor, the lawyer. He still would not let himself be found. If he had been the errant husband of a client in Rome, I would have thought he was avoiding me.

I found out where the dead Librarian had lived and went to search his quarters. I should have done this before, but there had been no opportunity. I discovered nothing that might explain his death, though the apartment was sufficiently spacious and well furnished to show just why there was keen competition to inherit Theon's post. Subdued staff showed me around meekly. They told me when the funeral was to be – over a month away because of mummification. It was clear they were upset at losing him. I thought it was genuine and saw no need to make them suspects. A personal secretary, who seemed a decent fellow, had written to the family and packed up Theon's private possessions, but he had had the sense to keep them here in case I needed to see them. I looked through all the packages and again found nothing of interest.

'Did he say what he would be working on at the Library, the evening he died?'

'No, sir.'

'Were any Library documents kept here?'

'No, sir. If the Librarian ever brought work home, he always took it back next day. But that was rare.'

'Who cleared his office at the Library?'

'One of the staff there, I suppose.'

I asked if he knew of any anxieties Theon had, but a good secretary never tells.

XXIII

I had some time before I had arranged to meet Helena. I went to the Library and managed to find my way back to the Librarian's room.

The damaged lock had been repaired and polished. The doors were closed. Even with the lock-bar off, they were hard to budge. I used my shoulder to barge my way inside, nearly damaging myself and landing in a heap. 'Bull's balls! I wonder if Theon kept the doors so tight to discomfit visitors?'

I had asked the question of Aulus, whom I found in the room by himself, sitting in Theon's chair, with an enormous scroll half unrolled. He had made himself at home, with his sandals kicked off and his bare feet on a footstool. The scroll lay across his lap as if he was genuinely reading it. He looked like a classic sculpture of an intellectual.

'If you stay here long enough, Aulus, you may see which of the notable scholars slips into the room to measure himself for Theon's fancy chair.'

'I thought we knew who wanted the job.'

'No harm in a double-check. What are you reading?'

'A scroll.'

I had played that game when I was young and silly. Camillus Aelianus knew I was asking the title – just as I knew he was being awkward on purpose.

'Cut out the daft answers; I'm not your mother.'

I could not read the title tab the way he was holding it. Instead I walked over to an open cupboard from which he had presumably lifted the scroll. The rest of the set were equally heavy and ancient. Three deep on their shelves, just one series took up all the cupboards. I started a rough count. There must be a hundred and twenty. I whistled. These were the legendary Pinakes, the catalogue begun by Callimachos of Cyrene. Without doubt they were the originals, though I had heard that men who could afford it had copies made for their personal libraries. Vespasian wanted me to find out about that. With the going rate for top-quality scribes at twenty denarii per hundred lines, somehow I could not see the old man opting for a new set.

I lugged a few down. There was a broad division into poetry and prose. Then there were subdivisions, into which Callimachos had placed each writer; I guessed that these must correspond with the shelf system in the great rooms where the scrolls were stored. In full the catalogue was called, *Tables of Persons Eminent in Every Branch of Learning, with a List of their Writings.* The authors were bunched together according to the first letter of their name.

'I've written stuff myself. Do you think they'll have me in, one day? *"Investigator and genius. He studied at the Museion of Real Life"* . . .'

Aulus was staring across the room at me as I mused happily. 'You are listed now. I looked you up – since, Marcus Didius, an author of your standing will not want to be so immodest as to search for himself.'

'You looked me up!' I was astounded. 'Camillus Aelianus, I am touched.'

'The Pinakes are claimed to be comprehensive. It seemed a good test. Your play was publicly performed, wasn't it? *"Phalko of Rome, father Phaounios; prosecutor and dramatist."* They only credit your Greek play, not any Latin legal speeches or recital poetry: *"His writings are: 'The Spook Who Spoke'".* There isn't a section for Ridiculous Nonsense, so you are categorised as a Comedian. So appropriate!'

'Don't be snide.'

Aulus seemed depressed, and not just because the

celebrated Library at Alexandria was prepared to acknowledge any old tosh just so long as it was written in Greek. 'We don't have time to read the Pinakes,' he said, rolling up his scroll. 'I've been in here for hours, just absorbing the style. I've barely tasted one volume. Creating the Pinakes was a flabbergasting feat, but it says nothing about how Theon could have been killed, or why. I'm giving up.'

I was back poking about in the cupboard. 'The collection of Miscellanea even has cookbooks. I'd like to be listed here too, with my *"Recipe for Turbot in Caraway Sauce"*. That's worth immortality.'

'It may be,' growled Aulus. 'But it's my sister's recipe.'

'Helena will never know. Women are not allowed in the Great Library.'

'Some bastard will tell her, knowing your luck. *"Oh Helena Justina, didn't I see your husband's name on a fish recipe, when I was browsing through the Pinakes?"* Or a copy will be made for Vespasian's fancy new library and she'll see it there herself. You know her; she will go straight to the incriminating evidence on opening day.' As he grumbled on cantankerously, I wondered if he had a hangover. 'Still, plagiarism has a grand old history here.'

'How do you know that?'

'While you think I have been sitting on a bench doing nothing for three days, I have been diligently applying myself to research.'

'Really? I imagined you munching in the refectory and wasting your time at lewd plays. Did you like *Lysistrata*?' He snorted. I sat on a stool, folded my arms and looked bright. 'So what's your thesis?'

'I had no instructions for a thesis.' Tossing back his hair, Aulus knew how to sound like an unsatisfactory student.

'Aulus, be inspired by your own area of interest. You need to find some previously untouched subject and pursue it independently. You may have been rubbish as an informer at street level, but now you are embellished with an expensive education so we expect better things . . . Just ask me before you run off and waste a lot of effort, in case I think your research is pointless – or I want to pinch it for my own. You mentioned plagiarism, I believe.'

'Oh there's a story that everyone here seems to be told. One Aristophanes of Byzantium, once a Director of the Museion –'

'*Not* the Athenian playwright called Aristophanes?'

'I said Byzantium; do try to keep alert, Falco. Aristophanes the Director systematically read every scroll in the library. Because of his well-known reading habits, he was asked to judge a poetry competition in front of the King. After he had heard all the entries, he accused the students of plagiarism. Challenged to prove it, he ran around the Library, going straight to the shelves where the right scrolls were. He gathered them up, completely by memory, and showed that every entry in the competition had been copied. I think this story is reiterated to new scholars as a dire warning.'

'They would cheat? Appalling!'

'Indubitably, it still goes on. Philetus can't know. Unless you have the right calibre of man in charge, who will be capable of telling whether work is original or a blatant steal?'

I was thoughtful. 'People speak well of Theon. Any indication that he had accused some scholar, or scholars, of plagiarism?'

'That would be a neat solution,' Aulus conceded. 'Unfortunately, no one knows of him doing it.'

'You asked?'

'I am thorough, Falco. I can see logical connections.'

'Keep your ringlets on . . . I wish I knew whether Theon was looking at the Pinakes that night.'

'He was.' Aulus had an annoying habit of withholding information, then dropping it into the conversation as if I already ought to know.

'How can you tell?'

153

He stretched his sturdy legs. 'Because.'

'Come on; you're not three years old! Because what, you flitterbug?'

'I got to the Library before opening time this morning, talked my way in and found the little knock-kneed slave who always cleans the room.'

I kept my temper. I had dealt with Aulus for some years. When he gave me a report he always had to make himself look good. Simply relating the facts was too simple – yet it would generally be a good report. I gave my body some exercise, pulling my joints systematically and adding in a head-rub just to show I could be patient.

'One!' Aulus liked order. 'When he first turned up with his sponges that day, he says the room was locked. Two! He came back, after people had broken in and found the body. He was told to tidy up.'

'How long have you known this?' I thundered.

'Just today.'

'How long have I been in this room and you didn't tell me?'

'Philosopher, does a fact take on substance only when Marcus Didius Falco knows it, or does information exist independently?' He had posed, gazing at the ceiling, and was speaking in a comic voice like a particularly tedious orator. Aulus enjoyed the student life. He stayed up late and went unshaved. In fairness, he enjoyed thought too. He had always been more solitary than his younger brother, Justinus. He had friends, whom his family thought unsuitable, but none were especially close. My Albia knew more about him than anyone and even that was a long-distance friendship. We let her correspond so that she could practise her writing. Presumably he answered her out of kind-heartedness. 'Anyway, I'm telling you now, Falco.'

'Thank you, Aulus. Who gave the order to tidy up?'

'Nicanor.'

'The lawyer. He should have known better!'

'Nicanor had come over from the Academic Board meeting. He told the cleaner to straighten the room and said the body would be taken away later. The slave could not bear to touch the corpse. So he did everything else just as he would have done normally – swept the floor, sponged the furniture, threw out the rubbish – which included a dried-up dinner wreath. There were a few scrolls on the table; he replaced them in cupboards.'

'I don't suppose he can say which they were?'

'My first question – and no; needless to say, he cannot remember.'

In fairness to the slave, all the Pinakes scrolls looked similar. The situation was tantalising; if the scrolls were relevant, I would have given a lot to know which Theon had been reading. 'Did he find any other writing? Was Theon making or using notes?'

Aulus shook his head. 'None on the table.'

'So that's all?'

'That's all he said, Marcus.'

'You asked this slave, I presume, whether it was he who locked the door?'

'Yes. He's a slave. He doesn't have a key.'

'So when Nicanor broke the door down, was he up to anything?'

'I can't see what. Thank Zeus you're the brains of our outfit, Falco, so I don't have to worry. The lock isn't broken now.'

'It was, after the death – didn't you notice? They have a handyman. The Librarian's room will take priority for repairs.' I posed my next question as cautiously as possible: 'Do I need to interview this slave myself?'

'I can talk to a cleaning slave and be trusted to get it right!' he answered, with resentment.

'I know you can, Aulus,' I answered back gently.

XXIV

I left Aelianus and went to meet his sister.

The Serapeion stood on the highest point of the city. This rocky outcrop in the old district of Rhakotis could be seen from all over Alexandria. It was a landmark for sailors. It would have made a fine Greek acropolis – so instead we Romans had installed a Forum at the back of the Caesarium. Now there was a civic focal point of our choosing, while a huge shrine to the invented god Serapis occupied the heights. Uncle Fulvius had told Helena that the Egyptians paid little attention to Serapis and his consort, Isis; as a religious cult, the couple were held in more regard at Rome than here. That may have been because in Rome this was an exotic foreign cult, whereas here it passed unnoticed amongst the multitude of old pharaonic oddities.

The precincts of the Serapeion did stand out. This site of pilgrimage and study was a large, gorgeous complex, with a huge and beautiful temple in the centre. Foundation tablets from the reign of Ptolemy III celebrated the establishment of the original sanctuary. Two series, set up in gold, silver, bronze, faience and glass, recorded the foundation in Greek letters and Egyptian hieroglyphics. 'Even now,' commented Helena thoughtfully, 'nobody has added Latin.'

Within the temple, we found a monumental statue of the synthetic god – a seated male figure sporting heavy drapes. His barber must be bursting with pride. Of hefty build, Serapis was lavishly equipped with hair and a flowing primped beard, with five fancy screw-curls lined up across his broad forehead. As a head-dress he wore the characteristic inverted quarter-bushel measure that was his trademark – symbolic of prosperity, a memento of Egypt's abundant corn fertility.

We paid a guide a bunch of coins to tell us how a window was arranged high up, through which sunlight streamed at break of day, falling so the sunbeam seemed to kiss the god on the lips. It was a device created by the inventor, Heron.

'We know of him,' I said. Aulus and I once did a job where I had him in disguise as a seller of automaton statues, all deriving from the crazy imagination of Heron of Alexandria. 'Is the maestro still practising?'

'He is full of ideas. He will continue until death stops him.'

I muttered under my breath to Helena, 'I wonder if Heron does magic with door locks? Might be worth exploring.'

'You boy, Falco! You just want to play with toys.'

We were told that beneath the temple ran deep underground corridors, used in rites connected with the god's afterlife aspect. We did not investigate. I keep out of ritual tunnels. Down there in the dark, you never know when some angry priest is going to run at you wielding an extremely sharp ritual knife. No good Roman believes in human sacrifice – especially when the sacrifice is him.

Outside, glorious sunlight filled the elegant enclosure over which the god presided. The precinct was surrounded internally by a Greek stoa – a wide colonnade, double height, its columns topped with fancy capitals in the Egyptian style that characterised Ptolemaic building. In a standard Greek market, there would be shops and offices around the stoa, but this was a religious foundation. Nevertheless, the sanctuary was still used by some citizens in the traditional manner as a place of assembly, and being Alexandria it was lively: we were told that this was where the Christian called

Mark came ten years ago to set up his new religion and denounce the local gods. Unsurprisingly, it was also where the mob then gathered to put a stop to that. They set on Mark and had him torn to pieces – rather more persuasive than intellectual chastisement, though well in the spirit of hot-headed Greeks whose gods had been insulted by upstarts.

Generally, the stoa had a loftier, more peaceful purpose; there was ample space for the book-loving public to stroll with a scroll from the Library. They could already read a first-rate translation of the Hebrew books treasured in the Jewish religion, which was called the Septuagint because seventy-two Hebrew scholars had been closeted in seventy-two huts on Pharos Island and instructed by one of the Ptolemies to produce a Greek version. Maybe one day browsers would read something by the Christian Mark. In the meantime, people were happily devouring philosophy, trigonometry, hymns, how to build your own siege warfare battering ram, and Homer. Sadly, in the Serapeion Library they could not borrow *The Spook Who Spoke*, by Phalko of Rome.

Don't think I was so immodest. Helena asked for me. That way we learned our first hard fact about the Daughter Library: it contained over four hundred thousand works, but they were all classics or bestsellers.

When we met Timosthenes, we congratulated him on the flourishing academy he ran here. He was younger than some of the other professors, slim and olive-skinned; he wore a shorter beard than the old fellows, had a square jaw and neat ears. He told us he had reached his high position after working on the Great Library's staff. From the look of him, despite his Greek name, he might actually be Egyptian in origin. There was no suggestion that this would make him more sympathetic to our task or likelier to betray confidences, however.

I let Helena talk to him first. Settling your interviewee is a good trick. Lulling him into a sense of false security would only work if he did not realise what was going on, but either way, it allowed me to watch him silently. I knew Helena thought I was subdued because we had not found my play. The truth was, I always enjoyed watching her in action.

'I know you must be asked the same questions all the time, but tell me about the Daughter Library,' Helena urged. She looked bright-eyed and curious, yet her cultured senatorial voice made her more than a mere tourist.

Timosthenes willingly explained that his Library at the Serapeion acted as an overflow, carrying duplicate scrolls and offering a service to the general public. They were barred from the Great Library, originally because using it was a royal prerogative then because it was the select preserve of the Museion scholars.

Mention of the scholars led to a distraction, though I put it down as accidental. 'Someone told me,' Helena said, 'there are a hundred accredited scholars. Is that right?'

'No, no. Closer to thirty – at the most fifty.'

'So my young brother, Camillus Aelianus, was fortunate indeed to be allowed to join them!'

'Your brother is an influential Roman, connected with the Emperor's agent. I heard, too, he came with a very good reference from Minas of Karystos. The Board is happy to grant temporary accreditation for someone with such pulling power.' Timosthenes was wry; not quite rude – yet close.

Helena's heavy eyebrows had shot up. 'So was Aelianus approved by the Academic Board?'

Timosthenes smiled at her acuteness. 'He was admitted by Philetus. Someone put it on the agenda afterwards.'

Helena tossed in, 'Raised a complaint, I imagine!'

'You have seen how things work here.'

'Who called Philetus into question?' I asked.

Timosthenes clearly regretted mentioning this. 'I believe it was Nicanor.' Aulus did study law. So their legal head objected? 'Nicanor was being difficult on principle.'

Helena said stiffly, 'My father, the Senator Camillus Verus, is set against corruption. He would not want my brother to use unfair influence. My brother himself is unaware that special pressure was applied.'

Timosthenes soothed her. 'Be calm. The admittance of Camillus Aelianus was discussed and retrospectively agreed by all.'

'Tell me the truth,' ordered Helena: *'Why?'*

Helena could be forceful. Timosthenes looked taken aback and fought it with frankness. 'Because Philetus, our Director, is terrified of whatever the Emperor sent your husband here to do.'

'He is shit scared of *me?*' I interrupted.

'Philetus is accustomed to run in circles after his own tail.'

That was something. We had induced the man to reveal an opinion.

Timosthenes was a good educator. He was eloquent, content to discuss things with women, revealed no burning grudges. At the same time, he did not tolerate fools gladly – and he obviously put Philetus in that category.

Helena dropped her voice: 'What makes Philetus so frightened?'

'That,' replied Timosthenes in a mild tone, 'he has not shared with me.'

'So you do not work in harmony?'

'We co-operate.'

'He sees your worth?'

I chuckled. 'He *fears* it!'

'I exercise toleration towards my Director's defects,' Timosthenes informed us, po-faced. A short lift of the hand instructed us not to trespass further. Continuing would have been impolite. Saying 'my' Director emphasised that this man was bound by professional loyalty.

I decided to be formal. I asked about his hopes for Theon's post. Timosthenes admitted at once that he would like it. He said he had got on well with Theon, admired his work. But he saw his own chances of being referred for the post by Philetus as so slim that this could not have been a motive to harm Theon. He expected nothing from the man's death.

'As Librarian at the Serapeion would this not be a natural career progression? Why does Philetus despise your qualities so much?'

'It is,' said Timosthenes heavily, 'because I achieved my post through the administration route, as a member of the Library staff, rather than as an eminent scholar. Although Philetus is himself a priest by background − or perhaps because of that − he is imbued with snobbery about "professors". He feels it adds to his own glory if the chief of the Great Library is famous for his academic work. Theon was a historian, of some note. I am self-taught and have never published any writings, though my interests are in epic poetry. I am primarily an administrative librarian, and Philetus may feel my approach is at odds with his.'

'In what way?' asked Helena.

'We might place different values on books.' He shrugged off the problem, however. 'It has never arisen.'

Clearly he was reluctant to continue. I then asked where Timosthenes was when Theon died.

'Here in my own Library. My staff can confirm it. We were conducting a scroll count.'

'Any particular reason for this inventory, or is it routine?'

'Checks are carried out from time to time.'

'Do you lose books?' Helena asked him.

'Sometimes.'

'Many?'

'No.'

161

'Enough for concern?'

'Not in my Library. Since works are available for public consultation, we have to be rigorous. Members of the public have been known to "forget" to return things, though of course we always know who has borrowed what, so we can remind them tactfully. We find scrolls mis-shelved occasionally, though I have a proficient staff.' Timosthenes paused. He had been conversing with Helena, yet he looked at me: 'You are interested in scroll numbers?'

I played bored. 'Tallying and ticking off lists? Sounds dry as desert dust.'

Helena pursed her lips at this interruption. 'And how did the count go, Timosthenes?'

'Good. Very few were missing.'

'Was that what you expected?'

'Yes. Yes,' replied Timosthenes. 'That was as I expected.'

XXV

Sometimes during an investigation, Helena and I just stopped. When the flow of information became over-whelming, we turned away. We fled the scene. We bunked off to the country for a few hours, without telling anybody. Students of rational science might find the fact odd but forgetting all about the case for a time could, by a mys-terious process, clarify the facts. Besides, she was my wife. I loved her enough to spend time alone with her. This was not the traditional way to view a wife, but as the noble Helena Justina often said, I was a surly beggar who just loved to break the rules.

Of course I was never surly to her. That's how tradi-tional husbands let themselves down. We two had a union of lustrous tranquillity. If Helena Justina saw a moment of uncharacteristic surliness coming on, she would stalk from the room with a riffle of skirts and a sneer. She always knew how to get in first.

We both pursed our lips over Timosthenes. We agreed he was high quality and almost certainly ethical, but we thought he was keeping things back. 'Men who take refuge in scrupulous good manners can be hard to break, Helena. I can't put the Serapeion Librarian up against a wall and mutter threats in his ear.'

'I hope you don't generally work like that, Marcus.'

'I do when it gets results.'

The Serapeion lay close to Lake Mareotis. We had picked up transport – a horse and cart, with its driver whom I had bargained with when I saw them sitting glumly in Canopus

Street. Uncle Fulvius was using his conveyance today. You can't blame a man for wanting to use his own palanquin. (I *would* blame him if I found out he had lent it to my father – an unpalatable thought, which was unfortunately probable.)

When we left the sanctuary, found our cart and faced that moment of having to decide where to go next, it took no time for us to choose a little afternoon trip. The driver was happy. Even his horse perked up. 'Outside city' had a higher rate.

He took us to the lake first. There, close to the city which it bordered, we marvelled at the size of the inland harbour. The driver claimed the lake itself stretched for a hundred miles east to west, cut off from the sea by a long, narrow spit of land that ran for miles, away towards Cyrenaïca. Canals provided links with other parts of the delta, including a large canal at Alexandria. Here on the north lake shore we found a vast mooring pool that seemed even busier than the great Western and Eastern harbours on the sea side. The surrounding countryside was obviously fertile, swept annually by the Nile inundation with its burden of rich silt, and as a result everywhere close to the lake was well culti-vated. They had grain, olives, fruit and vines so although at first this seemed an enormous, lonely area, we saw large numbers of oil presses, fermentation vats and breweries. Lake Mareotis was famously the home of endless papyrus beds, so it had all the necessities of the scroll-making industry. Boys paddled up to their knees in water as they cut the reeds, calling out to each other and stopping to stare at us. From the lake itself huge quantities of fish were caught. Then they had commercial quarrying and glass-blowing, plus numerous pottery kilns for the lamp industry and amphora-making for the wine trade.

It was one of the most frequented waterways I had ever seen. Outside the huge harbour, ferries plied both north–

south to and from the towns on the southern edge of the lake, and also east–west. The fringes of the lake were extremely marshy, yet lined with jetties. Flat-bottomed punts were everywhere. Many people lived and worked from houseboats moored in the shallows – whole families, including infants who at crawling stage were tied on with a rope around the ankle that just gave them enough play to keep safe. 'Hmm. I wonder if it would be frowned upon if we tried short tethers with our own dear mites?'

'Julia and Favonia could undo a rope in about five minutes.'

The driver refused to stop among the marshes. He said the tall papyrus reeds were full of paths and dens used by gangs of criminals. This seemed at odds with the multitude of luxurious out-of-town villas to which rich Alexandrians migrated for leisure in the countryside. Playboys and tycoons don't put up with brigands in their neighbourhood – well, not unless they themselves are brigands who have made their pile and settled in huge villas on the proceeds. The tycoons' spreads here worked like the grand holiday homes in the coastal strip between Ostia and the Bay of Neapolis – close enough to be reached from town in the evening by weary businessmen, and close enough too for obsessive workers to feel they could nip back to the courts and to hear the news in the Forum without ever growing out of touch.

We had left the harbour behind us and driven out on the long narrow land spit between sea and lake. After a time the driver decided the reeds in these parts were not the dangerous kind out of which brigands might rush to steal his horse. They looked the same as the others to me, but you bow to expert local knowledge. The horse itself was game to plod on, since it made progress at an undemanding pace, allowing itself time to gaze around at the views. But the man needed to get down and fall asleep under an olive tree. He made it plain we required a rest stop, so we obediently took one.

Fortunately we had brought drinking-water and snacks to keep us occupied. Herons and ibises paraded themselves. Frogs and insects kept up low background noise. The sun was hot, though not sweltering. While the driver snored, we took advantage of the peaceful spot. He may have been acting and hoped for intimate behaviour to spy on, but I was alert to that. Besides, sometimes catching up on a case is even more alluring.

'I had a long talk with Cassius this morning, when you abandoned me again,' said Helena, who liked to be part of everything. Her complaint was light-hearted. She was used to me disappearing on interviews or surveillance. She never minded me doing the boring routines, so long as I let her play dice when the game hotted up.

'I was with your dear brother part of the time, looking at the Pinakes.'

'How commendably academic. Oddly enough, Cassius and I were talking about the catalogue.'

'I hadn't seen him as a scrollworm.'

'Well, neither had I, Marcus, but we know very little about him. We just assume Cassius was once some beautiful, vacuous young boy Uncle Fulvius picked up in a gym or a bath house – but he is probably not that young.'

I laughed lazily. 'So you think he's an intellectual? Fulvius chose him for his mind? When nobody is looking, they sit together and intently discuss the finer points of Plato's *Republic*?'

Helena biffed me. 'No. But he is his own man. I think Cassius must have received an education – perhaps enough to have wanted more, but his family could not afford it. I'm sure he comes from a working background, he's too sensible not to. Anyway, so does Fulvius; your grandfather had the market garden. Now it's Fulvius who takes the lead in their business activities. I reckon that while Cassius is kept hanging around waiting for Fulvius to clinch some deal, he may sit in a corner and read a scroll.'

'Perfectly possible, my darling. It is what I would do myself.'

'You would buy drink,' scoffed Helena. 'And eye up women,' she added balefully. I could not deny it – though of course it would be only for comparative purposes.

'Not Cassius.'

'Well, I expect he can read and drink . . .'

'And eye up men?'

'I suppose that would depend how near Fulvius was . . . do you think men who live with men are as promiscuous as men who live with women?'

I dropped my voice. 'Some of us are loyal.'

'No, all of you are men . . .' Despite her tone, Helena laid a hand on my arm as if exonerating me. Like many women who understand the male sex, she took a charitable view. She might say, women had to do that or live as spinsters – though she would say it kindly. 'Anyway, do you want to hear what he says?'

I stretched out on my back in the sun, hands clasped behind my head. 'If it's relevant.' It had better be exciting, or I would nod off.

'Listen, then. According to Cassius there are tensions in the academic community. When the Museion was first set up, it was a magnificent centre of learning. The scholars who came to live in Alexandria all carried out new scientific research and lectured; great men published great papers. On the literary side, they conducted the first systematic study of Greek literature; grammar and philology were invented as subjects of study. At the Library, they had to decide which collected scrolls were original, or closest to the original, especially when they had duplicates. And of course there *were* duplicates, because the books came from various collections which must have overlapped or, as you know, darling, plays in particular have more than one copy. When you wrote *The Spook Who Spoke*, you were scribbling in a hurry – so errors may have crept in, even to your

master copy; plus the actors made their own scripts, sometimes only bothering with their own characters and cues.'

'Their loss!'

'Oh of course, dearest.'

To retaliate for her sarcasm, I made a lunge; despite her
pregnancy, Helena managed to shuffle quickly out of reach.
Too drowsy for another attempt, I contributed: 'We know
how the Library collection was gathered. The Ptolemies
invited the leaders of all the countries in the world to send
the literature of their country. They backed that up like
pirates. If anybody was sailing near Alexandria, teams of
searchers would raid their ships. Any scrolls they found in
luggage were confiscated and copied; if the owners were
lucky they got back a copy, though rarely their own original. Aulus and I saw some of that today – such works are
listed as "from the ships" beside their titles in the Pinakes.'

'The story is true then?' Helena demanded. 'I suppose
you wouldn't argue with a Ptolemy.'

'Not unless you wanted to be tipped into the harbour.
So what's the controversy nowadays?'

'Well, you know what happens with copying, Marcus.
Some scribes make a bad job of it. At the Library, the staff
examined duplicates to decide which copy was the best. In
the main, they assumed the oldest scroll was likely to be
most accurate. Clarifying authenticity became their
specialism. But what started as genuine critique has become
debased. Texts are altered arbitrarily. People who feel
strongly say that a bunch of ignorant clerks are making
ridiculous alterations to works they just don't have the intel-
lect to understand.'

'Scandalous!'

'Be serious, Marcus. Once, literary study in Alexandria
was of a very high standard. This persisted until recently.
About fifty years ago, Didymus, the son of a fishmonger,
was one of the first native Egyptians to become an accom-
plished scholar. He wrote three and a half thousand

commentaries on most of the Greek classics, including the works of Callimachos, the Library's own cataloguer. Didymus published an authoritative text of Homer, based on Aristarchus' well-regarded version and his own textual analysis; he wrote a critical commentary on Demosthenes' *Philippics*; he created lexicons –'

'Did *Cassius* tell you all this?'

Helena blushed. 'No, I have been reading up myself . . . It was a time of excellence. Didymus had contemporaries who were superb literary commentators and grammarians.'

'All this is not so very long ago.'

'Exactly, Marcus. In our parents' lifetime. Scholars here even made the first contact with Pergamum, which in Ptolemaic times had always been shunned by Alexandria because its library was a rival.'

I changed position. 'You're saying that only a generation ago, Alexandria was leading the world. So what went wrong? Piss-poor commentaries are being produced by hack reviewers, with ludicrous emendations?'

'That seems to have happened.'

'Is it our fault, Helena? We Romans? Did Augustus cause it after Actium? Did that start the rot? Don't we take enough interest, because Rome is too far distant?'

'Well, Didymus was later than Augustus, under Tiberius. But maybe with the Emperor as patron and so far away, Museion supervision has failed somewhat.' Helena had a careful way of trying to keep things right. She spoke slowly now, concentrating. 'Cassius blames other factors too. Ptolemy Soter had had a glorious ideal. He set out to own every book in the world, so that all the world's knowledge would be gathered in his Library, available for consultation. We would call that a good motive. But collecting can be obsessive. Totality becomes an end in itself. Possession of all an author's works, all the works in a set, becomes more important than what the texts actually say. Ideas become irrelevant.'

I puffed out my cheeks. 'The books are simply objects. It's all sterile . . . I haven't seen any direct controversy about that. But the librarians here do have a fixation with scroll numbers. Theon had a choking fit when I asked how many scrolls he had, and Timosthenes has been stock-taking.'

Helena pouted. '*I* asked Theon how many scrolls he had.'

'Right! It doesn't matter which of us asked –'

Oh yes it did matter. 'Now you are being dismissive. I hit upon a lucky question – I admit it was lucky.'

'Purely characteristic. You always count the beans.'

'So you say *I* am unpleasantly pedantic, while *you* have intuition and flair . . .' Helena was not really in the mood for a quarrel; she had something too vital to say. She brushed this niggle aside briskly: 'Well, Cassius told me that from what he and Fulvius already knew about Theon, before he came to dinner with us, there *is* an ethical controversy and Theon was part of it. He was fighting the Director, Philetus.'

'They quarrelled?'

'Philetus sees scrolls as a commodity. They take up space and gather dust; they need expensive staff to look after them. He asks, what intellectual value do ancient scrolls have, if nobody has consulted them for decades or even centuries?'

'Can this be relevant to the budget Zenon so carefully kept from me? Is there a financial crisis? And is it the difference of approach that Timosthenes was talking about? I can't imagine *him* ever seeing scrolls as dusty wastes of space . . . How does our Cassius know about this?'

'That was unclear. But he said Philetus was always haranguing Theon about whether they need to keep scrolls nobody sees, or more than one copy. Theon – who already feared his role was being undermined by the Director, remember – fought for the Library to be fully comprehensive. He wanted all known versions; he wanted comparative study of duplicates to be carried out as valid literary criticism.'

I was not entirely sympathetic to that. I dismissed scholars who spent years narrowly comparing works on a line by line basis. Minutely searching for the perfect version seemed to me to add nothing to human knowledge or to the betterment of the human condition. Perhaps it kept the scholars out of the taverns and off the streets – though if it had led directly to Theon being given an oleander nightcap, he might have done better to be away from the Library, just having a dispute about the government with five fishmongers in a downtown bar. Or even staying longer at our house, eating pastries with Uncle Fulvius, come to that.

'There are others feuding,' Helena said. 'The Zoo Keeper, Philadelphion, resents the international kudos that is given to the Great Library at the expense of his scientific institute; he wrangles, or wrangled, with both Philetus and Theon about uplifting the importance of pure science within the Museion. Zenon, the astronomer, thinks studying earth and the heavens is more use than studying animals, so he tussles with Philadelphion. For him, understanding the Nile flood is infinitely more useful than averaging how many eggs are laid by the crocodiles which inhabit the Nile's banks.'

I nodded. 'Zenon also knows where the purse pinches – and he must resent having to examine the stars from a chair he made himself while, if what Thalia says is right, Philadelphion can lavish gold on every last breed of fancy ibis. From what you say, love, the Museion is seething with animosity. Our Cassius seems to keep up with gossip. Any other nuggets?'

'One. The lawyer, Nicanor, lusts after the Zoo Keeper's mistress.'

'The fabulous Roxana?'

'You are salivating, Falco!'

'I have not even met the woman.'

'I see you would like to!'

'Only to evaluate whether her charms might be a motive.'

At this point, perhaps luckily, the hot, restless breeze that had got up while we were conversing began to agitate the undergrowth more wildly, to the extent that it woke our driver. He told us this was the Khamseen, the fifty-day wind that Zenon had speculated might have upset Theon's mental stability. It certainly was becoming gritty and unpleasant. Helena wrapped her stole around her face. I tried to look brave. The driver hurried us back to the cart and set off for the city, regaling us on the way with tales of how this wicked wind killed babies. There was no need to lure us back with sensational stories. We were ready to go home and check on our daughters.

XXVI

We arrived back in the city in early evening. The wind had blown across us all the way and was now terrorising the streets, grabbing at awnings and bowling rubbish ahead of its strong gusts. People were holding scarves and stoles across their faces, while women's long clothes twisted against their bodies, men cursed and children wailed. My throat grew scratchy. My hands, fingers and lips felt dry; the dust had worked into my ears and scalp. I could taste the stuff. As we drove along the harbour road, as long as the light lasted we could see choppy waves tearing over the water.

At my uncle's house, I paid off the driver outside the courtyard gate. Immediately we got down and the porter opened up for us, our driver was nobbled by that fellow Katutis who sat outside on the kerb trying to badger us every day. Out of the corner of my eye I saw them with their heads together, engaged in a deep conversation. I could not deduce whether Katutis was complaining or just curious. I had only a glimpse, but I reckoned he would soon know from today's driver everything about where we had been. Was he spying on us? Or just jealous that some other fellow had been successful in winning our custom? Today's driver had been a completely chance pick-up for Helena and me. There was no reason for these two similarly clad, similarly whiskery men to know one another. I could see no reason for them to discuss us so intently. In some places I might shrug and say it was a small town – but Alexandria had half a million inhabitants.

On the threshold, Helena and I shook the dust off ourselves and stamped our feet. We went up slowly. We were glowing from the sun and wind-blast, our brains relaxed and our relationship reasserted. We could hear no particular screaming from children. Everywhere seemed peaceful. Faint welcoming scents came from the kitchen area as we passed. The thought of a wash, followed by stories with my daughters, a quiet dinner, some gentle talk with my older relatives, even a drink with Pa – no, forget that – and an early night was extremely attractive.

But work never stops. First, I had a visitor.

Cassius and Pa had been entertaining him for me. Both seemed mildly surprised by their own co-operation. This was not a commercial contact: I had been tracked down by Nicanor, the Museion lawyer. Etiquette required that such a visitor should not be dumped alone in an empty room, but neither of my relatives was at ease with his calling and in return I could see him looking down on them. Cassius and Pa handed him over to my custody then left us alone together with unlikely speed.

Titbits and wine had been served previously; a slave brought a goblet for me. While Nicanor and I settled, Helena came in briefly and gave him her greeting as if she was the matron of the house, but even she excused herself, saying she had to see our little daughters to bed. She palmed some of the titbits as she left us to it.

The lawyer had only nodded pompously to Helena's good-mannered greeting. That was when I started to dislike him. No; thinking he had tried to do down Aulus, I already did. The feeling would grow, and not just because he was a lawyer. He trailed a cloud of self-esteem, just as some men waft overpowering hair unguent. Mind you, he had the unguent too. Though not effeminate, he was painstakingly manicured and groomed. I'd snort that lawyers can well afford it, but that really would sound like prejudice.

Nicanor had a long face with extremely dark brown soulful eyes. He looked like a Romanised Jew. His deep voice was certainly Eastern. He was cradling his winecup, now half full, not quaffing with the gusto I associated with lawyers. I slowed my own drinking pace to match his. Automatically I found myself adjusting my attitude too. I became more guarded than I had been with the other academics.

'I hear,' began Nicanor, who reckoned himself lead prosecutor, 'you have been asking after me.'

If he was just responding to my enquiries, it was disappointing. At the necropsy, I had invited people to give me clues and dish the dirt. I had hoped that high-flown members of the Academic Board would race to land their colleagues in midden-shit. Snitches are not always accurate, but it gives an investigator somewhere to start.

Patience, Falco. There was a reason for him coming. We just had not reached it yet.

I assumed the necessary posture of gratitude. 'Well, thanks for turning up. Just a couple of questions, really. I have asked most of your fellow Board members: first, the obvious.' I was pretending to assume he was a fellow-expert in crime enquiries. 'Where were you the evening Theon died?'

'That old cliché. Minding my business. What else?'

I noted he failed to provide an alibi – and he was rude about it. Somewhat sourly, I added my second question, 'I would like to know your interest in the Library post.'

'Of course you would! The shortlist is announced, I presume you know!' He was enjoying his power in telling me.

'I was out of town today.' I refused to lose my temper. I really would have liked to have heard this in private circumstances. I bet Nicanor saw I was annoyed. 'So who made the list?'

'Myself –' No false modesty there. He put himself in first. 'Zenon; Philadelphion; Apollophanes.'

Hmm. No Aeacidas, no Timosthenes. I would have included them both and dropped the toady.

'When was this list unveiled?'

'Special Board meeting this afternoon.'

Damn. While I was half asleep at the lakeside. 'Any reactions?'

'Timosthenes walked out.' Nicanor said it in a tone of disgust.

'He has a point.'

Nicanor humphed, though quietly. 'He never stood a chance; it would be cruelty to put his name forward. The way he stormed off surprised me, though . . . Normally he accepts being sidelined. Still, he's a realist. He must know he cannot even console himself with "it is not his turn"; he is never going to have a turn.'

'Is that because he came up through the staff route – or is it literary snobbery, because he studies epic?'

'Dear gods, does he? Oh he would, of course . . . His type always think nobody but Homer can write.'

Call me old-fashioned, but I could see a case to have a library headed up by a man who believed that. 'Can Timosthenes appeal?' Or could I appeal on his behalf, I wondered.

'If he wants another rejection . . . So, Falco, who do you think will get it?' Nicanor came straight out with the question. Some people would have dropped their voice or looked at the ground modestly. This man stared straight at me.

Some men, answering, would diplomatically name him as top choice. I don't use such flattery. 'Wrong for me to comment.' I let a pause niggle. 'What are the odds at the Museion? I assume it's buzzing.'

'When the list goes to the Roman Prefect, Philetus will tick his own recommendation, but will he be so obvious as to favour his sidekick? If he names Apollophanes, I imagine – I hope – he'll be wasting his time. Philosophers are out of favour in Rome. Theon was a historian. The Prefect may decide the arts have had enough influence; he may opt for a scientific discipline. If so, Zenon does not come over well in public. The money is on Philadelphion.'

'Seems about right.' I shrugged, still meaning that to be noncommittal. 'Still, elections rarely turn out as expected.'

I had not meant it as an invitation. Nicanor jumped in immediately: 'Well, now you know my interest – and you know why I am here, Falco.'

It took me a moment. When I worked out his meaning, it was so blatant – and for me so unexpected – I almost choked.

Fortunately I was trained by years of working with unrepentant villains, sharp Forum scammers and side-steppers who would try anything to load the scales of justice. Usually, what they tried was beating me up – but the other method had been known. Some villains have no shame.

'Nicanor! You think I have influence with the Prefect over this appointment?'

'Oh come on, Falco! The others may be calling you an "agent" as if you are an oily palace bureaucrat, but any imperial freedman would be twice as deadly and about five times as smooth. You are a common informer. Of course I know how that works. You appear in the courts. You bring prosecutions. I am your natural candidate.' Now Nicanor was implying we shared the same creepy networks, the same soiled obligations – the same two-faced standards: 'So how much?'

I tried not to gape. 'You are canvassing? You want to buy my vote?'

'Even you can't be so slow! Normal aspect of patronage.'

'Not exactly my experience.'

'Don't play the innocent.'

'I had somehow assumed that the award of a world-renowned academic post was different from vote-rigging the Senate.'

'Why?' Nicanor asked baldly.

I backed down. Why indeed? To pretend that the apparently high-minded intellectuals here were above begging for votes, if they could see how to do it, was hypocritical; he was right. At least he was open.

'What could you have against me?' he persisted. He must be a nightmare in court. He probably thought I was holding out – hoping one of the others would offer more than he did.

I sat up straighter. 'I certainly would like to know why you tried to blackball the accreditation of Camillus Aelianus to the Museion. What was wrong with him?'

'Minas of Karystos. That poser and I have been at odds for two decades . . . What's this to you, Falco?'

'Normal aspect of patronage,' I quoted back to him. 'Camillus is my brother-in-law. I suppose he should have bought you off first?'

'Smoothing his path would be polite – call it correct procedure. So does that increase your price in my business?'

This man was unbelievable.

I told him I would bear his request in mind. It must have been obvious I did not mean it. 'That's a no, then?' He seemed unable to credit it. 'You are backing *Philadelphion*?'

'I think him a good candidate, but I never said that.'

'This is stitched up?'

'I am sure you can have every confidence in a fair hearing.' Nicanor did not believe my demure promise, and so we parted company.

If this writ-rat won, I would not only spurn his cash; dear gods, if he was given the post, I would be joining Theon in an oleander snack. I knew the world was dirty. I just did not want to think it could be quite as depressing as that.

XXVII

Me being offered a bribe by a lawyer caused hilarity in my family. I warned Fulvius, Cassius, and – without much hope he would listen – my father, that this information ought to stay private. They all assured me such stories were only useful to businessmen if they could implicate someone who *took* a bribe. A mere offer was so commonplace it never counted.

'Well, keep quiet anyway,' Helena instructed the three reprobates. They were lined up on a reading-couch like naughty schoolboys: Fulvius cleaning his nails prissily, Cassius neat and collected, Pa sprawled on one end with his head back against the cushions as if his neck ached. Travelling had finally affected him. His untidy grey curls seemed thinner. He actually looked tired. 'I don't want Marcus knocked down in the rush,' Helena continued, 'if all the candidates race to bring him presents.'

'No presents! If I do it, I shall only be swayed by cash,' I said. 'I'm sick of tat. I don't want a bunch of unpleasant silver wine coolers with crass mottoes engraved on them; you can't rely on professors for taste. If gifts are to be lavished on our household, I want Helena to choose them.'

The three magi debated my chances. Their opinion was that neither the astronomer nor the philosopher would be good for much; Cassius thought the philosopher was bound to give me a tunic in a hideous colour, like a trembly aunt of eighty-five, murmuring 'Here is a little something for yourself, dear.' (So Cassius had aunts, did he?)

'This is philosophy at work? So "Know yourself" at Delphi means "Know your best dress colour"?' Helena quipped. Fulvius, Cassius and Pa surveyed her, troubled by this advanced thinking.

They reckoned the Zoo Keeper should have been a good bet, since he probably had income from people whose goats he cured as a sideline, but they knew Philadelphion was spending all his spare cash on his mistress.

I quibbled at that: 'The impression I have of the supposedly luscious Roxana is that she is more giving than demanding.'

'I've said it before,' groaned my father. 'This boy is so innocent, I refuse to call him mine!'

'Just because Marcus Didius has a nice nature, does not make him soft,' Albia reproved him. 'He needs to be an optimist. Many times he is the only honest man in a sea of filth.'

That silenced even Pa.

The banter continued through an early supper. My family are excellent at picking on some fool who has revealed a funny story that he ought to have concealed. They would never let go. *The time the lawyer offered a bribe to Marcus* was all set to become a classic festival favourite.

That was not what made me restless. Knowing the short-list for Theon's old post had been announced made me want to hear what everyone was saying at the Museion. Helena saw it. I never needed her permission to bunk off on work, but sometimes I held back and waited for her sanction, as a courtesy. Neither of us mentioned it out loud: she just tossed her head slightly and in return I winked at her. I slipped away discreetly. Albia saw it. The others didn't notice I was going.

Uncle Fulvius was staying in. Business must be coming to him tonight. As I went downstairs, I passed a man going up. That was the difference in Egyptian town houses: a classic Roman home has a line of entry straight ahead from the porch, crossing the atrium if there is one. It offers a show-off vista from the street – and a certain degree of space and choice; you can go either way around the peristyle garden, for instance. Here, it was all vertical. Anyone coming or going used the stairs. That could work two ways. With a house full of guests, in the commotion you might manage to infiltrate an extra person unnoticed. But if the house guests were prone to milling about, there was no chance of receiving a secret visitor.

So I not only saw the man, we exchanged nods. I pressed against the wall to give him room. He pulled his satchel in to avoid brushing against me, with his left arm clutched against the leather so I would not hear the money chink. He will have seen a good-looking foreigner, neutral tunic, Roman haircut, clean-shaven, pleasant manner, in command of himself. I saw a thickset trader-type, who did not meet my eye. Sometimes you know instinctively that whatever a man of commerce is selling, you do not want it.

One of Fulvius' servants was waiting at the top of the stairs to shunt this man into a private side room, probably the same salon where they put Nicanor earlier. Lying below the family rooms, it had a couple of basic couches, a tripod table just large enough for a drinks tray, a rug you could buy anywhere and no ornaments worth stealing. I kept a room just like it in my own house in Rome. I used it for clients and witnesses, allowing them access to my home as a good patron traditionally did for trusted members of the public. I never trusted anyone. If they came out of the room and pretended they wanted to use the lavatory, a slave who always just happened to be in the corridor would 'show them the way'; he would just as helpfully show them the way back too.

Downstairs, the courtyard porter saluted me obsequiously.

I nodded after the visitor. 'Who was that?'

'I know not his name. Fulvius knows.'

'No doubt . . .' I had no intention of letting Fulvius see I had any interest. 'Is the palanquin here?'

'You want Psaesis? Has gone. Here again tomorrow.'

Typical.

I half hoped the driver who took us to Lake Mareotis would be out in the street, even if he was still muttering with the dogged hanger-on Katutis. They were both missing. It must have been the first time since we arrived that I managed to leave home without being accosted.

I walked to the Museion. It took me back to my early years as an informer, when I had walked everywhere. That was all I could afford then. My legs were older now, but held up.

The wind was still whipping dust everywhere. There were plenty of people on the broad streets. Life in the Mediterranean is lived out of doors, on the pavement or at least on the thresholds of businesses. As I passed leather shops, furniture-makers, coppersmiths, I could see into lit interiors where families hung around. Wafts of grilled and roasted foods were borne on the restive gusts of the Khamseen. Dogs of all sizes enjoyed being part of the street life. So did cats, long lean creatures with pointed ears who were viewed as sacred creatures; I avoided them, lest I be like that Roman who killed a cat on the streets of Alexandria and not unexpectedly was torn to pieces by a mob.

I missed my dog. She was left behind with my mother, but she would have loved sniffing around here. Mind you, taking Nux anywhere near the zoo would have been a nightmare. As for the revered Alexandrian cats, Nux would have added a few to the total of sacred pussies who needed to be mummified.

Thinking about Nux kept me occupied until I reached the Museion complex. Here it was much quieter. The grandiose buildings had a spectral presence after dark.

Their long white porticoes were poorly lit by trails of oil lamps at floor level, many of which had gone out. A few men strolled through the gardens, in small groups or alone. There was a sense of activity still carrying on, although real toil had been ended for most of those who lived here.

This must have been the peaceful atmosphere when Theon returned that night after dinner. His subdued steps may have been the only ones. The sound had been unusual enough to make the astronomer glance over from the observatory, though not so rare as to cause Zenon to continue watching once he saw it was just the Librarian. I wondered whether Theon had known or guessed that somebody had noticed him. I wondered if it gave him a sense of fellowship, or increased feelings of isolation. I wondered if he was going to meet someone.

I retraced what must have been Theon's route. As I walked, I checked for oleander, but none of the bushes that adorned the walkways were of that type. It was our fault, then. Whether suicide or murder, he died because of his dinner garland. Finding out what happened was, therefore, my responsibility.

When I came to the main door of the Great Library, the two enormous portals were securely locked. I turned away. That answered that question. There was bound to be a side door but admission would be monitored, or by special key.

I walked slowly back down the porticoes towards the refectory. I was intending to try to find Aulus. If I was not allowed in, I would ask someone to go and look for him.

There were people about. Sometimes I heard low voices talking, sometimes just a footfall. Once someone passed me and politely said good evening. Once or twice I heard others cross paths and greet each other in the same way. I was alone, however, when the commotion started.

It was coming from the zoo. I heard voices shrieking for help in obvious hysteria. An elephant began trumpeting alarm. Other animals joined in. The human voices had seemed to be both male and female. As I started to run towards them, things changed, so for a few moments there was only a woman, screaming.

And then silence.

XXVIII

I had no weapons. Who goes into a seat of learning armed to the teeth? All you expect to need are knowledge, clarity and the gift of irony.

I managed to pick up a couple of oil lamps; their glimmer hardly lit the shadows and probably drew attention to me. I stood listening. The animals had ceased to trumpet, though I heard restless movements in their various enclosures and cages. Something had definitely disturbed them. They were listening too. They may have had a better idea of what had happened – or what could still happen, but with me doing the shouting – than I did. Like me, the agitated creatures all sounded certain they did not like the situation.

I thought I heard a long rustle, close to me amongst nearby shrubs. I turned, but could see nothing. A purist might say I should have gone in among the foliage to investigate, but believe me, nobody with any imagination would.

I started to explore the deserted paths. Everywhere lay in darkness. My lamps created a tiny circle of gloom. Beyond it, the blackness seemed all the more threatening. Part of the zoo's benign regime for the animals was to let the precious creatures have their natural amount of sleep. Not tonight, though. As time passed I could still hear them, awake and all apparently watching my progress.

Or watching out for something else.

The largest zoo in the world was indeed spectacularly big. Searching took ages. I forced myself to examine each area as best I could, in a hurry, in the dark. Whatever I was looking for, I knew would be obvious once I came across it. Those terrible shrieks had not been tipsy students larking about. Somebody had suffered terribly. Horror was still rippling along these deserted pathways with the wind that hoarded dust into patches like puddles against the raised kerbs. I thought I could smell blood.

And still I fancied I could hear something behind me, stalking. Every time I whipped around, the noise stopped. If this was Rome, I would walk casually around a corner and lie in wait, holding my knife ready. No; if I had been on a street, let's be honest, I would have nipped into the nearest bar and hoped the fear would go away while I downed a beaker.

I had no knife this evening. There was no handy street corner and no bar. What I did find, quite suddenly, was half a dead goat.

It was lying on the path. It had been butchered – skinned and beheaded. The bisection was neat. There was a long rope tied around the half-carcass, stretched out along the path as though someone had towed the meat from a very safe distance. The bloody lure lay close beside a gate. That was damaged and stood wide open. The gate was supposed to close off the fencing where my two little girls had clambered, when they were trying to see down into the deep pit where Sobek, the crocodile, lived. Just inside the broken gate a long earthen ramp started, which gave the keepers access to him. At the bottom there was probably another gate. I felt sure now that if I went right down the ramp I would find that open too.

I did not bother. I knew the crocodile was not at home. He had left his compound. Sobek was now out here with me.

XXIX

I could not see him, but I reckoned he had me under very close observation.

I did wonder briefly why Sobek had not snapped up his half a goat. Perhaps something tastier was on offer. Now it could be me.

I gathered up the rope in loops and towed the meat with me. I have had better luggage. I kept remembering stories Philadelphion had told to thrill my daughters: Nile crocodiles' persistence when trailing a victim; their great speed on land when they rose up on their legs and started running; their wiliness; their colossal strength; their vicious killing power.

Soon I found what Sobek really liked for dinner. The next horror lying in my path was a man's body – though only part of it. Chunks of the corpse had been torn off. There was a lot of blood, so he had been alive during some of the agony. Sobek must have ripped off and gulped down the missing pieces. I wondered why he had left the feast. I guessed he would return for his prey as soon as his reptilian stomach rumbled. He had just gone to catch more.

Ominous scrapes and rustles still sounded close by in the darkness. The mighty beast must be circling around me. I thought of scrambling up the fence but Philadelphion had told us they kept Sobek in a pit because he could climb short distances. He was such a size he could certainly rear up quite high.

Then I heard a new noise – different, human, disconcerting.

I stared around, but saw nobody. Still, I had definitely heard a subdued whimper. My voice was hoarse: 'Who's there? Where are you?'

'Up here . . . Help me, please!'

I looked up as instructed, and saw a distraught woman.

She was halfway up a date palm tree. Sheer fright must have propelled her up the tree; she had her arms and legs clasped desperately around the trunk, in the way boys shin up to collect fruit bunches, and was clinging on for dear life.

'All right – I'm here.' Not much comfort if she saw how scared I was. 'Can you hang on?'

'Not any longer!'

'Right.' I assumed she knew the crocodile was still about. No point stating the obvious. 'Can you slither down?'

She could; in fact, at that moment her strength gave way, her grip on the trunk failed and she tumbled to ground level, landing at my feet. I helped her up, like a polite informer. She threw herself into my arms. It does happen.

Fortunately I still had one oil lamp, which facilitated a discreet inspection. My heart was pounding, but that was nervousness about Sobek. If she felt it, she was too distracted to notice. Her heart was pounding too – I could see it was, because her ruined gown had been flimsy in the first place; thanks to the hard stubs of palm trunk, her garments now hung in rags. She was covered with blood, where the sharp edges of vicious old leaf spurs had cut her. She must have disturbed insects as she fled up, and she may have known that palm trees are a favoured haunt of scorpions. None of that would have bothered her, because she had seen the part-eaten corpse that now lay at my feet. My guess was that the poor woman also witnessed exactly how the dead man had died.

I would have wrapped her in a cloak for comfort and modesty, but on a warm night in Alexandria only wimps wear cloaks. I had not been expecting to rescue distressed women. She had, if it's relevant, dark eyes emphasised by cosmetics, masses of slithering dark hair that had come loose from various ivory hairpins, the figure of a still young woman who had never borne children and who took care of herself, pleasant features and a winsome manner. Only one piece of information was missing; she supplied it: 'My name is Roxana.' No surprises. Well, she was running around the zoo at night, looking spruce. She was not bad now, in this terrified state, and must have been exquisite when she first set out. No doubt she came to the zoo to see her lover, Philadelphion.

I understood why everything male at the Museion hankered for this beauty. Philadelphion, that silver-haired charmer, had all the luck. She was still young enough to be an extremely appealing prospect.

'I am Falco. Marcus Didius Falco.'

'Oh gods in heaven!' she squealed in alarm, and immediately started to shoot back up the tree.

Olympus. My name may be ignoble, but it normally causes only mild contempt . . . But at once I realised what had caused her to scramble for safety. I too looked around madly for a refuge. There was only one palm tree, and since Roxana's strength had dwindled, she was not far enough up it this time to leave any room for me – not if I wanted to be out of reach of the giant jaws of the thirty-foot-long angry crocodile that had suddenly appeared out of nowhere and was rushing at me.

I whirled the goat on its rope, once, and chucked it. Sobek stopped to take a look. Then he decided I was better.

We had been told of his enormous length, but I wouldn't volunteer to measure him with rulers. He stretched twice the distance of a fancy dining room, three times as long as mine at home. His four short, muscular, splayed legs had covered ground at a gallop in his first rush forwards; he looked happy to carry on at that speed if he had anyone to chase. I was not sure how long I could muster the same stamina – not long enough. When he opened his mouth, about sixty teeth adorned his yawn; they were all shapes and sizes, and all sharp-looking. The stench of his breath was terrible.

Roxana, more of a game girl than I had dared to hope, began to yell very loudly for help.

XXX

Sobek kept coming.

My instinct was to run like Hades. *'When crocodiles rise up on their legs, Julia, they can easily outstrip a man . . .'*

So don't run, Falco; you'll just encourage him . . . I was about to scram regardless, when a shout stopped both of us. I leapt to one side. Distracted, the crocodile snapped his vast jaws, ripping off a large square of my tunic. Then he swung his great head towards the new arrival.

Thank Jupiter! Someone who was good with animals.

Out of the darkness burst my old friend Thalia, drawn by the noise. She looked rumpled even by her standards, but at least she had grabbed a spear and a heavy coil of rope. She threw me the spear. I caught it somehow. 'Settle down, boy . . .'

Sobek might be pampered, but he despised endearments. He jerked from side to side, weighing up which of us to kill first. Excited voices were approaching; rescuers were unlikely to arrive in time. 'We're not going to lead him back home with a barley cake – Jump him, Falco!'

'What?'

Sobek chose me.

As he decided, I rammed the great spear into his open jaws, trying to keep it vertical to wedge his mouth open. Useless. It was a heavy old-fashioned implement, but he splintered the wood like fine kindling and spat it out. He had disliked me before; now he was badly annoyed. Thalia

191

yelled. She had lungs like an arena wrestler. Sobek's jaws seemed to take on a sneer.

The pause was enough. As he lunged, I obeyed orders, dodged around and flung myself across his back. The reptile was all muscle. He twisted violently and threw me off as if I weighed no more than a puff of goose-down. Every bone in my body came close to a fracture as I landed. Then he jerked around to come for me.

Luckily, helpers turned up – Chaereas, Chaeteas, Thalia's staff. Hard hands grabbed my leg and hauled me away as those terrible teeth closed. Both Thalia and Roxana were shouting at the tops of their voices. Winded, I scrabbled for safety, while Sobek turned on people who were flinging nets and ropes on him. Lashing his gigantic tail, he broke free as if these restraints were skeins of sewing thread. A rope end lashed me across the face. Nonetheless, I tackled him again, narrowly avoiding a ferociously stamping leg with claws that could have ripped me open.

Somehow I bestrode him again, clutching on just behind the eyes atop his skull. Others bravely seized his angry limbs. They were pressing down with all their weight. It was now or never. I threw both arms around his jaws, at full stretch, my face pressed to his ghastly leather skin, my body prone on the pulsating muscle that would soon thrash me senseless. I had never experienced anything so strong. I was blind to my companions, had no time to even think what they were doing. I squeezed tight – and whatever the Zoo Keeper had said about a man being able to close a crocodile's mouth with a small effort, he was wrong. How wrong I cannot begin to describe. Hercules knows how I hung on to Sobek.

I had sensed more people arriving. They knew the routine. Sobek had to watch and avoid them. I kept clamping his jaws shut, on the verge of fainting from the effort. But the situation was changing. The crocodile tried a stupendous roll, but his plummeting was hindered by the sheer weight of bodies restraining him. People must be hanging on all along his legs and tail. I could still feel him thrashing.

'Don't let go!' I heard Thalia chirp.

You are bloody joking! I thought, unable to reply or raise a Roman quip of suitable nobility. Still I gripped on – as I explained to Helena much later, holding the jaws shut from behind *very* firmly.

'Got him! Loose your grip, Falco. Falco – loose him *now*!'

I could not let go. My arms were locked. Terror kept me there, in my sordid embrace with Sobek. 'Oh, somebody separate them!' Thalia's voice growled, as if she was ordering a bouncer to break up a pair of rivals who were fighting for a sweet girl acrobat. Finally I unclenched my arms just enough to slide off. Chaereas, I think it was, had the courtesy to catch me.

There was still work to do, roping the beast, before we all had to tow his tremendous weight back into his personal compound. At no point was he entirely safe. We were sweating with fear the whole time. We manoeuvred him in, then on a command all sprang back and scarpered, leaving him to break free of his ropes. It took him no time. I squatted on the path, put my head between my knees and tried to recover, as close as I had ever been to total collapse, both physically and mentally. Someone was banging new timbers across the gate. Philadelphion – where had he come from? – set a guard on the crocodile compound.

When I raised my head, somebody – Chaeteas? – gave me a hand up.

People were looking over the fence to see what Sobek would do. He snapped a few times, but then began a slow waddle down the long ramp back to his quarters. 'Good as gold!' some wag remarked. Another man hurled the half-goat down to him. He ignored it.

By this time lights had been brought and those who dared were gingerly approaching the butchered corpse I had found near Roxana. Nobody could bear to touch the dead man. It *was* a man; you could tell by the legs.

Thalia, in a spangly tunic of such brevity it took bravado for even her to wear it, started eyeing up the Zoo Keeper's mistress as if Roxana was a dog with a killer reputation. Roxana, who by the light of newly-arrived lamps appeared not as youthful as I had first thought, glared straight back as if everything was Thalia's fault. Even though she had ended up scratched, bruised, tattered and terrified, the Zoo Keeper's mistress showed admirable style.

Despite the numerous witnesses, Philadelphion abandoned discretion and had the kindness to turn to his female friend with murmurs of comfort. Obviously concerned, he enveloped Roxana in his arms and took charge of her. I saw Thalia sneer. As he gazed around the scene, I wondered dispassionately just what he made of it.

The commotion had roused the scholars. Camillus Aelianus arrived and pushed through the press of onlookers as if he had official rights. He was coming to me, but as soon as he spotted the body, he veered and knelt alongside. I saw his expression and roused myself to get over there. When I reached him, he looked white.

'Who is it?'

'Heras, Falco.' Aulus was shaking. He must have recognised what remained of the young man's clothes. 'My friend Heras.'

XXXI

Someone threw a cover over the corpse. Not before time.

Aulus stood up. He seemed fine for a moment, then turned aside and violently vomited.

In an ideal world, we would have begun questioning people then and there. That was impossible. I was too exhausted, my assistant was in shock, witnesses were hysterical and crowds were milling everywhere. I wanted to get as far away from the crocodile as possible. I muttered to Philadelphion tersely that I would require to see his mistress and his staff first thing next morning, with no excuses. I exchanged a nod with Thalia. I could trust her to keep a discreet eye on the zoo area; I would speak to her tomorrow before I saw anybody else. I took Aulus home with me. We managed to hitch a ride on a cart; our journey passed in complete silence.

Aulus was devastated. He had seen corpses before, but as far as I knew, never that of a friend. The young man Heras had died terribly; Aulus was envisaging just how bad it must have been. As soon as we went indoors, I sent him to bed with a drink. He remained morose. I was none too chatty myself.

Next day, Helena woke me at dawn. She was gentle but persistent. Although this was what I wanted, it was difficult to rouse myself. My limbs were stiff and I was covered in grazes and bruises, so I ached all over. As she slathered on ointment, Helena knew how to hide her concern, but after nearly losing me she insisted on accompanying me when I went out. We left her brother sleeping. Albia and Cassius had been primed to look after him, once he woke in his own time. 'Let him come to the Museion and help, if that seems to be what he wants.'

'Will that make him feel better?' Albia had a scornful way of speaking sometimes.

'It may help Aulus,' Helena answered. 'Nothing can be done for the dead young man – Marcus Didius understands that. But there are other considerations. We need to find out what happened.'

Albia backed down. She was brusque but practical: 'To know what happened for his family, to prevent similar accidents . . .'

Answers might help me too.

Helena and I crossed the city back to the Museion as the bakers were riddling out their ovens ready for the first loaves of the day. Sleepy-eyed workers were already walking to their places of business in the Mediterranean way. Women with no weight on them were shouting at slovenly, flabby men, who cursed back grumpily; heavier and older females swept or mopped pavements outside half-open premises. Horses stood between the shafts. Passers-by could already buy pastries. Way across the bay, the Pharos was entirely hidden, sheathed in thick mist. It explained why they needed a lighthouse.

Even at the Museion people stirred. News of last night's tragedy had percolated the dormitories. Some of the dreamers would take a long time to find out what had happened; others were eager to gossip straight away. I urgently needed to start my enquiries, before rumours stuck and became accepted fact.

We found Thalia glumly sipping at a scented concoction in a beaker, flopped in the doorway to her fantastic marquee. Nothing like the ten-man military tents with which I was familiar but closer to a huge bedouin dwelling-place, it was

196

a long, dark red construction, colourfully swagged and flagged on every seam and guy-rope. The tent alone confirmed how well she was doing financially.

All kinds of water and food containers were cluttered outside. Amongst the clutter, in a large basket beside her lurked Jason, the python; I recognised his tall woven container and could tell from Thalia's awakening grin that she would tease me about him. Jason's idea of fun was to slither up behind me and stare under my tunic. I hated that. Helena quite liked him and was liable to ask to have him let out of the basket.

Folding stools were fetched and we joined Thalia. I ended up next to the snake basket; I could feel Jason thumping against the side, anxious to come and alarm me with practical jokes as usual.

Thalia was completely covered up; she had a warm woollen cloak wrapped around her, keeping her decent from ankle to throat. This strange decorum showed even she thought the recapture of Sobek had been a dangerously close business. 'That was a disaster last night, Falco!' Her voice croaked harshly as her sombre mood returned.

'Are you all right?' Helena asked.

'Women's business.'

Refreshments had been brought for us. I cradled a beaker, in the black mood of a man who had been recently knocked half senseless and who had not recovered his equilibrium. 'I have had more relaxed evenings . . . What's the word?'

Thalia took her time. Eventually she said, 'I sent some of my people over there this morning – take a look, ask about. The story is, Sobek grew suddenly keen on a day trip to Lake Mareotis. He broke out before his keepers noticed. The young student came across him unexpectedly, then was killed trying to intervene to save the woman. Who knows why she was cavorting there? But all a sad accident.'

'Her name is Roxana,' Helena informed Thalia, in an

innocent tone she used sometimes. I knew better. Helena had picked up that Thalia harboured some grudge against Roxana. Possibly she just hated members of the public who caused problems with animals; perhaps there was more to it.

'So I believe,' returned Thalia, sounding sour. I put down this definite needle as contempt for fancy dolls who tripped around in the dark, having to be rescued. Thalia had a jaded view of the public's lack of common sense.

'Had you met her before?' Helena enquired.

'I don't mingle with that sort.'

'How did the gates get broken?' I asked. 'Did Sobek smash them?'

'That's the story.'

'Do I believe it?'

'Believe what you like!' Thalia was definitely not herself today. 'Crocodiles are unpredictable, they are intelligent and skilful, they have devastating strength –'

'I don't need to be reminded!'

'And if he wanted to eat half a gate, Sobek could do it.'

Thalia relapsed into silence so Helena filled in more for herself: 'On the other hand, the zoo has had Sobek almost all his life and the keepers say he is fifty. Confinement must be all he can remember. Sobek is thoroughly pampered, fed daily with more treats than a wild crocodile ever dares to hope for. His keepers love him and regard him as tame. He is very intelligent – so why would he try to leave?'

'Who knows?' Thalia grunted. 'Once he did get out, he had a fine time – but that's what any croc would do. Perhaps he really did want an expedition and a little rampage. The lad was there in his way. I dare say he tried to run – well, Sobek would have only one reaction to that. It was just an accident.'

'So that's the official story. You believe it?' I asked.

'Yes, I do, Falco.'

'Well, I don't. Calling this an accident is sheer nonsense.

198

Somebody lured Sobek out deliberately, with a piece of goat on a long rope.'

'Whatever you say, Falco.' Thalia unaccountably lost interest.

I trusted Thalia. Nonetheless, as Helena and I walked to the Zoo Keeper's quarters after we left the circus tent, neither of us said much. Perhaps we were both pondering how tricky it is when somebody you have liked and trusted for years starts closing up suspiciously.

XXXII

We inspected the crocodile's enclosure. Sobek was lying at the bottom of the pit, feigning sleep. To encourage him to stay there, several chunks of new meat had been thrown down. Chaeteas was watching over him. Like his comrade, Chaereas, he was a pleasant-featured man of middle years and calm temperament, who looked to be of native Egyptian origin; they were so similar, they were possibly related. I had always received the impression these two were content with their work. They seemed genuinely fond of the animals and keen on the pursuit of science. At the post-mortem they had behaved with a discretion that seemed to come naturally. They appeared to have a close relationship with Philadelphion. He relied on them and they had respect for him. These qualities are plainly desirable, yet in my experience, between employers and their staff neither occurs frequently. In many professions it never happens. Mine, normally.

I examined the damaged top gate by daylight. It was mainly of wood, since the crocodile was never intended to reach it. It certainly looked as if it could have been chewed by a vicious reptile, though there could be equally persuasive alternatives. The way struts were torn out and one side smashed off its hinges could just as easily have been done with an axe (say). I lacked the forensic skill to distinguish; so would most people, as a villain might realise. Newly splintered wood is newly splintered wood. 'Are you satisfied,' I asked Chaeteas, 'that Sobek did this?' He nodded.

'If so, why did he break out?'

As if he had been with Helena and me yesterday when we were told about the Khamseen, Chaeteas blamed the disturbing effects of the fifty-day wind.

Chaeteas offered to take me down to see the lower gate as well. Under Sobek's evil gaze, I was satisfied to squint at long distance.

The other gate was made of metal and had not been so badly mangled. It looked a bit buckled, but the enormous Sobek could have thrashed it with his tail as he passed through. Chaeteas admitted sheepishly that a chain and padlock had inadvertently been left unsecured last night. I gave him a straight look. He then confessed this was not the first time – though he claimed it was the only occasion Sobek took notice and escaped. Philadelphion normally found and corrected the error when he made his nightly rounds.

According to Chaeteas, he and Chaereas always tended the beast together. Zoo routines forbade anything else. Sobek was so big, no one ever took solo trips down to his pit. It was impossible to say which of the pair had been responsible for not fastening the padlock as neither could remember.

'And what,' I asked, 'is your explanation for the goat on a rope I found?'

'Someone taunted him. Maybe the young fellow who died.'

That jarred with me. Helena, who had been listening in silence, also thought it seemed an easy way of making out that Heras had brought death on himself. 'He was not the type for taunting,' she retorted bitterly.

Helena and I went to see Philadelphion. When we arrived, he was being harangued by the Director. Philetus would happily reprimand his colleagues in front of strangers, however eminent those colleagues were. 'I have warned you! Your association with this woman brings the Museion into disrepute. You must end it immediately. She is not to enter Museion premises again.'

Philadelphion had been receiving his rebuke with pinched lips. In some respects he looked like a schoolboy whose misdemeanours had caused many a teacher's tantrum before. As the Director paused for breath, the Zoo Keeper's hand-some features flushed, however; I suspect because we were listening. 'You may be on my shortlist –' Philetus made no attempt to curb the nastiness in his tone – 'but do remember, I can only recommend a man of unsullied principles!'

Whirled by his own moral superiority, Philetus flew from the Zoo Keeper's office. He whipped up a breeze with his robe so angrily, a scroll on the desk began unrolling. Helena put out a slim hand and steadied it.

'As you see,' Philadelphion remarked to me, once the man had left, 'I am formally forbidden to present Roxana to you at the zoo this morning!'

He assumed a slight smile, the kind that often means a patient man is thinking how dearly he would like to throttle the bastard who has been insulting him. How slowly he would draw out the death, and how much pain he would inflict . . .

I spoke gently: 'I gather senior members have to be above reproach?'

'Senior members,' grated Philadelphion, now letting all his resentment show, 'can be fools, liars, cheats or buffoons – well, you have met my colleagues, Falco – but they must never reveal that they are having a more pleasant life than the Director.'

Helena's chin was up. I flashed her a grin, including the Zoo Keeper. 'So do what you like, but don't let him find out?'

Philadelphion bridled. 'The lady Roxana is intelligent, well-bred, well-read and a charming hostess.' That sounded next best thing to a courtesan. When I met her she certainly came over as a game girl. The way she shot up that palm tree did the lass credit. I believed him that the sweet Roxana could discuss Socrates at the same time as serving a plate of fig fancies. I could imagine the rest of her talents too.

'Philetus objects to your charming friend visiting you here?' asked Helena, coolly.

'She never does,' Philadelphion said. 'I see her at her house.'

'But she came here last night?'

His face shadowed at the correction. He almost looked guilty. 'Exceptionally.'

'By appointment?' I queried.

'No. She must have had some reason to speak to me urgently.'

'You don't know what?' Helena took it up again. Philadelphion shook his head, as if she was a fly tormenting him.

My turn: 'So where were you last night?'

He looked as if he was about to say something different, then: 'In my office,' he answered, so firmly it sounded unreliable. 'Until I heard the commotion and came running.'

'In your office – doing what?' I pressed him.

'Catching up on the zoo accounts.' He indicated the scroll on his desk, which was indeed sitting next to an abacus. Cynically I wondered if the abacus had been placed there this morning deliberately. Helena picked up the scroll, as if unaware she was doing it; almost idly, she unravelled a little of the end, while I continued the questions.

'Any idea what the young man Heras could have been doing in your zoo last night, Philadelphion?'

'None. Maybe students came for pranks, but we found nothing.'

Young men's pranks seemed to be the Museion's excuse for anything unusual. 'We met him. Heras did not seem one to lark about.'

'I know very little about him,' said Philadelphion. 'He was not a science student. I understand he was in Alexandria

203

to learn rhetoric, intending a public career. Someone said he came with you to the necropsy of Theon.'

'He was friends with my young brother-in-law. Did he know Roxana?'

'Not at all.'

'You asked her?' Helena put in. It made Philadelphion pause. When this pause lasted a long time, Helena altered tack: 'Well! Can we discuss the shortlist for the post of Librarian? Many congratulations on being included – but the obvious questions are, how do you rate your own chances and how do you feel about your rivals?'

Philadelphion had previously been disposed to gossip; he did not fail us now: 'Zenon is the dark horse – who knows what Zenon thinks, or how he will perform? Philetus obviously wants to give the post to Apollophanes, but will even our Director be so brazen as to recommend his own satellite? You could see Philetus starting to try to manipulate the list when he talked to me just now. He was threatening me – looking for excuses to support another candidate.'

'Marcus Didius and I were disappointed not to see Timosthenes given a chance.'

'Not as disappointed as him. He took his omission very nastily.'

'What of Nicanor?' Helena prompted.

'Nicanor thinks himself well qualified.'

'What do *you* think?' She did not mention Nicanor's offer to bribe me, in case he thought she was hinting.

'A bully. Frankly, I shudder at the prospect of working with him.'

'Someone suggested that Nicanor admires Roxana,' Helena put forward quietly.

'Many people who know her admire Roxana,' Philadelphion snapped back tetchily.

Helena had a tricky expression. Quickly, I weighed in and returned to asking what Roxana had told her lover about the Sobek incident. His version ran: she had come to find him; on the way, she heard odd noises; she bravely ventured to investigate and found Sobek killing and eating Heras. Roxana yelled, so the crocodile left the body; she realised the beast was about to attack her too, so she climbed the tree and shouted for help. Then I came along – 'For which Roxana and I must thank you, Falco, most sincerely.'

Helena purred that that was unnecessary; no doubt when we saw Roxana, she would thank me herself.

Chaereas was deputed to take us to Roxana's house.

On the way there I asked Chaereas about last night and he told me the same stuff we had heard from Chaeteas. *Exactly* the same. He too blamed an uncharacteristic escape by Sobek. He too called the death of Heras an accident. He had no explanation for the goat.

'Had you and your colleague perhaps used the meat to feed Sobek?'

'Oh no,' Chaereas assured us.

On arrival, he left us to go in by ourselves. Roxana had rooms in an anonymous building, up a dusty staircase, off an uninspiring street. This was typical of Alexandria. In Rome it would have told us she was a struggling manicurist, with five children by three fathers. Here, it meant nothing.

Inside was quite different. Discreet servants padded about a large apartment that was decorated with subtle, extremely feminine opulence. There were rugs everywhere; there were seats formed from enormous cushions; there was much gleaming copperware, ivory and elaborate small pieces of furniture carved from rare woods. I could not see any scroll boxes to confirm the claim of intellectual competence, but I was prepared to believe philosophy and plays were hidden away somewhere. Either Roxana had inherited money or she had had a rich husband – whether living or deceased; or a lover, or more than one, spent a lot on her. Helena was making an inventory scathingly.

Cleaned up, the Zoo Keeper's ladyfriend looked like a Vestal Virgin's younger sister. When she appeared (which took some time), Roxana wore discreet robes in dark colours, a plain hairstyle and little jewellery. She moved into the room in a quiet hum of unnerving perfume, but was otherwise not exotic. Mind you, she gave the impression she *could* make herself just about as exotic as anybody wanted, if she chose.

Helena Justina failed to warm to her. Somehow I expected that. Helena's presence at my side clearly surprised the lady. I must be the first good-looking man who, on coming to see Roxana, brought his wife. Well, that just showed her what clean-living persons Roman husbands were. And how well supervised.

Roxana's evidence about the Heras tragedy was as well thought out and organised as her appearance. She told us exactly the same story as Philadelphion. They corroborated one another as tightly as Chaereas and Chaeteas had done. Rarely can descriptions have been so mathematically co-ordinated. My instinct was not to waste much time here.

It was Helena who took charge of the situation.

'Thank you, Roxana. That was, if I may say so, an extremely clear and beautifully expressed witness statement.'

Throughout our interview so far, Roxana had given the impression of being slightly pent-up, but at this warm-hearted praise she relaxed, at least technically. If anything, she seemed puzzled, as if unsure how to take Helena. I enjoyed watching these two engage so stiffly.

Helena then turned to the servant who had placed herself near the doorway in the attitude of a chaperon. Placing a hand delicately on her pregnant belly, my trusty assistant begged sweetly, 'I am so sorry to be a nuisance, but could you possibly organise something to drink for us – just water will be absolutely fine, or mint tea would be delectable . . .' The maid withdrew, muttering darkly, then

Helena snapped upright. 'Marcus darling, stop jiggling about like a three-year-old. If you want to stretch your legs, go and do so.'

I never jiggle. Still, I knew a big hint when it hit me. I shuffled from the room with a shifty expression – then applied my ear to the door.

Helena must have turned back to Roxana. 'Right! Now we are quite alone, so you can be frank, my dear.' Perhaps Roxana had fluttered her eyelashes. Waste of time. Helena was crisp. 'Listen to me, please. My husband was nearly killed last night and another poor young man did lose his life most terribly. I want to know who caused that and I am not interested in pathetic taradiddles, cobbled together to preserve people's reputations.'

'I have told you what happened!' Roxana cried.

'No; you have not. Now here is what will happen. You can tell me the truth now, then you and I, like sensible women, will work out how to handle it. Otherwise, Marcus Didius, who is neither as stupid nor as susceptible as you obviously think, will explode your false evidence. Of course you thought he swallowed your story. Believe me, he doubts every word. Being a man, he won't say so to a pretty woman's face. But he is utterly competent and always direct. If – that means, *when* – Falco uncovers the truth of what happened at the zoo, he will make it public. He has no choice. You must see that. He is the Emperor's man and must be seen to expose lies.' Helena dropped her voice. I could hardly hear it. 'So, I suppose Philadelphion bullied you into telling us this tale. Is it him you are afraid of – or someone else, Roxana?'

I never have much luck. At this point, the damned servant decided to mooch back with a beaten-up tray of skinny refreshments. For several minutes I was locked in a sign-language tussle with her. In the end, the only way I could get rid of the inept factotum was to shoo her off as if sending a bunch of heifers through a hedge; it must have been fully audible from inside the room.

I had seized the tray myself from her clammy grasp. I knocked quickly and entered the room just as Roxana exclaimed, with heartfelt drama: 'Somebody let out Sobek deliberately. They cannot have known I would be there with that boy, Heras.'

'What – up to no good with him?'

'I deny it! Normally Philadelphion would have been going around to check on all the animals – so what you should be considering is that *somebody* was trying to make the crocodile kill *him*!'

The ladies turned their gaze on me. 'And who might that have been?' I enquired, mildly. 'Who wants Philadelphion dead?'

'Nicanor!' blazed Roxana. 'You fool, Falco – it's obvious!'

I put down the tray on a small table and set about serving mint tea for everyone.

XXXIII

'A guilty lawyer – oh I like that!'

'Don't say I told you!'

'Trust me, lady!'

Helena's eyes sweetly accused me: *you dog, Falco!* She let me continue the questioning, however.

According to Roxana, Nicanor's hatred of the Zoo Keeper was all to do with her. Nicanor was not simply a silent rival, lusting from a distance; she said he had been approaching her on the sly for months. He had publicly sworn to snatch her from Philadelphion, whatever it took. She found his persistence a menace. She was a little scared of him; he had a harsh reputation. The Zoo Keeper refused to tackle Nicanor, feeling himself secure in possession of Roxana's favours and not wanting quarrels at work. She, of course, had always known it would end badly.

She was a self-centred piece. It was only because she dimly understood that stressing her own importance might reflect badly upon her, that Roxana allowed a possible contributing factor: Philadelphion being favourite on the Chief Librarian shortlist. She knew Nicanor felt fervid professional jealousy. I asked how Philadelphion really felt about the post, given his known resentment that the Library attracted more attention than the zoo, where his heart clearly lay. Roxana thought he saw taking over the Library, if it happened, as potentially a way for him to right the balance. Whether that would make him a good Librarian I doubted, though I could not see Nicanor doing any better. He too wanted the post for personal reasons – his raw ambition.

If he could snatch Roxana from Philadelphion as well, that would double his triumph.

In my experience lawyers make good haters and they never flinch from revenge. However, they are skilled and subtle, rarely descending to violence. They don't need to. They have other, more potent weapons.

It would be easy to dismiss Roxana's claim as a flight of fancy. Lack of evidence at the scene made it difficult to accuse Nicanor – or anybody else – of setting Sobek loose. If somebody did it, their plan was extremely risky. Yes, Philadelphion was known to make his rounds at night to check on the animals, but actual events showed all too clearly that other people might be blundering around the zoo as well. Besides, even if the Zoo Keeper had found the croc, Sobek might like Philadelphion. He might just have waddled up, wagging his tremendous tail and hoping for treats.

On the other hand, if someone really had let Sobek out to kill, their plan had a simple glory: but for them abandoning the goat, the resulting death would convincingly have looked like an accident. If only Sobek had slaughtered the right man, it would have been perfect. This argued for a bloodthirsty killer. The victim died a horrific death. Anyone sufficiently mad and vindictive to arrange it would have enjoyed those screams.

Anyone that mad, I thought, might try to strike again.

I assured Roxana all her claims would be investigated. I would do it in the true Falco style: discreetly, effectively and as soon as possible. Meanwhile, she was not to approach Nicanor, nor admit him to her house. She should warn Philadelphion of her fears for his life, but discourage him from tackling the lawyer. I would approach the man – at the right moment.

In fact, when Helena and I left, I said that I would first want to consider whether anybody else had a big grudge against the Zoo Keeper. 'What did you think about the doting mistress?'

'I thought,' replied Helena acidly, 'the lovely Roxana was a tribute to the powers of a good night's sleep.'

'Really? You mean, she had just seen a young man die a hideous death, with herself and me nearly killed too, yet she was not beset with nightmares?'

Helena was scornful. 'Where were the puffy eyes? The signs of weeping? The gaunt cheeks? The ravages to the complexion? Marcus, that woman has no conscience.'

We both then had the same intriguing notion about the luscious hostess: would *Roxana* have had any motive to let Sobek out?

When I suggested it might be useful to investigate Roxana further, Helena Justina scoffed. 'No need! I think we know *exactly* what that woman is all about!' I concurred meekly.

She was obviously tired. I sent her back to my uncle's house in his palanquin, which we had borrowed that morning.

On the excuse of discussing the late Heras, I took myself back to the Museion to see Philetus. Heras was already on his mind when I was let into his office. 'As Director of the Museion, I shall have to write to tell the parents what has happened.' He was soon in full flow, lamenting his time-consuming responsibilities and the burden of trying to keep order among the young scholars.

'Had Heras come to your attention before?'

'I try to know all our scholars personally.' So he had never heard of the young man.

'Was he a model student?'

'His tutor says so. Hard working and well liked.' That was the natural response to an unexpected death. It had no value. I bet the tutor could barely remember which one Heras was.

'What is known of his background?'

211

'His father owns land and collects taxes.' That fitted what Heras himself had told me. 'Of course everyone of any standing in Egypt farms and collects taxes, Falco – but I am told the family is respectable and of good repute.' Surprisingly, Philetus did seem to have done some home-work. Perhaps he was not all bad – or perhaps some minion winkled out the facts. A diplomatic letter was needed for the family, to protect the Museion's reputation. Philetus was clearly nervous that an angry father would storm here, demanding answers and trying to apportion blame. I wondered if his anxiety was based on prior experience.

If there had been negligence, I wanted no part in any cover-up. I changed the subject. 'I'd like to tap your wonderful knowledge, Philetus –' I managed not to choke myself.

'You are stuck then?' he rasped. I nearly decided not to ask him anything. Still, he was right to some extent.

'May I speak in confidence?' Philetus nodded, eager to see how much trouble I was in. 'I have one death that looks like murder, but which may be suicide. Another looks like an accident, but I believe it was attempted murder.'

'What? Who would have wanted to murder Heras?'

'Nobody, as far as I know. The suggestion is, another man was the intended victim. Heras died by mistake. Apparently you have a slew of feuds among your shortlist candidates.'

'Oh that's no secret, Falco!'

I tackled the subject as delicately as I could. 'I could not help overhearing your pleas with Philadelphion to set aside his mistress. She seems a liability! I am looking at her care-fully in case her involvement last night is suspicious.' As I expected, that thrilled the Director. He was so pleased, I even wondered if he had wooed Roxana himself and been rejected. 'Can you tell me any more about the woman?'

'A papyrus merchant's widow. He was wealthy, it goes without saying. It wouldn't surprise me if her husband was helped on his way – though the story was, he died of a tumour. Somebody should have made sure Roxana remarried and was kept firmly out of trouble – but who would have her now? Several of my junior colleagues pay her far too much attention. She enjoys it and will not be discouraged.'

'Are members of the Museion allowed to marry?' I enquired.

'No reason why not. Nobody has ever suggested,' Philetus pontificated, 'that a man may not copulate and think at the same time, Falco.'

I stayed calm. 'Nor that a rich sex life lessens mental facility. Men with fine minds often rush to lower themselves – and being known for their minds seems to increase their chances. Power is a fast-acting aphrodisiac. Women find high position an attraction in a man – and busy men feel extra virile.'

'Some of us know how to control our urges.'

'Oh good!' I was no prude but I flinched from the idea of Philetus controlling his urges. 'So your objection to Philadelphion's flirtation with Roxana is purely moral – he is supposed to be a family man. Others, I am told, resent it out of pure jealousy.'

'A woman with such a soiled reputation? I cannot see the attraction,' Philetus sniggered.

'Not tempted?' I bet he was! 'What about Nicanor? People say he lusts after her.'

'A man of upright principles.'

'An honest lawyer?' I let a smile show. 'Well, I do not think Nicanor would risk his grand career over a woman. However, he has vile ambition. He might do absolutely anything to obtain the prestigious librarianship.'

'Would he? You had better ask him, Falco.'

I probably would do eventually. At the moment, seeing I had no evidence, Nicanor would simply deny it.

*　　*　　*

213

'So give me a steer, Philetus: now you have announced your shortlist, which of your four candidates is the hot name?'

'What do you think of them, Falco?' As always, the slippery Director dodged the ball, throwing it straight back to me. If he was being discreet I could have borne it, but he was just indecisive.

'Philadelphion must be the front-runner – though would you relish working closely with him? Apart from the black mark for Roxana, is there anything else against him?'

'I shall be perturbed if it comes to light there was something amiss with zoo security last night. It appears,' mused Philetus grimly, 'at the very least there must have been carelessness in locking up the crocodile. I now have to see whether Philadelphion is running his zoo properly . . .' So count him out! Philetus could not leave it alone: 'He is too quarrelsome, anyway. He was always wrangling with Theon and he continually argues with Zenon, our astronomer.'

'So what of Zenon?'

Philetus' eyes narrowed. 'Extremely competent.' That was terse. I got it: Zenon knew far too much about the financial background. Zenon was dangerous to Philetus.

'We were talking about Nicanor. Is he as good as he thinks he is?'

'Too reluctant to make contributions to discussions. He holds back – and thinks himself very clever and manipulative.' That was such a good assessment I thought Philetus must have filched it from someone else.

'Apollophanes? You get on well with him, I think?'

Now I had pleased him. 'Oh yes,' agreed the Director, like a feral cat who had just stolen a particularly rich bowl of cream from a bunch of pampered house pets. 'Apollophanes is a scholar I always find congenial.'

I left, thinking how very much I would have liked to see Philetus dead, embalmed and mummified on a dusty shelf. If possible, I would consign him to a rather disreputable temple where they got the rites wrong. He festered. The man was only good for a long eternity of mould and decay.

XXXIV

This was a mess. At risk of increasing the slurry, I went to the Prefect's palace and told the staff not to allow any movement on the Library appointment until my investigation finished.

'The Director is nagging us for an early announcement, Falco.'

I smiled serenely. 'Let him nag. You are the bureaucrats. Your prime task is to find convoluted systems that necessitate delay.'

Anything that avoided work seemed clever to the aides-de-camp.

'When the Director sent through his list, did he tick his preferred candidate?' I recommend you make additions.

'Philetus? Make a decision?' Even the senatorial wide-boys laughed.

They had passed the list in to the Prefect like a red-hot brick. Knowing how to take care of himself, he biffed it straight back out and asked them to brief him on what action to take. It was too important to remain in an in-tray. They were stuck. They asked me.

'If in doubt, consult the Emperor.' That could take months. 'The list is a travesty, incidentally. I recommend you make additions.'

'*Can* we add names?'

'A Prefect can always call in extra candidates. He should do so. It demonstrates that he is exercising his judgement and experience, not just acquiescing weakly to whatever is put in front of him.'

'He will like that! Who should he call in?'

'Timosthenes, for one.' They wrote it down. Beneficiaries of fine educations, they could write. I was pleased to see it. 'When the old man asks why, say: *"Timosthenes is already holder of a similar post at the Serapeion. He runs that library well. He is not so academically eminent as the others, but a solid candidate, so in view of the Emperor's preference for appointments made on merit, you advise that Timosthenes should be considered."'*

They wrote that down too. One of them could do short-hand. 'Sounds good.'

'I am an informer. We earn our fees.'

'Anybody else?'

'If the Prefect – or his noble lady – has ever shown a particular interest in tragic drama, suggest a man called Aeacidas.'

'His wife enjoys lyre music. He follows gladiating.'

'Goodbye, sad tragedian then!'

The Palace was cool. Out of doors, the Khamseen had dropped but without the wind we had a stonking hot midday which made me just as stressed. Wherever I decided to go next, even home for lunch, I would find myself sweating and debilitated. I faced this prospect with mild depression.

Fortunately, I spotted Numerius Tenax, the centurion. I told him if he could find an excuse to go for lunch so I could pick his expert brains, I would buy him the drink he had offered to buy me when we first met. He pretended to be unravelling the clauses in my offer. But he appreciated drinking on my imperial expenses (as he thought). When he took me to his local bar, we raised a toast to Vespasian.

I relayed the latest developments. Tenax grimaced. 'I'm glad you're in charge, not me.'

'Thanks, Tenax! The gods know where I go next.'

We drank, and ate saucers of savouries, in silence.

Tenax had nothing to tell me about the intellectuals'

217

feuds. However bitter their rivalries, it would be a war of words. Only if they started throwing punches would the military be involved; that was unlikely. 'They tend to fix things themselves. When I saw you at the Museion the other day, Falco, it was my first visit for ages. The Prefect leaves them alone. We never get involved.'

I mentioned my theory that there were financial difficulties. 'Anything cropped up on audit, do you know?'

'What audit? The Museion is given a big fat annual budget; it's from the imperial treasury now, of course. They can spend the money how they like. The Prefect doesn't have the staff to oversee an institution of that size. Not in any way that would be meaningful.'

I swirled my drink. 'Someone was afraid the Prefect – or higher – was about to start taking notice. They all seem scared stiff of my appearance on the scene.'

Tenax surveyed me. He pulled down the corners of his mouth. 'Scared of you, Falco?' he mused whimsically. 'Gods in Olympus, however could that be?'

I produced a dutiful grin and ate more olives. Maybe the salt would rebalance my tired body.

Tenax went on thinking about it. 'The way it looks from here, the current Director has a poor grip. You know from the army how that works.' How did he know I had been in the army? 'Once people get a hint supervision is a bit limp, everyone overspends madly. One tribune orders himself a new desk, probably because his is genuinely riddled with woodworm, then the next man along sees it and wants one, and next minute, gold-handled desks with ivory-inlaid tops are being sent halfway across the Empire in multiple quantities. Then headquarters asks a question. Immediately, there is a crackdown.'

'At the Museion, the crackdown hasn't happened yet?'

'I can't see that it will, Falco. The Museion is run by that miraculous system called self-certification.'

We both laughed hoarsely.

Tenax did remember some kind of incident involving the Great Library, maybe about six months ago. He had not bothered to involve himself. 'I never went down there. It faded out, as I recall. I can ask my boys . . .'

I did not wait around to hear what his legionaries might have to say. I had already seen Cotius and Mammius. Not much chance of obtaining a significant lead through them.

I thanked the centurion for his time and advice. Chatting with a like-minded professional did me good. I returned to my investigation feeling much more vigorous.

I entered the Museion complex on a route that took me near the Great Library. I passed through its pleasant colonnades, enjoying the shade and the beauty of the gardens. My attention was drawn when I noticed a man I recognised. He had passed out of sight by the time I remembered who he was: the trader who had called last night to visit Uncle Fulvius. I wondered idly whether he merely used this as a route elsewhere, or if he had had business here. Although he had fitted in well with my uncle's circle, he seemed an incongruous visitor to the Museion. Still, it could be on his way to the Forum.

Then as I came through to the open area in front of the porch, I stopped wondering about him. I spotted Camillus Aelianus, so I set off after him. Aulus must have subconsciously recognised my footfall, for once in the Library porch, he slowed and looked back over his shoulder. I caught him up on the threshold of the great hall. Concerned, I checked him over. He looked pale but calm.

We might have stepped back away from the study area to exchange greetings and news, but we became aware of excited activity in the reading hall. A crowd of scholars and library staff were milling around to our left, at the far end. Aulus and I exchanged a glance, then at once moved towards the commotion. Some of the staff were urging the others to move back. They seemed to need little encouragement.

A small stampede occurred. As we arrived, we discovered the reason: a strong, distinctive smell. My heart sank.

Even before we could see anything, I realised we were about to encounter yet another corpse.

XXXV

Flies zoomed, in the way only flies who have been laying eggs in a corpse do.

Pastous, the assistant we had met on our first visit, pushed out through the crowd, one hand covering his mouth. Previously so calm, he stumbled towards us, horrified and agitated. He stopped when he recognised us, his expression a mixture of relief and anxiety.

'Pastous! Smells like you need an undertaker – better let me take a look.'

People were falling over themselves in their haste to retreat. Aulus told the staff to clear the hall completely. We waved away everyone except Pastous, then cautiously approached. We batted at the flies with ham-fisted motions; they were not interested in us, however.

The commotion had centred on the table where I had been told the man called Nibytas worked. It had been moved – in a hurry, scarring the floor marble. Behind it stood a stool and beside that lay the body. We leaned over, but failed to see enough. I nodded to Aulus; we took an end of the table each, heaving the furniture towards us then swinging my end sideways to leave a clear path.

'People tried to pull the table; he must have been propped against it, so he fell.' Gazing at the dead man, Pastous whimpered faintly.

'That is Nibytas?'

'Yes. He was just here as usual, apparently working . . .'

He must have been 'apparently working' for a long time after he was actually dead.

Pastous stepped back, leaving Aulus and me to investigate. 'Jupiter,' I confided. 'I could have done without this!'

'What do you think, Marcus? Suspicious circumstances?'

'Died of old age, by the looks of it.'

That would be *very* old age. The dead man looked a hundred and four. 'A hundred and four, plus about three days he's been sitting here, I'd say.' Aulus was suddenly the expert.

I held one forearm over my nostrils. 'The last time I smelt decay that bad was –' I stopped. The dead man had been close to Helena and Aelianus, an uncle of theirs; I was not supposed to know his fate. That was nearly seven years ago. I was respectable now; other people could clear up the mess this time . . . Aulus had looked up, curious. I avoided his gaze, in case he worked out just what it had meant over the past years, being the Emperor's man. My job had its sombre moments. 'Best not remembered.'

Nibytas was shrunken, papery, desiccated with age and self-neglect. His shoulders were hooked in a drab tunic; his skeletal legs were mottled. He must have been a stranger at the refectory, though entitled to eat there. Like many old folk, he probably skimped on baths too. Thin feet dangled in oversized sandals. We could tell that he had barely lived, by our standards, while he was alive. No wonder nobody had noticed for days that he did not move. The corpse lay on its side now; it must have stiffened at right angles, but was flexible again. The slight fall from his low seat had simply left him as he must have been sitting when concerned helpers finally disturbed his last reading session.

When moving the table nudged him off his stool, the usual bodily substances leaked everywhere. That must have been the moment when we saw everyone recoil. Thank the gods the Great Library was cool.

His skin was discoloured but from a brief examination – not too close – I could see no evidence of wounding. A stylus was still clasped in his wizened fingers. Unlike the

Librarian, he had left no garland on his table, nor could I detect any vomit. The mass of scrolls and crazy scribbled notes looked exactly the same as when I had inspected his work station only the other day. It gave an impression that this table must have looked the same for thirty years, or even fifty. Now the old man had simply gone to sleep for ever in his accustomed place.

I crooked a finger, calling Pastous. I held him lightly by both shoulders, making him look at me. Even so, his gaze could not help sliding downwards to Nibytas. I let him look. Feeling unsettled might help him open up to questions. Aulus rested his backside on the dead man's table. Both of us managed to look as if we were unmoved by the spectacle and repulsive odours.

'So, Pastous. In this venerable library, a respected old scholar can pass away, poked in an out-of-the-way corner. Nobody notices for several days. He must have been locked in every night. Even your cleaners passed him by uncaringly.'

'We cared, Falco. It is deeply unfortunate –'

'It looks bad,' I growled. Aulus put out a hand in protest, playing the kind-hearted one. I half turned and glared at him. 'Looks like a bloody great disaster, Aelianus!'

'Marcus Didius, Pastous is upset –'

'He should be! They all should be.'

Aulus marshalled me aside. He spoke kindly. As a senator's son he had no need for bombast; he had been brought up to be polite to people at all levels. Everyone was his inferior, but sometimes he overcame his snootiness. 'Pastous, this sad ancient character appears to have died from old age. If so, we are not interested in why he remained undiscovered.'

'Pass it off as a consequence of having no Chief Librarian!' I muttered.

Aulus continued to be civil and unthreatening. 'What we *must* ask about is that we heard Nibytas was the subject of disciplinary enquiry. What was that about?'

Pastous did not want to tell us.

'Don't worry,' I told Aulus conversationally. 'I can go out and buy a large hammer and drive nine-inch nails into the Director's head until Philetus sings.'

'We could simply hammer nails into Pastous,' replied Aulus, who could be not-so-nice very easily. He was looking at the library assistant in a thoughtful way.

'At one time,' Pastous confessed quickly, 'we thought Nibytas might be abusing his privileges and taking out scrolls.'

'Taking them out?'

'Concealing them. And not returning them.'

'Theft? So you called in the soldiers!' I snapped. The assistant looked flustered, but nodded. 'What happened?'

'The matter was dropped.'

'Why?'

'Only Theon knew.'

'Useful!' I cracked out. I stared at the table where the old scholar had worked. The litter of written material was almost a foot high, all over the surface. 'Why would he need to steal books, when he was allowed to have so many here to work with – and obviously to keep them for a long time?'

Pastous lifted his shoulders in a shrug, raising both hands helplessly. 'Some people cannot help themselves,' he whispered. He addressed the issue sympathetically, however much he deplored it. Then he suggested to us, also in a low voice, 'You might perhaps look at the room where Nibytas lived.'

Aulus and I had both relaxed. 'Know where it is? Can you show us – discreetly?' Pastous willingly agreed to take us.

On the way out we gave instructions that the end of the great hall should be roped off. Anyone who wanted and who was made of stern stuff was free to work in the other area. After listing them, Pastous would return all the borrowed library scrolls to their proper places; I asked him to gather up all the notes Nibytas had made and save this material. Undertakers should be called in to collect the body; if they were asked to bring the necessary equipment, they would clean up. They would know how to do it properly and how to sanitise the area.

I knew ways to get rid of inconvenient corpses, but my ways were crude.

We walked to the dormitory hall in subdued mood. Nobody spoke until we got there. A porter let us in. He did not seem surprised that officialdom had come with heavy steps to Nibytas' quarters.

The main building had splendid communal spaces in the marble-clad pharaonic style. Beyond were pleasant living quarters. Each scholar was assigned an individual cell where he could retreat to read, sleep, write or pass the time thinking of lovers, brooding on enemies or munching raisins. If he chose to munch pistachios instead, a cleaner would remove the shells the next day for him. These rooms were small, but furnished with what looked like comfortable beds, X-form stools, rugs on the floor to step on in the morning when barefoot, simple cupboards and whatever jugs, oil lamps, pictures, cloaks, slippers or sunhats each man chose to import for his personal comfort and identity. In a military camp it would be all weapons and hunting trophies; here, when the porter proudly showed us several of the bedrooms, we were more likely to see a miniature sundial or bust of a bearded poet. Homer was popular. That's because scholars at the Museion were sent their poets' busts as presents from loving little nieces or nephews; statuette-makers always make lots of Homers. Nobody knows what Homer looked like, as Aulus pointed out; he was inclined to be pedantic on Greek matters. I explained that the statuette-makers liked us not knowing, since nobody could criticise their work.

There were scroll boxes and loose scrolls in most scholars' rooms. One or two fancy boxes, or a small mound of assorted documents. As you would expect. They were personal possessions, their prized works.

The room used by Nibytas was different. It had a sour smell and a dusty air; we were told he refused ever to admit the cleaner. He had been there so long, his cantankerous ways were tolerated just because they always had been. The housekeeper could not face an argument, especially since the authorities were bound to cave in. Nibytas had got away with it for too long, and was too old to be taken in hand.

We knew in advance he had been an eccentric. Just how eccentric only became obvious when the porter found the door key. He had to go away and hunt for it, because Nibytas had been so adamant he would never have people in his room to spy on him.

The room was absolutely full of stolen scrolls. It was so full, it was difficult to see the bed; there were more scrolls under that bed. Nibytas had amassed scrolls in papyrus stalagmites. He had lined the walls with shoulder-high ramparts. Scrolls were piled in the window recess. We had to carry those out to the corridor, to let in some light. When I opened the shutters, so fresh air would clear the turgid atmosphere, I put my hand through enough spiders' webs to staunch a deep spear wound.

We must have been the first people into that room, apart from Nibytas, for decades. When Pastous saw the hoard of stolen property, he let out a small, piteous cry. He went on his knees to examine the nearest mound of scrolls, blowing off dust tenderly and lifting them to show me that they all bore end-tags from the Great Library. He clambered upright and darted about, discovering others from the Serapeion, even a small number he thought might have been lifted from scroll shops. The regime under Timosthenes must be stricter than that at the Great Library, while commercial premises are strictly geared to preventing loss of stock.

'Why would he have all these scrolls, Pastous? He cannot have been selling them.'

'He just wanted to possess them. He wanted them close to him. They cover all subjects, Falco – he cannot have been reading them. It seems Nibytas just crazily removed scrolls, as and when he could.'

'Theon suspected he might be doing this?'

'We all feared so, but were never sure. We never caught him at it. We never thought it could be on such a scale . . .'

'Nibytas had reached the agenda of the Academic Board, though.'

'Is that so?'

'This very week.' For a long time, probably, but Philetus ducked out of discussing the sensitive issue.

'There was always uncertainty about how we could tackle the old man. We never managed to witness him taking a scroll. He must have been very clever.'

'It seems he had years of practice!' chortled Aulus.

'Was he ever confronted at all?' I asked.

'Theon had a word once. He got nowhere. Nibytas denied it and got very upset at being challenged.'

'So who brought it to the attention of the Academic Board?'

Pastous thought. 'I think that must have been Theon.'

The Academic Board were shrinking from it, under Philetus' strong leadership, but Nibytas would not have known that. If he believed the game was up, he must have been in turmoil. He would have been facing not just the penalty for theft, but public and academic disgrace. I guessed the biggest threat to him would be that of being debarred from the Great Library. Where would he go? How would he survive without the financial support of the Museion and the stimulus he found in his fanatical work? His life's study would have been terminated, doomed to remain unfinished. His future existence would have held little meaning.

One thing was clear. That threat would have provided Nibytas with a motive for killing Theon.

XXXVI

Aulus and I went home. The old man's sad life and death depressed Aulus, especially as he was still brooding about his friend so much. First I took him to a congenial bath house I had discovered near my uncle's house. We were early, so it was fairly quiet. A noisy group of stall-holders arrived almost the same time as us; you learn to hang back and let such a crowd go ahead. They did not linger; they were cleaning up after a day's work and were eager for home – or, for the ones who had to moonlight for financial survival, their next job.

We sat for a long time in the steam room. Aulus was working through his unhappiness. I was content to be left alone to think.

I was not surprised when eventually Aulus took up an almost oratorical posture: 'Marcus Didius, I am trying to decide whether to say something.'

'My normal rule in such circumstances is: don't speak out.' I allowed a slow beat. 'Though unless you say what you are on about, now you'll drive me mad.'

'Heras.'

'I thought it might be.'

Being Aulus, once he decided to broach it, he went ahead doggedly. 'I knew that he was going to the zoo.' He screwed up his face. 'Actually, I knew he had an assignation. Heras was not there by coincidence. He had told me in advance, he was meeting Roxana.'

"They cannot have known I would be there with that boy" . . . That had slipped out under stress. Roxana would

deny any prior association with Heras if we tackled her.

Thoughtfully, I drew a breath. Aulus scooped up cold water and let it trickle down his chest. I rubbed my eyes, massaging my forehead with my fingers. 'So Heras fancied her. What did he tell you?'

'He had a heavy crush.'

'You warned him off?'

'I had never seen the woman. I didn't even know Heras himself all that well.'

'But you could see the potential for trouble? A student trying to take up with a senior academic's floozy? At the very least, Roxana was going to dump him hard, and sooner rather than later.'

Aulus smiled drily. He understood. He stood on the brink of greater maturity than Heras had possessed, though close enough to appreciate his friend's innocent hopes. 'I thought he was in for a let-down. I never imagined she would even show up . . .' I had taught Aulus something then. 'Heras said Roxana had always ignored him, but that day he had met her earlier and she had seemed restless; Heras tried his luck; she led him on. He begged to see her. She promised to meet him at the zoo.'

'Seems amazing. I've seen her, Aulus. This is a pert, rich widow, in her middle thirties, courted by all sorts of eminent professors.'

'I agree. Heras, poor fool, believed she had suddenly found him attractive. I thought,' said Aulus glumly, 'she must have had a row with Philadelphion.'

'Then you are my kind of cynic . . . So choosing the zoo for a secret liaison could have been a sweet act of revenge?'

I hated this kind of affair. Roxana saw Heras as a boy – and the selfish madam was about to make him a boy with a broken heart. Deliberate cruelty. Why did she need to do that?

'Heras was aware she wanted to make Philadelphion jealous. She made no secret of that.'

'What? Did she intend Philadelphion to come across them in each other's arms, while he was doing his nightly rounds?'

'Heras just thought his luck was in, so he didn't ask. He was so happy he didn't care.'

I remembered how solicitous Philadelphion had been to Roxana when he came upon the scene. I bet he took charge of her so firmly that night so he could get her away from other people and ensure she told the story he wanted. Until now, I had been imagining he was afraid of awkward questions about the lapse of security at Sobek's compound. But his solicitations could have been more personal. *Why* was Roxana so annoyed with him in the first place?

'There's a lesson, my boy,' I told the downcast Camillus Aelianus. 'Stay away from fancy women.'

'Like you do, Falco?'

'Absolutely.'

All the same, when we went to Uncle Fulvius' house, I left him to talk to Albia while I bounded up the stairs to the roof, all too eager to see *my* fancy woman.

Late afternoon was verging on early evening. Across the bay, the Pharos was still hidden in the mist. The day's heat was just beginning to alleviate up here; it would be a wonderful night to eat out of doors with my family. Helena was relaxing in the shade. Favonia, our solemn, private one, was asleep alongside, pushing against her mother like a small dog, while Julia, our imaginative spirit, was playing quietly by herself, some long absorbing game that involved flowers, pebbles and intense conversations in her secret language. I ruffled her hair; Julia scowled at the interruption, half unaware she had done so but also half conscious that this was the father she tolerated. Father, the source of treats, tickles, stories and excursions; Father, who would kiss bruises better and mend broken dolls. Father, who in a few years could be blamed, cursed, despised for fuddy-duddyness, hated for meanness, criticised and quarrelled

230

with, then nonetheless called upon to get her out of scrapes, pickles and the inevitable love disaster with the lying wine waiter . . .

Helena Justina raised a hand vaguely. Helena was doing what she liked most, apart from private times with me. She was reading a scroll. It might be from her luggage; she could have been out and bought it. Or, since she got through so many, it was just as likely she had borrowed this one from a library in Alexandria. She looked up, saw me dreaming sentimentally, then escaped back hurriedly into the scroll.

I sat nearby, content to be among my own, not disturbing them.

XXXVII

Mammius and Cotius came to see me next morning. Being soldiers, they had been up and about since dawn. They made sure they arrived while we were eating. They had already been fed at their barracks, but I knew the rules. I let them sit down for a second breakfast. Uncle Fulvius was never at ease with the military, so he escaped with Cassius. Pa stuck it out annoyingly. He had a way of listening in on private conversations that made my bile rise.

In return for our food and a sit-down, the lads would have told me anything. I suggested they stick to facts, however.

The centurion Tenax had sent them, following his conversation with me, because they were the pair who had responded to a request from the Great Library six months ago. Theon had called them in. 'About lost scrolls?'

Yes, but to my surprise, it was nothing to do with the eccentric old scholar Nibytas.

'Never heard of him. This was a strange upset. A heap of stuff from the Library had been discovered by a member of the public on a neighbourhood rubbish dump. The Librarian had gone incandescent. If you like volcanic explosions, it was pretty to watch. Then we all trogged along to pull the dump apart —'

Helena pulled a face. 'That cannot have been pleasant!'

Mammius and Cotius, two born sensationalists, enjoyed themselves describing the joys of Egyptian rubbish dumps. Both passed over the ordinary mass of combs, hairpins, pot shards, pens and inkwells, oil lamps – with and without oil spillage – the occasional perfect winecup, many an amphora, even more jars of fish-pickle, old clothes, broken brooches, single ear-rings, solo shoes, dice and shellfish detritus. They listed more eagerly the half-rotten vegetables and fish-ends, they spoke of bones, grease, gravy, mouldy cheese, dogshit and donkey-do, dead mice, dead babies and live babies' loincloths. They claimed to have unearthed a complete set of currency-counterfeiting implements, perhaps discarded by a coiner who had had a fit of conscience. They had barked their shins and grazed their knuckles on spars, bricks and bits of roof tile. Then there were layers of love letters, written curses, shopping lists, laundry lists, fish-wrappers and discarded pages from lesser-known Greek plays. Amongst these documents, which were clearly chucked out from private houses, had been a great jumble of tagged scrolls from the Library.

'So how had those ended up in a dump?'

'We never found out. Theon dug them back out himself, brushing off the dirt as if they were his personal treasures. He bundled them on handcarts from the Library and wheeled them back safely. To begin with everyone made a great fuss. There was supposed to be a full enquiry, but next day a message came for Tenax that the Librarian had uncovered what it was all about, so our intervention was not needed.'

The thought of these two lumpish red tunics poking around the sacred cupboards of the Great Library, fingering the Pinakes with their stubby, filthy digits, then noisily shouting dumb questions at bemused scholars and fraught staff, told me just why Theon had dropped it officially. But had he then pursued this incident himself?

'If venerable works have been walking off the shelves in murky circumstances, I can see, darling,' Helena suggested to me, 'why people at the Museion might have thought Vespasian was sending you to Alexandria to be an auditor.'

'But Theon would have been well aware he had *not*

233

bumped up the issue to imperial level. He hadn't requested an official recount.'

'Is that what you do, Falco?' Mammius asked, all sceptical innocence. 'Go into places and count things?'

'Is it, Marcus?' Helena ate a roll stuffed with goat's cheese in an extremely mischievous manner. I would get her for that later. She was still thinking about Theon. 'He was the one who choked with horror when I asked him how many scrolls there were.'

'Maybe he was very sensitive to criticism. Perhaps he was scared he would be blamed if other books had been lost . . . So what did you think had been going on?' I asked the soldiers.

They were just square-bashers. They had no idea.

'Sounds like somebody weeded the cupboards and storage stacks without asking the Librarian first,' scoffed Aulus.

'And the Librarian did not like their choice,' agreed Albia.

I grunted. 'It sounds to me as if the Librarian asked some half-baked assistant to reshelve some outstanding returns that had been littering up the place for months. Instead of sorting out the mess, the assistant just filed the scroll mountain in the "Not needed" skip, to avoid doing any work.'

'You have such a jaded view of underlings,' Albia tutted.

'That's because I have known so many.'

Mammius and Cotius seemed to feel they were being got at. They stuffed a few last chunks of bread into their fists, saluted and made off.

My father had eavesdropped without interruption, but now he just had to weigh in. 'Seems you were brought here to dig out a swamp of corrupt practices.'

I served myself a new slice of smoked ham, a task that required silence and concentration lest I cut myself on the very sharp thin-bladed knife. While I was at it, to prolong the activity I did slices for Helena and Albia. Aulus held out his bread too.

'All right,' agreed Geminus patiently. He recognised my delaying tactics. 'You weren't brought here for that. I believe you. You came on an innocent holiday. Problems just float up to you, wherever you take yourself.'

'If I attract problems, it's inherited, Pa . . . What's your interest anyway?' As usual when talking to my father, I immediately felt like a surly teenager who thinks it is beneath his dignity to hold a civil conversation with anyone over twenty. I had been one once, of course, though I did not have the luxury of a father to be rude to at the time. Mine had run off with his lady love. When he reappeared, renaming himself Geminus instead of Favonius, he behaved as if all those intervening years never happened. Some of us would not forget.

Pa produced a sad smile and his personal brand of annoying forbearance. 'I just like to know what you are up to, Marcus. You are my boy, my only surviving son; it's natural for a father to take an interest.'

I was his boy, all right. Two days in the same house and I understood why Oedipus had felt that burning urge to strangle his kingly Greek papa even without recognising who the bastard was. I knew mine too well. I knew that behind any interest he took there must be a suspicious motive. And if I ever met him in a chariot at an isolated crossroads, Marcus Didius Favonius, known as Geminus, might disappear, complete with his chariot and horses, and no need to waste time on dialogue first . . .

'Settle down, Pa. I don't know what you're wheedling for. I'm here because Helena Justina wants to see the Pyramids –' She favoured us with her own little knowing smile. 'You go and get on with whatever tricks you are up to with Fulvius. Don't fret about any convoluted Egyptian schemes that have been going on at the Library. I can sort out a few book fiddles. Their days are numbered.'

'Is that so?'

Pa consulted Helena with a sceptical look. Her word was

law with him. He had convinced himself that a senator's daughter was above practising deceit, even for the usual family reasons.

'That's right,' she confirmed. She was extremely loyal – and hilariously inventive. 'We expect to have the full facts any day now. A report for the authorities will be cracked out straight away. Marcus is on to it.'

Helena had just imposed a time constraint, though I did not know it yet.

XXXVIII

Aulus and I went to the Museion together. When we first left my uncle's house, we found Mammius and Cotius were still in the street, giving a shake-down to the muttering man who always lurked outside. On the excuse of routine public order enquiries, they had him pinned against a wall and were scaring him silly.

'What's your name?'

'Katutis.'

'A likely tale! Pat him down, Cotius –'

We grinned and quickly walked on.

By now the familiar route to the Museion seemed much shorter. I said little on the way, planning my next moves. I had a number of lines I was eager to pursue, and a job in mind for Aulus. As we walked through a colonnade together he suddenly asked, 'Do you trust your father?'

'I wouldn't trust him to squash a grub on his lettuce. Why do you ask?'

'No reason.'

'Well, let's have a pact: I won't dwell on any deplorable relatives you may have – and you can keep your high-class disapproval away from mine. Geminus may be an auctioneer, but he has never actually been arrested, even for passing off fakes – and you are not a praetor yet. You won't be either, until one day you trudge your noble boots back to Rome and levitate yourself like a demigod, up through the *cursus honorum* to the dizzy heights of the consulship.'

'You think I could make consul?' Aulus could always be

sidetracked by reminding him he had had political ambition once.

'Anyone can do it if enough cash is spent on them.'

He was a realist. 'Well, Papa has no money at present, so let's go and earn some!'

At the Library, we found Pastous, looking anxious.

'You asked me to preserve the papers Nibytas was working with, Falco. But the Director sent across this morning and asked for everything. I'm told he wants to send personal effects to the family.'

'What family did Nibytas have?'

'None I know of. '

'You let those notebooks of his go?'

Pastous had discovered a liking for intrigue. 'No. I claimed you had taken everything. I decided that if they were so urgently in demand, they must be significant . . .'

'Is the stuff here?' Everything off the table where the old man worked had been secreted in a little back room. 'I want Aelianus to go through it.' The noble youth pulled a very ignoble face. 'If you have free time, Pastous, maybe you can help. You don't need to read every line, but decide what Nibytas thought he was doing. Aulus, just give us an overview, as rapidly as you can. Pull out anything significant, then the residue can be dispatched to Philetus. Jumble it up a bit to keep him busy.'

Before I left them to it, I asked Pastous to tell me what he knew about scrolls being found on rubbish dumps. It was clear the assistant was uneasy. 'I know that it once happened,' he admitted.

'And?'

'It caused much unpleasantness. Theon was informed, and he managed to reclaim all the scrolls. The incident made him extremely angry.'

'How had the scrolls got there?'

'Junior staff had selected them for disposal. Unread for

238

a long time, or duplicates. They had been instructed that such scrolls were no longer needed.'

'Not by Theon, I take it! What do you think of the principle, Pastous?'

He stiffened up and sailed into a heartfelt speech. 'It is a subject we discuss regularly. Can old books that have not been looked at for decades, or even centuries, justifiably be thrown out to increase shelf space? Why do you need duplicates? Then there is the question of quality – should works that everyone knows are terrible still be lovingly kept and cared for, or should they be ruthlessly purged?'

'And the Library takes what line?'

'That we keep them.' Pastous was definite. 'Little-read items may still be requested one day. Works that seem bad may be reassessed – or if not, they are still needed to confirm how bad they were.'

'So who ordered the staff to clear the shelves?' asked Aulus.

'A management decision. Or so the juniors thought. Changes are always happening in large organisations. A memo comes around. New instructions appear, often anonymous, almost as if they fell through a window like moonbeams.'

What Pastous said seemed all too familiar.

Aulus had less experience than me of the madness that infects public administration. 'How can such things happen? Surely someone would have double-checked? Theon cannot have allowed such important and controversial instructions to be given to his staff behind his back?'

Four days had passed since Theon died. In an organisation, that counted as eternity. His loyal staff, once completely tight-lipped, were already prepared to criticise him. Pastous himself seemed more confident today, as if his place in the hierarchy had changed. He admitted to Aulus, 'Theon had not been much in evidence. He was going through a bad patch.'

'Illness?'

The assistant gazed at the ground. 'Money worries, it was rumoured.'

'Did he gamble on the horses?'

I had asked this before, when we first met Pastous, and he had avoided the question. This time he was more forthcoming. 'I believe he did. Men came here looking for him. He disappeared for a few days afterwards. But if there was trouble, I assumed he cleared it up, because he was back at his post when a civic-minded member of the public came to report finding the dumped scrolls.'

'So how did Theon tackle that?'

'First priority was to reclaim them. Afterwards, he confirmed that Library policy was to keep all scrolls. And I think – though of course it was done very discreetly – he had a terrific argument with the Director.'

'Had *Philetus* sent the scrolls to the rubbish dump?' Pastous answered my question only with a weary shrug. Staff had given up any hope of loosening the Director's grip. Philetus was stifling their initiative and their sense of responsibility.

Aulus could always be relied upon to give delicate subjects a big thumping push. 'Was there any crossover between Theon's personal money worries and Library finances? I mean, did he –'

'Certainly not!' cried Pastous. Fortunately, he liked us enough now not to flounce off in horror.

'That would have been a terrible scandal,' I remarked.

I was thinking it was the kind of scandal I had come across too many times – the kind that could have fatal results if it got out of hand.

Leaving Aulus and Pastous to wade through the morass Nibytas had bequeathed to us, I decided to try to tackle Zenon once more about the Museion's accounts.

He was in the observatory on the roof again. He seemed

to hide up there as often as possible, tinkering with equipment. Remembering how he went for me last time, I made
sure I kept his sky-scrutinising chair between us. He
noticed.

'Getting anywhere, Falco?'

I sighed dramatically. 'In my dark moments, my enquiries
here seem particularly futile. Did Theon kill himself or was
he killed? Did Nibytas die of old age? Did young Heras
die by accident and if not, who killed him, was he the real
target or did they intend to murder someone else? Are any
of these deaths linked, and do they have any connection to
how the Museion and the Great Library are run? Does it
matter? Do I care? Would I ever let a child of mine come
here to study in this crazy home of warped minds, with its
once-fine reputation apparently now hanging in tatters due
to incompetence and maladministration on a monumental
scale?'

Zenon looked slightly taken aback. 'What maladministration have you found?'

I let him wonder. 'Tell me the truth, Zenon. The figures
are a mess, aren't they? I am not blaming you – I imagine
that however hard you struggle to impose sound business
practice and prudence, still others – we know who –
constantly thwart you.' He was letting me talk, so I pressed
on. 'I haven't seen your accounts, but I hear that at the
Library things have got so bad, even penny-pinching measures like clearing out old scrolls have been attempted.
Somebody is desperate.'

'I wouldn't say that, Falco.'

'If funds are tight, you need a concerted effort to
economise. This can't be co-ordinated properly during a
full-blown disagreement about holdings policy. What? –
The Director sneaks in behind Theon's back to clear out
old scrolls *he* reckons are not worth keeping. Theon violently
disagrees. The spectre of the Librarian on hands and knees
in a rubbish dump, retrieving his stock then wheeling it

back here through the filthy streets in handcarts, is quite unedifying.'

'There is no financial crisis calling for the Director's measures,' Zenon protested.

'It was all pointless, anyway,' I growled. 'Savings would have been minimal. Tossing out a few scrolls and closing a few cupboards would never achieve much. Staff still have to be paid for. You still have to maintain your building – not cheap when it is a famous monument, constructed on a fabulous scale, with four-hundred-year-old irreplaceable antique fittings. All that happened was that the staff ended up depressed, feeling that they work for a declining organisation that has lost its prestige and energy.'

'Calm down,' said Zenon. 'All that was just Philetus trying to upset Theon.'

'Why?'

'Because Theon refused to be pushed around by a fool.'

'He objected to short-sighted policy?'

'He objected to the whole current regime. What can we do? Do *you* have the power to overturn it?' asked Zenon, clearly without much faith in me.

'Depends on the root cause. One man's ineptitude can always be altered – by removing the man.'

'Not if he is in a post for life.'

'Don't give up. Under Vespasian, incompetents who thought they were fireproof have nevertheless found themselves uplifted to occupy absolutely meaningless positions where they can do no harm.'

'It will never happen here.' Under the current Director's stifling rule, Zenon, like Theon before him, had become a black defeatist. 'In Alexandria we have our own ways.'

'Oh that old excuse! *"We are special. Everything here is different!"*'

'The Museion is in decline. Fewer true intellectuals come to Alexandria than in its heyday. Little new scholarship occurs. But Philetus represents the future.'

I kept trying. 'Look – ever heard of Antonius Primus? When Vespasian was aiming to become Emperor, Primus was his right-hand man. While Vespasian himself remained safely here in Alexandria, it was Primus who brought the Eastern legions through the Balkans to Italy and defeated their rival, Vitellius. He could have argued he took all the risks and did all the work so he deserved huge recognition. But Primus had no judgement, success went wildly to his head and he was driven by misplaced ambition – any of that sound familiar? He became a liability. It was dealt with. It was – I can tell you, Zenon – dealt with *extremely* quietly. Who has ever heard of him since? He just disappeared from the scene.'

'That will never happen here.'

'Well not if you all keep caving in!' Zenon's defeatism was making me depressed too. 'I suppose Theon was pretty demoralised by those attempts to get rid of unwanted scrolls?'

'Theon was upset, certainly.'

'You and Theon were on friendly terms, you said. So what do you know about his personal gambling debts?'

'Nothing. Well, he sorted it all out.'

'He paid off the men who were hounding him?'

'I never heard it got that bad . . .' Zenon was oblivious to gossip – or that was what he wanted me to think. 'He had a temporary cash problem – could happen to anyone.'

'Did you ask Theon *how* he solved it?'

'No. People keep their debts to themselves.'

'Not necessarily – not if they are friends with the man who controls the Museion's enormous budget!'

'I resent your insinuation, Falco.'

He would resent my next question even more, because by now I had lost my temper. 'So is the Museion bankrupt – or merely run by a bunch of monkeys?'

'Get off my roof, Falco.'

This time, the astronomer was so sad at heart he did not

even try to manhandle me. But I knew it was time to leave.

'How do you feel about being on the list for Theon's job?' I called back at him, when I was at the head of the stairs.

'Vulnerable!' Zenon retorted with feeling. When I cocked my head in enquiry, even this buttoned-up near-mute lost his laconic style: 'The rumour machine in the refectory says what happened at the zoo two nights ago was a bungled attempt to reduce the number of candidates! Of course,' he added bitterly, 'there are people here who would maintain that murdering academics is ethically more acceptable than getting rid of scrolls! The written word must be preserved at all costs. Mere scholars, however, are untidy and expendable.'

'So the Library appointment led to Sobek being on the loose?' I scoffed. 'No, I see that as a messier-than-usual end to a love triangle. Besides, I hope any expensively educated scholar intent on murder would do it in an elegant manner – some allusion to classical literature – and an apt Greek quotation pinned to the corpse.'

'There is no scholar at the Museion,' complained Zenon, 'who could bring off a murder. Most need a scale diagram and instructions in three languages even to lace their shoes.'

I gazed at him, both of us silently acknowledging how practical *he* was. He could certainly have worked out how to sneak away some goat's meat and lure Sobek from his pit. Moreover, unlike the unworldly men he was deriding, Zenon had no qualms about violence. I skipped down the stairs before he could make another of his attempts to throw me headlong from his sanctuary.

XXXIX

I went to see Thalia.

As I was setting off for her tent, I noticed the Director leaving the Library. He was in the company of a man I recognised: the same man who had come to see my uncle and whom I also had spotted yesterday, walking through one of the colonnades here.

Philetus and the businessman had definitely been together, though they immediately parted company. I nearly followed the trader, but I had yet to discover enough about him to feel ready. So I went after Philetus.

He bustled along like a worried rabbit and had reached his office when I caught up. I tapped his shoulder to hold him up, in the classic Forum manner. I went straight to the point: 'Philetus! Don't I know that man I just saw you with?'

He looked annoyed. 'It's Diogenes, a scroll collector. He makes a menace of himself, trying to sell us works we don't want or need. Poor Theon was always trying to get rid of him.'

'Diogenes,' I repeated, chewing it over slowly, the way people memorise names. The Director was now trying to shake *me* off, determined not to let me indoors with him. We stood on the steps of his building like a couple of pigeons having a stand-off over a scatter of stale crumbs. He was just puffing up his feathers to look big. I was manoeuvring to get at the barley cake. 'I wanted to ask you about scrolls.' I made my voice casual. 'Explain about the time poor Theon discovered all those Library scrolls on the midden-heap. Somebody told me you had ordered it.'

'Just a minor housekeeping exercise,' Philetus sniffed.

'Theon was not there and his staff went to extremes.' Trust Philetus to coerce juniors and then blame them. The weakest kind of management. 'When Theon found out and he outlined his reasons for keeping the documents, naturally I bowed to his expertise.'

'What were you trying to do – save money?'

Philetus looked abstracted. He was behaving like a man who had realised he might have left a lit oil lamp in an unattended room. I smiled at him reassuringly. That really scared him.

'So! That was Diogenes . . .' I murmured, as if it was highly significant. Then I could not bear Philetus and his vacillations any longer so I let the bastard go.

Thalia was with Philadelphion, the Zoo Keeper, though he left as I was approaching. They had been hanging over a fence and looking at a group of three young lions, just bigger than cubs, the long-bodied male starting to show a ridge of rough fur where his mane was coming, the two females having rumbustuous play-fights.

I said I hoped I had not driven Philadelphion away.

'No, he had to get on, Falco. Things to do and he's short-handed. Chaereas and Chaeteas have gone to their grandfather's funeral.'

'So people still use that tired excuse for a free day off?'

'Well, it's better than "got a stomach upset", even if you can only use it twice.'

'Informers don't have that luxury – nor you, nor anybody self-employed.'

'No, it's funny how your stomach goes back to normal very quickly when you don't have any choice.'

'Talking of upsets, are you fit, Thalia?' I asked affectionately. 'You seemed a bit off-colour yesterday morning.'

'Nothing wrong with me.'

'Sure? Not that I would blame you after Sobek's escapade.'

'Leave it, Falco!'

'Fine.'

I changed the subject and reconfirmed with Thalia her impression of the zoo's financial health. She reckoned they had plenty of money. They could purchase any animals they wanted; there was no pressure over fodder and accommodation bills; the staff seemed happy, which meant there were enough of them and they were well treated.

'Sounds satisfactory . . . Are you buying those lions?'

'I think so.'

'They are beautiful. You're bringing them to Rome?'

'A lot of beautiful animals will be having a very short visit to Rome, Falco. When the new amphitheatre opens, thousands will be slaughtered. Why should I lose out? If I don't take these three, someone else will – or, since the zoo cannot keep too many full-size lions, they will end up in one of the arenas in Cyrenaïca or Tripolitania. Don't weep for them, Falco. They were doomed from the day they were captured as cubs.'

I was musing aloud: 'Could the zoo be involved with some scam – procuring wild beasts for arenas?'

'No. Stop fantasising,' Thalia told me frankly. 'There is no scam. Traders and hunters acquire rare beasts down south and in the interior. They show good specimens to the zoo first. That's what they have always done, since the pharaohs. If the zoo turns them down, the hunters move on to sell elsewhere.'

'And your three lions?'

'Were kept here as a public attraction while they were cute cubs. Now they are a handful and Philadelphion is glad I'll take them.'

'I'd better go and find him,' I said, concluding our conversation. 'I have to ask the silver-haired charmer whether one of his colleagues might want to kill him.'

'Scram then,' rasped Thalia.

'I don't suppose you know anything about the Zoo Keeper's love life?'

'Wouldn't tell you, even if I did!' replied Thalia, laughing coarsely.

Well, that sounded more like her old self.

XL

I tracked down Philadelphion.

'I won't keep you long. I hear your men are at a funeral . . .' He gave it a nod, but made no other comment. 'What are they – brothers?'

'Cousins. What do you want, Falco?' He was terse. Perhaps he felt harassed, having to slop out enclosures and heave around feed buckets. When I found him, he had his sleeves rolled up to the armpits, straw in his hair and was doling out fruit to the baby elephant.

I asked if it was true that he had quarrelled with Roxana the day Heras died. Philadelphion denied it. I said there was supposed to be a feud between him and the lawyer Nicanor, with Nicanor making threats to steal Philadelphion's mistress. 'Roxana herself told me. And I know he is determined to defeat you in the race to become Librarian – using any unfair means.'

'You think that pumped-up dandy let out my crocodile? Sobek would have crunched him up on the enclosure ramp.'

'That then raises this question, Philadelphion: did you suspect Roxana might be meeting a rival at the zoo – so did *you* let Sobek out?' Philadelphion guffawed but I kept at it: 'You would know how to do it. Did you think Roxana was meeting Nicanor, and was *he* supposed to die?'

'Falco, what kind of world do you live in?'

'Sadly, one where it is necessary for me to insist you tell me where you were the night young Heras was killed.'

'I told you before. Working in my office.'

'Yes, that's what you said.' I toughened up. 'Now let's

have the truth.' I was sick of being treated like a dunce. I was sick of traipsing to and fro across this magnificent complex just so one arrogant scholar after another could think he was bamboozling me. 'I've heard false alibis before. Stop prevaricating. A thirty-foot crocodile escaped and savagely killed an innocent young boy. Heras was flirting with your lady love – who had lured him here to annoy you. What do you and Roxana want – the army to arrest you both for perverting the course of justice? Either you cough up what really happened or you'll be in custody within the hour. Your affair will be exposed and it will finish your chances of becoming Librarian. The Director will be absolutely thrilled to drop you.'

'Flirting with *Heras*?' Philadelphion interrupted, apparently amazed.

'My source is impeccable.'

'I know nothing about that.'

'So what *do* you know?'

'Does Roxana say this happened?'

'Roxana denies it.'

'Well –'

'That clinches it for me. She's a lying little madam. She and Heras had an assignation; I have an independent witness who knows it was pre-arranged. So Roxana is a liability for you – and a suspect for me. Forget being wounded by her skittish behaviour and confess what went on that day.'

Philadelphion straightened up. 'Roxana and I quarrelled, yes. It was about Nicanor. The minx uses his interest in her to cajole me into spending more time with her, bigger presents, better outings . . .' 'Minx' was too soft. Still, better men had been bewitched by cunning Egyptian temptresses. 'This business with the shortlist has just brought everything to a head over Nicanor. I loathe the man; I make no secret of that.' The Zoo Keeper shook his head in wonderment. 'But I don't see, Falco, why Roxana would have been with somebody like Heras –'

I could see it. 'Because she wanted to make you sorry for something. If she had encouraged Nicanor instead, he would have been very difficult to shed once she finished with him. A woman of Roxana's perception would know not to use Nicanor as a temporary dupe. With him, it would be all or nothing. Toy with such a man, and the consequences would be grim. Heras, though, poor Heras seemed a safe plaything.'

'Roxana is not like that.'

'She is as tough as an army nail,' I said. 'And trouble. Take my advice – dump her.'

'Oh but she's such a pretty little thing!' wheedled the Zoo Keeper. I nearly decided the Director was right: this man's judgement was faulty. Still, if candidates were turned down just because they were linked with unsuitable women, no high positions in the Empire would ever be filled.

The baby elephant was not receiving its fruit fast enough. It began to circle us with its tiny trunk in the air, trumpeting petulantly. If Hannibal had used such little creatures in the Carthaginian armies, the Roman legions would have stood their ground going 'Coo, aren't they cute?' – though only until the babies came at them. This one was half my height but he carried enough weight to make us scamper out of his way when he charged.

We took refuge behind a fence. As a way to interview a suspect, it was not ideal.

The Zoo Keeper made a feeble joke about how sweet they were when their ears flapped. Then, crouching out of the little elephant's sight, he knuckled under and confessed: Roxana had been spiky because *she* thought *he* was playing around with another woman.

'What other woman?'

'Oh, nobody.'

I groaned. As a couple Philadelphion and Roxana seemed made for each other. Both tangled themselves in complications. But according to him, Roxana was ridiculous to doubt him. He maintained his complete innocence and her irrational fears – right up to the point when he decided to admit that after all, he did have an alibi for the night Heras died. I could hardly believe his effrontery; he came out and said it was Thalia.

I went back to see Thalia.

'Oh you again, Falco!'

'Routine enquiries . . . Can you confirm for me, please, that two nights ago a certain Philadelphion, Zoo Keeper of this locality was – as he is now claiming – engaged with you for several hours in innocent discussion of an animal he calls a catoblepas?'

Thalia looked vague. 'Oh yes; now you mention it, we might have been.'

I seethed. 'Never mind. What in Hades is a *catoblepas*?'

She drew herself up. This was always impressive. 'A kind of wildebeest, Falco.'

'Philadelphion called it legendary.'

'Maybe yes, maybe no.'

'This strange dispute kept you entertained all evening?'

'He refused to see it my way. He told me what he thinks – and I put him straight. The beast hails from Ethiopia, has the head of a buffalo and the body of a hog – or is it the other way around? The name means it looks downwards, anyway. Rumour says its horrible stare or its breath can either turn people into stone or kill them.'

'That sounds like rubbish.'

'In my opinion,' replied Thalia, 'with which, when I put it to him properly, the Zoo Keeper agreed, a catoblepas is the same as the bloody big antelope I know as a gnu.'

'A what?'

'A g-n-u.'

'Fabulous . . .' I controlled my lungs, while wishing *my* breath could kill people. 'So you pair were locked in debate about the origins of this suppositious creature for how long?'

'*Suppositious?* Don't come here with your big words, Falco.'

'How long?'

'Oh . . . about four hours,' wheezed Thalia.

'Don't even begin to hope I'll believe that.'

'Falco, when I visit Alexandria, we always observe the customs of the desert. Perhaps we aren't actually *in* the desert – but it's close enough. So most of the time the Keeper and I were sitting cross-legged in my tent, having a respectable bowl of mint tea.'

'Mint tea? Is that what they call it around here?' I demanded caustically.

'You do go on, Falco.'

'I know you of old. You said most of the time. And the rest?'

'What do you think?'

'I think I feel sorry for Davos.'

'Davos isn't here to complain. Jason got a bit jealous – snakes can be touchy – but he knows it wasn't serious and he's all right about it now . . .'

'When I first asked, you implied you hardly knew Philadelphion.'

'Oh, did I?'

'Don't mess me about. I assume you have in fact known him well for years?'

'Professional contact. Since before his hair went white.'

'Roxana presumably knows that. So her suspicions of him were fully justified?'

'Oh Roxana!' Thalia grumbled. 'Can't she overlook a little bit of fun between old friends?'

'Your "fun" got a boy killed by mistake.'

Then a shadow did darken Thalia's face. Whatever her attitude to adult behaviour, she always had tender feelings for the young.

XLI

This was turning into a drear morning. Either people gave me the run-around or they came clean with stories I preferred not to know.

Next, I tracked down the lawyer. That was never going to cheer me up.

Only a fool would expect Nicanor to confess to anything. I knew if he did, there would be some tricky technicality that would get him off – probably with me looking stupid. I was spared that: he denied everything. According to him, he had never looked at Roxana and had no desire to beat Philadelphion to the librarianship. 'Let the best man win, I say!'

I asked if he had any kind of alibi for the night Heras died. Again, I was wasting my breath. Nicanor declared he had been alone in his room at the Museion. Since he was a lawyer, he knew this was completely useless. His arrogance made me wish I had the key to the padlock on Sobek's enclosure and a goat to lure the crocodile out to eat Nicanor.

That made me wonder who did have the key to the padlock. I wasted more time returning to the zoo to ask, only to remember I had been told. Philadelphion had one complete set of keys which was with him in Thalia's tent when they were 'drinking mint tea'. The other set hung in his office for the use of his staff. Chaereas and Chaeteas would have taken it when they visited Sobek to tuck him up for the night but they said they returned it. However, while Philadelphion was dallying the office had remained open, so anybody could have removed the keys again.

I asked about the half goat. Food for various carnivores came from local butchers, generally unsold stock that was on the turn. Until use, it was stored in a shed, which was kept locked to prevent the poor stealing the meat for food. The key was on the same bunch that was kept in the office.

Disheartened, I went to dig out Aulus, to take him for a late lunch. Helena Justina arrived with the same idea as I was walking to the Library. We all went together, along with Pastous, who took us to a fish restaurant he recommended. I calmed down on the walk there. There was really no need for Helena to send me that look of hers saying, *Do not tell Pastous your opinion of lousy foreign fish restaurants.* Which is: that you can never tell what anything is because fish have different names everywhere; that the waiters are trained to be rude and blind and diddle change; and that eating fish abroad is the fast way to experience whatever killing diarrhoea that town is famous for.

Pastous was right, however. It was a good restaurant. It had enthralling views over the Western Harbour, where the mist had cleared today and we could see the Lighthouse. Among more mysterious names were recognisable varieties – shad, mackerel and bream.

While we were eating, Aulus and Pastous told Helena and me what they had managed to deduce from the old man's note-tablets. They were full of complaints. Nibytas had left a haphazard jumble. His handwriting was particularly difficult. Not only did he run words together without spaces, but his cursive frequently deteriorated into little more than one long squiggly line. Sometimes, too, he used the papyrus back-side up.

'You know papyrus, Falco,' Pastous explained, as he spoke adeptly taking apart a fish he had called a tilapia. 'It is made by cutting thin strips of reed, then placing two layers cross-ways; the first goes top to bottom, the next is placed on top of it, running from side to side. These layers are compressed until they coalesce; to make a scroll, sheets are glued together so each overlaps the one on its right. For preference, people then write on the side with the grain running sideways and the joins easy to cross. This is smooth for the pen, but if you reverse it, your nib constantly hits ridges. Your writing is rough and your ink blurs.'

I let him tell me all this, though in fact I knew it. I must have been enjoying my lunch so much it mellowed me. 'So Nibytas was becoming confused?'

'Obviously had been for years,' declared Aulus.

'And could you make any sense of what he was doing?' asked Helena.

'Compiling an encyclopaedia, all the world's known animals. A bestiary.'

'Everything,' elaborated Pastous in some awe, 'from the aigicampoi (Etruscan fish-tailed goats) and the pardalo-campoi (Etruscan fish-tailed panthers), through the sphinx, the androsphinx, the phoenix, the centaur, the Cyclops, the hippocampus, triple-headed Cerberus, the bronze-hoofed bull, the Minotaur, the winged horse, the metallic Stymphalian birds right up to Typhon the winged, snake-legged giant.'

'Not to mention,' added Aulus gloomily, 'Scylla, the human-cum-snake-cum-wolf hybrid, who has a snake's tail, twelve wolf legs, and six long-necked wolf heads.'

'And no doubt the legendary catoblepas?' I could show off too.

'Whatever that is,' Pastous confirmed, sounding as depressed as Aulus.

'Most likely a gnu.'

'A what?' Aulus looked scathing.

'G-n-u.'

'G-n-obody has ever seen one?'

'G-n-ot as far as I know.'

Pastous remained serious. 'The old man's method is not acceptably scientific. Nibytas wrote a strange mixture; he included both true technical data and far-fetched nonsense. Made available to others, such a collection would be dangerous. The quality of the best parts would convince readers that they could trust the myths as factual.'

'He evidently managed to pass himself off well,' Aulus said. 'He corresponded with scholars all over the educated world – even some old fellow called Plinius in Rome consulted him quite seriously, some friend of the Emperor's.'

'We had better warn him off,' Helena suggested.

'Do not be involved,' Pastous advised her, smiling. 'These dedicated scholars can be surprisingly unpleasant if you cross them.'

'Did Nibytas ever snap?'

'He became very worked up sometimes.'

'Over what?' I asked.

'Small things he felt were being organised badly. He had high standards, perhaps the standards of a past age.'

'So he made complaints?'

'Constantly. Perhaps he was right, but he would be so angry and he made so many complaints, in the end no one took him seriously.'

This made me thoughtful. 'Can you remember any of these complaints, Pastous? Who did he complain to, can you tell me that?'

'The Librarian. He had been badgering Theon a lot recently, though I cannot tell you what about. I overheard an exchange, but it was only part of the conversation; I think they realised I was nearby and both of them dropped their voices. Nibytas, the old man, snorted fiercely *"I will go over your head about it to the Director!"* Theon did not try to stop him; he just replied in a rather sad voice, *"Believe me, there will be no point."*' Pastous paused. 'Falco, is this important?'

I could only shrug. 'Without knowing the subject, how can I say?'

257

Helena leaned forwards. 'Pastous, would you say the Librarian was depressed about this conversation?'

'He seemed in deepest gloom,' Pastous answered gravely. 'As if utterly defeated.'

'He did not care?' asked Aulus.

'No, Camillus Aelianus; I felt he cared very much. It was as if he thought to himself, let Nibytas make a fuss if he wanted. Dissuading Nibytas was too hard. Speaking to the Director would achieve nothing, but there was nothing to lose by it.'

'Did you feel the Librarian himself might already have raised the subject – whatever it was – fruitlessly with Philetus?'

Pastous considered. 'Very likely, Falco.'

I picked my teeth discreetly. 'I saw Philetus earlier today, leaving the Library. Is it like him to make visits?'

'Not in normal times – though since we lost the Librarian he comes along to see us. He walks around. He inspects the scrolls. He asks if there are any problems.'

'You could say that was good practice!' Helena murmured, being fair.

I scoffed. 'Or think he was up to something! What does inspecting the scrolls entail?'

'Gazing at the shelves. Making little notes on a tablet. Asking what the staff believe are trick questions, to see if they are doing their jobs.'

'How's that?'

'He requests peculiar books – old works, material in unusual subjects – then when we produce them, he just makes one of his notes and sends them back to be reshelved.'

'Hmm. Pastous, what do you know of a man called Diogenes?'

Before he answered, Pastous laid his knife in his bowl and pushed the empty bowl away from him. He spoke very formally: 'I have had no dealings with this man. So I have nothing against him.'

Aulus picked up on that, grinning slightly. 'But you think you ought to be suspicious!'

Pastous smiled back. 'Should I?'

I said, 'The first time I saw this Diogenes, I immediately felt I would not like what he did. Occasionally people have that effect. Sometimes, it is just unfortunate for them that they give such a bad impression – but sometimes the gut feeling they inspire is exactly right.'

'Who is he?' asked Helena.

'Philetus calls him as a scroll-seller.'

'He buys too,' stated Pastous, with an air of infinite sadness. He had both palms against the edge of the table where we were sitting, while he stared at the board about a foot from his hands, not meeting anybody's eye.

I let out a low whistle. Then I said, matching his regret, 'Don't tell me: he tries to buy scrolls from the Library?'

'I have heard that, Falco.'

'Theon used to give him the bum's rush – the Director sees it differently?'

'Whatever Philetus is doing,' answered Pastous, his voice now extremely gentle, 'I have no idea. I am below the level at which such an important man would share his confidence.'

He was a library administrator. His life there was quiet, orderly and on the whole free from anxiety or excitement. He worked with the world's knowledge, an abstract concept; it could cause dissension, though rarely to the extent of physical violence. If library staff ever see anyone attacked – and of course it must happen, for they are dealing with the public, a mad crew – it tends to be a sudden, inexplicable outburst from someone who is mentally unstable. Libraries do attract such people; they act as a refuge for them.

But deliberate harm is almost never levelled at librarians. They know time-wasters, book thieves and ink-spilling desecraters of great works – but they are not targets for hit-men. It was all the more chilling, therefore, when this open, clearly honest man at last raised his eyes and looked at me directly.

'There is one other thing I overheard, Didius Falco. I heard Theon give a warning to the old man: *"Take my advice and keep quiet. Not because these matters should be concealed – indeed, they should not, and I have tried to correct things. But whoever drops the white handkerchief to start this race, Nibytas my friend, needs to be a brave man. Whoever speaks out will be placing himself in the gravest danger."* Falco, I cannot help remembering,' Pastous ended quietly, 'that both of the men who had that conversation are now dead.'

We had a fine meal. I said afterwards, the proprietor must have been the library assistant's cousin, giving us special treatment.

'No Falco; I am not specially known here,' Pastous replied seriously.

XLII

I handed Aulus cash to settle up for lunch, and led Pastous aside. 'Be very careful. Theon was right: speaking out against your superiors is always risky. I am very unhappy about what we are dealing with here.'

If this Diogenes was involved in murky business, aided and encouraged by the Museion Director, and if both Theon and Nibytas had found out, that would explain much. Bad feeling, at the very least. But Philetus could well claim that as Director he had full authority to sell off scrolls if, in his judgement, they were no longer required. Who had the power to overrule him? Probably only the Emperor, and he was too far away.

What was going on might be no more than sleazy. Philetus might be turfing out work by writers he personally hated, discredited material, outdated books that would never be looked at again. He might well call this routine house-keeping. Any difference of opinion on the philosophy behind it could resolve itself when they appointed a new Librarian. In any case, if weeding out works was decided to be more than just unorthodox, if it was deemed to be wrong, then Vespasian could issue a directive that no scrolls held at the Great Library were ever to be sold. Only one thing deterred me from making such a recommendation at once: the famously stingy Vespasian might like the idea. He was more likely to insist scrolls were sold in large numbers, with the money raised all sent to him in Rome.

It could be assumed that if Philetus really was selling off scrolls to Diogenes, the income was used for the overall benefit of the Museion or the Library. But if Philetus was removing books on the sly and taking the money himself, that was different. It was theft, no question.

Nobody had suggested that. Nobody had given me any proof of it either. But perhaps it never crossed their minds that a Director could do such a thing.

There could be worse. Trouble about the scroll-selling could have led to foul play. We had two recent deaths at the Library. I would need the strongest kind of evidence to suggest a scroll fraud had caused them. Most people would guffaw at it. To proceed on my suspicions would mean going over the head of the Director, since he appeared to be involved. That meant taking matters to the Roman Prefect.

I was not stupid. Unless I found proof, it was out of the question.

I made Pastous promise simply to observe. If he saw Diogenes in the Great Library, he was quickly to alert Aulus or me. If the Director appeared again, Pastous was to watch surreptitiously what Philetus was doing, keeping a record of scrolls he asked to see.

Aulus and Pastous went off to finish reading the old man's documents. I took Helena home to my uncle's house. I wanted to discuss with her, alone, the other aspect of this story: Diogenes was connected to Uncle Fulvius.

'If Diogenes is a trader,' Helena mused, 'he could be involved in all sorts of commerce with numerous people. It doesn't follow that what he is doing at the Library also involves your uncle.'

'No, and the sun never sets in the west.'

'Marcus, we could ask Fulvius about it.'

'The trouble with Fulvius is that even if he is completely innocent, he will give us a tricky answer on principle. And what am I to do, love, if I find out there is a scam – and a member of my own family is in it? Possibly more than one member.'

'You are thinking of Cassius?'

'No,' I said grimly. 'I meant Pa.'

All three were out when we arrived home. That saved me having to tackle them.

When they rolled in, we could tell they had all been at a *very* extended business lunch. We could hear them coming even before they wove unsteadily into the outer courtyard. Crossing it took about half an hour from when they staggered in through the gateway telling the porter that they loved him. All of them were extravagantly good-humoured, but almost incomprehensible. I had given myself the task of interrogating three elderly degenerates who had lost all reason, plus any semblance of manners or bladder control. We would be lucky if none of them suffered a stroke or a heart attack; even more lucky if no irate neighbours came to complain.

What do pensioners do for vandalism? Write graffiti on a Temple of Isis in very neat Greek? Untie a row of donkeys then put them all back in the wrong places? Chase a great-granny up the street, threatening to give her a little kiss if they catch her?

Pa was in the lead. He took a run at the stairs and managed to propel himself as far as the salon. He aimed at a couch, missed, landed face down on a pile of cushions and immediately fell asleep. Helena insisted we turned him on his side lest he suffocate. I poked him hard, just to be sure his sleep was genuine. For me, he could choke.

Fulvius stumbled and fell down as he came up the stairs. This made him even more woozy, and there was a chance he had broken his leg, which had twisted awkwardly beneath him. Cassius spent a long time trying to get Fulvius first to their bedroom and then into, or at least on to, the bed. Fulvius was cursing and being unhelpful. Cassius was cursing back and, I think, weeping mildly. Various household slaves were watching goggle-eyed from doorways, always dodging out of sight the minute anyone invited them to lend assistance. I offered. Either nobody heard me in the kerfuffle, or nobody was capable of taking in what anybody else said.

I removed to the roof with my family. We read *Aesop's Fables* to the children. Eventually we ran out of fables and just enjoyed the sun's last evening rays.

Cassius had been, perhaps, the least intoxicated. Eventually, he joined us up there. He burbled a few apologies, interspersed with momentary snores. Somehow he got himself on to a daybed, while we all watched in silence.

I walked downstairs. Fulvius and Pa were alive, but completely out of it. I rooted out the staff and politely requested a meal for those of us who were able to eat.

Back on the roof, I sized up Cassius and decided he at least could answer questions. 'Good lunch?'

'Ex-cell-ent!' He was so impressed with his enunciation, he continued to say the same thing several times.

'Yes, I think we can see that . . . Were you with that trader, Diogenes?'

Cassius squinted at me, though he was not in the sun. 'Diogenes?' he mumbled blearily.

'I heard Fulvius knows him.'

'Ooh, Marcus . . .' Cassius was wagging his finger at me, as if he knew even through the drink that I had asked something forbidden. The finger wavered wildly, until he poked himself in the eye. Helena gathered up the children (who were fascinated by the extraordinary adult behaviour) and moved with them to the furthermost part of the roof terrace. Though she could be a disapproving little piece, Albia stayed with me. 'Have to ask Fulvius about *that*!' decreed Cassius, when he finished wiping his watering eye on his arm.

'Yes, I will . . . So did Diogenes give Fulvius a good deal then?'

'*Ex-cell-ent!*' answered Cassius. Too late, he realised his mistake.

Albia looked at me and shuddered. She was right. This was dire — the sight of a man in his fifties, hunching up and hiding his face behind his fingers while he giggled at us like a guilty schoolboy.

XLIII

Far be it from me to be self-righteous.

The fact was, every generation hates the others to have fun. Human nature makes us deplore bad behaviour in the young – but bad behaviour in the old is just as grim. It was clear I would never get much sense from any of this intoxicated trio that evening, and by tomorrow, if they survived and started to sober up, they were unlikely to remember who they had been entertaining – or who had been entertaining them – let alone what anyone had said or what agreement they shook hands on.

If I could persuade them to back out of the deal, that might be just as well.

The rest of us had a subdued evening, as tends to happen when half a household has had a great adventure and the other half has not. I went to bed early. We all did. The girls were so good, Uncle Fulvius would be sorry to have missed it.

Next morning, Helena and I woke gently, entwined in love but wary about what the day might bring. My family ate breakfast together, Helena and I, our daughters and Albia. There was no sign of our elders. Even if they had begun to come round and realised that a new dawn had broken, daylight would hurt, recollection would be fleeting and troublesome. If they had all come round, they probably decided to keep out of the way until they could compare notes. I had no doubt they would be unrepentant.

Helena said she would take the girls out sightseeing. She

would come home after lunch, to check on the debauchees, see if medical attention was required and try to get sense out of them.

'You are a martyr to goodness.'

'I am a Roman matron.'

'She will give them a strong dressing-down,' suggested Albia, hopefully.

I grinned. 'You can be there to watch, so you will know how to do it yourself, one day.'

'I shall avoid sharing my house with wicked old men, Marcus Didius.'

'Don't say that. You never know what Fortune will dump on you.'

'I can handle Fortune. Are you going to see Aulus?'

'If Aulus is where I am going, I shall see him, certainly.'

'You have to make a riddle out of everything.'

'So where exactly are you going, Marcus?' put in Helena.

I told her I was starting at the Library. This business with the scrolls seemed the most profitable line to pursue. The episode with the crocodile seemed unconnected, probably just a domestic tiff gone hideously wrong. I said I expected to be home early, hoping to grill Fulvius and Pa about their involvement with Diogenes. But a lot was about to happen before I made good that promise.

Helena thought events could be turning nasty; she wanted me to take a sword. I refused that, but I sharpened my knife to please her.

As I left the house, the muttering man leapt to his feet but I passed by him with an angry face and left him trailing. He dogged my footsteps, but I kept going. I stared ahead, and although for a while I fancied he had stayed behind me, by the time I reached the Museion I saw no more of him.

Pastous was in the Library, but not Aulus.

'Have you finished up?'

'Yes, Falco. There was nothing more of interest among

the documents. In among the last batch we sorted, we found this.' He held up an object. 'It is the key to the Librarian's room.'

The lock had now been replaced but the diligent Pastous had rooted out the broken one. The key was portable, though heavy – made of brass, with a sphinx decoration. I tried it. Despite the damage to the lock, it turned in both directions. According to the assistant, Theon had found the key too cumbersome to carry about with him except when he left the building. When he was in attendance at the Library, he hung it outside the room on a discreet hook.

'So if he was working in his room, anyone could have come along and locked him in?'

'Why would they do that?' asked Pastous, who was something of a literalist. He had a point. 'But it was the Librarian's key – Nibytas should never have had it.' He looked troubled. 'Falco, does this mean that the old man may have killed Theon?'

I pursed my lips. 'As you just said – why would he do that? Tell me, when you overheard them arguing that time, did it sound as though Nibytas was very angry – so angry he might come back late at night and attack Theon?'

'Not at all. He went off grumbling to himself, but that was normal. We often had complaints from other readers that Nibytas made a noise, talking to himself. That was why he had been given a table at the far end of the room.'

'Old men do mumble.'

'Unfortunately Nibytas gave the impression he was annoying on purpose.'

'Ah, old men do that too.'

I asked where Aulus had gone. Pastous' face clouded. As usual, he seemed ill-inclined to gossip, but concern drew the story out of him. 'A man came. Camillus was with me at the time. It was Hermias, the father of Heras, the young man who died in the zoo. Hermias has come to Alexandria

268

to learn what happened to his son. He was extremely upset.'

'No doubt!' I hoped the Director had had the sense to have the remains rapidly cremated, Roman-style. Philetus had told me he would write to the family in Naukratis, which was just under fifty miles to the south. The messenger must have travelled at speed; the father had dropped everything and rushed here just as fast, no doubt spurred by grief, anger and raging questions.

'Plenty of young men are grabbed by crocodiles along the Nile,' sighed Pastous, 'but the distraught father realises this should have been preventable.'

'Aulus and Heras had been friends, briefly. So did Aulus talk to the father?'

'Yes, I suggested they went into the Librarian's empty room. They were there a long time. I could hear Camillus Aelianus speaking quietly and kindly. The father was highly agitated when he arrived; Aulus must have calmed him. He is so impressive –' *Aulus?* I would like to tell Helena that strong verdict on her brother. 'When they came out, the father looked at least more resigned.'

'I hope Camillus did not reveal why Heras was there that night.'

'You mean Roxana? No, but after the father left, Aulus told me.' Pastous wore his anxious expression again. 'I hope you are not angry, Falco – Camillus Aelianus is a grown man. He makes his own decisions –'

Now I was nervous. 'He is an idiot sometimes . . . Cough up – what has Aulus Camillus done?'

'He has gone to see the woman,' said Pastous.

'Oh no! He has taken Hermias to her?'

'He is not that much of an idiot, Falco.'

This was far worse. *'He has gone on his own?'*

Pastous looked demure. 'I do not visit such a person. Besides, I am on duty now. I cannot leave the Library.'

XLIV

Finding Roxana's house again took a long while. The anonymity of her street and her building had me running around in circles. I kept asking directions from bemused locals, who were either deliberately awkward or failed to understand either my imperial Latin or my polite Greek. Everyone here spoke Alexandrian Greek, a bastard version that was heavily accented with Egyptian vowels and peppered with dialect vocabulary; they pretended not to understand the standard pronunciation that is beloved of Roman teachers. I was wary of using Latin; people could be hostile.

Everywhere looked the same: narrow streets with occasional little shops or artisan premises, street stalls, blank-walled houses. There seemed to be no distinguishing street furniture, no fountains, no statues. I rushed into two wrong apartments, frightening several groups of women, before I found the right place. It took so long, that by the time I was standing outside Roxana's place, wondering just what to say, Aulus walked out.

When he saw me he reddened. Bad news. I tried to pretend I had not noticed. I felt a deep need to discuss this situation with my best friend Petronius Longus, back home, safe in Rome. I would once have said, discuss it over a large drink, but the behaviour of my supposedly mature associates last night put me off that.

'Greetings, Aulus Camillus!' Delaying tactics.

'Greetings, Marcus Didius.' He seemed calm.

'If you have been to see Roxana, we shall need a heart-to-heart.'

'Why not? – A bar?'

'No thanks.' I might never drink again. 'I am suffering from a monumental hangover, in triplicate – not mine. I'll tell you later about that.'

Aulus raised his eyebrows gently. We chose a tiny caupona and ordered bread and goat's cheese. He asked for a beaker of fruit juice. I said I would manage with water. Even the waiter seemed surprised. He wiped the desert dust off a bench for us and brought us a complimentary dish of gherkins.

'So – tell me about Roxana, Aulus.'

'Don't look like that. There is nothing you need report to my mother.'

'It's your sister I'm scared of.' I bit in half one of the gherkins. They were so wizened I knew why the waiter was giving them away. I wondered how much Aulus knew about the time I was held responsible for their younger brother, Justinus falling in love ill-advisedly when we were out in Germany.

'Nothing to tell my sister either.'

The bread came.

'That's good. So the amorous Roxana did not try to seduce you –'

A slow grin crept across Aulus' face. It was rather unlike him. 'She tried.'

My heart sank. 'Titan's turds! – as my horrible father would say. I do hope you rebuffed her boldly?'

'Would I not?' The cheese came.

'Wonderful! You are a good boy!'

Then Aulus Camillus Aelianus gave me a look that I found distinctly unreliable.

If we had any more conversation on this subject after the juice and water came, obviously it was in absolute confidence. So you will not hear it from me.

XLV

No, sorry, legate; I meant that. Absolutely *sub rosa*.

XLVI

Of course, although Aulus swore *me* to secrecy, other people were not in on our bargain.

He and I ate our lunch. The anguish of Heras' father had deeply upset him; after he unburdened himself about that, I took him home with me to my uncle's house. There, matters had progressed – far enough for Cassius to have innocently owned up to Fulvius that he had admitted that Fulvius and Pa knew Diogenes. Helena informed me that immediate ructions blew up. Flouncing had occurred, together with angry words, horrible insults and loud door-slamming. Fulvius quarrelled with Cassius, then Pa woke up and quarrelled with Fulvius. All three had now gone to sulk in separate rooms.

'That should keep them under control temporarily. And what did you do, sweetheart?'

'I told you this morning; I am a Roman matron. I had purchased cabbages to cure their hangovers. So I made broth.'

'Did they have it?'

'No. They are all being stand-offish.'

Well, that suited Aulus and me. We took a couple of trays up on the roof together and tucked into the excellent cabbage broth. Albia joined us. Still upset, Aulus described to Albia how he had had to face Hermias, the father of Heras. Amazingly, he then let slip how he upped and visited Roxana. If visiting her had been stupid, it was nothing to the folly of mentioning it to Albia.

More flouncing and door-slamming occurred.

In the midst of this hurricane, we had a visitor. Nicanor, the lawyer, had come for a legal confrontation with Aulus. This was when we discovered that details of our lad's interview with Roxana were no longer as secret as he wished.

When he went to her apartment, Aulus took it upon himself to inform Roxana just how distressed the father of the late Heras was. He had dwelt upon Hermias' grief, his desperate yearning for answers and his wish for compensation – all fully understandable, Aulus had maintained. Money could never replace Heras, a good, clever, hard-working son who had been loved by all – but recognition in a court of law that Heras died unlawfully would help assuage the parents' misery. Screwing the bolts as tight as he could, Aulus had announced that the bereaved father intended suing Roxana for luring Heras to his doom. The only possible deterrent, Aulus claimed, might be if she speedily co-operated with my enquiry and admitted everything about the night in question.

When Aulus and I had discussed it over our goat's cheese, we agreed this was first-class informing. The bluff was justified. (It *was* a bluff; Aulus had in fact persuaded Heras' father to go back sadly to Naukratis.) When dealing with unhelpful witnesses, small untruths that help to break them are acceptable, if not compulsory. Roxana had it coming. Putting the frighteners on her had results too: she did admit to Aulus that she had seen someone in the zoo that night, someone who must have been the murderer. Sadly, in the dark, she failed to recognise him – or so she maintained. According to her, her eyesight was poor.

Aulus and I had discussed whether we believed her. We put a marker to perhaps interrogate her again later. I reckoned she was holding out; for the right inducement, Roxana would suddenly find herself able to name the culprit after all. As a witness, her safety gave me some qualms. Still, Aulus had had the sense to warn her to tell no one that she saw the man. If the killer thought he had been identified, it could be dangerous.

I had congratulated Aulus on his diligent pursuance of our fine profession. What neither of us had expected was that once Aulus left (after whatever further formalities) (according to him, he never touched her), while brooding alone on her plump silken cushions, Roxana reconsidered her legal position. The ridiculous woman then bustled out and consulted Nicanor about the presumed compensation claim.

'She is not as intelligent as she thinks herself,' scoffed Helena. 'And she is *far* dimmer than all her lovers believe.'

Helena burst out with this denunciation in front of Nicanor.

As he turned puce, I said to him pleasantly, 'Don't be insulted. Technically, according to your own witness statement, you are not Roxana's lover – though I concede you may count as such, since so many other people have sworn that you wanted to be.'

The once-suave scholar threatened to burst a blood vessel. Emotions ran so high, he must have forgotten that I was supposed to have influence with the Prefect over the appointment he also coveted. 'You bastard, Falco! What are you implying?'

'Well, you are hardly suitable to give Roxana impartial advice.'

'I can tell her she is the victim of a trumped-up charge! I can warn her it was certainly made for duplicitous reasons – thus rendering invalid any evidence she was induced to provide to your asinine assistant.'

'Fear not,' said Aulus, with his ugliest senatorial sneer. 'The woman will never be made a witness. Any judge would denounce her as morally unreliable and – by her own admission – she is short-sighted.'

'She says you threatened her with Minas of Karystos!'

'I merely mentioned that the eminent Minas is my teacher.'

'Eminent? The man is a fraud. What's he teaching you?' jeered Nicanor. 'Fish-gutting?'

Apparently Minas had taught Aulus how to remain calm under brutal cross-examination. He smiled patiently and said nothing.

'She wants compensation,' Nicanor snarled. This just proved how muddle-headed it can be to set out on a legal course, even with the aim of squeezing a witness. One thing always leads to another. We had no time to mess about in lawcourts, and certainly no spare cash to cover it. 'For nervous stress, slander and wrongful accusation.'

'Of course,' mocked Aulus. 'And I shall make my counter-claim – for shock and bruises inflicted on a free Roman citizen's body, when the lecherous madam jumped me.'

'*She what?*' shrieked Helena, in big sister mode.

'She is shameless, but I fought her off –'

We then learned just how passionately the predatory Nicanor lusted for Roxana. He let out a roar, leapt from his seat, fell on the noble young Camillus, grabbed him around the throat and tried to throttle him.

XLVII

The commotion was so rowdy it drew Fulvius, Cassius and Pa from their hiding-places. They all recovered from their sulks enough to launch into the action, fists whirling. Aulus was outraged, so once I pulled Nicanor off I pinned down Aulus and tried to reason with him. No senator's son needs a reputation for fisticuffs, even if the fracas was not his fault. Being thought a bruiser might win votes in Rome, where the mulish electorate always goes for thugs, but we were in Alexandria where we would merely be despised as fractious foreigners. Aulus broke free of me at one point, but Helena backed him up against a wall with her well-used instruction: 'Remember, darling, we are guests!' He had socked me in the liver, but he was polite with her.

Nicanor also refused to be subdued, but was pushed around and abused verbally by the pensioner gang. They hustled him down the stairs in fits and starts, then bullied him until he did reluctantly capitulate. I said sternly that *nobody* was taking any legal action. 'Please remember, Nicanor, you have just proved yourself capable of violence to a young man who *rejected* Roxana's advances – so any jury will know what you might have done if you had caught Heras actually in her arms.' Pa sniggered. I think Nicanor was composed enough to hear me. To put us in the clear as non-aggressors, I sent the man away in my uncle's palanquin.

That was a mistake, as it meant the palanquin was missing when I needed it.

Fulvius, Cassius and Pa then realised how much their heads hurt. They all went to lie down, while Helena and Albia ministered to them with cabbage broth. I was in charge, so when a shy messenger came for Fulvius, it was to me that the lad reported, 'Diogenes is making your collection tonight as agreed.' Fortunately, he was as timid as a wood mouse and whispered in a nice quiet voice. Only I knew he was there.

I was unable to reconnoitre even with Aulus, or Fulvius and company would have known. Instead, I slipped out of the house discreetly, telling no one.

Of course the muttering man with the evil eye, Katutis, saw me leave.

The rendezvous was at the Museion. The shy boy had given me directions. Diogenes would be by the Library, not at the main building but a separate place alongside. Without transport, I had to walk there. I went fast. That was none too easy. It was evening; the streets were thronged with people, going home, going out, meeting friends or colleagues, just enjoying the atmosphere of this fabulous city. At this hour, the crowds were thicker than in daytime.

As usual, when I first set off I thought I was tailed by Katutis, though by the time I reached the Museion grounds, I had lost sight of him. There, strollers had gathered in considerable numbers, admiring the gardens and loitering in the colonnades. I saw members of the public, including a few young families, as well as men who were obviously scholars, none of whom I recognised. The heat of the day lingered just enough to keep things pleasant. The sky was still blue, though the richest depth of colour was about to be sucked out of it as the sun hovered, then sank out of sight below the buildings. Nothing in the world beats the atmosphere of a seafront Mediterranean city on a long fine evening; I could see that Alexandria was among the best.

I went to the Great Library. It was of course locked up.

Any faint hope of coming across Pastous faded. He would be long gone, home to wherever he lived and whatever life he had. I was on my own with this.

Behind the Library were various ancillary buildings; eventually I worked out which annexe had been described to me. It was of an age with the main reading rooms, though built on a considerably smaller scale and much less ornate. This must be either a scroll store or a workroom, perhaps where damage was repaired or cataloguing happened. I stood outside for a moment, watching and listening.

Here, at the back of the monumental complex and the elegant, formal grounds, hardly anybody was about. There were gravel paths and service rooms, delivery points and rubbish skips. If vagrants lurked in the Museion grounds at night, this would be where they bedded down. Not yet; it was still too early. Nor did the public come here. It was remote enough for loners or lovers, yet an unattractive venue. The quietness was unwelcoming, the isolation scary. I myself felt out of place, a trespasser.

Sometimes a moment makes you catch your breath. Doubt settles on you. Dear gods, why did I do this job?

There was an answer. If, like me, you were born to a poor family on the Roman Aventine, there were very few options. A boy with a father in trade could be introduced to a guild and might be allowed a lifetime of hard effort in some unrewarding industry; you needed an introduction – and I had had an absent father. No grandfathers. Uncles all too old or with no decent contacts. (As a bitter example, one had been Fulvius – at that time far away, cavorting on Mount Ida, hoping to castrate himself as an act of religious devotion . . .) The only alternative had seemed good to a teenager: the army. I had joined, but found that in legionary life neither the bloody tragedy of war nor counting boots and cooking pots in the comedy of peace had suited me.

So here I was. Independent, self-employed, favoured

with a job full of challenge yet leading a life of madness. Informing was only decent if you liked standing in a doorway for hours by yourself, while everyone with any sense was cosily at home, enjoying dinner and conversation, prior to sleep or love or both.

That could have been me. I could have learned to use an abacus or taught myself to be a seal-cutter; I could haul logs or run an apple stall. I could be a bakery owner's bread-oven-paddle-poker or a butcher's offal-bucket-toter. Right now, I could be sitting in a wicker chair, with a drink on a side table and a jolly good scroll to read.

Nothing appeared to be going on, but I was patient.

As far as I knew I was observing a fraud, nothing dangerous. I had on decent boots, a knife tucked in one of them and a belt I was fond of. The weather was fine. The night was young. I was clean and fed; I had trimmed finger-nails, an empty bladder and money in my arm-purse. Nobody close to me knew where I was, but otherwise my situation was comparatively good.

As soon as I arrived, I noticed at the side of the building a discreetly parked, typical Alexandrian horse, between the shafts of a typical Alexandrian flat cart. It seemed unattended. The knock-kneed off-white horse was waiting with his head down as they generally do, his mouth halfway down his nosebag for comfort, though he was not bothering to eat. He was thin, yet not visibly abused. Perhaps people loved him. Perhaps at the end of a long day, plus half a night when his man was moonlighting, he went home to a tolerable stable where the water in his old bucket would be not too dirty and his manger hay was part-way decent. He was a work-horse. He would not be spoiled, though it was in no one's interest to make him suffer. He led the life his master led: hard work that he had always known and that would last until he collapsed and ceased existence.

Close by, in a shadowed doorway, a door stood ajar.

Eventually a man staggered out of the doorway, pulling behind him a loaded hand-barrow. He was moving backwards at first, in order to haul the barrow over a bumpy threshold. Then he turned around and pushed it to the back of the cart, where he began, slowly, to unload small bundles and lift them on to the cart. A second man soon followed him and even more slowly moved more bundles. They had to reach across the tailgate awkwardly. Neither thought of climbing up and taking the items from his colleague so they could pack them more easily. Neither had bothered to let down the tailgate. They had no sacks to collect up the items they were shifting, but handled them two or three at a time. It was a tedious process.

Before they returned indoors for another load, they both went and patted the horse. He leaned his head towards them, so they could whisper in his flicking ears. You could call it endearing, though whoever was employing them would probably not say so. One of them started to eat a bread roll.

Typical. If Uncle Fulvius and Pa were involved in this, they had mixed themselves up with an outfit that lacked even basic efficiency. Trust my relatives.

I watched the two clowns saunter back inside, chatting together, then they came out again, having reloaded their barrows. Abruptly the scene changed. Our friend Pastous walked around a corner. He saw the open door, though perhaps did not take in the clowns with the cart. Before I could signal or call out, he rushed inside the building.

The men with the hand-barrows looked at each other apprehensively, then bolted after him.

Groaning, I wrenched myself from the security of my doorway, to follow all of them. My situation, previously so good, was now turning dirty.

Inside the building, I found one large room. It was murky but still dimly lit by the evening sun. Upon various work-tables and the floor stood piles of scrolls. These were what the two fellows had been transferring to the horse and cart. Their labours were being supervised by the unsmiling man called Diogenes. He might employ clowns, but he was better quality. Though neither tall nor agile, his thickset, pear-shaped body was strong; he looked like a man nobody should cross. In short sleeves today, he had an old scar from his shoulder to his elbow, and large hands. His tiny eyes seemed to notice everything. I put him at forty-five, grim-natured, and from the thick black eyebrows that met in the middle, I thought he probably came from the north side and eastern end of the Mediterranean.

When I walked in, Diogenes had knocked Pastous to the ground and was tying him up. He must have reacted extremely fast. He was using cord he must have brought to gather scrolls into manageable bundles.

He looked up.

'Evening,' I said. 'My name's Marcus – nephew to Fulvius. My word, I don't know what you were doing with the old fellows yesterday. They got your message, but they are all flaked out like a row of squashed slugs today. I've been sent instead.'

I made a show of looking at Pastous; I favoured him with a large wink, in the manner of a no-good, cheeky cabin boy. Ashamed of letting himself be captured, he said nothing.

Diogenes scrutinised me suspiciously while he tightened knots on Pastous. I stood and waited. I just hoped Fulvius and Pa had kept quiet about me. They could certainly be secretive.

Did Diogenes remember he had passed me on the stairs that night? Had he then asked Fulvius about me?

He grunted. 'You're from Fulvius?'

'And Geminus,' I answered meekly.

I passed his test, it seemed. Diogenes bent over Pastous, ripped off the hem of the assistant's tunic and gagged him with it. Before he was reduced to helpless gurgling, Pastous managed to come out with the old cliché. 'You won't get away with this!'

'Ah, but we will!' Diogenes told him with mock-sadness.

Silenced, Pastous glared. I reckoned this rather literal man now thought that I must have been working with the trader all along. His antagonism suited my act.

Diogenes seemed to accept that I could be trusted. He ordered me to set to and help the other men. So, in this strange fashion, I found myself unexpectedly working for relatives, as I could have done for the past twenty years if life had been different.

Before the room had been emptied, the cart was laden. Diogenes told his two men to wait there until a fresh cart came. He climbed up to drive, indicating that I was to go with him and unload the scrolls at the destination. Tracking the cargo suited me, so I obeyed. Only after we had left the Museion and were driving through many streets, heading westwards, did I ask casually, 'Where are we going?'

'The box-maker's. Weren't you told?' Diogenes glanced at me. I detected a sardonic note.

Now I was stuck with my role: the family idiot, the one to whom nobody ever bothered to give explanations. So I sat quiet, clinging on to the cart as if I was nervous I would fall off, while I let the trader take me wherever he was going.

If this went wrong, my adventure could have an unpleasant, very lonely outcome.

XLVIII

We travelled for ages, or so it seemed. Now I learned just how large a city Alexandria was. Journeys through unknown streets always seem interminable.

We kept going west, into what I knew must be the district called Rhakotis. This part, peopled by the native inhabitants, was an area Uncle Fulvius had warned me never to go to. This enclave had always been a bolthole for descendants of the original Egyptian fisherfolk Alexander displaced when he decided to build his city. They were at the bottom of the pecking order, almost invisible to the rest – Romans and Greeks, Jews, Christians and the multitude of other foreign immigrants. According to my uncle, these were also the descendants of the semi-pirates the Ptolemies had encouraged to pillage ships, looking for scrolls in all languages which they commandeered for the Great Library. According to Fulvius, they had never lost their ferocity or their lawlessness.

The street grids were like all of Alexandria or any planned Greek city, yet these alleyways seemed more sinister. At least in a poor district of Rome, I knew the rules and understood the dialect. Here, lines of drab washing were hung from the same kind of crowded apartments, but the barbecued meats smelt of different spices while thin men who watched us pass had distinct local faces. The usual half-starved donkeys were impossibly laden, but the middens were scavenged by long-legged dogs with pointed noses, mongrels that looked interbred with aristocratic golden hunting hounds; instead of Suburra sewer rats, skeletal cats swarmed everywhere. Human life was normal enough. Semi-naked children squatted in gutters playing marbles; sometimes one bawled after a brief squabble. Tears of indignation trickling through the dirt on a scabby child's face are the same anywhere in the world. So is the flaunt of a couple of girls, sisters or friends, walking down the street in similar scarves and bangles, wanting to be noticed by the male population. So too the malevolence of any hooked, black-clad old lady, muttering at shameless girls or cursing when a cart passes, just because it is occupied by foreigners.

After enough time passed, the unfamiliar became familiar. We drove through now seemingly ordinary streets where people carried on regular occupations: bakers, laundries and dye-fullers, garland-weavers, copper-beaters, oil-lamp-sellers, oil and wine merchants. We passed down one magical alley where, by the light of hot fires, glass-blowers produced their jewelled flasks, jugs, beakers and perfume bottles. We reached roadworks and building renovations, where trenches, implements, piles of sand and heaps of bricks or cobbles impeded progress, but as soon as we were spotted, work stopped and our horse was led through safely with impeccable courtesy.

Once I stopped feeling anxious, I saw that this district was busy but conventional. A great number of people, mainly at subsistence level, lived and worked here; suffered; made others suffer; reached the end of their span and died. Just like anywhere.

Diogenes pulled up the horse.

We were in yet another side street with washing lines threading over it. Two men were playing dice with murderous intensity – though they looked up whenever a woman hove into view. Any women excited them, even grandmothers. A noisy trio of youths were dashing about with a melon for a football. A dilapidated bath house stood on one corner, with a small temple diagonally opposite.

Each had a very old man sitting on a stool outside, either attendants or just lonely octogenarians who had staked out good places to stop people for enforced conversation. They looked as if they had fought at the Battle of Actium and would tell you all about it if they could grab a chance, drawing diagrams in the dust with their wobbly walking sticks.

The box-maker came out. He worked from a traditional one-room lock-up with a large shutter. It was only half open when we arrived, giving the place a secretive air such workshops normally do not have. I could see lights inside, but no clustered family. The man himself had a pale, gaunt face with an unpleasant twist to his mouth. He kept his lips together all the time as if he had bad teeth. He was not introduced to me, nor I to him.

Diogenes started to act as if there was urgency. He himself marched to and fro, unloading the scrolls from the cart, while he ordered me to start putting them into the boxes. These had been made in advance, simple round *capsae* with flat bases and lids, in the same form as the elaborate ones made from silver, ivory or rare, scented woods in which rich men guard their valuable scroll sets. Diogenes had bought very basic containers, just enough to protect the scrolls on shipboard and make them look respectable for selling on. Bothering to buy boxes meant he expected to make a lot of money.

Indoors with the box-maker, I tried chatting: 'Where are all these going, then?'

'Rome.'

I unrolled one, holding it upside down as if I was illiterate. The end-tag proved it came from the Library. It seemed to be a play, Menander by the look of it. He might be a raging bestseller in all the Roman theatres, but I was never keen on Menander. 'Who for?'

'The people of Rome,' grunted box-maker. 'Get on, and don't waste time.'

I packed scrolls into boxes. Nowadays only one public benefactor was allowed to splurge gifts on 'the people of Rome'. Their Father, their Chief Priest, their Emperor. I was beginning to see what the plan might be.

The box-maker looked up. Diogenes had come back into the workshop with the next armful of scrolls. 'He asks a lot of questions. Where did you find him?'

'He says he's Marcus.' Diogenes finally introduced me. I did not like his tone of voice. 'He says he works with Fulvius – but Fulvius told me different.'

He knew. He had known all along. Both men were now glaring at me, the impostor.

So Fulvius *had* told Diogenes his nephew worked as an informer. It could even be my fault that getting these scrolls removed from the Library then packed up and shipped tonight had become so urgent: my father could well have reported that Helena had assured him I was close to uncovering the scams at the Museion.

Now I was in trouble. The box-maker had grasped the situation. He stood up. In his right hand appeared a small knife that he must use for box-making; its narrow, shiny blade looked hideously sharp. 'What did you bring him here for?' he demanded accusingly.

'To get him away and deal with him,' Diogenes replied.

The workshop and its rectangular doorway were about six feet wide; with the shutter half pulled, Diogenes filled most of the doorway, blocking escape that way. He had no weapons on show, but looked tough enough not to need one. He yanked the shutter further towards him. I was now trapped indoors with them, and any cries for help would be well muffled.

This was no time to hesitate. I half turned, hoping for the possible one chance – yes, at the back of the workshop, uneven wooden stairs ran up. I bounded up them fast, fully aware this could put me in a worse trap. I came through a hatch into the dark living-room-cum-bedroom such places often have, where the workman can live cheaply with his family. I grabbed the bed. One built into the wall would have failed me, but this one was free-standing. I shoved it hard down the hatchway, jamming the legs as best I could so it blocked the stairs. There was another way up, little more than a vertical ladder. It brought me one floor higher, in among old boxes and box-making materials. At first I thought I was stuck. But we were in Alexandria; the place had access to the roof. The door was barred, but I managed to free it. I pushed my way out into fresh air, under the night sky.

I could hear Diogenes and the box-maker coming up hard behind me. Nothing for it but to shin over a parapet wall on to the next roof. I ran straight across and clambered through some kind of reed screen. I kept going. From then on, the buildings were separate, but along the street they were so close together I could take a breath and leap. So I continued from one house to another – not always easy. People had gardens up there; I fell into giant flowerpots. They stored furniture; I hurt my legs on chairs and beds. I startled moths. A stork flew up and frightened me. At the far end were select apartments where family occupiers led leisured evening lives. At one, enormous women sat out on long, battered cushions, drinking from small copper cups and chattering. When I flew down among them like an ungainly owlet trying out his wings, the shocked ladies squealed, exuding sour breath and raucous laughter. But they heard my pursuers coming and at once blew out several oil lamps so they could hide me quickly among their husky-scented soft furnishings. I lay there trying not to choke. Diogenes and his companion thumped on to the roof and were sent on their way with extravagant curses.

Emerging, I faced a tricky moment with a crowd of excited women who appeared to think the gods had sent me as a mercurial gigolo. But amidst many giggles and painful pinches, they sent me down a narrow stair, which let me out at street level. It must be the way they admitted their lovers, I thought (admiring the stamina of men who could deal with such heavies). But they were women with good hearts, quick to grasp an emergency. I had thanked them genuinely.

I emerged in a dark alley. It smelt the way they all do, with some extra strong Egyptian whiffs. I had no idea where I was. I recognised nothing. I saw nobody from whom I could ask directions, even if I dared trust them. My pursuers could at any moment burst from some other doorway.

Suddenly, a cat meowed. I started. 'Get lost, filthy moggie. I'm a Roman; you're not sacred to me.' I flattened back against a wall, breathing hard.

While I listened for trouble, I thought grimly about Vespasian and my supposed 'mission' as his agent. In fact I had no mission, not in the paid sense. My reasons for visiting Egypt were exactly as I had told everyone: Helena wanted to see the Colossus of Rhodes, and the Pyramids and Sphinx; because of her pregnancy we had had to travel as soon as possible. Uncle Fulvius had made us a convenient offer to stay with him. The Emperor meanwhile was completing his new overspill Forum, called the Forum of Peace; in it would stand a new Temple of Peace, while dominating the temple forecourt would be two beautiful public libraries, one Greek, one Latin. All Vespasian had said to me was: 'If you are in Alexandria, Falco, take a look at how the Great Library works.' There was no mention of scrolls. I reckoned he had not thought ahead as far as making acquisitions for his new buildings; it was, of course, a good moment for an entrepreneur to turn up in Rome offering cheap books.

No way would the Emperor *pay* me to come and look at the Great Library. The mean old beggar was making no contribution to my travel expenses and the only reason I would actually complete a report for him would be a vague hope of future gratitude. Helena believed that in return for a good brief (which she had promised to write), the Emperor would give me a big thank-you. I thought he would just laugh. He had a reputation as a joker. Trying to screw payments out of Vespasian was the biggest joke on the Palatine.

So for this nebulous concept – a job that had never existed – I was now being hunted down by the hostile confederate of my scheming relatives. They knew nothing about the trouble they had landed me in; they were ensconced at home with their feet up, while doting women tended them with dollops of hot broth.

I now saw what their scheme was: acquiring scrolls cut-price from the twisting Museion Director, shipping them across the sea then presenting them in Rome as an easy-buy, save your on-costs, complete package for the so-far empty libraries of the Temple of Peace. If I knew Pa and Fulvius, they would recoup seven times their investment. The grim-faced Diogenes would want a large cut – but that shifty pair would still make an enormous profit. Was any of it illegal? It was certainly illegal in *intention*, for everyone from Philetus and Diogenes to Fulvius and Pa.

I was implicated as a relative. Since I was staying in the same house, it looked doubly bad. I doubted that even the eminent Minas of Karystos could get me off charges of guilt by association.

Furious, I walked to the end of the alley and surveyed the street in both directions. I was hoping for a donkey that I could 'borrow' – better still, if I saw a man with a horse and cart, I would offer him a large sum to take me back to the centre; I could name somewhere he would be bound to know, the Caesarium, for instance, or the Soma, Alexander's Tomb . . .

But my surveillance remained unfinished. I wanted to discover what ship Diogenes was using. It could already be half laden. I also needed to stop him conniving further with

Fulvius and Pa – and stop him telling them that I was on to their project. I would like to arrest Philetus and Diogenes, but saw no way to do that without involving my relations.

Walking about, at last I recognised the street where the box-maker lived. All members of the public had now dispersed; both the baths and the temple looked closed for the night. As I turned up, a second horse and cart was arriving with the two clowns I saw at the Library, bringing a whole load more of scrolls. Despondently I parked myself in the shadows. A donkey came trotting by, carrying two men who from their build and manners looked like brothers, similarly dressed in black desert robes, with head-dresses they had wound up to cover their faces as if a sandstorm threatened. They stopped and looked at the box-maker's, but rode on. Nobody else was about now, not at street level. I could hear woozy music from behind closed shutters, and voices from inside houses or shops. People had hung up lights, though at infrequent intervals.

As I continued to watch, the two clowns loaded up the first cart with filled boxes. Once all the boxes were in place, Diogenes came out and assumed the driving seat. As the clowns began unloading loose scrolls from the second cart and carrying them indoors to be packed by the box-maker, Diogenes set off.

The horse was tired and went quite slowly. I followed on foot. At one point, cursing, I had to stop to pick a sharp stone out of my boot. As I leaned one-handed against an awning support, fiddling madly, a donkey passed me, with two riders. It was the one I saw earlier. A while later, when the same donkey was drinking from a horse-trough, I overtook them again. The two men did not look at me; I wondered if they knew I was there. Somehow, I hoped not. I was starting to ask myself whether, just as I was tailing Diogenes, the two donkey-riders might be following both of us.

Diogenes went on in one direction, apparently aiming

for the Western Harbour. He had turned north towards the ocean. Somewhere ahead must be the canal which I knew came through to this harbour from Lake Mareotis. To our right at the far end of its causeway stood the dark shape of the Lighthouse, topped at this time of night by the mighty glow of its signal fire, reflected out to sea but eerily lighting up the topmost turret. Diogenes turned on to Canopus Street, unmistakable in its porticoed grandeur. We were very near the Moon Gate; due to the city's orientation, this end of Canopus Street lay quite close to the sea. The horse picked up speed. I saw Diogenes glance back over his shoulder. I ducked into the portico. When I dodged back out through the columns, I had lost him.

He could not have got far. I nipped along, trying to catch him up. Very soon, I saw the cart, recognisable by its load of scroll boxes. The horse was standing still, the driver's seat was empty. Six feet away from the cart, someone else had abandoned a donkey.

My heart thumped unevenly.

XLIX

When completely stuck, ask passers-by.

'Did you see where this driver went?'

'That way! To the market.'

Simple.

'And the men off the donkey?'

'That way too.'

'Walking?'

'Walking. All walking.'

'Very fast?'

'Not fast.'

Never impose unnecessary complications. People often try to impede investigations. But if they don't know who you are, they will often help.

I asked the man to keep the cart and its load safe in his yard at the back of his shop. I gave him money and promised more. If he was kind-hearted he might even feed the horse. 'Someone will come tomorrow.'

'What are these?' he gestured to the scroll boxes.

'Just some old fish-wrappers.'

'Oh – dirty stories!'

He thought it was my private hoard of pornography. Apparently my grinning helper had met Roman travellers with scroll collections before.

I rushed after Diogenes and his two mysterious trackers. When I caught up, he was moving along briskly, but as if he was disguising the fact he was trying to get away. The men in desert clothes were following about five strides behind, one on each side of the road. I kept them all under observation until Diogenes hit the agora.

The market lay close to the heptastadion, the Pharos causeway. It was a huge square enclosure, open to the skies, as large as you would expect in a city devoted to international commerce, which had been established by a Greek. They love their markets. Since Alexandria was a city that hardly slept, most of the stallholders were still working. A rich odour of street food hung like a smoky cloud above the area. Shouts resounded. Wheels rattled. Footloose musicians, barefoot and threadbare, pattered on hand drums and tooted peculiar pipes. It was well-lit and vibrant, somewhere that a trader who knew his way around the city, might well feel he could lose a couple of wild men in dark cloaks who were harassing him.

At first it only looked like a man moving fast between the stalls, with others perhaps trying to catch his attention so they could all go for a drink. I was bemused but game. Where they went, I followed.

Soon it became more sinister. Diogenes began to show panic. Dropping all pretence that he was just walking somewhere and had not noticed any pursuit, he knocked into the corners of a couple of the stalls; he clattered through a pile of metal cauldrons; he kicked aside giant sponges; he annoyed people; he was chased by dogs. I fixed on him. One or other of the two men in cloaks was visible from time to time. It became apparent they were stalking Diogenes as if it was a game. They could have caught him at any time, but they were teasing – they let him think he had lost them, then swooped bat-like out of nowhere, so just as his heart started to settle, he had to be off again.

I suspected Diogenes knew them. He certainly knew what they wanted. The way he had taken off, abandoning the precious scrolls, said it all. A man who had struck me as afraid of nothing was now extremely worried.

The pursuers worked well in tandem. They seemed close-bonded. Perhaps they were Rhakotis residents, or perhaps they had fished and hunted wildfowl together in the great reed-beds of Lake Mareotis. Perhaps they came from those houseboats, where the driver had told Helena and me murderous gangs lived, unchecked by the authorities.

People began to notice the chase. The few women present gathered their children and hurried away, as if they feared trouble. Men stood and watched, though guardedly. Roaming dogs were harshly ordered back. One or two then stood by their owners' stalls, barking defiantly. A man caught my arm and pulled me to a halt; he shook his head, wagging a finger to warn me not to involve myself. I broke free and heard him mutter a baleful comment as I went on.

I saw a flash of red: soldiers. They were making their way towards Diogenes, though more curious than purposeful. A man with a great basket of apples barged into their way, perhaps deliberately, and sent fruit bowling crazily in all directions; the soldiers just stood there while he let out a cascade of complaint. If Diogenes spotted the military, he made no attempt to appeal for help. He was near enough, but instead moved on. One of his pursuers appeared, but Diogenes grabbed the awning ropes of a tunic stall, heaving over the whole edifice to block the man; entangled in garments, he let Diogenes flee. I jumped over a display of ceramic bowls, tripped on wet vegetable leaves, dodged around the end of a long row of ornament stalls, forcing a path through the crowds as best I could. When I lost sight of Diogenes, I kept going forwards and I had him in clear sight when he made what seemed to me a big mistake: ducking his head and running at a lope, he left the market on the seaward side. He set off down the enormous causeway, the heptastadion. I was so close at that point, I even yelled his name. He looked back, his face anxious, then turned away and speeded up.

The heptastadion looked long enough in daylight; it must

be almost half the distance of the city north to south. I was tired, and this chase was not of my making. I decided to return to the agora and alert the soldiers. Let them catch Diogenes. Legionaries could put a roadblock on the causeway and flush out the fugitive at their leisure.

What stopped me was a dark huddle of men outside the agora gate. The rough inhabitants of Rhakotis had answered some call; they were drifting in and suddenly I saw that the gathering was being orchestrated by the two cloaked figures who had chased Diogenes. They were gesturing in his direction as he headed out across the long mole. Poor as they were, I knew the descendants of the scroll pirates would be armed – and vicious. Uncle Fulvius said they were considered very dangerous. When the first few began to make a move, I turned back and on to the causeway.

With no real plan – was I warning him, helping him or hunting him down myself? – I too began running down the heptastadion after Diogenes.

It was a serious hike. The mole was a man-made granite structure, easily as long as its name said: seven stades. At least it was good underfoot. On it ran a decent road, well built to take the fuel convoys for the Pharos and the many daily tourists. Now, in the dark, it seemed almost deserted. Diogenes took it steadily. So did I. So too did the desperadoes behind us. To anybody watching from the shore, or from the packed vessels in the huge Western and Eastern Harbours, we must have looked strung out like a group of athletes in a Pan-Athenian race stadium. We adopted that steady, long-distance pace marathon runners have, saving ourselves at this stage, nobody yet making his move to overtake.

It was a wonderful night. A cool breeze was in our faces, the sky now dark overhead but fizzing with a multitude of tiny stars. Thousands of ships were moored to right and left of us, dark hulks whose rigging made interminable noises, their bumboats splashing and bumping against them in the gently lapping harbour waters. Occasional cries sounded from the dark shore or indignant seabirds let out squawks as their privacy was disturbed. It was too late for casual strollers. If there were lovers or fishermen out there in the gloom, they lay low and kept quiet. On the far side of the Eastern Harbour, I made out buildings faintly lit – the palaces, administrative quarters and other monuments where no one made economies in lamp oil. Any junkets, recitals or concerts would now have ended. Only night-watchmen would be walking the silent marble corridors, though perhaps in some lonely room, by light from a fine wax candelabrum, the Prefect wrote his interminable reports on nothing, to let the Emperor believe he did some work.

I could have been a clerk. I could have allocated sacks and scrawled on dockets. I really could have been a poet. I would have been a poor man, with starving children, but danger would never have approached me . . .

I stopped thinking.

Down seven stadiums' length we ran, until breathing hurt my chest and my legs felt as heavy as waterlogged wood. I reached Pharos Island. Everywhere was dark. I could no longer see Diogenes. The road forked. Somewhere to the left was a Temple of Poseidon, the great sea god of Greece and Rome, guarding the Western Harbour's entrance. To the right lay another temple, that of Isis Pharea, the Egyptian protectress of ships. Beyond her, was stationed the Lighthouse, forming the mighty endstop. I went right. The Lighthouse, which must be manned at night, seemed the less lonely destination.

Pharos Island was a curved rocky outcrop, far enough beyond the city to feel like a wild citadel out in the thundering seas that famously beat upon the long, low shores of Egypt. Here, Homer said, Menelaus and Helen were beached during their journey home after the fall of Troy; at that time they found only a lonely fishing village on the island, with seals basking on the rocks. Apart from the Lighthouse, the place seemed uninhabited now, though I could not bank on it.

At the Temple of Isis, I glanced in just in case the fugitive had sought sanctuary. All lay still. No parades of priests in long white robes, no sistrums sounding, no chants. An enormous statue of Isis, big-breasted and striding forwards, held a swelling sail in front of her to symbolise catching the winds for sailors' benefit. The dim, lonely interior began to unnerve me. I left.

Ahead of me rose the enclosure for the great tower. The Pharos itself had been built as a tall, slim eagerly sought landmark for sailors to aim at from far away, one clear point in an otherwise famously unmarked coastline. It was taller than other lighthouses, perhaps the tallest structure in the world – fully five hundred feet. The walls of its square enclosure were dwarfed by the Pharos within, though when I crept up to one of the long landward sides I found those walls were formed of enormous ramparts with huge gates and corner towers.

Helena had told me how the entrepreneur who organised the twelve years of building had sneakily outwitted a regulation that forbade leaving his personal mark. He had an inscription carved on the eastern walls; on a covering layer of plaster he proclaimed the customary praise for the Pharaoh: when the weather-beaten plaster ultimately peeled off, black twenty-inch letters said: *Sostratus, son of Dexiphanes, the Cnidian, dedicated this to the Saviour Gods, for the seafarers.* I hoped his protection would extend to me.

The Pharos was a civic building, frequented by workers who tended the fire and even by sightseers. Its entrance was occupied by only a couple of Roman soldiers. Diogenes had got past them. The guards were chatting with their boots on a table when I burst in. I introduced myself as an imperial agent, assured them I was neither drunk nor crazy, and warned them to expect trouble. One, named Tiberius, made an effort to appear alert.

'An unruly crowd is galloping here from Rhakotis. Call for back-up!' I ordered. 'Send your oppo if you have to – can you communicate with the mainland?'

'We *are* at the world's biggest signal tower!' Tiberius commented sarcastically. 'Yes, sir. We can send a message – if anybody over there is looking in our direction, we can talk to them quite chattily . . . Titus! Find the torches. Signal *Send reinforcements.*' He sounded ready to help. Out here among the endless sea spray, any excitement was welcome. 'This will be my first riot! What's up in Rhakotis?'

'Not sure – lock up, if you can.'

'Oh I can lock up, tribune – though I'll be locking in the workers who mostly come from Rhakotis themselves.'

'Do your best.'

I limped through the gatehouse to the vast courtyards, where forty-foot-high statues of pharaohs and their queens in colossal pairs dominated the scene. Movement caught my eye: a dwarfish figure I thought was Diogenes. He was climbing the huge ramp into the main tower.

The entrance door was set a couple of storeys above ground level, for defensive reasons. A long ramp, supported on arches, led steeply up. When I myself reached the top, gasping, I found that a wooden bridge crossed from the ramp to the door. I was already feeling afraid of heights – and I had hardly started yet. The doorway was nearly forty feet high, its architraves faced in classic pink Egyptian granite. The same pink granite had been used elsewhere, an aesthetic contrast to much of the rest of the building, which was composed of titanic blocks of white, grey-veined Aswan marble.

The first tier of the building was an enormous square structure, aligned to the four quarters of the compass.

Looking up, I could see it was topped by a huge decorated cornice that seemed to replicate the waves that I could hear pounding the outer walls, with massive tritons blowing their horns from each corner. This great tower tapered slightly, for stability. Above it stood a second tier, which was octagonal, and high above that, the circular fire tower, crowned with a tremendous statue. Row after row of rectangular windows must light the interior; I could not stop to count but it looked as though there might be nearly twenty floors in the first tier alone.

When I went inside I found that the interior was a vast space dominated by a central core that bore the weight of the upper storeys. There was what seemed to be accommodation for the keepers just inside the door. They resented disturbance, but unlike the soldiers they could pretend not to understand any languages I tried out. I could get no sense out of them.

I knew the basement housed stores for arms and corn. This place was vast enough to house several legions, if threatened. But currently there was no permanent garrison.

Long ramps wound up the inside walls. Up those ramps, which were wide enough for four beasts abreast, trains of donkeys toiled slowly, taking combustible materials for the light – wood, with which Egypt was poorly supplied, mighty round amphorae of oil and bales of reeds as supplementary fuel. Once they reached the top of the grand spiral, they unloaded, turned around and plodded back down again.

Nothing for it. I climbed to the top of the first, square tower. It was much the largest stage. The donkeys stopped here. Men unloaded their heavy packs and took the fuel manually up the remaining distance.

Doors led out on to a big, railed observation platform running round the exterior. Food and drink were being sold to visitors – of whom I found more than I expected. The view was staggering. On one side was the distant sweep of the city, faintly picked out by the glimmer of thousands of tiny lights. On the other, the dark emptiness of the Mediterranean, its ominous night presence confirmed by the sounds of fierce surf breaking on the rocks far below us.

Up here were lamps, men with trays, guides spouting facts and figures, and a festival atmosphere. I had never been anywhere like it that was man-made. The Lighthouse had always been a tourist attraction. Even at night, supper parties must come out here in fine weather. Rich fathers arranged birthday and wedding celebrations. Ordinary families came sightseeing, for education, fun and striking memories. There were people up here now – not throngs, but enough to make it dangerous if Diogenes had brought trouble – enough people for me to have lost sight of him and not to know either whether his two cloaked pursuers had followed him this far.

I walked around, on the way meeting Tiberius, the tough soldier from the gatehouse, together with Titus, his companion, who was carrying signal torches and what I recognised as the codebook. We failed to find Diogenes at this level, so while the soldiers cleared a space on the viewing platform and began to send their message shoreward, I left them to it, gritted my teeth and began to climb up inside the next tier.

L

Now I was making my way up the octagon.

By the time I staggered out on to the next viewing platform, I was nearly done in. For those who wanted to make this additional climb to the top of the eight-sided tower, and who could find the stamina, a smaller balcony gave a truly spectacular view. This must be over three hundred feet above the sea. It was wonderful and horrific at the same time. Anyone here needed a head for heights that I unfortunately lacked.

Far down below in the courtyard, men swarmed like insects. On the wind came faint ululating cries. I had heard such sounds in terrible places and situations – the rebellion in Britain was the worst; remembering, I shuddered. As I leaned over, way down there on the ramp to the main door, it looked as if one scarlet blob – Tiberius? – held the riot at bay, a latter-day Horatius defending the wooden bridge. If I made it out correctly, as men from Rhakotis ran across sporadically, they were whacked and tipped off the ramp. The spectacle added to the madness of this unexpected night.

On the first viewing platform below me, I saw the soldier Titus diligently shepherding the public inside the tower for safety. On his own, he was not having much luck. People were milling about hopelessly, of course.

Drawn by the crackle of the great fire, I climbed into the cylindrical lantern area, just as a bunch of the stokers came pushing out in panic. Not waiting to say what disturbed them, they scattered down the octagon.

At the top, I found a frightening scene. I had entered the eerie, perpetually mobile, orange light of the beacon. A strong steady wind blew constantly, its noise lost in the roar of the fire. I was sure I could feel movement. The lantern tower was substantial but it seemed to sway.

The Pharos had stood here for three hundred and fifty years – but the Greeks and Egyptians never had a beacon fire. It was our introduction; we Romans added it, because ever-increasing night-time sea traffic required better safety features. Cassius had given my children a model lantern, which they loved and used as a nightlight. That showed the ancient design; it was topped by a pillared tower, covered by a cupola – a feature that still lived in folk memory and would probably persist. But to accommodate a massive fire-basket, which had to be open to the skies, the round turret's roof had now been dismantled. The open top of the Pharos glowed like a lurid scene from Vulcan's forge, with dark figures tending the terrific fire.

On my face I felt the burning heat, a blaze so fierce it was barely approachable. You wouldn't toast your lunch bap here. Sweating stokers tended the fire with long metal rakes. Behind, from my viewpoint, stood an enormous curved metal reflector. Mirror-bright, it gleamed red in the light of the beacon. From out to sea, some said a hundred miles away, this light would shine like a huge star, low on the horizon, bringing hope for anxious sailors and a dramatic statement of Alexandria's power and prestige.

To my astonishment, I made out Diogenes. Even more out of breath than me, he had staggered to the foot of a colossal statue, a leftover that had once topped the old covered tower – Zeus? Poseidon? One of the heavenly twins, Castor and Pollux? It was no moment for art appreciation. Diogenes was slumped and on the verge of collapse.

Suddenly, from behind the reflector leapt one of his tormentors. Bat-like and shrieking, the wild figure ran at the trader. Diogenes stumbled to his feet, trying to flee.

Cowering away from the cloaked figure, he tipped over a low wall that contained the beacon and fell right into the roaring flames. He began to scream. Ablaze from head to foot, he floundered there; but it can only have been moments before he desperately clambered out. Intentionally or not, he launched himself towards his assailant, a fiery human torch. The man in black lost his cloak as he tried to get away. Holding up an arm to shield his face from the beacon's hot glare, he ran blind. He crashed against the outer balcony parapet. Unable to regain his balance, his momentum toppled him right over. His cry was lost as he vanished.

Diogenes fell to the ground. His clothes, hair and skin were alight. By the time I reached him, a stoker had aimed the contents of a fire-bucket over the writhing figure, but in that great heat the water sizzled uselessly. We dragged the attacker's discarded cloak over the prone man, then people brought more water pails. But some fool pulled the cloak away, so the flames broke out again spontaneously. At last stokers dragged up a heavy fire-mat and rolled Diogenes in it; they must have had experience or training. He was still alive when we finally put him out, but his burns were so bad he could never survive. Ghastly shreds of skin from his back and arms just fell away. I doubted he would even make the journey down to ground level.

Sickened, I crouched beside him. 'Diogenes! Can you hear me? Who were those men? What did they want you for?' He mumbled. Someone put a flask to his charred lips. Most of the liquid ran away down his neck. He struggled to speak. I strained to hear.

'Stuff you, Falco!'

He sank into unconsciousness. Despairing, I left the stokers to bring the body down.

I stumbled my way off the fire tower and back down the octagon. When I reached the public viewing platform at the top of the big main tower, it seemed deserted. I felt cold and desolate. This night had turned as sour as it could be – and still gave me no answers.

People who had been shepherded into the interior were crowding on the spiral ramps. White-faced, they gazed upwards in terror, aware that some tragedy had unfolded high above.

'Everyone stay inside, please – for your own safety. Make your way quietly down to the bottom now. Leave this to us!' One of the soldiers, Titus, came out on to the platform with me. We took lamps and searched the four long sides of the observatory area. Together we found the motionless form of the man who had gone over.

Titus bent. 'He's done for.' He twisted and looked up at the lantern, high above us. 'Must be what – eighty feet?' Who knows? He was guessing. 'No chance.'

'There was another man.'

'Must have scrammed.'

Titus moved back. I bent to inspect the dead man's face. *'What?'*

'Know him, Falco?'

'That's unbelievable . . . He works at the Museion zoo.' I looked twice, but there was no doubt. It was either Chaereas or Chaeteas. That took some comprehending. Whatever had turned those two calm, competent zoo assistants into vengeful furies, hunting a man to his death? Risking their own lives to do it, too. 'I'll have to go after the one who's made a run for it – how can I get out of the building safely? Are those rioters in the courtyard?'

'All be sorted by the time you reach the door.' Titus looked over to confirm: I joined him, though with trepidation. My nerve had vanished up on these windy platforms where I had just seen two men die.

Titus was right. All the men from Rhakotis were running for home. A red column of soldiers, so far away it looked stationary, was marching through the enclosure. 'Landed by boat, Falco.'

The way the waves beat against the Pharos base, that could not be easy. I was surprised they had arrived here so quickly, but of course Titus took the credit for his dextrous signalling.

'You're whacked, Falco. You'll do no more good tonight. Tell us who the other fellow is, and let the military track him down.'

Those words seemed as sweet as a lullaby.

LI

Even the worst nights end eventually. So, although my head still thronged with images of dark figures gesticulating against towering flames, I awoke to the hard clear sunlight that for several hours had been streaming through an open shutter. It must be mid-morning, maybe later. Subdued murmurs told me that my little daughters were close by, playing quietly on the floor together. When I had had adventures, they would often creep up near me while I recovered. I lay for a while, drowsily fighting wakefulness, but then let out a grunt to tell Julia and Favonia they could now scramble on to the bed with me. Helena found us all cuddled up together when she brought a tray of food for me. One arm around each, I kissed the children's soft, sweet-scented heads and gazed at Helena like a guilty dog.

'I am in disgrace.'

'Was it your fault, Marcus?'

'No.'

'Then you are not in disgrace.' I smiled at my tolerant, wise, forgiving girl with all the adoration I could muster. As smiling goes, it was fervently meant, though perhaps rather pallid. 'Don't do that again,' she added waspishly. ' – *Ever!*'

I remembered that I was delivered home by soldiers, filthy and exhausted. I thought it had been in the dead of night, though Helena reckoned closer to dawn.

'You were sensible enough to order people to look for Pastous at the Library. He was found safe, incidentally. A message came from Aulus. Aulus is coming here later, to see what needs doing.'

She propped me up on cushions while I ticed down a late breakfast. I had little appetite. I let the children steal most of it. Helena perched on a stool, watching without comment. When I pushed away the tray and slumped wearily, she told the girls to run off to see Albia, then we two settled down alone to catch up on all that had happened.

I tried to narrate the story logically, to make sense of it myself. Helena listened, her great dark eyes thoughtful. It all took time. My words came sluggishly. Left to myself I would have lain still and closed my eyes again.

No use. I had to decide what to do.

'So . . . where are Fulvius and Pa?'

'They went out, Marcus.' Helena appraised me. I must look a wreck, but she was cool, clean, beautiful in garnet red and a russet stole. Her face seemed pared and hollow, but her eyes were clear. Although she wore no cosmetic tints, she had dressed her fine hair meticulously, holding it in place with a full pantheon of long ivory pins, topped with little goddesses. Her custom was to be carefully groomed after I had had a scrape – to remind me that I did have someone worth coming home to. 'I had told them you got into trouble in a bar . . . they believed it very readily. Perhaps you should buff up your reputation, dearest.' She spoke as a long-term partner discussing work, reasserting her own importance. I knew that attitude. It posed no threat. Her sniping tone would be temporary. 'I believe they are hoping to meet Diogenes.'

'He won't turn up!' I shifted about; every joint ached. I found it impossible to get comfortable. 'The military will try to keep a lid on what happened – the Pharos is remote enough, but there were members of the public all over the place. Rumours will leak out.'

'Well, when you came back last night, I rushed down and took over. I have done my best to hide what happened.'

Helena had been magnificent: alarmed, naturally, she pretended to be coping with a reprobate husband; shooed everyone else back to bed. I had heard her rapid enquiries of my escort, their sheepish answers. I remembered her scanning me for wounds, or possibly wicked women's perfumes.

That made me smile at her, a long, deep smile of reassurance and love. Accepting it, Helena hauled herself from her stool, and came across to me. After moving the tray to a side table, she took our daughters' place in my arms, as we held one another for comfort, reconciliation and relief. Once it would have led to more. I was too exhausted; she was too pregnant; we were too intrigued by our enquiries. We lay there, thinking. Don't sneer until you've tried it.

Aulus turned up. He said he had told Pastous to go into hiding – it was either that or protective custody. The fish restaurant where we ate lunch the other day had rooms for hire; Pastous was now secretly staying there. I gave Aulus directions and cash for reward purposes, then sent him across the city to recover the cartload of scrolls that Diogenes abandoned in the street last night. Albia went with him for the adventure.

'I warn you, the man took it into his head I was entrusting him with pornographic literature.'

'I wonder why he would believe that?' mused Helena.

I went to the baths as soon as they opened, then spent the rest of the morning at home. Once I would have bounced back faster, but I had reached an age when a whole night of strenuous activity – *not* the kind involving women – left me in deep need of recovery time. I consoled myself that Egypt was famous for its sensual baths and exotic masseurs – only to find that the baths near my uncle's house had nothing better to offer than a miserable washing-slave from

Pelusion, who slathered me in sickly iris oil then gave me a half-hearted neck massage while he endlessly told me his family problems. It had no effect on my aches and made me utterly depressed. I advised him to leave his wife, but he had married her for her inheritance, which due to the complicated Egyptian inheritance laws, where property was divided between all the children, came to thirty-three two-hundred-and-fortieths of their building.

'Nevertheless, trust me – leave your wife and get a dog. Choose one who has his own kennel, then you can share that and live with him.'

It went down badly.

Chewing gloomily on a quid of papyrus he sold me, I crawled home to Helena. She met me in the courtyard with a warning that the old men had come in; they had gone into a huddle upstairs. Cassius had told her they had heard that Diogenes was in a coma, in military custody, and it was certain he would not live. Before they could tackle me, I commandeered the palanquin and fled. Helena came with me; we set off for the Museion.

LII

Philadelphion was gazing at a herd of gazelles, perhaps trying to seek solace in the company of animals. Gazelles were not the best choice; they grazed in a spacious enclosure, indifferent to his mournful scrutiny. Occasionally they would stiffen, heads up, then bound away from imagined danger. He simply continued to stare across their pasture.

We dragged him away, chivvying briskly. I was in no mood for melancholy.

'Leave me alone, Falco. I've already had that centurion down here, making my life dreadful.'

'He told you one of your staff died last night at the Pharos?'

'It was Chaeteas. I identified the body. Since his cousin seems to have gone missing, I shall take responsibility for a funeral . . .' The man who had seemed so competent and restrained when he conducted the necropsy – when was it? – only six days ago – had sunk into unexpected misery.

Helena and I led him in a quick march to his office. Philadelphion halted outside, as if reluctant to enter this scene of so many conversations and experiments, shared with his two assistants. 'I had known them since they were boys. I taught them all I knew . . .'

'So you cannot explain why they were roving through the city in chase of Diogenes yesterday?' Helena asked gently.

The handsome, silver-haired man looked at her sadly. 'No idea. Absolutely no idea . . . This business is incredible.'

311

'It was all too real at the time!' I growled. 'Get a grip. I want to know what they had against the trader.'

'I know very little about him, Falco –'

'What would Chaereas and Chaeteas have to do with a scroll-seller?' Losing patience, I shoved Philadelphion on to a stool and loomed over him. 'Look, man – enough people have died in murky circumstances at the Museion! First your madcap pair were implicated in Sobek's release –'

'Oh that was merely carelessness. They had their minds elsewhere – Roxana saw them standing by the crocodile enclosure talking together so earnestly they were not thinking properly about fastening the locks.'

'Talking about what?' Helena asked.

She deliberately used a mild tone and the Zoo Keeper answered, 'Their grandfather.' Immediately he looked as if he regretted it.

'He had died?' I remembered we had been told they were at a funeral, shortly after the Sobek tragedy. 'They were upset?'

'No – no, Falco, they had not learned about their grandfather at that time –' Philadelphion was flapping his hands, apparently torturing himself.

I gave him a slight shake. 'So what were they discussing so intently? Did the gorgeous Roxana eavesdrop?'

'No, of course not.'

'Still,' Helena helped me put on pressure, 'I think you know what the conversation was about. You must know what was troubling Chaereas and Chaeteas. You had a long relationship with them. When they had a problem, they would bring it to you.'

'This is very difficult,' Philadelphion whimpered.

'We understand.' Helena soothed him. Fortunately for him, I was too weary to wring his neck. 'I suppose they told you in confidence?'

'They had to; it could have caused a great scandal . . . Yes, Helena Justina, you are correct. I know what was troubling my assistants – and troubling their grandfather.' Quite suddenly Philadelphion straightened up. We relaxed. He would tell us the story.

At his best once again, he kept it succinct. Elements of this story sounded familiar. The two cousins' grandfather was a scholar who had been working in the Great Library; once, unobserved, he overheard the Museion Director arranging to sell library scrolls privately to Diogenes. The grandfather took the story to Theon, who had an inkling already of what was going on. Theon attempted to dissuade Philetus, with no success. Then Theon died. The grandfather was at a loss what to do, so he turned to his grandsons for advice.

'Chaereas and Chaeteas told him to report it to you, Falco.'

'He never did so.'

'But you know?'

'I found out myself. I really could have used this grandfather's testimony,' I complained. 'Who is he, or should I say, who was he?'

Philadelphion looked astonished. 'Why he was Nibytas, Falco! Nibytas was my assistants' grandfather.'

By this point, I was half expecting it. 'Nibytas? The ancient scholar, who died in the Library of old age?'

Philadelphion pursed his lips. 'Chaereas and Chaeteas convinced themselves it was not old age that killed him. They were certain he was murdered – killed at his table by Diogenes to stop him speaking out.'

'Evidence?'

'None.'

'Dodgy!'

Philadelphion agreed. 'I was sure they were wrong. They agitated for me to conduct a necropsy, but – as I believe you know, Falco – the body was too decomposed. The funeral had to be held the next day; mummification was impossible.'

'So what form did burial take?'

'Cremation.' Damn. 'Only solution,' Philadelphion told us tersely. As a man who lived with animals, he was unsentimental.

We were all silent, then, as we thought about those two bereaved men: how Chaereas and Chaeteas must have become increasingly disturbed, going over what they believed had happened to Nibytas and fretting that nobody else, not even Philadelphion, would help them to expose the truth. I wished they had consulted me. Instead, they conspired to exact revenge themselves. Hence the way they chased down Diogenes last night – and his real fear of them, because he undoubtedly knew why they had come for him.

If they were wrong, the two cousins had driven a man to his death prematurely. Diogenes may have been engaged in criminal activities, but we had laws to deal with that. Chaeteas himself had died on the tower pointlessly. Chaereas, who presumably knew about his cousin's fatal fall, was now a fugitive.

'Where may Chaereas have gone?' asked Helena. Philadelphion shrugged.

'They had connections in Rhakotis? Or would he flee to the desert?' I persisted.

'To some family farm, more likely,' Philadelphion now replied sadly. 'He will hide up until he believes you have left Egypt and the matter of the scrolls has been resolved.'

'He could give a statement,' I barked. 'Chaereas could ensure that his grandfather and cousin did not die in vain. What Nibytas overheard would be third hand, but it could weigh the balance against Philetus. He is slippery and powerful –'

'Undeservedly powerful!' That was Helena, who had no tolerance for greed. 'Will you tackle Philetus, Marcus?'

I shook my head. 'I want all my lines clear first.'

The Zoo Keeper volunteered, 'Philetus knows what has happened to Diogenes.'

I could live with that. It might panic the bastard. With Pastous in safe hiding and me keeping mum about my last night's adventures, the Director would struggle to discover details. He would not be sure just how much of his malpractice was known. Soldiers were looking for the box-maker, using what I could remember about his whereabouts. They would also search for the second cartload of scrolls, while Aulus had, with luck, now retrieved the first. I would quarantine Fulvius and Pa. The Director was about to find himself very much alone.

'I'll come to Philetus as soon as I am ready. Let him sweat.'

LIII

Next, I wanted to see Zenon.

Helena was tired, feeling the weight of her pregnancy and delayed effects of her anxiety about me yesterday. She stayed sitting on a shaded bench in the gardens, gently fanning herself, while I went up to the observatory alone. I climbed the stairs very slowly as my thighs and knees protested about yet more mountaineering. It would takc me days to recover. I was hoping the astronomer would be pleasant and not try anything physical.

As I concentrated on my climb, the light was blocked out. A huge man was coming down towards me. I paused politely at a landing. The last time I squeezed past a stranger on a flight of stairs, it was Diogenes; that thought now gave me goose-pimples.

'Falco! Why, it is Didius Falco! Do you remember me?'

Not a stranger. Instead, a terrifically overweight figure; I looked up and recognised him. Worldly, sophisticated and just a touch devious, he must be the largest doctor practising anywhere in the Empire – all the more ironic since his method was to recommend purges, emetics and fasting.

His name was Aedemon. After twenty years addressing the putrefying innards of credulous Romans, he had agreed to be recalled to his home town, to serve on the Board of the Museion. At the meeting we went to, we had heard he was coming. It must be a genteel retirement for a well-respected professional. He could teach occasionally, write learned papers in staccato medical prose, revisit friends and family he had not seen for years and criticise from a distance the bad habits of his former patients.

After exclaiming over this chance meeting with genuine pleasure, Aedemon's next remark was that I looked in need of a laxative.

I felt a big grin spread across my face. 'Oh it makes a change, a wonderful change, Aedemon, to meet an academic with a practical attitude!'

'The rest are whimsical slobs,' he agreed at once. Helena and I had liked him. 'They need me to line them up and dispense wild lettuce and common sense.'

I gave Aedemon six months, then the inertia and in-fighting would wear him down – but I did trust him to have a good stint first.

We were still on the stairs. Aedemon had wedged his tremendous backside against the wall for support while we chatted. I hoped that wall was well built. 'What were you doing up aloft, doc? Do you know the starry-eyed Zenon, or did he call you for a consultation?'

'Old friends. Though his yellow bile needs correcting. I want him on a strict regime to cure that choler of his.'

'Now listen,' I said. 'I trust you, Aedemon – so tell me, please, can I trust Zenon?'

'Absolutely straight,' Aedemon responded. 'His bodily humour means he is prone to bad temper – but equally, he is of impeccable moral virtue. What did you suspect he had done?'

'On your say-so – nothing!'

'Well you can trust him with your life, Falco.'

'He tried to throw me off the roof,' I reported mildly.

'He won't do it again,' Aedemon assured me. 'Not now. I've put him on a regular decoction of myrrh to cleanse his rotting intestines – and I am about to prepare his personal regime of ritual chants.'

This mystic lore hardly fitted with the pure science that

Zenon had always protested, but friendship can overturn many barriers.

'He will be farting too much to lose that temper,' Aedemon confided in me – with a rather wide grin.

As we were about to part, I asked, 'Did you know the late Librarian, Theon?'

Aedemon must have heard what had happened. Maybe Zenon had just told him. The big physician looked sorrowful. 'I met Theon many years ago. Now *he* was a black bile man. Morose. Irritable. Prone to lack of confidence. A sink of putrid matter clogging him.'

'Suicidal?'

'Oh, easily! Especially if he had been thwarted.'

Regularly, by Philetus, for instance.

Even without a purge or emetic, I felt inspired as I went up to the roof.

The astronomer, that man of few words, turned away on principle.

'Just one question, Zenon. Please, just answer one for me: has Philetus been injecting cash into the Museion's funds?'

'No, Falco.'

'No money has been realised from selling Library scrolls?'

'You had your one question.'

'Aedemon calls you a pillar of morality. Humour me. Don't be pointlessly pedantic. Confirm the supplementary, please.'

'As I said – no. The Director has not boosted our accounts with income from his secret scroll-selling. I've been waiting to receive it – but he keeps the money himself.'

'Thank you,' I said sweetly.

Zenon smiled. I took it as encouragement for my enquiries. Aedemon's cure must already be working. Or had the celestial stars and planets foretold to Zenon that the downfall of Philetus might be imminent?

The Director was about to bring doom on himself. Just

at that moment we spotted from the observatory roof a column of alarming black smoke. Zenon and I were horrified. The Great Library was on fire.

LIV

The emergency loosened up my stiff joints and sinews.
I made it down the stairs ahead of Zenon, then we raced
to the Library in tandem. We pounded into the main hall,
but everywhere seemed clear. Readers looked up from
their scrolls and glared at us for disturbing them with
indecorous behaviour. So far at least, the famous monument was in no danger. We shouted 'Fire!' to alert the
assistants. If the fire spread from its seat – wherever that
was – we knew the peaceful atmosphere could change in
moments.

We rushed back outside. We could smell the smoke, but
not see it. Scooping up the young scholars who always
loitered in the portico, we hurried around the main block
to the utility area where I had been yesterday. The fire was
in the very building where Diogenes' scrolls had been
stored, prior to removal. The Khamseen was blowing today,
which unsettled us and fanned the flames.

A crowd had gathered, watching dopily. Zenon and I
mobilised those who looked handy, instructing the rest to
scram. With the helpers we had brought, we did what we
could. The scholars responded well. They were young, fit
and eager for practical experiments. They used their minds
to devise sensible activities. Anything that could beat out
flames was fetched quickly; some eager exhibitionists
stripped off and used their tunics. Buckets were found –
perhaps, like the fire platform at the Pharos, the Library
had equipment stored in case of such an emergency. Its
cleaners would have buckets too. Our lads soon organised

a human chain to manhandle these after filling them at the great ornamental pool in the forecourt.

They did well, but the Library was an enormous construction. Zenon muttered that the marble would not burn. I reckoned he was wrong. Even marble crumbles, if it becomes hot enough; the surface splits off, so flakes the size of dinner platters crash down. Even if we could save the building, this fire might be disastrous for its historic fabric.

By the time buckets reached us, much of the water had sloshed out. The fire had taken hold, unnoticed, before we even started. Thick smoke impeded us. After yesterday, I was half unmanned by the heat, desperately trying to ensure that nobody was burned. The hideous spectre of the badly disfigured Diogenes swam in visions before me as I worked.

We were losing the battle. Any moment now, the flames would break through the workshop roof. Once that went up, fire would leap to other nearby buildings, carried over by the wind. Anyone who had seen a city blaze must have been aware we were on the brink of tragedy.

I wished we were in Rome where we could call on the vigiles. Other cities in the Empire had no fire brigades; they were discouraged, since emperors feared allowing remote foreign provinces to run any semi-military organisations. If word reached the Prefect's palace, whatever soldiers were in Alexandria could come and help us, but most of the legionaries would be in their camp, outside the city. Any message would be too late. All we could expect were dregs. I sent a lad who had long legs to run for help anyway. If we were about to lose the Library, the news would rush around the world. Once the recriminations started to fly, official witnesses would be a benefit.

Panic set in. Hopelessness quickly followed. The first bursts of youthful energy had run out. Our efforts were starting to seem pointless. We were tired and dirty, running with sweat and steam. The heat was beginning to drive us back.

Zenon rallied the young men for one last strenuous attempt. I directed them where the flames were worst. The buckets kept coming but what we achieved was pitiful. We were close to exhaustion, barely managing to hold our own. Then, trundling through the glorious porticoes, I made out the dim outline of a large, unsteady cart. Double lines of straining young men towed it on hauling-ropes. As this cumbersome edifice emerged through the smoke and teetered on a corner, I was astonished to see that my own Helena Justina led the way. Seeing me, she cried, 'Marcus! I noticed this in one of the lecture halls. The engineering students were to have a demonstration – this is based on the siphon pump invented by Ctesibius, three hundred years ago, with modern modifications by Heron of Alexandria –'

Nobody knew how to operate the beast. They had not heard their lecture yet. But my best friend in Rome, Lucius Petronius, worked with the vigiles. So I knew.

Fortunately the water tank was full, in preparation for planned demonstration. This would be better. This was for real.

We put up a couple of the most powerful students, one each end, where they had to work the two great levers of the rocker arm up and down on its central post.

'Go steadily!' I ordered as they creaked into action far too fast. They soon mastered the right pace. The hosepipe turned on a universal joint; it could be adjusted in any direction. Directing the pipe gave no trouble to inquisitive, practical lads who had come to Alexandria hoping to become mad inventors. They all wanted to be the new Archimedes, or at best follow Heron, their mentor. As the rocker arm creaked and brought the two pistons into play, advice from me was unnecessary. They were soon spraying away with the hose nozzle as if they had just come from a vigiles' training exercise in the Fourth Cohort's station yard. So, as the jealous boys on the bucket chain redoubled their efforts to compete in glory, I dared mouth to Zenon, 'We may be winning!'

True to form, he made no answer.

Eventually, the water tank on the siphon engine ran bone dry. But the blaze which had threatened to overwhelm us was now reduced to glowing embers. Buckets fell from numb hands as our helpers collapsed, completely played out. The young men lay on the ground, groaning loudly after their unaccustomed effort. Even those who practised athletics had been severely tested; I could see they were astonished at how depleted they felt. Zenon and I flopped on a stone bench, coughing.

Helena Justina, fetchingly besmirched by smuts, sat on a small patch of grass, clutching her knees. Dreamily she lectured us: 'Ctesibius, the son of a barber, was the first head of the Museion. His inventions included an adjustable shaving mirror, which moved on a counter-weight, but he is best known as the father of pneumatics. To him we owe the water organ, or *hydraulis*, and the most efficient version of the lawyer's water clock, or *clepsydra*. His work on force pumps enabled him to produce a jet of water, for use in a fountain or for lifting water from wells. He discovered the principle of the siphon, which we have had demonstrated with such good effect today! However, it may be said that setting fire to the Great Library was a drastic way to illustrate pumping princi-ples. This empirical approach may have to be rethought in future.'

Her listeners cheered. Some recovered enough to laugh.

'Ctesibius,' Helena added, her voice assuming self-mockery as she ventured into propaganda, 'had the advantage of working for benign pharaohs who supported invention and the arts. Fortunately, you now have a similar advantage, since you live in the reign of Vespasian Augustus, who was of course first brought to power in this wonderful city of Alexandria.'

'The scholars have shown today that they fully appreciate their good fortune,' I croaked. I too could sound priggish.

'Many thanks to all of you for your bravery and hard work,' cried Helena. 'And look! – Now the excitement is all over, here is the wonderful Academic Board coming to congratulate you on saving the Library!'

Through the thinning smoke, we beheld Philetus. He waddled at the head of a small bearded entourage: Apollophanes the philosopher, Timosthenes from the Serapeion, Nicanor the lawyer. On the bench at my side, Zenon growled in the back of his throat. Neither he nor I stood up. We were begrimed with smoke, our eyes red and stinging. Neither of us was in a mood to tolerate a condescending idiot.

Philetus moved among the youthful firefighters, placing a hand approvingly on one, murmuring praise to another. If he had thought to bring garlands, the oily sycophant would have draped their necks or crowned their sooty heads like triumphal Olympians. The scholars knew better than to shy away, but they looked nervous. I had worked out just how hypocritical Philetus was being about this workshop fire.

He ignored Zenon and me. He side-stepped the siphon engine too, as if appreciating mechanics, and the beauty of utility, was beyond him.

He approached the burnt-out workshop. Heat that the ancient stones had absorbed still beat off the pharaonic blocks, so Philetus only ventured as far as the granite threshold. He looked in. 'Oh dear! There seems to be nothing left of the contents.'

I stood up. Behind me, the astronomer stayed put, but he folded his fingers together like an eager member of a popular audience who is about to watch a prize-winning play.

I crossed to Philetus and sounded apprehensive. 'Really! What contents would those be, Director?'

'We were storing a large quantity of library scrolls in this building, Falco –'

'Oh no! Are you sure?'

'I had them put here myself. They are all lost!'

'We were able to save nothing from inside, sadly,' I told him, apparently full of regret.

'Then a great many valuable works of culture have been burned to ashes.'

'Are you saying so?' I stiffened up. 'Good try, Philetus!'

'What?' He was about to resort to bluster – too late.

Apollophanes, Timosthenes and Nicanor pulled back from supporting him at the same moment. Those three worthies saw where we were heading. All were up for the post of Librarian – and if Philetus fell, they would be scratching for the directorship as well. Mental repositioning began right there. The candidates were ready for huckstering even before the old Director saw that he was finished.

'Those would be the scrolls,' I spelled out slowly, 'that were taken away from here last night by a trader called Diogenes. Philetus, you sold them to him – wrongfully, secretly and for your own benefit. Not only did you dispose of irreplaceable material that had been collected over centuries, you personally took the money.'

He was about to deny it. I stopped him.

'Don't add to your misdemeanour by publicly lying. Diogenes was taken while in commission of your theft. Now the scrolls are in safe custody. They will be returned to the Library. Dress up what you have done, Philetus, however you like. I call it fraud. I call it theft.'

'You exaggerate!' He was too foolish to recognise that the end had come.

Before I could speak, someone else drawled laconically, 'Sounds good to me!' Hardly believable: that was

Apollophanes, the Director's own sneak. He was a worm – but worms, it seemed, could turn.

I strode right up to Philetus and dragged him inside the smouldering store. The charred walls still glowed, as I kicked aside the burnt remains of a table. We could barely breathe in the smoke, but I was so angry I managed to speak. 'What did you say – *"Oh dear – there seems to be nothing left of the contents"*? You hoped not, of course. You wanted them to seem gone, to hide that they were missing.'

I gripped the scared Director by the tunic edge and hauled him towards me on tiptoe. 'Listen to me, Philetus; listen well! I bet you had this building torched. Why don't I arrest you here and now? Only because I can't yet prove that you had this fire set. If I ever do find evidence, you are done for. Arson to a public building is a capital offence.'

He gurgled. I dropped him. 'You disgust me. I cannot even bear to spend my time on an indictment. Men like you are so insidiously evil, you destroy everything; you drive everyone who has to deal with you to inertia and despair. You are not worth my trouble. Besides, I truly believe in this institution that you have misgoverned and plundered. The reason for the Museion lies in those young men lying exhausted outside. Today they used their knowledge, their vision, their application. They were courageous and dedicated. *They* justify this place of knowledge – its learning, its invention, its devotion to ideas and its development of minds.'

I shoved him out into the air. 'Send your resignation to the Prefect tonight. It will be accepted. Do it yourself is my advice. Otherwise –' I quoted words of his own back to him: '*"Occasionally we might suggest a very elderly man has become too frail to continue."*'

Philetus would go, even if under protest. It would obviate the need for enquiries, recriminations, petitions to the Emperor, and, above all, scandal. He might yet be given a pension, or keep his right to a statue in the line of former directors, those great men whose impressive administrations had been instituted by Ctesibius, the father of pneumatic science. Who knows? Philetus might even keep his reading rights at the Library. I knew life was full of ironies.

I hated this, but I was a realist. I had served my Emperor long enough to know the style of action Vespasian wanted. Resignation would be painless and tidy, limiting awkwardness and adverse public comment. And it would be immediate.

LV

Alexandria might be the foremost training place for the mind, but it was ruining me physically. I looked for Helena, hoping we could gather ourselves together and go home. 'Home' was beginning to have a Roman resonance, even though we were nowhere near finishing with Egypt.

I was downhearted to see her on her feet, talking avidly to an elderly man. He was a typical Museion greybeard, though older than most and leaning heavily on walking sticks. Though gaunt and probably in pain, he had that look in his eye of a thinker who refused to give up while there was still any chance he might crack one of the world's great puzzles.

'Marcus, come quickly and be introduced – I am so thrilled!' For the cool and refined Helena Justina to gush was unexpected. 'This is Heron, Marcus – Heron of Alexandria! It is such a privilege to meet you, sir – my brother Aelianus will be so excited: Marcus, I have invited Heron to dine with us.'

I bet she had not told the great automaton-maker that her brother once spent weeks trailing around the New Rich of remote Britannia, trying to sell those deluded culture-seekers dud versions of Heron's moving statues. One of the statues accidentally killed someone, but we hushed it up with the excuse that the dead man was a bath-house installer. Maybe Heron would enjoy that; he was human, for he pierced me with merry eyes and said, 'If you are Marcus Didius Falco, the investigator everyone talks about, I want a word on a professional matter – but, as your wife says, let us talk in a civilised fashion over good food.'

Clearly our kind of man. And as we all made our way to my uncle's house on a hired cart – Heron crippled, Helena pregnant, me completely whacked – he even made jokes about us being borne home like a bunch of walking wounded after life's battles.

Aulus and Albia had arrived back. Vast numbers of scrolls from the Library had been recovered in Rhakotis and transferred back to where they came from, under military guard.

Fulvius and Pa, looking tense, were going out. Cassius confessed to Helena that my conniving relatives were desperate to snatch back money they had paid over to Diogenes. They wanted to find where he had stashed the cash. Knowing traders, retrieving their deposit might prove impossible. His banking would be done in cunning hideaways; the money might even already be tied up undetectably in a knotted skein of investments.

Cassius said there would be plenty of food and drink for us to entertain our famous visitor. There was indeed, and so we had a memorable evening. It was nowhere near as formal as the night we dined with the Librarian, but all the more enjoyable for that. Helena and I, Aulus and Albia were delighted by Heron, who was so secure in his enlightened cleverness he could freely share his enjoyment of ideas with anybody who would listen.

This was the mental conjuror who invented the self-trimming oil lamp, the inexhaustible goblet and slot machines to dispense holy water. Not for nothing was he known as the Machine Man. We already knew of him from his work with automata, famous devices he made for theatres and temples: noises like thunder, automatic opening doors using fire and water, moving statues. He had produced a magic theatre, which could roll itself out before an audience, self-powered, then create a miniature three-dimensional performance, before trundling away to resounding applause. As we sat enthralled, he told us how he once made another that staged a Dionysian mystery rite; it had leaping flames, thunder and automatic Bacchantes who whirled in a mad dance around the wine god on a pulley-driven turntable.

Not all of his work was frivolous. He had written on light, reflection and the use of mirrors; useful stuff on dynamics, with reference to heavy lifting machines; on the determination of lengths using surveying instruments and devices such as the odometer that I had myself seen used in transport; on the area and volume of triangles, pyramids, cylinders, spheres and so forth. He covered mathematics, physics, mechanics and pneumatics; he was the first to write down what was called the Babylonian method of calculating square roots of numbers. He collected information about military war machines, particularly catapults.

The most fascinating gadget he told us about was his *aeolipile*, which he modestly translated as a 'wind ball'. His design for it used a sealed cauldron of water, which was placed over a heat source. As the water boiled, steam rose into pipes and into the hollow sphere. As I understood it, this resulted in rotation of the ball.

'So what could it be used for?' asked Helena intently. 'Some kind of propulsion? Might it move vehicles?'

Heron laughed. 'I do not consider this invention to be useful, merely intriguing. It is a novelty, a remarkable toy. The difficulty of creating sufficiently strong metal chambers makes it unsuitable for everyday applications – but who would need it?'

Eventually, it became impolite to demand yet more stories. Heron was willing to talk, a man eager to spread his knowledge and deservedly keen to report his own ingenuity. Still, he must find himself asked the same questions over and over again; that must become tedious. He could probably dine out every day of the week with devotees, though I noticed he ate wisely and drank only water. We all liked him. He flattered us by seeming to like us. Helena was particularly impressed that he encouraged us to let the children run around. 'What is the point of knowledge, but to improve the lot of future generations?'

Since they were allowed to be with us, the novelty of being amongst the adults soon palled; Julia and Favonia quickly took it as natural and were for once well behaved. I wished Uncle Fulvius had seen it. Mind you, they might have sensed his attitude; things could have been very different.

Time for business.

'Heron, before we break up this delightful party, you wanted a word with me, you said – and I would like to pick your brains about a puzzle too.'

He smiled. 'Falco, we may have been beguiled by the same problem.'

Aulus jumped in: 'Marcus, are you going to ask how the Librarian came to be found dead in a locked room?'

I nodded. We all fell silent as the great inventor settled down once more to fascinate us. He certainly liked to be the centre of attention, yet had a winning attitude that made his holding court endurable.

'I knew Theon. I heard about how he was found. A locked room – its lock worked from outside – and its key missing.'

'We have now found the key,' Aulus quickly informed him. 'The ancient scholar Nibytas had it.'

'Ah – Nibytas! I knew Nibytas too . . .' Heron let his quiet smile suffice as comment. 'I have considered deeply how this mystery can be explained.' He paused. He was wickedly keeping us in suspense. 'Could it be ropes and pulleys? Could Theon have worked some pneumatic device from within his private sanctum? Could some incredibly impractical criminal have set up a crack-brained mechanical killing machine? Impossible, of course – you would have found the machine afterwards . . . Besides, this is

331

outside my sphere,' he said tactfully, 'but most murderers tend to act on impulse, don't they, Falco?'

'More often than not. Even premeditating killers are often quite stupid.'

Heron acknowledged this and continued: 'When I was told that the eminent Nicanor had been first on the scene, my mind took flight extravagantly, I must admit. I know Nicanor also –' He favoured us with his sweetest, most mischievous smile of all. 'I have often thought I would like to harness Nicanor's bluster. That energetic material would surely work some miraculous device!'

Heron paused again so we could all laugh at his joke.

'So do you have a theory?' Helena prompted gently.

'I have a suggestion. I will call it no more. I cannot prove my idea with mathematical rules, nor to the high legal standard you would require, Falco. Sometimes, however, we should not seek answers that are intricate or outrageous. Human nature and material behaviour may suffice. I took myself to the Librarian's room, to inspect the scene of this mystery of yours.'

'I wish I had been there with you, sir.'

'Well, you may visit again and test my ideas at your leisure. I propose nothing complicated. First,' said Heron, making it all sound so logical I felt ashamed not to have seen this myself, 'over the centuries, the great Library has suffered many times from the earthquakes we experience here in Egypt.' Young Albia squeaked and bounced about; Aulus nudged her quiet. 'The building has withstood the shocks –' He chortled. 'So far! One day, who knows? Our whole city lies on low land, scored and silted by the Nile Delta. Perhaps it may yet slip into the sea . . .' He fell silent, as if troubled by his own speculations.

It was Aulus who worked out where the original comment had been heading. 'The doors to the room stick – one very badly.'

Heron revived. 'Ah, excellent young man! You catch my

drift. The door sticks so much, I myself could not open it. Earthquake damage has shifted the floor and doorframe; routine maintenance has failed to address this problem. Were that my room, I should devote myself to arranging some system of artificial exodus, in case I found myself trapped one day . . .'

'So you think Theon found himself stuck?' suggested Albia.

'My dear, I think he never knew the doors had been locked. I suspect his death was entirely coincidental to what happened with the key.'

'I am more and more inclined,' I said, 'to call Theon's death a suicide.'

'That would be like him.' Heron nodded soberly. He sank into reverie.

After a while, I nudged him on: 'So the doors stick . . . ?'

Once again, Heron roused himself, throwing off his moment of melancholy. 'Consider the scene. Theon, finding his struggles with life unbearable, has decided to end everything; he has made sure he closes the doors firmly, so he will not be disturbed. Then, let us imagine, along comes Nibytas. I do not know – perhaps nobody will ever know – whether the Librarian is already dead inside his room. Nibytas is very agitated; he wants to urge Theon into action, but Theon has already shown reluctance. Nibytas is elderly in any case; he may be confused, easily made to panic when things do not go all his way. He comes to the double doors; he cannot open them. He lacks the strength to force them –'

'I nearly put my shoulder out,' I confirmed.

'Less youthful than you, Falco, less fit and more clumsy, Nibytas just cannot budge the doors. It is late; he knows Theon may not be in the building. He wonders if the lock has been engaged. The key is hanging on its hook. Nibytas fails to see that this means Theon must be around some-where and the doors not locked – he tries the key anyway.

We can see him in our mind's eye, fumbling, perhaps growing angry, thwarted, concentrating on his preoccupations – well, you know what happens when a lock is difficult. This is what I mean about human nature. You forget which way the key turns.'

I took up the idea. 'So you think Nibytas turned the key one way, then the other, becoming frustrated. The lock was working; the doors were simply jammed. Theon did not come to help him – he was probably already dead inside the room. In the end, Nibytas stormed off, taking the key with him – probably by accident. And in his muddle, he had left the doors locked.'

'I cannot prove it.'

'Perhaps not. But it is neat, logical and likely. It convinces me.'

I told Heron that when he tired of academic life, there would be a job for him as an informer. The great man had the courtesy to say he did not have the brains for it.

LVI

Once sluggish cases start moving, a dam-breaking cascade will often burst. Well, Aulus poked about with a stick and made a muddy mess.

The noble Camillus decided this was the moment to challenge Roxana about her doubtful sighting on the night that Heras died. I should have stopped him, but he was acting out of friendship. He felt he owed it to Heras, so I gave him his head.

We went to see her together. Helena and Albia insisted on that. They both wanted to come with us but we men took a firm line that we needed no chaperons. Nonetheless, under the influence of Heron, we used our common sense.

Roxana received us meekly enough. She seemed subdued, and told us that her relationship with Philadelphion had foundered. Apparently, he now had to consider his career – though the bounder had actually claimed he was over-come by wanting to do right by his wife and family. Roxana said she knew a lie when she saw one. Aulus and I glanced at one another, but did not ask how she knew. She would never admit to telling fibs herself, but would blame her dealings with men for teaching her about deception. We were men of the world. We knew that.

We discussed the night of the crocodile. I let Aulus do the questioning. 'We have been told that on the night in question, you saw Chaereas and Chaeteas, the zoo assis-tants. True?'

'Locking up the crocodile,' Roxana agreed.

'Well, *not* locking him up, it transpired,' Aulus told her grimly. 'They were busy talking?'

'Intently.'

'Why did you not mention this before?'

'It must have slipped my mind.'

'You were near enough to overhear their conversation?'

'Is that what you were told?' asked Roxana narrowly. 'Then I must have been.'

'You tell me.'

'I just did.'

I shifted. I would not have wasted any time on her. But Aulus was determined, so I let him be.

'This time, try and remember everything. You told me you had also seen a man, near to Sobek's enclosure, just before you and Heras realised the crocodile was loose.'

'He was right there. Doing something by the gate.'

'And were you still very near the gate?'

'No,' said Roxana, as if explaining to an idiot. 'When I saw the two assistants, then I was close by, on my own, looking for Heras. By the time I saw the other man, they had gone. Heras had arrived, so when we thought there was somebody coming, we took evasive action.'

'What exactly?'

'We jumped into the bushes.' She said it without a blush. Well, this was a lady who would climb up a palm tree if her life was threatened.

'So you were ashamed of being with Heras?'

'I am not ashamed of anything.'

Aulus sneered. That was unprofessional, and Roxana smirked at him. 'So who came along? I am sure you know really,' he admonished her sternly.

Roxana was a stranger to admonishments. She looked puzzled at his tone.

'Was it Nicanor?' asked Aulus. In court, Nicanor might have denounced that as a leading question.

'Well, yes,' faltered Roxana. She made herself sound

reluctant. 'It probably was.' Even women who say they are ashamed of nothing may balk at naming a murderer – especially one whose professional expertise means he may get himself off any charges and released back into the community, burning for revenge. 'He hated Philadelphion – perhaps enough to kill him. Yes, I suppose it must have been Nicanor.'

LVII

Uncle Fulvius and my father decided I had no work to do, so I could help them. They confessed they were trying to find Diogenes' coin hoard. He had lingered, but had now died of his burns. He expired without regaining consciousness, which spared him great pain but left our pair in a big loss-making situation. Since he seemed to have been a loner, their chances of discovering what he did with their cash were slim.

'You paid him up front?' I emphasised my astonishment.

'Who – us? We just paid him a little deposit, Marcus. Showing good faith.'

'You lost that then!' I said, without much sympathy.

I refused to be inveigled into helping. Since living in the same house as such a moaning bunch of martyrs then became unbearable, we did what we had come to do. I took Helena, and all the rest of my party, to Giza to see the Pyramids.

I am not writing a travelogue. Phalko of Rome, long-suffering son of the conniving Phaounios, is a Greek comedy playwright. All I have to say is that it was near enough a hundred miles. It took us two weeks in each direction, travelling at a suitable pace for a family with a pregnant wife and young children. Twenty days of leisure with my dearest relations is of course an unbroken delight for me, always a good Roman, model husband and affectionate father. Trust me, legate.

When we got there, a sandstorm was blowing. Sand

whipped across the raised ground where the three enormous Pyramids were placed all those centuries ago. The sand hurt our bare legs, stung our eyes, tore at our clothes and made it even more difficult than it would have been anyway to deflect the attentions of the guides, with their interminable inaccurate facts, and the leather-faced local hawkers, who were lying in wait to fleece tourists. It was all exhausting. The best way for visitors to avoid the misery of the storm, was to turn their backs on the Pyramids.

We saw the Sphinx the same day, of course. In the same weather.

We stood about, all trying not to be the first to say, 'Well there it is, so when can we go home?'

'Juno!' cried Helena breezily. 'Who is having a good time then?'

That was her mistake. Several of our party told her.

LVIII

Theon, the deceased Librarian, was given his funeral just after we returned from our journey to Giza. It was forty days since he had died; in the Egyptian tradition his family had had his body mummified. In those forty days, he had been washed in Nile water, emptied of organs (already removed from him once, at the necropsy), packed with natron to dry and preserve the remains, washed again, repacked with his preserved organs, moisturised with scented oils and wrapped in strips of linen. Spells had been said over him. A scroll with more spells from the Book of the Dead had been placed between his hands, before more bandaging. Amulets were secreted in the bandages. A lifelike painted plaster image of his face was attached to the mummy, which received a golden victor's crown as a sign of his great status.

I suspected more care was now lavished on the corpse than had been shown to him in life. If family, friends and colleagues had paid greater attention to a man whose mind was unbearably troubled, would Theon still be with us, instead of passing into the afterlife pampered only with the ritual processes of his embalming? There was nothing to gain by dwelling on such thoughts publicly. I had made a report to the Prefect, in which I deduced that the Librarian was despondent about his work and took his own life. I told the Prefect exactly why his work depressed him. That was in confidence. Theon's professional unhappiness was kept quiet, of course, though anyone who was alert might notice the simultaneous departure from office of the Museion Director.

Plenty of people came to bid farewell to Theon. Philetus was not among them. We heard he had gone south, to whatever ancient temple complex he first came from.

The funeral took place in a large necropolis just outside the city where, because of his high status, Theon had commissioned a magnificent tomb for himself. Had this been designed and constructed before he actually died? It seemed impolite for casual acquaintances to ask. It was cut from native rock, though parts were decorated with painted stone courses, in different colours, to create a pretence that it was a building. We descended a flight of rock-hewn stairs into an open atrium; there an altar stood beneath the blue sky for the formal ceremonies. Throughout, we observed a curious mixture of Greek and Egyptian decoration. Ionic pillars framed the atrium, but lotus columns flanked the burial chamber. Mourners dined with their dead in a chamber where seats had been carved out, upon which were placed mattresses for comfort. The coffin lay in a sarcophagus that was ornamented with Greek motifs – garlands of vines and olives. It would rest in a painted room where one row of scenes from Greek mythology (the capture of Persephone by Hades as he rode out in his chariot from the Underworld, according to Helena) ran under another scene of traditional mummification procedures. Dog-headed gods and Medusa heads shared the task of protecting the tomb from intruders – but the statue of the Egyptian god was wearing a Roman uniform. Winged Egyptian sun-disks extended over doorways, while a new statue of Theon stood outside the burial chamber, represented with a decidedly Greek fashion for the lifelike – his features familiar, his hair and beard rich and curly. 'Richer and curlier than I remember!' I muttered.

'Allow him a little vanity,' reproved Helena.

I found his funeral a miserable business. Remembering how we had met him that night, I thought of how he must all the while have been concealing his depression, perhaps even planning how the night would end with his death. We had not known him well enough to see that, nor grieve for him fully now. I refused to have a bad conscience about it. We had listened to his complaints about the Museion; had Theon wanted, he could have warned me of the Director's wrongdoing and sought my help.

After a while, I was too uncomfortable to stay. I slipped away, again climbed the steps into the necropolis and hung about restlessly. Helena would do our duty. She saw formal attendance today as a reassurance for his relatives and a healing process for his colleagues. I thought it all hypocritical. I was too glum to go through with it.

The undertaker was outside. Petosiris.

I hesitated when I saw him. The last time we met, Aulus had hustled him, while I beat up his two assistants. They were here as well, the pair Aulus had named Itchy and Snuffly – still scratching and snuffling. None of them seemed to bear me ill will, however, so we exchanged quiet nods of recognition.

'Hope you brought the right body today,' I said, on the presumption that jaded professionals always like to have jokes at interments.

We passed the time of day courteously, as you do, when you are hanging around a burial ground waiting for a funeral to drag to its close.

When I first emerged, the three mortuary men had been holding a fairly serious conversation. They had broken off when they saw me. Now for some time they went on chattering among themselves. Most of their remarks were in a language that I did not speak. I understood the tone, however. I knew they were talking about me.

Even so, I was surprised when Petosiris cleared his throat and assumed an almost apologetic manner that I recognised. In the course of my work, other men had approached me in this style, often bringing me some piece of information they claimed I needed. Usually they asked for payment. Sometimes they told me rubbish. But often it was perfectly good information.

'These lads think I should tell you something, Falco.'

'I am listening. Go ahead.'

'I did that Nibytas the other day. The old man who died in the Library.'

I pulled a face to commiserate. 'I saw the body. I heard you had to cremate him.'

'Not popular with the relatives,' Petosiris bemoaned. 'A burnt man cannot be reincarnated. Of course,' he said, 'not everyone believes in rebirth nowadays. But for them that do, getting just an urn of ashes can be heart-breaking.'

'Does the urn go into a tomb?'

'Numbered shelves. Further down the necropolis. We pack them in a bit, to save space. Not as gracious as this, obviously.'

I nodded, thinking again of that wild night when Chaereas and Chaeteas hounded Diogenes. The manner of their grandfather's burial would have added to their anger. 'So what's to tell me?'

'The thing is . . .' Petosiris tailed off. 'Those boys, his grandsons – they were upset about the cremation, of course, but there was something else. I thought I had to tell them what I found.'

'It might be helpful if you told me.'

'That's what we were all just saying . . .'

Petosiris made a sudden gesture. Two gestures. He placed his hand once on his throat with his fingers splayed, then with both hands he made a quick snap, as if dividing a chicken's wishbone.

I whistled gently. 'The bone in his throat had been broken?'

Petosiris nodded. He knew I understood: there is a bone that breaks during strangulation. His grandsons were right. Nibytas did not die of old age. Someone murdered him.

I thought they were probably right too about who did it.

Helena had a point. Funerals are always worth going to.

Philadelphion was among the small group of academic luminaries who attended. When these mourners emerged, I collared him discreetly. I told him I reckoned he probably knew where Chaereas had taken refuge. He need not tell me, but it would do Chaereas a good turn if we knew – and believed – this news from Petosiris. It would not make the old man's death any easier to bear, but it did mean the cousins had some justification for their actions against Diogenes. Chaereas had not been at the top of the Pharos, so no official action would ever be instituted against him. He could return to the zoo and carry on with his life.

Chaereas might feel that Chaeteas had died in a good cause. I knew what I thought about that, but I passed no judgement. 'How are you managing without them, Philadelphion?'

'Rather enjoying it! Reminds me of my roots. This kind of situation starts you reassessing.'

'A rethink? What's this about?'

'I don't really want the librarianship,' Philadelphion said. 'I like what I do too much.'

All the same, he made no threat to withdraw from the shortlist. The handsome man had too much social ambition, whatever he was now saying.

'Well, good luck, whatever happens . . . Helena and I have been away travelling. Help me catch up, Philadelphion. What happened about Nicanor, after Roxana landed him in trouble? I heard he was arrested, but nothing of what happened after that.'

Philadelphion laughed shortly. 'Nothing. She retracted her evidence.'

As I feared. I would have to tell Aulus this just showed the danger of squeezing a short-sighted flibbertigibbet who must have had her conscience sucked out by skilled embalmers. 'How did that happen?'

'Roxana went to see him —'

'Nicanor?'

'Nicanor. She was upset to have caused him trouble, so the dear little thing went to apologise. It all ended with her and Nicanor becoming good friends.'

'Soft cushion tête-à-têtes for the lawyer? No chance of a reconciliation for you then?'

Philadelphion looked shifty. Against all credibility, it seemed that Roxana and he had in fact made up their differences. Openly guffawing, I demanded how that had been achieved with the famously jealous Nicanor. Easy: her two lovers had formally agreed to share her.

'Well, you amaze me,' I confessed. 'It does leave one vital question unanswered, however. Did Roxana really see a man letting Sobek out? Was some madman making an attempt to do you harm? If so, why and who was he?'

'She saw someone, I believe that,' Philadelphion agreed. 'Not Nicanor. I am being extremely careful, just in case this person tries again – but nothing odd has happened. I think he must have given up.'

'I think you are in danger. I insist on finding out who did it —'

'Let it go, Falco,' the Zoo Keeper urged. 'Now Theon is in his tomb, let us all quietly resume our daily lives.'

LIX

We were leaving Alexandria. Our ship was booked; much of our luggage – now increased by many exotic purchases – was already loaded. We had been to say goodbye to Thalia, only to find that she and her snake Jason had already packed up and moved on to whatever new haunts would be graced by their vivid presence. I had made my peace with Pa and Uncle Fulvius, who both looked too smug; I guessed they had traced their supposedly lost deposit, surprisingly, and had begun some terrible new scheme. They would remain here. So for the time being would Aulus, though from various discussions, I reckoned his period of formal study would soon end and we would be seeing him again in Rome. For Helena and me, Albia and the children, our adventure in Egypt now drew to its close. We would sail out under the mighty Pharos, back to the familiar: our own house and the people we had left behind. My mother and sisters, Helena's parents and her other brother, my pal Lucius Petronius, my dog Nux: back home.

Now it was all fixed up, we experienced the last ridiculous pang of travellers' melancholy, wishing we could stay after all. No use: it really was time to go. So, for the last time, Helena and I borrowed my uncle's far-from-discreet purple-cushioned palanquin. We slipped out of the house past the muttering man, who still sat in the gutter hoping to accost us. Of course we ignored him. We had one last thing to do: I took Helena to return her library scrolls.

Unable to use the Great Library, she had been borrowing

from the Serapeion's Daughter Library. Don't ask whether taking out scrolls was really allowed; Helena was a Roman senator's daughter and she wielded her charm well. So we jogged there in the palanquin, jumped out, entered the stoa – then I had to go back to our conveyance because we had forgotten the scrolls. Someone was talking to Psaesis, the chief litter-bearer, but whoever it was scuttled off.

By the time I reached the Library with my armful, Helena was talking to Timosthenes. I handed in the reading-matter like her trusty pedagogue, while she continued her conversation. 'Before we go, Timosthenes, did I hear a little rumour that your name was on the shortlist now for the Great Library post? We both want to congratulate you and wish you well – though sadly, it seems Marcus and I will have left Alexandria by the time they make the appointment. These things take so long . . .'

Timosthenes bowed his head gravely.

Helena could not resist lowering her voice to say, 'I know you must have been very disappointed not to have been included in the first place. But it is good that despite the efforts of a certain party, the Prefect was alerted to the error.'

'By Philadelphion!' said Timosthenes.

I saw Helena blink. 'Oh! Did he tell you that?'

Timosthenes was sharp. He had caught her surprise. 'Well, I believed so – when my name was added he said to me, "I always thought you should have been on the list".' We watched Timosthenes reassess the remark, realising it could have been mere politeness from the Zoo Keeper. For a fraction of a second, I thought his eyes took on a new coldness.

'We *all* thought that!' Helena told him crisply.

I was studying Timosthenes. He wanted the post; I remembered him saying so. He had thought the Director's prejudice counted too much against him, because he was a professional librarian not an academic. Even so, people had told me that when the original shortlist was announced by Philetus, Timosthenes was so livid, he threw a tantrum and flew out of the Academic Board meeting. I tried to remember if I had ever told him that I believed Philadelphion was the favourite candidate . . .

Timosthenes was contained now. His manner was almost arrogant. I felt concerned for him; yes, he should be on the list, though he probably stood little chance. He was younger than the other candidates, must be less experienced. Yet I could see he believed he should get the job. He had convinced himself. To an old soldier like me, his certainty was dangerous. His yearning showed in the merest flicker of an eye, a slight tension in the muscles of his cheek. But I saw it there and was perturbed by the strength of feeling.

He noticed me watching. Perhaps he also saw Helena slip her hand into mine. It was a natural enough gesture, to anyone who had seen us both together. What he would not have detected was the extra pressure of her thumb against my palm and the mild squeeze as I returned acknowledgement.

She sighed as if weary. I said we had to go. We said our formal farewells. I took Helena to the palanquin. I kissed her cheek, told Psaesis she must be taken home, then without further comment, I went back across the stoa on my own.

Timosthenes was walking away from the great temple trio: the dominant shrine of Serapis, flanked by a smaller temple to his consort Isis and a much smaller one to their son Harpocrates. I saw him enter a place I had previously noticed, and dreaded: the passage down to the oracle. I followed him, despite a horror of underground spaces. In all the godforsaken provinces that I had ever visited, if there was ever a hole in the ground where a man could be terrorised, I ended up going into it. Ghostly tombs, eerie caverns, cramped and unlit spaces of all kinds just waited to unnerve me with their claustrophobic interiors. Here was another one.

*   *   *

This was built by the pharaohs so it was civilised. It had a clean smell and was almost airy. A long, limestone-lined corridor sloped away under the stoa. Like all pharaonic structures, this passageway was beautifully built – roomy, with a good rectangular shape. The steps were shallow and felt safe. From what I knew, it probably led to a subterranean chamber used for the cult of the Apis Bull. That had rituals with similarities to Mithraism and in Egypt was connected to the cult of Serapis. The rituals for initiates took place underground; I could guess they involved darkness, fear and gore.

There were plenty of people out in the stoa but down here we were completely unobserved. I refused to go far. I stood close to the entrance and called out.

Timosthenes must have been expecting me. That meant he had lured me underground on purpose. I had supposed I would be compelled to chase after him into the fearsome dark, but at my shout he stopped and turned around pretty quietly. His behaviour had a strange, unnerving courtesy.

'This is a secret way to our oracle, Falco.' He stood still while he spoke. 'Perhaps it will tell me who is to be given that post.'

'There is something you should know.' My voice was cool. We had liked him once, but now I knew better. 'The night that the crocodile was set loose to kill, a witness saw a man nearby.'

'The woman Roxana. She named Nicanor.'

'She has reconsidered and denied it was him. I think she can be persuaded to confess the truth. So who will she name then, Timosthenes?'

I expected him to try something. All Timosthenes did was shrug, then he began to move towards me. I was still near the exit. There was room for him to pass.

I was happy for him to leave without trouble. I let him go by, then I quickly turned to follow. In this great city of contrived effects, it was intended that those emerging from the underground into the bright upper world would be dazzled. As soon as I faced the exit I was blinded by the natural sunlight. Timosthenes had judged it perfectly.

He thumped me so hard I was winded. He shoved me so fast that I fell. I had no time even to curse. With the same pedantic logic that had made him try to kill the Zoo Keeper with his own beast, he tried to kill me with my knife. He must have spotted it earlier, close against my calf; he went for it instantly. I had barely begun to reach down for it myself. We fought briefly at close quarters, struggling on the steps. The knife was pulled out by one of us. It slipped through my fingers; it skittered past his hand too.

Someone let out a grunt. I heard three blows, each hard. None of them punched into me.

Timosthenes fell off me. Everything went quiet.

I was alive. If you are stabbed, you do not always know at once. I moved gingerly, testing. I sat up, easing myself by stages against the wall behind me, uncertain what to expect. Here near the exit there was enough light to see that Timosthenes was dead. I had been rescued.

I knew him. Squatting beside the body with a pleased expression, my saviour was middle-aged, scrawny, in a long grubby tunic. He looked unwashed and seedy, all starvation and beard-shadow. As ever, he seemed both sinister and desperate. Grinning, he wiped the blood off my knife on to his tunic, then offered it back to me, handle first.

'*Katutis!*' I gave him a good long stare, then took the knife. I could not manage Egyptian so I spoke to him in Greek. 'You saved my life. Thank you.'

'At the Pharos too!' he told me, sounding excited. 'I saw you going. I ran to the Palace. Sent soldiers over to help you!' Well, that explained how they arrived so quickly. So much for military signalling. Amazing.

'Very well, Katutis, I give up. Don't mess about; you have your chance at last: just tell me what you want.'

'Work!' he pleaded. He said it in Latin. His accent was awful, but then so was mine to anyone not from the Aventine. At least he had spoken clearly, without muttering or cursing. 'I need work, legate.'

'I live in Rome. I am going back to Rome.'

'Rome!' enthused Katutis. His eyes shone with eagerness. 'Great city. Rome – yes!'

Why does it happen to me? This was not what I had expected yet I recognised its ring of doom. 'What can you do?' I ventured despondently.

'Perfect secretarial Greek, my legate. I read, I write. Every letter fully formed, all the lines straight –' He knew I had no need of him, but his need of me would beat me down. As I sat helpless, he hit his stride and sang out joyously, 'Good copies, Phalko – I can copy many scrolls for you!'

LX

Rome.

A month later we were home. I had soaked in enough old-world Eastern luxury. Here in the modern thriving West, the sun was clear, the skies were blue, the Forum reeked satisfactorily; it reeked of lassitude, fraud, rumour, corruption and depravity. There was nothing exotic about it; this was our own home filth. Now I was happy.

About another month passed before we had a letter from Uncle Fulvius. In fact it was written by Cassius. He and Helena had struck up one of those friendships in which news is passed to and fro with delightful flippancy. Fulvius and Cassius were still at Alexandria, though my father was said to be now on his way home to us.

'Oh how can we wait? – Read out the rest, Helena, if it won't upset me.'

Helena and I were relaxing under our own rose-clad pergola in our rooftop garden. She was ready to produce, so I spent a great deal of time close by, ready for the domestic crisis. My cautious support seemed to amuse her; it also helped fend off my hysteria.

'I could call your secretary to read this to you.' Helena Justina teased me without mercy.

We had cleaned him up, but it would take much more than hot water and a new tunic before Katutis matched the suave factotums other men employed. I growled that Helena was prettier and had a better voice; besides, I claimed, Katutis was busy co-ordinating my memoirs. 'I have put him to flattening papyrus, which you do – any stationer will tell you – by sitting on it . . .'

'Oh hush, Marcus! This is important – Cassius has sent us the list of appointments at the Museion!'

I was picking my teeth with a twig, which generally superseded most things, but I sat up. Then Helena read out the news to me: 'Here is the first announcement. The Librarian of the Great Library is to be – Philadelphion.'

I tossed my twig. I folded my hands and put myself into full assessment mode. 'Lucid, steady, good with staff, popular with students – on the surface an all-round decent candidate. Since all the Library readers are men, his belief in his good looks and his womanising will not be relevant. Unfortunately, academically he only cares about experimental science. His understanding of a great collection of written literature, much of it philosophical, may be inadequate . . . He was the only man to come out and tell me that he did *not* want the job.'

'The natural choice,' Helena cynically said.

'This is the dark side of public appointments.'

'Those who chose him may feel that any man who wants the post too much is bound to bungle it. This could be a sophisticated way around that.'

'Or a complete rat's arse.'

'Well, you know how everything works, Marcus. It's not choosing the best candidate, but avoiding the worst. It cannot have been easy, picking through the idiots and incompetents, not to mention one candidate who escaped execution for murder only because he was already dead.'

'I left behind a very clear briefing note. I don't know how palace secretariats justify their salaries . . . Who is next?'

Cassius must have a wandering style. Helena searched before she said, 'Additions to the Academic Board, promotions to fill vacancies. Two new faces. Aedemon, our medical friend, which we already knew, plus Aeacidas, the historian.'

'Could be worse.'

353

'Oh here is another. Nicanor is made head of the Daughter Library at the Serapeion.'

I groaned. 'Cobnuts! Nicanor? A bent lawyer – if that isn't a tautology. This is useless. All flash and pyrotechnics. What does Nicanor know about sanctuary libraries? He will just regard it as a sinecure, a useful step to worm his way into more senior positions. I see it all. He will never take decisions, so he never does anything for which he can be criticised. The Serapeion is well run and flourishing; from now on it will deteriorate. Everything will just stagnate.'

Helena gave me a look, then unravelled more of the letter from Cassius. 'He is, however, to have our friend Pastous as a special assistant.'

'Promotion on merit – an innovative concept, my dear, but it could just work! Whenever Nicanor is away, playing about with Roxana or defending some utter crook in court for an exorbitant fee, the excellent Pastous can fix up all that needs doing. Just let's hope his dire position never wears him down. Or perhaps Pastous can somehow organise a fatal accident for Nicanor; he will be well placed to take over . . .'

'Nothing for Zenon. Cassius says, Zenon's fate is to be a permanently disappointed man. Still, he will have foreseen that, if he is any good at star-gazing.'

'Old joke! The kind I like, however.'

'He should have spoken up.'

'Man of few words. They are always shoved aside.'

There was a small silence. Helena gave a woeful sigh. 'Brace yourself, darling. Here we have it: the new Director of the Museion. Ugh. I dread what you will think about this, Marcus.'

'What could be more horrible than we have heard already? Tell me the worst.'

She laid the scroll in her lap. 'Apollophanes.'

'Well, there you are.' Sadly, I applied my characteristic

phlegm. 'There is no justice. That must be absolutely the worst, most depressing solution any bunch of ludicrous, remote, ignorant officials could possibly dream up. I assume they decided this nonsense when they had all just reeled back from a five-hour drinking bout, all paid for by luxury goods importers who want the Prefect to do them favours.'

Helena drew upon her natural fairness. 'Let us try to be optimistic, Marcus. Perhaps Apollophanes will rise to it. There are men, men with limitations at the outset, who nonetheless defy opinion and grow into a new position.'

I said nothing. I would not argue with my wife, lest it brought on premature birth-pangs and our mothers laid the blame on me.

Besides, she was right. The new Director was a creep but a serious scholar. He might come good. In the terrible satire that is public life, you have to have some hope.

THE POWER OF READING

Visit the Random House website and get connected with information on all our books and authors

EXTRACTS from our recently published books and selected backlist titles

COMPETITIONS AND PRIZE DRAWS Win signed books, audiobooks and more

AUTHOR EVENTS Find out which of our authors are on tour and where you can meet them

LATEST NEWS on bestsellers, awards and new publications

MINISITES with exclusive special features dedicated to our authors and their titles

READING GROUPS Reading guides, special features and all the information you need for your reading group

LISTEN to extracts from the latest audiobook publications

WATCH video clips of interviews and readings with our authors

RANDOM HOUSE INFORMATION including advice for writers, job vacancies and all your general queries answered

Come home to Random House

www.rbooks.co.uk